THE TIMELE⟨

Marged Evans and the Pebbles of Time

JOHN DINGLEY

John Dingley

Published by Gwenwst Books 2014

19 Oakley Avenue #3

St Paul, MN 55104

Cover design by Dan Sexton.

Chapter illustrations design by Dan Sexton.

Manufactured in the United States of America

Library of Congress Registration TXu 1-845-276

Library of Congress Tracking 505370094

ISBN 978-0-9914423-0-0

E book ISBN 978-0-9914423-1-7

To the memory

of

Janet Lee Cody

A great lady, a great friend and a great
niece of a great American legend

ACKNOWLEDGEMENTS

This writer's journey has been like driving a bus in the dark to an incredible destination and the bus itself loaded with navigators without whom the destination would not have been achieved.

The encouragement received has been wonderful. First, from my sister Snowy, her husband Jeff, who ordered me to stick with it and follow through, and the rest of the crew at Tremaen and of course my enthusiastic sister Jane.

Thanks to La Rana, Decorah, where the idea took shape and the first notes were made.

A very special thanks to Liz Williams, Alltmawr, my Wales editor, who had been after me for years on my visits home to write. Her persistence has paid off and also, thanks to her friend Glenn Horridge.

And a big thanks to my artist friend Nancy Christiansen for her advice and art instruction.

The readers who waded through the first draught, that included Bill Watkins of Celtic Childhood fame. His observations were very informative. Richard Meredith, augmented my knowledge of Mid Wales and its people and drew the map. Bob Anderson took time out from the Raptor Resource Project and his work with the Decorah Eagle Cam. He indicated that I may have a future as a writer. Then there is Tom Dahill and Ginny Johnson who read between forays into the Twin Cities music scene. They want more.

There were many more including the fabulous bank manager Emily Darling. The Eagle Cam helpers and others in Decorah. Also among the many who have encouraged me are Jordan Parker, Eileen Kerr,

Tom Tulien, Erin Hart, Eric Hazen, Kathie Luby, Adam Stemple, Jim Womeldorf, Gary Smith, David Hecht, David Taylor, Eirwen Davies and Church, Sadie Jenkins, Wayne Nobes, Patrick Barrington-Coates and "Madam Librarian" Kristin Torresdal. Also readers from the populous that the book is aimed for and they are, Maddie in Decorah, Jackie and Lauren in St Paul and others.

The insights from my story editor Irishman, Professor Patrick O'Donnell will never be forgotten. He has a great understanding of a story and its telling.

Chris Kelsey's copy editing was meticulous and reminded me that I should have paid more attention to English classes when in school.

My special thanks to the following: Teresa McCormick for the photograph portrait for the cover and help with formatting. Mike Faricy, a St Paul, mystery fiction writer, for his advice on publishing and formatting while at the same time cooking me a dinner. Also Charles Sobcjac the Florida writer for his publishing advice and Dan Sexton who took on the task of cover design and the formatting of the chapter illustrations, a man with awesome skills.

Finally, members of the Midwest Independent Publishers Association, particularly Sybil Smith of Smith House Press, who teaches and guides all writers who contact her on their journey to publication. She has been my encouraging, main guide through the publishing process.

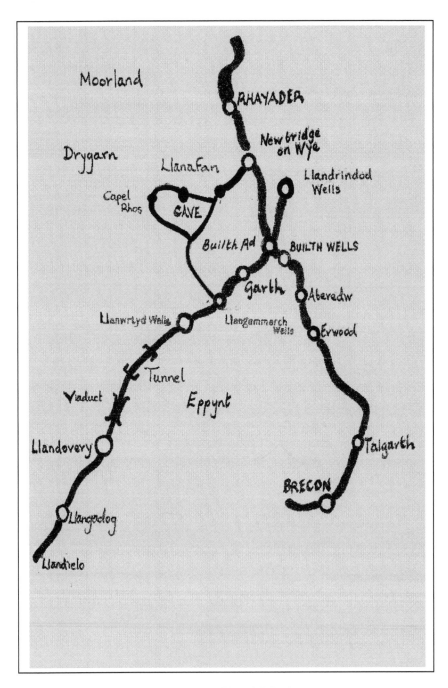

Marged's Mid Wales

THE

TIMELESS

CAVERN

Marged Evans and

the Pebbles of Time

John Dingley

Prologue

Erbury Canter appeared in front of the timeless cave keepers and waited for their words.

Although there was no keeper more powerful than another it was always the same one who did the speaking and made statements that sounded like orders.

"Erbury Cantor, you have the knowledge to move through caves and times' dimensions so we have chosen you to watch and disrupt the activities of a clever girl.

"This girl is called Marged Evans and she will soon disrupt the histories of times that have pleased us most.

"Your task is to disrupt *her* efforts of disruption so that she will reconsider and give them up. Her support from Caradoc you cannot stop, so it is outside the cave where your work will be. Seek her in the multiverse and we are sure you will have success."

The last sentence he spoke didn't sound much like a confident request.

CHAPTER 1

Myths and legends that perk your ears
Are all a part of histories' years.
Dragons red and breathing fire,
The English yoke and princes' ire.
Do not lose touch of what's gone before
The past and future to explore.

1936

"**W**here did he come from?"

"Well, he said he came out of your cave, Evans."

The policeman was bundling the handcuffed man into the back of the police car as all who were at the meeting watched, amused.

"I have heard that he has been around on other occasions over the years. I was told that someone like him was around here a hundred years ago."

The man dressed in medieval costume had shown up at the meeting claiming to be Owain Glyn Dwr. Everyone present was laughing. How could he be Owain Glyn Dwr? The man had surely died in the beginning of the fifteenth century. It was now 1936 and it seemed that this man had, indeed, shown up at other times.

Evans turned to the group as the police car drove away with the strange prisoner. "Perhaps he did come out of the cave. There are many legends about that cave and I am sure you have heard many of them. What he would have been doing going in and out of there for over 500 years, I have no idea."

Everyone laughed and went back indoors to continue the planning meeting for the upcoming agricultural show.

2004

It was after one o'clock in the afternoon and the family had finished dinner. Dinner was always at mid day on the Welsh hill farm. Lunch was for pubs, restaurants and institutions.

Emrys Evans, the head of the household, had gone outside to tend a cow that was due to calf. Megan, his wife, was in the spacious farm kitchen loading up the dish washer. She shut the large door on the machine, pressed the button and gazed out of the window. As she took in the pristine, blue sky she could hear the television.

Megan shook her head, turned and marched into the living room and stood in front of the offending box facing her two children, Rhys and Marged. "What do you think you are doing? You've been cooped up here for almost the last week because of the rain. And now, on a beautiful day like this, you are still here watching television. Well, no more." She turned and switched off the set.

Marged, who was nearly 11 years old and would be going to the high school for the first time when school started again in September, objected. "Mam, that was good."

"Marged, I don't care how good it was. You two are going to go outside and enjoy the day. There's a whole farm to explore, the forestry and the old cave. You haven't been to the old cave since your father took you there a few years ago. You should go there again, who knows what you might find."

The brother and sister stared at her and knew that they had better obey their determined mother, although, Rhys frowned.

Megan continued. "Rhys, you will go with your sister, you can be her guide. Now, when you return I want you to start doing more to help your father. You are 13 and you should start taking on a more responsible role on the farm. Your father could use the help. Alright, off with the both of you. Rhys, you should tell your sister about some of the myths and legends that surround that old cave."

Rhys and Marged got up in a wordless acceptance of their mother's orders and went into the hall to put on their wellies and coats. Megan watched. "Take a torch with you, you will see more in the cave that way. I will get one for you." Megan turned back to the living room and returned with a pocket-sized torch.

The two would-be explorers left the house. They looked in at the cow shed where their father was helping a new born calf to its feet. It was bedraggled and slathered down with birthing fluids. Seeing light for the first time it shook its drooling head as its mother turned with delicate mooings to give him his first cleaning and reassuring licks. The first lick almost knocked the new offspring over.

"What is it Father?" Rhys asked.

"It's a very fine bull calf, should fetch a bit of money in the market. So where are you two off to?"

"Mam told us to get outside."

"Quite right too, it's a lovely day. So where are you going?"

"Mam said we should go and see the old cave."

"Good idea. Be careful mind, things go missing in that cave and you could be gone forever."

Rhys smiled. "We'll be back for supper, pops."

"Pops, I am pops, now, is it? I suppose you heard that one on the television?"

"I don't remember."

"Off you are then and mind not to walk through the hay fields, you go around them. The hay is ready to cut and I don't want anyone trampling it down."

"We'll go round."

As they left the farmyard Marged bent to rub Roy, the collie's, ears. Roy just wagged his tail; he was getting older and was used only occasionally these days. He had won many prizes in sheepdog trials over the years and was in his usual spot in the yard, under the shading branches of the sycamore trees. They finished crossing the yard and entered the grazing field, where the small herd of cows were lying down and chewing their cud. Marged loved the cattle; she knew all of their names. There was Blackie and Brownie, May and Maisie, Winnie and Ginny, Sally and Daisy and many others. She even knew how old they all were. At the end of the first field they climbed a stile into the corner of the hay field. It was a landmark corner for miles because of the giant oak tree that grew there. It was said that the tree was over 400 years old. A nearby farm was named after it.

The edge of the field, where they had to walk along its top to stay out of the crop, was sheltered by an old overhanging hedge that had many different kinds of bushes, trees and brambles. Hawthorne, blackthorn and hazels were splashed along the entire length interspersed with wild rose, blackberry brambles and other plants. Sloes and haws were developing on the branches, so too were nuts on the hazels. The roses had finished flowering and were developing hips, although a faint rose smell lingered in the branches. The blackberry fruits were bulging, about to turn black, and be ready for picking. Marged's mother would soon make her delicious jams and tarts from these wild fruits.

Walking under the low branches they were next to the hay crop where the meadow grasses and flowers were in full bloom. A rare sight in the 21st century, indeed: a whole field of wild flowers with their multiple colours and aromas. Blues, bugle, scabious and harebells. Reds, campion, red dead nettle and clover. White stitchwort and others intermingled with yellow hawkweed, coltsfoot, toadflax and Welsh poppy. There were many more, but Marged couldn't remember all their names. She wished she could. The whole field resembled an impressionist painting.

The air buzzed with insects: Flies, bees, beetles and other families of the six-legged creatures all out scrambling over petals to get to the pollen and nectar. Their work in the bushes and trees was done and the field was getting their full attention.

Marged turned to her brother. "Are we going to see the cave?"

"Of course we are. "After all, Mam told us we should."

"What are these myths and legends, then?"

Rhys, who had become a very good story teller, even at his young age, began with a smile in his eye. "Well, it is said that thousands of years ago a giant dragon lived in the cave."

"Was it the Welsh Dragon?"

"No, no, the Welsh Dragon came much later."

"Was he a nice dragon?"

"Nobody knows for sure."

"What did he do? Did he breathe fire?"

"I don't know what he did. He must have breathed fire. He was a dragon, after all."

"It's not really very interesting is it?"

Rhys nodded. "No, I suppose not. "Anyway, I don't think there have ever been dragons, but lots of strange things have happened in the cave. Just after the Romans left Wales, there was much struggling between the old tribes. Soldiers from a tribe from South Wales, the old Silurian people I shouldn't wonder, made a camp on the river Wye where Builth Castle is today. They were chasing a few soldiers from another tribe who had raided into their territory. There were ten soldiers in the raiding party and they were being chased by a hundred from the South Wales tribe. They came up the valleys from the Wye and then up our valley, down below us."

"Is this true?"

"I don't know, but everyone says it is. Anyway, the ten soldiers found the cave and went inside, hoping not to be found and if they were, they would make a last stand there."

"What happened?"

"Well, this is where it gets interesting. An old shepherd, who was watching, probably from where our farm is today, saw the ten go into the cave. Then, a few moments later, he saw the hundred soldiers who were chasing them run into the cave as well."

"They all went into the cave?"

"That's what the old shepherd said."

"Isn't it too small for all those people?"

"That is true and that is what puzzled the old shepherd. He watched for the rest of the day and even stayed up all night to watch. The next day his curiosity got the better of him and he decided to take a look for himself. Very cautiously he made his way to the cave and listened. He could hear nothing. He could see the footprints going in and none coming out. He crept inside and there was no one there. At the end of the cave there was nothing except a dropped spear which he picked up and took home with him. The spear is said to be on display in the Cardiff Museum."

"What happened to them? I bet it was UFO's, I have heard about those things."

"No one knows how they disappeared, but here is the big mystery."

Marged was into the story now. "What, what?" She had been in the lead under the hedge row and had turned to face her brother, trampling some of the grasses on the edge of the hayfield.

"Mind the hay Marged," Rhys pointed out. "Watch where you are going."

"Oh, sorry. But tell me, tell me."

"Well, it was a thousand years later and a hundred soldiers with ten prisoners walked into Builth. The local people didn't know who they were. The dress was animal skins. They had swords and spears, some of them Roman. They thought perhaps it was a rag tag group of soldiers that had been fighting for Owain Glyn Dwr. They spoke Welsh, but it was a bit different from the Welsh the locals spoke, but they could understand one another. The leader of the soldiers shouted 'Where is your King?'"

"One of the townsfolk spoke up in answer. 'There isn't one here. There is one in London. Are you not with Prince Owain's army?'"

"'Londinium!' he exclaimed. 'What is your King doing in Londinium?'"

"'Well, that is where he lives and he is not really our King. Prince Owain is our man.' They told him."

"'Where is my camp? It was hereabouts this morning.'"

15

"The townspeople were gathering around. It seemed that they were in the presence of a whole crowd of nutters. Someone spoke up in answer. 'There hasn't been a camp here for hundreds of years. We have a castle that was built about two hundred years ago.'"

"The leader looked at the castle; he had never seen anything like it. 'That is where my camp was. What have you done with it?'"

"'We haven't touched your camp.' They replied."

"Anyway, they asked him where he and all his weird people had come from."

"He explained to them. 'We came from the south to kill these cattle raiders. We camped here and took after them this morning and chased them into a cave. There was a man in there who would not allow us to kill them. We could not lift our swords to do so. He allowed us to take them prisoner, which we did. The old man said that if the raiders gave back our cattle or replaced them, we were to set them free. If we did not, we would never be able to lift our swords in battle again.'"

"It was then that someone in the crowd, staring at these strange people, realized who they were, because he had heard the legend of the disappearing soldiers. 'They are the soldiers who disappeared into the cave a thousand years ago. Who else could they be?'"

"The people were shocked, was this possible? Disappearing soldiers showing up a thousand years later? There were many questions asked. The prisoners asked to stay in the Builth area and some of the soldiers decided to stay as well. Some say there are a lot of people in Builth who are descendants of those soldiers and their prisoners."

Marged's eye's opened wide. She heard the fantastic story, and now she was trying to see it. However, she didn't believe a word, but she wanted to. "What happened to the ones who didn't stay?"

"No one was completely sure. Some, it is said, went back to South Wales and some of them went back to the cave and were never seen again."

They reached the lower meadows that had a few damp places which they avoided as they walked in the direction of the cave.

"Are there any more stories?"

"There are lots of them. The one I like best is what happened to our great-grandfather about 50 years ago."

"Did he disappear too?"

"No, but some of his sheep did."

"What happened to them?"

"Well, he had rounded up some 20 ewes and lambs nearby, and instead of bringing them up through the fields to the yard to trim the ewes, tails and feet, he put them into the cave, as he had done many times before, and put a hurdle across the front, to stop them out. He then took a short cut back up to the house to have his dinner and came back later, with the tools he needed to work on the ewes. When he came back the sheep were gone. The hurdles were shut just the same as he had left them, but the ewes and lambs had disappeared. He went around the whole farm, looking for them in every field. He sent a dog around and through the forestry many times but turned up nothing. He asked the neighbours and they had seen nothing of them. He went to the police and asked if any stray sheep had been found or reported. They had heard nothing about them. He watched the markets for a year to see if they showed up at them, but they never did."

"Were they earmarked?"

"Yes, of course, the lambs were too, the same earmark as we use today on our sheep. Now what is interesting was that he was working nearby the cave two years later, almost to the day, when he looked up and out of the cave came the missing 20 ewes and lambs, looking the very same as the day they had disappeared. He was shocked. He put the dog around them and took them back to the yard and penned them up for a closer look."

17

"Were they the same?"

"Yes, exactly the same. He checked their mouths and the teeth told him that they were still the same age as when they had been put into the cave, two years before. Pitch marks and the faces on them all were identical. Of course he couldn't believe it. He told his friends in the pub that night and they laughed at him and would not believe him. Behind his back he could hear them whispering things like 'He's going a bit loopy' and other things not so nice."

"What did he do?"

"Well, he couldn't do anything. He shut up about it after that. Mind you, he would never pen anything up in the cave again, and no one else has to this very day, not even Father. Well, here we are."

The cave entrance was about six feet across and about eight feet tall. Cautiously, they entered. Marged grabbed Rhys' arm. "We won't disappear will we?"

"No, I don't think so."

"Put the torch on, it's dark further on."

Rhys took the torch out of his pocket and turned it on. He shone the light to the far end of the cave. The light reflected off the cave wall where it turned right and went deeper into the mountain. They walked religiously on, as if entering a church for a funeral. About 15 feet in, they turned and the torch shone on the rock at the end of the cave, 10 feet away. The floor was littered with leaves, small twigs, animal droppings, rounded stones of varying sizes and it smelled a mouldy damp. Rhys shone the torch onto every inch of the cave, not missing a thing. "See," he said. "Not a secret passage or door anywhere. There are a few bats though. See them hanging in the roof?"

Marged smiled as she scanned the cave roof. "Those soldiers would have been crammed in here like sardines in a tin! I don't believe those stories."

Rhys chuckled. "I don't know what to believe either. I am sure

18

hundreds of people have come in here over the years. I wonder if any of them disappeared and showed up later."

Marged looked around, "And probably thousands of animals as well and I wonder how many of them disappeared? Perhaps, if we sit here a long time, a person or an animal will appear right through the cave wall."

"No, I don't think so. Look." He picked up a stone and threw it against the end wall of the cave. It hit the solid wall of rock, bounced off and went clattering into another wall and rolled back onto the floor.

There were two big rocks inside, close to the entrance. They sat down and looked out down the valley with its pretty trout stream. After many minutes of silence Rhys spoke. "You know, Father told me that back about eight years ago a fisherman from London was fishing here. Father said hello to him and had a bit of a talk with him. He told me that he was a nice man, an important banker he was. He said a week later the police came knocking on the door and asked if Father had seen this man. They had a picture of him. Father told them he had seen him on the brook fishing and had talked to him. The police told Father that the man had not shown up at his bed and breakfast or his home or at his work four days later. There was a huge search for him; I remember all the police cars in the yard. They never found a trace of him, except a small box of homemade fishing flies which they found here in this cave."

"Do you think he will show up in the future like all the others?"

"I don't know, but he will have a shock if he does. What if he shows up in the past? There was a Roman camp in the field over there. What if he comes back in the past and walks right into their camp? He would think it was some sort of re-enactment like you see on the telly, and oooh, can you imagine the look on his face when he'd find that they were real and he couldn't understand their language? And what would they think of him with his waders on and carrying his fishing rod?"

They both laughed. They sat in silence once more, mulling over in their minds the stories of the cave.

"Well," said Rhys. "Let's walk up through the forestry and out on to the top. We can look down on the farm from up there and the views everywhere should be pretty good today."

As they began their journey into the wood they heard a noise and turned to see a small, stumpy man in old fashioned clothes enter the cave. Marged turned to Rhys. "Who is that?"

"I don't know, I've never seen him before. Let's go and see."

When they got back to the cave the man was gone. They looked around and Rhys shook his head. "He must have come out and gone on up the valley."

Marged was puzzled. "How could he have done that? We would have seen him"

"He must have done, because he is not in the cave."

They turned back to their intended journey through the forestry.

Twenty minutes later they were on the top of the hill overlooking the farm, their home. All the fields they knew so well were laid out before them. They could see the farm and buildings and that marvellous old oak.

They sat for a while to get their energy back after the steep climb and then they stood and slowly turned clockwise, taking in the panoramic view. To the south there was the open land of the Epynt and, beyond, the Brecon Beacons. Those distant Beacons in the heart of a National Park were bluish in colour, and their outline was plainly recognizable. Rain drained down from their southern slopes to form the South Wales Valleys. Those Valleys were the world's industrial heartland in the early nineteenth century. To the west were the hills, Drygarn Fawr and Gorllywn, the larger mountain lumps in the vast moorland of Mid Wales. A land of coarse grasses, rushes, bracken, stunted trees, sheep, lots of sheep, and Wild Welsh Ponies. To the northwest were the North Wales Mountains the main stronghold of language and culture. And to the east, one could almost see right into England.

Overhead two Welsh kites circled. It was good to see them.   They had almost completely disappeared throughout the British Isles and there were only a very few left in Wales. Due to hard-working conservationists their numbers were increasing and it was now the symbol of the county.

After an hour or so on the hill, taking in the scenery and plucking casually at the mountain grasses, they decided to make their way down and finish their walk by taking the long way around the farm, in the opposite direction to the way they had come earlier. On the way, Rhys counted the sheep in the top meadow. He would give the number to his father. It paid to count them regularly in case any went missing, broke through a hedge into a neighbour's field or were even stolen. There had been one or two incidences of sheep rustling in the area. They arrived home about twenty minutes before supper and flopped down in chairs in the living room. They were tired, even too tired to turn on the television. Their mother was pleased.

The food was served around the kitchen table. Rhys addressed his father. "We visited the cave, pops."

His father stared at him. "What is this blooming pops thing! Call me father or dad or something. Pops makes me sound like a fizzy drink."

Everyone smiled. Rhys apologised. "Sorry, Dad. We stayed in the cave for awhile before going to the top. The view was clear today. You could see for miles."

Emrys, smiled at his children. "You haven't been to that cave in a while, have you? When I was young you could hardly keep me out of it."

Marged smiled at her father. "Did you disappear, Dad?"

"Fortunately, no I didn't, but there have been a few that did."

Marged's smile continued. "Rhys told me about the soldiers that went in there and came out a thousand years later and then he told me about great-grandfather's sheep. Is that true, Dad?"

"It sounded very true to me when he told me. It was very believable."

"What about the fisherman?"

"Well, they searched for weeks and finally gave up. The man's two sons visited last summer. I'm sure you remember them. They had no idea what might have happened to him. They had investigated every move their father had made. They thought he might have been in some sort of trouble at the bank where he worked, but they found nothing, and he had no enemies. He had just vanished."

Rhys looked at his father curiously. "How many disappearances do you know about? To do with the cave."

"There's quite a few, but nobody knows if the cave connection is real or coincidental. There was a case, they say, of a hunt about 150 years ago. The hounds were in full cry and chased a fox into the cave, the huntsman and whipper-in followed them in, lying across the necks of their horses so that they wouldn't hit their heads on the cave roof. The other riders at the hunt saw them go in but when they got there, there was no sign of the fox, the hounds or the huntsman and the whipper-in. They had vanished. The other riders spread out to search for them.

"The hounds, which had been in full cry, had belonged to the squire at the Manor House. He was devastated. Not a better pack could be found anywhere in the whole country. He never saw them again. He had been dead a long time, when, seemingly out of nowhere, they showed up again. His grandson, who was a boy at the time of the disappearance, recognized the hounds, as he was the one who liked to feed them in the mornings on the days when they weren't hunting. He swore that they were the very hounds, he had known them well and this was 50 years later. The story goes that an old man in the cave was holding the fox in his arms and he had stopped the hounds from hunting forever. When the huntsman and whipper-in came out they found that they had grandchildren as old as themselves. Now, what do you think of that story, Marged?"

She smiled. "That's amazing. Tell us more, Dad."

"No, no, that's enough for now. Let's watch some telly."

"No, we want more stories about the cave. Oh, come on Dad. This is better than the telly."

Megan was smiling. "I think you had better. Anything that keeps them away from that old goggle box is good, so go on I know you have lots more to tell."

Marged's eyes gleamed. "Come on, Dad, tell us more."

He smiled. He never took a lot of persuading; he loved to tell the stories. "Alright, you have all learned the history of Owain Glyn Dwr who fought against the English, almost completely driving all the English Lords out of Wales. He conquered and held the great Harlech Castle in North Wales and the Castle in Aberystwyth for years, against almost overwhelming odds. But in the end he made a big mistake, he went into England to fight the English King and his armies. You see the Celtic peoples don't aggressively invade other countries unless they are forced or obligated to by another people, like the English. The English King, cunningly, starved them out and then ran them back into Wales and after that Owain's forces were slowly beaten and shortly afterwards Owain disappeared.

"It is said that he is buried just outside the Welsh border in the county of Hereford. However, there are some legends that say he found his way here to our cave and was never seen again. The English King wanted to capture him and take him back to London, where he would have been tortured and then hung, drawn and quartered. His head would have been put on a spike for all to see, as a warning not to rebel against the English Crown. They did that to our last prince, Llywellyn, in 1282, and they killed him not far from here. Perhaps he should have found our cave."

Marged was more attentive than she had ever been in school, or at any other time in her life. She could hardly contain herself and why should she, this was marvellous stuff! "Come on, Dad, do you think that Owain Glyn Dwr went into our cave and disappeared?"

Emrys, smiled broadly; he loved seeing his daughter this enthusiastic. "I think anything in those times was possible. Why not our cave? There is no evidence at all of where else he might have gone. They have never found his grave. Now, we come to the interesting bit.

"In 1936 a man was found ambling along the road past the Red Lion and everyone who saw him thought he was some old tramp. He was wearing a medieval costume and a big sword with jewels on the hilt. They took him into the pub and gave him a drink. They were puzzled. They could hardly understand a word of the Welsh he spoke and then he began to speak some sort of French, some thought it might have been Latin. Eventually the local policeman from Newbridge showed up in his car. It was one of the few in the area at the time.

"The policeman left the car running outside to save starting it up again when he came out. In those days there were no electric starters. Instead, there was a big handle in the front that you turned to crank the engine until it started. The policeman spoke to the strange man in Welsh and asked him who he was. It took a while and eventually the man said he was Owain Glyn Dwr, 'your Prince'. Everyone burst out laughing. Well, what would you expect, the man had been dead for over 500 years or at least they thought so!

"The policeman took him outside and when the man claiming to be Owain saw the car and the smoke coming out from the exhaust pipe, he drew his sword and held the hilt with both hands, pointing the blade at the car. He said something in Welsh to the car that was undecipherable and everyone laughed again. They tried to disarm him but he kept them and, in his eyes, the car at bay for some time, before someone was able to knock him on the head with a stick. He fell down. They took the sword off him and the policeman placed him in handcuffs and then bundled him into the back of the car. The policeman then took him to the hospital in Builth where he was strapped to a bed and sedated.

"They stripped off his clothes and had them examined. They found that they were indeed clothes from the time of Owain Glyn Dwr. They were puzzled that they could not prove that this man was not who he claimed to be. For a start, clothing like his was rare, even in museums. Enquiries were made of all the museums as to whether or not there were any medieval costumes missing but there wasn't. The sword was of the same era, and no amount of questioning would lead them in any direction other than what he was telling them. They took him to Talgarth to the mental hospital there, where he calmed down and after a few weeks they let him go.

"Someone in Builth went and picked him up and he stayed with them for a long time.

As the authorities could find no evidence that his medieval dress and sword was not stolen, they had to give them back to him. A week or so after that he went walking in a suit of that time, carrying his original clothes and his sword buckled on. He was last seen by a shepherd, who said he was heading up our valley and that was indeed the last time he was seen. No one ever saw him again. It seems that he went back to the cave and as far as anyone knows, he is still there to this very day. So there it is. No more stories tonight let's be off to bed."

Marged, who had been glued to her father's every word, was silent, expecting more until she realized that he was finished. She stirred herself back to the present. "Oh, Dad, come on, one more."

"No, that is enough for today. Anyway, I have to get up early in the morning and so do you, Rhys, because you are going to help me sort some ewes and lambs first thing. By the way you didn't happen to go anywhere near the far field and count the sheep there did you?"

Rhys smiled. "I did, all present and correct. All 200 ewes and lambs and none gone missing in the cave."

Marged suddenly started. Her mother looked at her. "Are you all right, Marged?"

"Yes, I just remembered. We saw a man go into the cave and we didn't see him come out. Didn't we, Rhys?"

"Yes, we did. He was strange, but he must have come out, because he wasn't there."

Marged looked seriously at her father. "Do you think he's the old man from the cave, Dad?"

Emrys smiled at Marged and raised his eyebrows. "You never know Marged. It could be him. Do you want to help us tomorrow?"

"Oh, Dad, no, I want to go back to the cave. Perhaps I can find out what happens to people that go in there."

Emrys chuckled. "Very well, you were both in there today and you didn't find or see anything unusual, did you?"

"No, I know, but surely there has to be something there with all the stories about it. I am going to see what I can find in it."

"Alright, don't go disappearing on us now, will you?" He laughed.

"No, I won't."

Megan, who had been quietly listening to the stories with a small amused smile on her face, spoke up now. "Alright, you two have a wash and get off to bed and don't keep the light on late reading."

"Alright Mam. We won't."

They left the room and went upstairs.

Megan smiled at Emrys. "That cave has more stories than an entire library and I have heard you tell many more. I had never heard the Owain Glyn Dwr one before. Is that true do you think, him showing up in 1936?"

"Yes, it is. Grandfather saw him at the pub."

"Really, the same grandfather whose sheep had vanished for two years and then showed up again at the same age as when they had gone into that cave?." She raised her eyebrow with a mischievous smile.

He grinned. "The very same. So, now then, what if Marged finds Owain in the cave tomorrow and brings him home to tea, medieval clothes, sword and all?" He laughed at his suggestion.

She laughed back. "Oh, yes and a hundred blooming soldiers and their prisoners and a pack of hounds that can't hunt and only knows what else she will find there!"

They both laughed some more. She looked at Emrys. "I am certain she will turn it into a great adventure. It will be good for her. She's been watching too much television lately."

"I agree. Alright *gel*, let's go to bed. Lots to do tomorrow."

CHAPTER 2

The rocks of Wales are hard and old.
They have seen the past and future hold.
In time's dimensions their presence felt
Deep in the heart of the land of Celt.
If you are trapped in time beware
Others from the past find there.

When Marged awoke the next morning and finished her breakfast she grabbed her small coat, put on her wellies and picked up the torch and put it into her pocket. "I am going back to the cave now, Mam."

Her mother shook her head. "Alright, you be careful. Be back for dinner." Then, laughingly, she said "You mind not to disappear on us now."

"I won't, Mam," and out the door she went. She was greeted by a yard full of bleating sheep and lambs kept in a tight bunch by two collies. Roy, her favourite, was lying in the background under the sycamore trees, his ears pricked. Even though he was an old dog, his instincts were very much alive. Her father and Rhys were ear-marking the new lambs. She watched for a while as her father skilfully snipped and cut pieces out of each ear to make distinctive marks for that particular flock. It was one of hundreds of different ear marks that were used to distinguish between flocks around Mid Wales.

She felt sorry for the lambs as they shook their heads and bloodied themselves and the bodies of their mothers. She said goodbye and moved on past the sheep and stroked Roy between his ears. She climbed over the gate at the end of the yard and walked through the field that she and her brother had walked through the day before. The cows were grazing; it was usually in the afternoon when they laid down to chew their cud. One of her favourites, Brownie, approached. Marged greeted her. "Hello, Brownie, how are you today?"

The cow sniffed at her outstretched hand and Marged moved closer and scratched the cow's hard head between the eyes. Brownie snorted with approval and then turned and walked away. The greeting was over. At the far corner of the field she once again climbed over the stile and walked around the edge of the hay field. Her boots had got quite wet. It had rained a bit in the night and the dampness was still in the grass. She continued to follow the same route as she had the day before.

In another ten minutes she arrived at the cave. Before she went in she saw the small, stumpy man again dressed in the old fashioned clothes. He approached her and in a strange voice he spoke. "You are

Marged Evans, are you not?"

She stared at him. He was creepy and made her nervous. The clothes he was wearing were black and very old fashioned. He even wore buckled shoes and gaiters. She thought, perhaps he was the Arch Bishop of Canterbury on holiday. His eyes were dark under bushy brows that looked out over plump, ruddy cheeks that were mostly covered in a thick, wiry, ashy coloured beard.

Her silent staring was too long for him and he asked her again in a louder voice. "Are you or are you not, Marged Evans?"

Her mouth was dry, but she answered. "I am Marged Evans. Who are you?"

The dark, deep eyes looked into her face. "You are better off not knowing me and if you explore this cave you will know me well."

She retaliated; after all he was a stranger on her parent's land. "I can explore this cave if I want to. It belongs to my parents. It is you that shouldn't be here."

The man huffed. "Oh, I should be here and have been here much, much longer than you could ever imagine." He leaned a little closer. She wanted to step back from him, but held her ground as he continued his statement. "Beware the dimensions of the cave, Marged Evans, I will be watching you." Then he turned away from her and walked off down the valley.

Marged watched him go until he was out of sight. Then the question crossed her mind. "Was *he* the old man from the cave?"

Taking the torch out of her coat pocket she turned it on and entered. She walked carefully to where the cave turned, but not as cautiously as she had the day before. She shone the torch to the far end after the turn and carefully examined the walls of the cave, taking in every nook and cranny of the ancient Cambrian rock. She spent almost an hour studying the walls, feeling the cracks and then began to examine all the loose stones.

After about fifteen minutes she noticed a stone that wasn't quite like the others and she bent to pick it up, but it was stuck to the floor. She kneeled down to take a closer look and tried to move it again but her hand slipped off it and then suddenly she heard a noise of scraping rock. Looking up she saw a section of the cave wall open before her disturbing some of the bats that were hanging in the roof. Her bottom jaw fell almost to her chest. She stood and stared through the opening. The space inside was huge and glowed. Where was the light coming from? It was certainly not sunshine. She whispered to herself, "Oh my gosh!"

She was riveted to the cave floor. She was scared. Had she discovered the cave's secret and were all the myths and legends true.

She had to go through. Very nervously she entered the opening and as soon as she was through, the opening quickly closed. Her nervousness changed to fear. She was on the inside. She was trapped. She turned and placed her hands on the wall of the cave where she had entered. It was solid, cold rock. The opening was no longer there. Standing there she was almost as petrified as the rock she was touching. She was very, very scared and then turned again to look inside. The cave was huge and as she gazed, she heard an old voice.

"Who has entered, be not afeared?
I am just a man with a long grey beard."

The voice came from somewhere deep inside. She could not see that far. She said nothing, she swallowed and the fear was terrifying. Then she heard the voice again, and it was closer this time.

"I know that there is someone there.
You are here and yet know not where."

She stared in the direction of the voice and after a few more seconds an old man with a grey beard and a velvet cloak appeared, coming toward her as if with destiny. On his head he had a square, floppy, black hat. His face was bold with sharp cheek bones. He had what seemed to be a determined mouth surrounded by his grey facial hair.

As he approached she could see his timeless blue eyes. His look was mesmerizing and he pointed at her green wellies.
"Who are you, the maiden with the odd clad feet?
I see no toes, do you have cleat?
There is another that you should meet.
His are bigger and have yours beat."

She struggled to speak. "I, I, er, I am Marged. Who are you?" she bravely asked.

"I am Caradoc the keeper of the cave.
You are welcome here, Marged, please be brave."

She was stunned. She had wanted to know if the stories she had been told had any truth in them. She didn't really expect to find anything, let alone find herself in her present situation. Staring at the strange old man she asked, "Ah, er, how did I get in here?"

"You touched the door stone of the cave, my dear,
And to open you are not more than sixteen year."

"How do I get out?"

"You move the stones to get you out.
But, place them right not all about.
If you are wrong you will not be where you should be,
And what you want out there, you will not see."

"You are not going to hurt me, are you?"

"No one can hurt another here.
We all move here without fear."

"I was told stories about the cave; my parents own it you know."

"Your parents owning is very small,
For the Time Tyrants have it all."

A look of fear flashed across his face and was gone. Marged saw it, even though he thought she hadn't, and felt that she had also seen a glimpse of sorrow. "Are there others here?"

"Oh, yes, there are many in this mountain's womb.
And some will never die to have a tomb."

"I think I should be going now."

"Marged you are a very brave young girl.
Come further in and knowledge to you I will unfurl."

"I, er, I don't think I should. I should be getting back, because my parents will be worried about me."

"They should not worry, this is no game,
You could be out there before you came."

"How can I be out there before I got here?"

"Out there, there is a before and later.
Here, now is all and nothing greater."

"You are a crazy man, I don't understand you. Why won't you let me go?"

"You can leave, I will not hold.
I want you to see, so please be bold."

"If I come with you, will I be alright?"

"You will be fine and as right as rain.
Come with me now, you will have much to gain."

He turned and she followed, albeit a little reluctantly.

Marged was astounded by the massive size of the cave. It was quite bright. There were people, lots of people and it was if they were all attending a major costume party. It seemed that all of history's years and events were depicted in the clothes that they wore. Throughout there were animals of all kinds moving around totally indifferent to their surroundings.

She nodded and smiled at the people and was admiring the variety of peoples dress. There were a few large dogs, which she would later learn were wolves, and snakes slithered across the floor. She didn't want to be anywhere close to them. Larger reptilian type animals, the like of which she had never seen before, were watching her. She kept an eye on them, making sure she knew where they were if they came near. "Will they bite?" she asked.

The old man reassured her.
"Nothing here will bite or scratch.
And nothing here will they catch."

At noon on the farm, dinner was on the table. Rhys and his father had come in, washed their hands and were sitting down to eat. Emrys looked around, "Where's Marged?"

Megan was seating herself. "She went off to the cave this morning and I haven't seen her since. You know what she is like when she takes an interest in something. She loses herself in time. She'll be here directly."

They finished dinner and the two males returned to their work outside. Five o clock came along and there was still no sign of Marged. Megan began to worry. She went outside to call her husband. "Emrys, where are you?"

He had been checking on the new calf and came out of the barn. "I am here. What's the matter?"

"It's Marged. She is still missing, and I am getting worried. Would you and Rhys go and look for her? If she shows up here, I will let you know."

Emrys and Rhys, split up in the yard and took different routes to the cave, calling as they went. They got to the cave and entered, still calling. There was no sign of her as they searched the entire area surrounding it and found absolutely nothing that would indicate what might have happened to her. They returned to the farm by different routes again. It was now after seven and Megan called the police.

Rhys looked at his father, "Perhaps she disappeared into the cave."

Emrys stared back with fury in his eyes, "Don't talk so dull boy, they were all stories. You've seen the cave. How could anyone disappear in there? The walls are solid rock. Something has happened to her. This is not like her at all."

"The fisherman disappeared didn't he?"

"Yes, but that was different. He was a grown man and could have gone anywhere to get away from his regular life."

Megan got off the phone, "The police are on the way. What are you two doing, sitting there? Go on, get out, keep looking." She went back to the phone and began calling the neighbours. No one had seen Marged.

Out they both went and decided to search the forestry until dark. When they got back to the house the police were talking to Megan.

There were two police officers and they gave all three individuals an interrogation they would long remember. A CID officer was called in and was briefed by the two uniformed officers and then he too questioned the three all over again. It seemed that in these types of cases the close relatives were the ones most likely to have the best knowledge of what might have happened. Their story was holding up and a full search was organized to continue through the night by police and volunteers.

The officers left the house for a while, leaving three exhausted, stressed and very upset people to find their way through the awful night ahead. They were unable to sleep and Emrys and Rhys went out to search every inch of the farm buildings. Nothing was found.

The next morning at dawn, a van and car loads of police began arriving on the yard. The CID officer came to the house and was shocked at the three stressed, tear stained faces that greeted him. He told them how the search was to be organised and asked them for some recently worn clothing to establish a scent for the tracker dogs to follow.

Megan turned and went into the house. She came back with a pair of pink socks. She was sobbing, "Will these do? She wore them the day before yesterday. Please find her."

"Thank you, Mrs. Evans. These will do very nicely. We will do everything we can to find her." He turned to Emrys. " Mr. Evans, we would like you to come down to the police station this afternoon. We would like to ask you some more questions."

Emrys was shocked, "Why do you want to ask more questions? Didn't you ask all the questions you needed to ask yesterday?"

"I am very sorry, Mr. Evans, but in these cases it is a matter of routine. You see we need to get a full picture of the girl's family background."

"Are you going to question Megan and Rhys as well?"

"Yes, we are. A police woman will do that here at the farm, while you are at the police station." He turned and took the socks over to the men who were holding onto a bloodhound each.

The two men took a sock each and held them for the dogs to sniff. They then placed each sock in a plastic bag and put them in their respective pockets. The dogs turned and placed their noses close to the ground and immediately yelped out to indicate they had picked up the scent. They moved off, pulling along a man each on the ends of their leashes. Through the cow field they went, the cows moving rapidly away from the yelping dogs. They reached the stile and the big dogs were helped over in turn and the tracking and yelping continued. The men could see the track that the girl had made the day before. The dogs were right on it. Ten minutes later, after crossing more fields, they arrived at the cave. The dogs led the men straight in and sniffed, scratched and howled at the rock base where it had opened. One of the men looked at the other. "You would think she had gone right through the rock the way the dogs are barking."

The other looked back. "Well, that is not likely is it? Let's try outside."

They moved out, struggling to get the dogs out with them. It seemed that the dogs knew where the girl had gone even if their handlers didn't. The dogs took up sniffing around outside the cave and soon picked up the girl's scent from the day that she and her brother were there. The men followed the dogs up through the forestry. They noticed that the scent was weaker there. They frowned at each other; these men were experienced dog handlers. One of them spoke, "Perhaps she was carried."

"Why on earth would someone want to carry her up here?"

"I don't know. It was just a thought."

They continued on with the dogs still on the fading scent and came out on top. With stops here and stops there the dogs followed the route that Marged and her brother had taken. The trail eventually led them right back to the front door of the house.

The CID man approached the two men, "Well, what did you find?"

"Can we put the dogs away and then talk?"

"Yes, of course, we can meet in the incident trailer; we have just had one set up at the entrance to the yard."

The dogs were put back into the van and the two men met the CID officer in the incident trailer. "So, gentlemen, what did you find?"

"Well, she went into the cave alright. The scent was very strong. We could hardly get the dogs out of there and when we did we picked up a weaker scent of her. We thought that perhaps someone was carrying her. But, if they were, they went out a long way doing it. The trail led up through that forestry and out on to the top of the mountain over there." He pointed in the direction of the mountain. "The trail lingered on the top for a while and in one place was quite strong. We thought that if she was being carried, the person carrying her might have put her down and rested. Then the trail came back down through the forestry and back on to the farm, following the borders of some of the fields. In that far sheep field over there the trail stopped again for a while and then continued on right up to the front door."

"Thank you, gentlemen. I really do not know what to make of this.

There are no discrepancies in the family's stories as to what happened. But, on your information I am going to have the house searched from top to bottom and I would like you to search with the dogs around and through the buildings, the garden, the dung heap and any other place you can."

"We can do that; let's get the dogs out again." The CID officer went into the house to ask more questions.

He found the family sitting in the living room accompanied by a sympathetic policewoman and informed them as to what the tracker dogs had found. He told them how the trail had led right back to the front door of the farm house.

Megan's eyes widened. "But, she didn't come back here, I would have known if she had."

Rhys spoke up. "I went to the cave with her the day before yesterday and when we left the cave we went up through the forestry to the top to look down on the farm and see the view. But I wasn't carrying her."

The officer thought for a moment. "Could you go with one of my officers and walk the exact trail you walked with your sister?"

An hour and a half later they returned and Rhys had followed the exact trail.

The searching and questioning continued for many days. Expert geologists were sent to the cave and spent an entire day there but found nothing that they would have considered as unusual. The CID officer revisited the files from the missing fisherman case to see if there might be a connection. The only thing the two cases had in common was the vicinity of the cave.

Marged's picture went up in every public place across the country.

The search dwindled and was eventually called off.

After three months it was hard for the three to stay on the farm with all the memories. So the farm was leased to another couple and Emrys, Megan and Rhys moved into a house in town. The adults got part-time jobs. Megan helped in a restaurant kitchen and Emrys drove a lorry. Rhys continued at school.

Caradoc led Marged into an area where light was coming from the surface of large rocks. He pointed to them.
"Take a look and do not fear.
The whole world's knowledge you will find here."

"What are they?"

"I know little of what's within.
But look you must, so please begin."

Marged approached one that had a brighter light than some of the others. "What does this one do?"

"For that one, I do not have a clue.
But I enjoy it when its light turns blue.
What many of these do I do not know.
I try to find out walking through them to and fro."
He pointed to another.
"That one will help you remember all.
The whole world's knowledge at your call."

"If that is true why don't you know how these things work?"

"They will not work but I have tried
Without success, until I've cried.
All the knowledge is in one of these.
It is confusing and quite a tease.
Come, my dear, now follow me,
You have many to meet and lots to see."

She followed him through rooms and caverns to a large area with a lot of people. He raised his arms and spoke to them. Most of them barely bothered to listen.

"Here is another to join your number,
Marged Evans, and like you here she'll never slumber."

39

He turned and faced her.
"Please speak to the people you see before,
When ready, I will meet you at the door."
He pointed in the direction of the rock door. She nodded.

The people before her were staring. They had never seen anyone dressed the way she was. She was wearing a pink sweater under a light weight, navy-coloured jacket, blue jeans and bright green wellies. A short, older man dressed in medieval costume, wearing a sword, approached her. "Where are you from?" he asked.

"I am from here," she answered. Her eyes widened, "Are you Owain Glyn Dwr?"

"No, I am not; I am the protector of our Llewellyn ap Gruffydd. Owain Glyn Dwr goes in and out and out he is."

She stared back at him with a firm look, "You didn't protect Llewellyn very well. He was killed."

"Of that I am ashamed. They had his head before I could reach him, and when outnumbered, fled I did. I could do no more. I stayed ahead of their pursuit and in great fear entered this cave to make a stand, but then the rock it opened and in I came. I have been out a goodly number of times but cannot find the world that I had left behind."

Just behind the protector, partially hidden by the people around him, she noticed a man in a plaid shirt and bright green waders. He was carrying a fishing rod with a tied fly on the end of the line. Looking at the waders she realized why Caradoc had been staring at her wellies. They were the same colour as the waders. She pointed to him. "Are you the fisherman? Were you fishing on the stream nearby?"

He stepped forward, "Yes, I was there this morning."

She stared at him. "No, you weren't. You went missing eight years ago. My father told me so. You were a banker from England, he said."

"That is true, I am a banker, but I only came in here today, not eight years ago."

A boy in scruffy, turn-of-the-twentieth-century clothes moved slowly toward her. Around his neck on a loop of string was a wooden block with the initials WN inscribed on it. "I am from here," he said. "If you are from here as well, why haven't I seen you here before?"

"What year was it when you came here?"

"Well, this year, 1904."

"If you came here in 1904 you have been here for a hundred years, because it is now 2004."

"You are a liar. That cannot be true."

"Why did you come here?"

"I ran away from school."

"Why?"

"Because, the teachers were going to beat me."

"Why would they beat you?"

"Because, I am wearing this." He held up the piece of wood.

"Why didn't you take it off?"

"You can't do that. The pupil wearing it at the end of the school day always gets beaten."

"But why? What's it for?"

"It's for speaking Welsh. The teachers are English and don't like you speaking Welsh. So when you hear someone speaking it, you hang this around their neck and when they hear someone else speaking Welsh, they take it off and hang it around that person's neck and the one wearing it at the end of the day gets beaten."

"That is terrible." Marged was shocked. "They are not allowed to beat children in schools anymore and they do teach Welsh in the schools in my time. I am taking classes in it and I am very good too."

41

"Well, they don't teach it in my school and I am always wearing this at the end of the day. Welsh is my language. I can't help but speak it, and every time at the end of the day I get beaten. I was so sore from the beatings I couldn't take anymore, so I ran away from there before school was over for the day."

"Have you been out from here?"

"Yes, and every time I do go out I am not in the right time because it's different."

She stood almost deathly still, while all that she had seen and heard sank into her brain. There were dozens of people there. She talked to many and found that they were all from different times. Most had been in and out several times trying to find their way back to their own time. They were free to come and go, but most came back to try again and again with little success. It seemed that they were trapped for one considerably long instant of time.

A few had gone and not come back, so they might have found their right time, or perhaps they had been captured or even killed. Then she made a realization. Would she be able to go back to the time she came in. She felt she could, but the thought of not making it scared her. She then asked the boy from 1904 his age. "How old are you boy, and what is your name?"

"I am nearly thirteen and my name is Rhys Edwards."

"I have a brother called Rhys and he is about the same age as you."

"Is he here with you?"

"No, he is on the outside."

In the midst of the people was a sight that seemed out of place. She could understand the variations in the dress of the people and the times they came from, but there were two individuals with reddish copper skin, long jet-black hair with feathers poked into it. They were wearing waist coats, what looked to be light-coloured leather trousers, and coloured, beaded slippers. One carried a spear with feathers on it and the other had a gun, probably a rifle, and there were feathers on that too.

She stared at them and they stared right back. She thought that they looked like Native American Indians. She was pretty convinced that they were, but what were they doing in a cave in the middle of Wales? She wanted to ask them, but they were deeper into the crowd of people and so she decided to talk to them later or on another visit to the cave.

She looked around a little longer and noticed seven men in very primitive clothes lounging by one of the cave walls. As they weren't blocked in by any others she went over to them. They stared at her with scared eyes. "Who are you?" she asked.

"We are warriors. We are here two times today. We came here first a hundred and captured ten of our enemy here. When out we went, our camp had gone. Strange men and women greeted us. A huge fort stood where was our camp. We seven fled, the others stayed. We have not seen one of them again."

"Oh, my gosh. Your other soldiers and your prisoners stayed in the town around the fort and lived out their lives there some six hundred years ago."

"That is not true. We came today, not six hundred years ago."

"No, you came here one thousand six hundred years ago and went out after a thousand years and six hundred years have passed since."

"What kind of witch are you? What you say is not true. Years ago we fought the Romans and they are now gone."

"Yes, they have gone, they have been gone for one thousand six hundred years, and," she added, "they haven't been back since." Then, she smiled. "I don't know how all this happens, but it seems you are all over sixteen hundred years old."

"Impossible." He pointed at one of the men, "He is only fifteen and the rest of us are in our early twenties. You are a witch, a sorceress."

"No, I am Marged and I am going to try and help you all. I am going to talk to that Caradoc and tell him to let you go in your proper time, because I have to go home at the proper time too."

Nearby the warriors there was a man in full armour sitting on a horse that was also in full armour. She stared at him. He was stoic. Behind him there were two women talking as they watched a girl playing with a wolf, and against one of the distant walls, she could see a man leaning there in the uniform of a German WWII Luftwaffe pilot. She knew this because she had seen them on the television. He had his German peaked cap on, a scarf around his neck and he was picking at his finger nails. "How did he get here?" she whispered to herself. Sitting on a large rock next to him were a boy and a girl and they didn't look very happy.

She left the crowd of people, who all seemed to think that they had just got there that very day and thought that she was mad. She went toward the door where Caradoc was seemingly waiting.

"What are you doing to all these people?" she asked. "It seems that some of them have been here forever."

"There never was, nor is, a forever here.
There is only now my lovely dear."

"How did *you* get here?"

"I am here by the Time Tyrants will.
My place is full under this old hill."

"Who are these Time Tyrants and what did they do?"

"From the beginning to their forever,
They are throughout and here never.
The power they have will never cease.
They do not choose between fear and peace."

Again she saw a brief look of sadness and frowned with disbelief. "I think you might be a bit bonkers. You have been here too long."

"Here I am and only been here now

And not one other to me will bow."

"What I want to know is why the people here can live for so long without really getting older."

"Only outside will they age.
In here is now and there is no gauge."

"Why can't you help these people get back to their proper time?"

"Because, the stones that open the rock door out,
Will not align when moved about."

"Why don't they work right?"

"Because, this cave's mountain moves you see
And you can only guess where the stones should be."

"Why can't you fix it?"

"This cave's mountain I cannot move.
To you I'll show and I will prove."

"Good. Show me, please. I want to leave now so that I can go home for my dinner." She looked at her watch. It had stopped. However, she thought it must have stopped when she came through the cave door. She felt as if she had just arrived but knew that time of some sort must have passed.

He led her to a wall of rock close to the door. The wall of rock had a ledge and on the ledge there were three sets of rounded pebble-like field stones of seven different sizes, a small one going on up increasing in size to a large one. Caradoc pointed to them.
"See those stones upon the ledge.
You move them back and fore not to the edge."
He pointed to the large rock in the left hand set and to the marks on the rock behind it.
"Move the rock one mark distant,
Outside a thousand of yours no cant.
The middle one is five cant
When moved for one mark distant."

45

She interrupted. "That is five hundred years, right? Cant is Welsh for a hundred."

"You are correct and should not be vexed.
It is the one cant rock that comes up next."

"What are the smaller ones, then?"

" Every set has a ten year reach.
And next to it a one year each.
They are followed by a monthly stone
And one week stones shaped like a cone.
The next is for a single day,
And the last is for an hour, I say."

"Are they the same as when I came in?"

"Yes, they are and out you'll go to a friendly day,
But what day it is I cannot say."

He placed his hands on the ledge and the rock door opened and out she stepped. As she went she turned and said to the long grey bearded Caradoc, "I will come back."

He smiled for the first time since she had met him.
"Oh, yes you will of that I am certain.
For your time out there is not behind a curtain."

The door closed behind her and she left the cave.

CHAPTER 3

Don't let a year in your life be still.
Grasp and use it to your will.
The past to keep and now to hold
Will open eyes to keep you bold.
Visit the past to see well ahead
And a full life's path you will surely tread.

As Marged walked up through the first of the fields she felt that she had left the cave a short while after she went in. Looking at her watch she found it had started again. She was not exactly sure of the right time, but the sun was shining high in the sky so it must be close to dinner time. As she went into the hay field and was just about to start walking she noticed that the hay had been cut and not only cut, it had been gathered in and very recently because she could still smell it. All that remained was a yellowish green stubble. All the flowers were gone. She said to herself, "I could have sworn this hay was not cut when I went through here earlier. Something is not right."

As it was cut she walked across the field through the middle diagonally. It was the shorter distance. When she got to the other end she went into the cattle field by the connecting gate. There were cattle in the field. She looked for Brownie and couldn't see her. She couldn't see any other cattle there that she was familiar with either. This was all very curious to her and she decided to ask her father about what had happened.

As she approached the farmyard she could hear no ewes and lambs bleating. When she had left in the morning, the yard had been full of bleating sheep. When she opened the gate onto the yard two strange sheep dogs rushed up to her barking. "Whose dogs are these?" she thought. "There must be someone visiting." Roy, her favourite was nowhere to be seen.

She crossed the yard, the strange dogs trailing behind her. They stopped when she walked straight into the house and took her wellies off in the hall. She noticed that the hall was different. She shouted out. "Mam, I'm home. I hope I am not too late for dinner."

She entered the living room just as a strange woman stepped out of the kitchen. The woman looked at Marged. "Who are you?" she asked.

Marged stared at her. "Where's my Mam?"

"I don't know. Who is your Mam?"

"She's my Mam, of course. She's the one that lives here."

"Well, I can tell you, there's only me and my Will living here, now."

Marged raised her voice; she was on the point of tears. "No! This is my house. Where is my Mam?"

"Alright, alright, I don't know who you are, but we live here now. So who is your Mam?"

"Well, she's Mrs. Evans."

"As in Emrys and Megan Evans?"

"Yes, where are they?"

"They live in town."

"How can that be, they were here just this morning."

"Well, they are not here now."

"Why?"

"Well they leased us the farm after their daughter disappeared." A look of shock and disbelief appeared on her face. "Oh, my gosh, you are her!"

"But I didn't disappear; I went to the cave this morning after breakfast." She glanced at the living room clock, which was unfamiliar to her, "And it's only twelve now."

"Oh, my goodness, come on you're coming with me." She led Marged outside after she had got her wellies back on and let her into the car, which, strangely enough, was very like the car her parents owned. On the way the woman introduced herself. "I am Gwyneth Jones and I am now taking you to your parents' house."

"I don't understand. What year is it?"

"Well, it's 2005."

"Oh, my gosh, I have been gone a year."

49

"Yes, it seems that you have. Where have you been?"

"I don't know, I went to the cave and I just got back. I thought it was the same day as I went. Caradoc said that this sort of thing happens to people who go into the cave."

"You mean the cave at the bottom of the land?"

"Yes."

"So, who is Caradoc?"

"He is the old man in the cave. He has been there since the beginning."

"Really. The beginning of what?"

"Time, he was placed there by the Time Tyrants at the beginning."

"Who are the Time Tyrants?"

"They are the ones that don't care about fear and peace and we don't know who they are or if they can be changed."

Gwyneth glanced at the girl from time to time very sceptically, as she drove. She had a feeling that she should get away from this girl, who she had begun to think was a bit of a nutter.

In about ten minutes Gwyneth pulled up outside a nice looking house on the outskirts of town. "This is where your mum and dad live with Rhys, your brother."

Marged got out of the car, quickly followed by Gwyneth who followed her up the steps. Marged was a little nervous about walking in, so she rang the bell.

Megan Evans came to the door and opened it. When she saw Marged she shrieked and put her hands to her head and started to jump up and down. Marged was astonished, it was her mother, but her hair and clothes were different, but it was her mother. Marged had been gone, in her mind, about two and a half hours but to her parents it had been a year. When Megan calmed down they just stared at each other. Gwyneth was standing behind Marged when Megan stepped forward and grabbed Marged and enveloped her with her arms. "Oh, my darling I thought I had lost you forever."

"Oh, Mam, where I have been there is no forever. Caradoc told me so."

Her mother held onto her and began weeping. "Oh, Marged, where have you been? What happened to you?"

Marged's head was pressed against her mother's chest almost suffocating her, but she answered, "Mam I just went to the cave and the rock opened and I went in; there were lots of people there. There was a man with a long grey beard and a robe, he was the keeper of the cave and his name was Caradoc. I met the fisherman who had gone missing and seven of the one hundred soldiers that had gone missing. I met a boy from 1904 who had a piece of wood around his neck to stop him from speaking Welsh. I met the soldier who was the protector of Llewellyn ap Gruffydd."

Megan was overjoyed to have her daughter back and yet confused with her outburst of where she had been. "Oh, my darling, it's alright, you are back, come in now, so that I can call your father to tell him that you are back safe and sound."

Megan thanked Gwyneth, closed the door and took Marged into the living room. Marged sat in an armchair while her mother called her father. Marged could tell by the interaction on the phone that her father could not believe what her mother was telling him. Then Megan blurted out, "She is here, speak to her yourself." She handed Marged the phone.

Marged took the phone and spoke. "Hello, Dad, it is me. Dad, I was only in the cave. I didn't know that I had been gone for a year."

"I am coming home," her father said. "Don't move." The phone went dead.

Marged handed the phone back to her mother, "Dad said he is on his way home."

"Oh, good. I am sorry, but I don't know how to handle this. It is so wonderful to have you back. You must be starving. When did you last eat?"

"This morning. You gave me Weetabix, remember."

Megan looked totally confused, "But that was a year ago."

"No, Mam, for me it was only this morning. I am hardly hungry."

"Marged that is silly, it has been a year. It has to have been a year for you too."

"No, Mam it hasn't. It's only been a couple of hours for me, honest."

Her mother stared at her and looked her over very carefully and then she spoke. Her voice was a little shaky and had a touch of fear in it. "You are wearing the same clothes as you wore when I last saw you."

"Yes, Mam, I am."

"Oh, my gosh. You should be a year older, but you are not." She burst into tears again. "I don't understand any of this."

Marged got up and went to her. "Mam, it did happen the way I said. Mam, it's alright, I am home now."

"Are you real? Are you some girl that looks like my daughter?"

"No. Mam, I am real."

"You are nearly eleven?"

"Yes."

"But, you should be nearly twelve."

"Yes, Mam, I know, but I am still nearly eleven."

The door of the house opened and in came her father, Emrys.

He took one look at Marged, strode over to her and wrapped his arms around her and picked her straight up off the floor. "Oh, my darling girl, where have you been?"

"Dad, I only went to the cave, honest." She realized that she was going to have to explain everything all over again to her father. When she was finished, he stared at her. "Are you lying to me, Marged? Now tell the truth, what really happened?"

Marged became frustrated and began to cry. "I have told you the truth; I went to the cave and nowhere else."

Megan spoke up. "Leave her alone, Emrys. I am just so happy to have her back."

He responded. "I am too, but look what we have had to go through because of her disappearance."

Marged was crying full on now. "I am not lying. I can't help coming back at this time. It is not my fault. Caradoc says it's because the mountain moves slightly all the time, and the stones that make the time right are not accurate anymore. Those hundred soldiers in the story thought that they had come out on the same day they went in, when actually 1000 years had passed. There are people in the cave that have been there for over 3000 years, but they think it's the same day as they went in. You have to believe me."

He stared at her in total disbelief and then Megan spoke to him. "Emrys, I don't know what to believe, but look at her. She is the same age as the day she left and she is still wearing the same clothes. We have to let the police know that she is back."

Emrys got up and headed for the phone. "I'll call them."

Megan stopped him. "No, let's leave it until tomorrow. It can't hurt if we do that."

He nodded. "Okay, it can't hurt; it's been a year, so another day won't matter. Oh, Marged, I don't understand any of this. We thought you had gone for good. We imagined all kinds of terrible things that might have happened to you and here you are a year later, safe and sound. The fact that you are the same as when you left is unbelievable and yet here you are. Can I pinch you to see if you are real?"

"If you want to," she snivelled, "But don't do it hard."

He leaned forward and pinched her arm gently. "You feel real to me."
He put a slightly mischievous smile on his face. "Alright, tell me all
about what happened to you again. Start at the beginning after you
left the house."

Marged repeated and described everything that had happened to her
even repeating the couplets that had been spoken by Caradoc.
Marged continued her story for over an hour. To the minds of Emrys
and Megan it was either true or their daughter had acquired the most
amazing imagination possible.

Shortly after Marged had finished her recollection, her brother came
in. He stood in the door of the living room his bottom jaw almost on
the floor. "Oh, blooming heck!"

Emrys scolded him. "Be careful of your language, boy."

"Sorry." He didn't take his eyes off his sister. "You came back, but
you're the same. You haven't altered a bit. Where were you?"

She made her tear-stained face smile at him; he was a lot bigger and
looked a lot different than when she had left. "I was in the cave all the
time."

"No you weren't, don't talk so dull. Come on, where were you really?"

"I am telling the truth. I have been in the cave, and in the cave time
stands still."

"Oh, come on. Dad, Is she telling the truth?"

"It seems like she is."

Megan spoke up. "Alright, alright, let's stop this for now. She will have
to go through it all tomorrow when the police will want to know what
happened. I am going to make something to eat."

They ate together and watched some television. Marged was

squeezed between her parents. They kept glancing at her, making sure it really was their daughter. Megan prepared a bed for Marged in a spare room where she had kept a few items of her clothing for sentimental reasons.

Marged slept well once she could get most of what had happened out of her mind. Her mother came into the room at about eight in the morning. "Marged, you have to get up and have your breakfast; the police will be here at ten to talk to you about what happened to you."

"Oh, Mam can't you tell them what happened?"

"No, I won't be able to do that; they are going to want to talk to you directly."

Marged resigned herself to what was ahead for her, got up, took a shower, dressed and went downstairs to breakfast. At ten a police woman and a man in a suit showed up to talk to her. The man was the CID officer D I Jones who had been in charge of the case. The policewoman was in uniform; her name was Julie. Megan sat with Marged on the living room sofa and the two officers sat opposite in armchairs. They introduced themselves.

The CID officer looked at Marged. "You have led us on a pretty wild chase young lady. So how did you manage to disappear like that without a trace and then show up back here as if nothing had happened to you?"

Marged stared back at him. She didn't like him very much.

He gave her a sickly smile, "Proceed, take your time."

Marged relayed the whole story. The officer was blatantly sceptical and began to ask questions in an annoyed voice. Marged answered truthfully, but he was having none of it. He began to be very firm, bringing her to tears.

The policewoman spoke, "Sir, you have asked enough, you have to stop now."

"Alright, I will, I will come back tomorrow and we will go over it again."

Marged perked up a little. She wasn't going to completely succumb to this man's badgering questions. "I will tell you the same thing tomorrow and everyday and if you don't believe me, why did I come back in the same clothes as I went in and at the same age as I was?"

He stopped and stared at her for a moment in total disbelief. This girl, he thought, must be hiding something, because he felt that she was leading him down the garden path. He then looked at Megan. "Tell me, Mrs. Evans. Is what she has just told me true?"

"Yes, she has come back the very same age and wearing the same clothes as she wore when she left."

"Could I see those clothes please?"

"Yes, of course, I will get them."

Megan got up and went upstairs. While she was gone the CID officer held Marged's eyes in a steely look, but Marged didn't flinch. She wasn't going to let this man beat her.

Megan came back with Marged's blue jeans, pink sweater and navy jacket and handed them to the officer. He examined them carefully, even though half of his attention was on the girl. The clothes were exactly as had been described to him by Megan on the day that Marged disappeared. "Can I hold on to these for a while? I would like forensics to examine them. The constable here will give you a receipt for them and when we are finished I will get them back to you. Now, young lady, I am going to send a complete team down to that cave this afternoon and they had better find something or you are going to have a lot of explaining to do."

As soon as the police had left Marged looked at her mother. "I don't like that man. I have told him everything that's happened. What am I supposed to do, tell him lies so that he will believe me?"

"Oh, Marged, I don't know what to think. Come on, let's have dinner."

They spent the afternoon watching television, interrupted every so often by relations and family friends stopping by to see if it was true that Marged had returned.

The specialist team found absolutely nothing so the CID man had a tracker dog brought in. The dog was given a sniff of the girl's jeans and led into the cave. In the cave he began to yelp and scratch at the rock wall and then followed the scent out of the cave. The dog tracked her through the fields and back to the house where Gwyneth confirmed that Marged had walked into the house, taken off her wellies in the hall and gone into the living room shouting for her mother.

The CID man was totally baffled. He had the handler and dog team check the area surrounding the cave for several hours. Not a whiff of scent was found except that which seemed to come out of the rock wall in the cave and lead up to the house.

The following day the police officers were back to question Marged further. She went through the whole thing again with not one indication of a discrepancy. The CID man was stumped. Marged was fed up with this man. Why didn't he believe her? But there again she wasn't convinced that her parents believed her either.

Finally the CID officer looked her in the eye and said, "Alright, Marged. If we take you to the cave this afternoon could you show us how you got in?"

"Yes. I am not sure if I can, but I will do my best."

That afternoon the entire family and a whole cadre of police officers visited the cave. If there was anything to this story then they wanted to be first-hand witnesses.

The CID officer walked into the cave with Marged by his side, followed by everyone else. They got to the end of the cave and the CID man said, "Alright, Marged. Now is the time to prove you are telling the truth. Show us how you did it?"

Marged wanted to prove it to get this man off her back, but decided not to. She didn't like him one bit so she thought she would put up with him until he gave up and decided to avoid showing him by handling the wrong rocks and not stroking the key rock, only grabbing it the way she did when it didn't open. "I don't remember which rock it is so we will have to stroke all of them until we find the right one."

There were over a hundred of them in the cave. She began grabbing and stroking them in turn and nothing happened. She came to the key rock and grabbed it firmly. Nothing happened; she was relieved until the CID man spoke up.

"You didn't stroke that one."

"Yes, I just did."

"No, you didn't."

"Well, if you don't believe me why don't you stroke it?"

"Alright, I will." He leaned down and stroked it several times. Nothing happened. She had remembered what Caradoc had said.
"You touched the door stone of the cave my dear,
And to open you are no more than sixteen year."

They spent a whole hour touching, grabbing and stroking stones but nothing happened. More and more the CID man felt he was being made a fool of. After another fifteen minutes he called the whole thing off. He was close to losing his temper. "I don't know what it is with you, young lady but I am done with you, I am finished with this. If you were an adult I would throw you in a cell until you came to your senses. Alright, everyone. This is over with. Let's get out of here. The girl has returned and I guess that's all that really matters. It will be up to the parents to sort this one out."

The police left and the four Evans' went back to the house in town.

The next day Megan took Marged shopping to buy new clothes, including a school uniform and school supplies. A complete young girl's wardrobe was purchased, including two pairs of new shoes. Next on their shopping list were the school supplies - note-books, pencils, pens, book bag, geometry tools and a ruler. Marged held the ruler in her hand and she stopped dead in her tracks and smiled. Her mother asked, "Is there something wrong, Marged?"

"No, I was just thinking," and she was. When she held the ruler in her hand and saw all the divisions of millimetres and centimetres, she realized that she could recalibrate the stones in the cave. She knew that she should go back as soon as possible, but how could she now that her home was in town and eight miles from the cave? The walk she wouldn't mind it was the possibility of being caught by someone before she got there. A way would have to be worked out to get there before anyone really knew she had gone. "Mam, I need some spare batteries for my watch."

"Is your watch working, now?"

"Yes, but I know that I will need batteries soon so I can put them in when the others run out."

"Alright, we'll get some." She stopped for a second. "Marged, are the batteries in your watch the same as when you went to the cave?"

"Yes. When I was in the cave, the watch stopped working and when I came out, it started working again."

"How long do the batteries last?"

"It says they last about half a year."

"Six months?"

"Yea."

"I bought you that watch in March last year for doing well at school, and you haven't changed the batteries at all?"

"No they are the same ones that came with it."

Megan thought for a while as they shopped. The watch was a very persuasive collaboration of her daughter's story. Perhaps all this did happen to her.

A week later Marged started taking her classes at the high school.

Every morning she walked to school about a mile distant and then walked back in the afternoon. Usually she was accompanied by two or three other students who were going in the same direction. Her brother usually left earlier to walk with his friends. One day on the return walk one of the girls, she walked to school with in the morning, was missing. She asked another what had happened to her. "Did a parent pick her up?"

She was told that the girl had a cousin on a farm out in the country and had taken that area's school bus out there to see the cousin. Marged's eyes twinkled. That was her way back to the cave.

A few days later, she had her plan. She found out which bus to take. She also started to make her own bed in the morning before going downstairs so that her mother wouldn't do it. Her mother was delighted with her daughter's new found responsibility. However, it was all part of Marged's plan.

Towards the end of the second week she got up early, made the bed and left her parents a letter in an envelope under the pillow. With a little luck they wouldn't find it before she was back in the cave. The letter read as follows:-

"There are a lot of things that I have to attend to at the cave so I am going back. Don't worry about me nothing can come to harm in the cave and that is the truth. I know you will be upset, however if what I am going to do there works out, I will be back before I left and you won't even know that I wrote this letter to you because you won't even know that I have left.

I am going back to the cave because I think I can help a lot of people get back to their right time. I know you don't believe this, but it is true. Please don't worry.

All my love. Marged.

PS: If this does work out you will have never left the farm."

She placed her basic school supplies, including the ruler, in the bag along with her wellies, jeans, pink sweater and the navy jacket that had been returned by the police. Also, she packed a small spray bottle containing bleach, along with some plastic bags. She went downstairs and had her breakfast and joined her brother and his friend for the early walk to school.

She took all her classes that day, occasionally glancing out the window to check on the weather. The weather, to her satisfaction, seemed good.

At the end of the school day she loaded up her bag and went out to catch the bus. She climbed aboard and the driver asked her if she had made a mistake and had got onto the wrong bus instead.

She smiled. "No, I am meeting my parents at the old farm, Derwen Mawr. You can drop me off there."

From there it would only be about a mile walk under a wood to the cave and she would be less likely to be seen.

On the bus she took from her backpack one of the plastic bags. She then took off her watch and placed it in the bag. A girl sitting in the seat opposite asked "What are you doing that for?"

Marged smiled. "I'll be walking through the woods to the farm and I don't want to get it damaged." She then took out her note-book and wrote down the day's date, the approximate time that she would re-enter the cave, folded it up and put that in the bag as well. She had put some new batteries in the watch so it would be good for about six months or so.

The girl opposite asked again "Why are you putting that paper in there as well?"

"It's a bit of a list. If I put it in with the watch I'll remember where it is."

Her answers satisfied the girl. Marged placed the sealed bag in her school blazer pocket and then took her wellies out of the backpack, took off her shoes and placed them in the bag and put the wellies on her feet. Then she smiled at the girl who had questioned her, who was still watching. "There," Marged said. "I am ready, now."

The girl smiled back and nodded.

The bus stopped at the school stop for Derwen Mawr and Marged stepped off, waving goodbye to the students who were still aboard and quickly let herself through a farm gate into a field. She walked close to the hedge at the top part of the field, the 200 yards to the forestry, stepping just inside the edge of the trees for cover. It wasn't long before she reached the cave; everything in her plan had gone perfectly.

There was one thing to do before she went in, she took the plastic bag with the watch out of her pocket and tucked it deeply into a pile of rocks to the side of the entrance. Then she took out of her bag the small spray bottle of bleach and sprayed the surrounding area where she had hidden the plastic bag. She hoped that if dogs were sent to search for her again it would be enough to stop them finding the bag. The watch was a crucial part of her plan. She stepped into the cavern and found the entering stone. She stroked it, properly this time, the rock door opened and she slipped inside and it closed behind her.

She smiled when she heard Caradoc's voice again coming toward her.

"Who has entered, be not afeared?
I am just a man with a long grey beard."

She called out, "Caradoc! It's me, Marged. I am back."

He came into view.
"Did you go back to your right time?
Or was it wrong with no bell's chime?"

"It was wrong. I was a whole year ahead of myself and they couldn't understand why I was not a whole year older. I have great news." She took off the backpack and held it up for him to see. "In here I have the tools that will help me recalibrate your pebbles, the Time Stones, but you will have to help me and I might need some help from some of the people here."

"All will help you with the rock.

For all their mysteries you'll unlock.
I know a girl who's brain is good
And provide all the help you need she could."

CHAPTER 4

When you can measure time and make it right
The days of loss are regained from plight.
No future gain to you will cost.
Your place in time will not be lost
And no place from you will ever take,
For in your time your place will make.

She took out the ruler. "Do you know what this is?"

"I do not know your marked stick.
I'm sure 'twill work if that's your pick."

She smiled, not like the first time she came to the cave. She was excited, because she knew that she could help and do good things. "With this stick, with its marks, I can make the pebbles, the Time Stones, accurate. Let me show you." From her backpack she took out a note-book and drew a diagram of what she intended to do.

He liked her scribble of description.
"I will bring to you the girl with brain,
Work she will to help you gain."

"Oh, Caradoc, thank you for letting me do this. I am excited and know that I can make the Time Stones work."

"I will go now and soon will appear
With the girl to help you, have no fear."

Off Caradoc went to find the girl. Marged took out her pens and pencils and a large roll of thick paper. She intended to record every mark on the wall behind the Time Stones and use it as a base to adjust those real marks on that rock wall at the back of the ledge. There was a large flat rock about three feet away from the Stones where she spread out the roll of thick paper and placed the pens and pencils to its side. It was then that she took her ruler and measured the marks, the gradations on the wall. She then transcribed them onto the thick paper. She found that every gradation, whether hour or millennium, was equal distance and realized that as a group they were affected by the moving mountain. It was the gradations and the stones that determined the times. What she had to do was establish an accurate time for one gradation mark. The stones had not been moved since she had left. So using the ruler, she drew a diagram on the thick paper to record an accurate position of the stones, so that if anyone moved them to find their time she could place them back again.

She had a feeling that the stones were reasonably correct for the years in thousands, the five hundreds, the hundreds, the fifties, the twenties and the tens. The year, the month and the rest were obviously not correct. What she had to do was to find out when the mountain moved, how it affected the Time Stones and, in turn, the days. If she knew how much the mountain moved, she could correct the calibrations, but she realized that would not be likely, so she had devised another way. She heard Caradoc coming back. He had with him a girl who looked to be about the same age as Marged. The girl was wearing very nice clothes that seemed to come from a time before the Second World War. She thought that they were expensive and that the girl was from a rich family.

Caradoc introduced the girl.
"Buttercup, is the girl you see,
And your assistant she will be."

Marged reached out her hand, the girl took it and they shook hands. "I am Marged. When did you come here?"

"Today," she said in a posh English accent.

This was frustrating for Marged. She put her hands to her head for a second. "No, what year was it when you came here?"

"1918."

"How did you come to the cave?"

"My mother and I were staying at the big house up the valley to get away from the bombs from the big German balloons in London and the sickness there that was killing lots of people. I fell ill and mother wanted to get me to a doctor down the valley. Our car had stopped working so we rode a horse down. Just above the cave the horse went terribly lame so we had to go the rest of the way on foot, but I was so ill I could hardly walk, so mother left me in the cave to go and fetch help. She will be back soon."

"Well, are you still ill?"

"No, I was sitting by some stones in the cave, not feeling very well, when I moved the rock opened and I looked up and there was Caradoc. I was scared to death, but I was too weak to resist when he picked me up and carried me inside. Once inside I wasn't ill anymore."

"Have you ever been outside since you got here?"

"No, I am just waiting for my mother."

"Well, with a little luck you might be able to go outside and meet your mother, but you have to help me first. Can you write?"

She answered with a haughty attitude. "Of course I can. I am a very good writer. My governess says that I write exceedingly good stories and I am very good at mathematics."

"Good, let me show you what I want you to do."

"Why should I help you? You are just a common Welsh girl with funny clothes on." She was looking Marged up and down with a disapproving expression on her face.

"If you don't help me you may never see your mother again."

Buttercup seemed to be on the verge of a tantrum. "That is not true. You are mean. My mother will be here, you'll see. Tell her, Caradoc."

Caradoc placed his hands on the girl's shoulders from behind.
"What Marged tells you is very true
And if it is your mother you wish to view,
You must help her here with all she asks,
For your mother you'll see with completed tasks."

She glanced back at him and then faced Marged again. "Oh, alright, what do I have to do?"

Marged turned and pointed to the big flat rock where she had copied down the gradations on the roll of paper and explained in great detail all that she had learned and what she intended to do. "Do you understand what I have told you?"

"I think I might understand. Is this all true, Caradoc?"

"The truth is in the words she says,
So help her find the times and ways."

Marged smiled and Buttercup gave a half smile in return as Marged went through her intentions. She handed Buttercup a notepad and a ballpoint pen. Buttercup held up the pen. "What is this for?"

Marged raised her eyebrows, "It's a pen to write with, silly."

"I am not silly. I have never seen a pen like this before. How does it work?"

"Just like this." Marged picked up another identical pen and pressed the button on the top so that the writing point was sticking out at the bottom. Buttercup did the same and a huge smile rolled onto her face.

Marged continued, "Then you hold it on the paper and begin to write."

Buttercup pressed the pen to the notebook page and wrote a letter A. "Where does the ink come from?"

"The ink is inside and it lasts for a long time."

"Can I have one of these?"

"Yes, you can."

"I can't wait to show this to my mother."

Caradoc spoke up.
"When you leave here the pen you'll lack.
You cannot take the future back."

Marged looked at him. "Why not?"

"The smallest thing makes a big world change,
To all the times across a great wide range."

She thought about what he had said and realized that every time she went out she would have to be very careful. "What about taking things to the future?"

"You can take many things more than one.
Because in the future the past is done."

Marged smiled. "Of course, I understand. We shall be very careful."
She then continued to explain what she intended to do. She pointed to
a line on the paper that had been marked in red ink. "This mark is
where I went out the first time and it wasn't my right time. It was a
year later. Because of that, my parents had moved from the farm to a
house in town. The farm reminded them too much of me, because to
them I had been missing a whole year. So what we have to do is
adjust the stones to make them work correctly."

She took the ruler and made some measurements. "I think about four
centimetres in this direction." She marked the paper. "Now if I move
this pebble, Time Stone, accordingly, I should be able to go outside at
close to the same time I came in this time. So let us try it." She
adjusted the stone. "Now you wait here, I shall be right back. I will
check outside to see how close we are to the right time." She turned
to Caradoc. "If I put my hands here where you placed yours will the
rock door open for me like it did for you?"

"All hands can open the door of rock.
Place them there and it will unlock."

She placed her hands where she had seen Caradoc place his and the
rock door opened and she went out through the opening and the rock
door closed behind her. When she searched the pile of rocks the bag
with the watch was not there. She glanced around, there were some
birds singing and the leaves on the trees were half out. It was spring,
but what year was it? Then she noticed in a distant field two figures
walking and ducked back a little so as not to be seen. She recognized
the figures as her father and her brother, Rhys. As she studied them
she felt that she was in the year, 2004. Suddenly another figure,
smaller, ran toward the other two. It was a girl and Marged gasped.
She was looking at herself. The girl was showing the other two figures
something. It was the watch that her mother had given her.

Marged was in shock at the distant scene, she even felt fear. What if
she should be discovered? That would never do. She rushed back

and stroked the stone, the rock door opened and she went back in. The door closed behind her.

She was out of breath following the rush of fear that had come over her.

Caradoc and Buttercup looked at her. Caradoc spoke.
"Ah, I see the look of self been seen.
And to see one's self is quite a scene."

Marged looked at Caradoc. "Oh, Caradoc, why didn't you tell me that I could possibly meet myself out there?"

"It rarely happens, so I didn't think,
But that will help the times to link."

"Yes, it will, knowing what I have seen, I can now make another adjustment to the stone." Picking up the ruler she measured a bit less than a centimetre in the other direction from the last time and adjusted the Time Stones accordingly. "Now let's see how close we are this time." She placed her hands where she had before and the rock door opened once again. "I shall be right back." She stepped out once more carrying the spray bottle with the bleach as she had before.

She got to the entrance and looked around, there was no one about, it was midsummer. She checked the pile of rocks the plastic bag was there and she opened it and took out the watch. The time was three days after she had gone in the first time on her second visit. It seemed to her that she only needed to make one more adjustment to make it close to exact. She put the watch back in the bag and hid it in the rocks once more and then squirted the area again with the bleach spray. Then suddenly she heard voices and dogs yelping, coming in the direction of the cave. They were looking for her. She could not afford to get caught. She ran to the entering rock and stroked it. The rock door opened and in she went and it closed behind her, just as the men with the tracker dogs entered the cave.

She was out of breath again and leaned against a rock. "Oh, my gosh."

Buttercup asked. "What happened this time?"

She got her breath back after a half a minute or so. Caradoc and Buttercup were staring at her. "I got out there exactly three days after I had come in the time before the last time. Tracker dogs were coming to the cave looking for me. If I had opened the rock door a minute later, they would have been in the cave and I would have been caught and who knows what might have happened." She smiled as she was calming down. "One more adjustment and it will be close to perfect."

Caradoc smiled.
"To you 'Your work is good' I say,
But if it is right, it's here you stay.
If you are right and you go out
It's yourself you'll meet without a doubt."

Marged's eyes widened. "Yes, of course, I can't go out if it is right, but how will we know for sure?"

Caradoc looked at Marged.
"Send Buttercup out to see if right
It will not harm her to see your light."

Marged leaned toward Buttercup. "Buttercup, will you do it, will you go out there to see if it is right?"

Buttercup hesitated as they waited for her answer. Then she looked at both of them with a half smile. "Yes, I'll do it. What do I have to do when I go out there?"

Marged nodded. "Yes, that is a good question. If we are right you will meet me right in the cave and if you do you will have to give her something that she will recognize and know that I am already here. I know, show her this." She reached in her bag and retrieved a coloured hair clip that her mother had bought for her while they were shopping. "Once she sees it you must tell her that I am already in the cave, doing what she intended to do. Do not let her in here whatever you do."

"What if she is not there?"

"If you don't see her, you must go to the pile of rocks near the entrance and find a plastic bag with a watch in it. The watch is digital and shows the time and date. Take the notebook and pen with you and write down all the numbers showing on the watch, put it back in the plastic bag and put it back where you found it , then come back in here as quickly as you can. Just a minute though, if the numbers on the watch are the same as these numbers," Marged wrote the exact time she had entered the cave in the notebook, "I want you to bring the watch back with you, so that we can use it to find another time."

Buttercup looked at the notebook and then at Marged, "What is a plastic bag? And what is digital?"

"Oh, dear, yes." Marged explained and Buttercup nodded as she understood each bit of new information.

"Alright, I think I can do that."

"Good." Marged turned and made some more measurements and moved the Time Stones accordingly and instructed Buttercup where to place her hands on the rock. She did, the rock door opened and out she went and it closed behind her. Caradoc and Marged smiled at each other.

Out in the cave Buttercup went over to the rock pile. Before reaching in, she cautiously looked around. She didn't see anyone. She retrieved the bag and looked at the watch. She had never seen anything like it in her life before. She checked the numbers and they were almost identical to the ones written in the notebook, so she decided to take it back into the cave with her. She looked up and she could see a figure in the distance coming through the woods. It was Marged. She almost panicked, but gathered her senses and ran back to the stone and stroked it. The rock door opened and she dashed through it and it closed behind her. She, too, was out of breath. She looked at Marged, "You are coming to the cave. The numbers are almost the same as what you wrote, so I brought the bag and the funny watch with me. But you, the other you, will be here right away, what are you going to do?"

Caradoc smiled.

*"The other Marged will not enter, do not fear.
She will enter not this cave right here."*

Buttercup stared at him, "Where will she go then?"

*"She will be here in parallel.
And be doing what you are as well."*

The two girls looked at him and then at each other. Marged spoke first. "How can there be two caves in the same place?"

*"There are many more than you will ever know.
It is the Time Tyrants and the worlds they sow,
You can be in all of them,
And each to its own, and each a gem."*

Marged stared at him. "I have seen stuff like this on television; I didn't know it was real."

Buttercup asked. "Marged, what is television?"

"Oh, my goodness. That is right. In your time, they haven't been invented yet."

"But what are they?"

"Well, a television is a box with glass on the front and inside it has wires and other things and it works through electricity. When it is on, it shows picture stories from around the world. It is amazing."

"Can I see one?"

"I would show you one, if that would be alright to do so." She gave Caradoc a questioning look.

*"She can see all the things found in the future.
But, none take back to her own culture."*

Buttercup lit up. "I wouldn't take anything back, honest. I just want to see." Then she remembered what they had been doing. "Marged, is the watch right?"

Marged checked the now stopped watch. "Yes, Buttercup, it is. We've done it, we've done it." They grabbed each other and danced around in front of Caradoc.

Caradoc smiled at the dancing girls and raised his hand.
"You now have solved a starting place.
To move ahead it will be your base.
You must continue to measure right,
To save all here from their plight."

The girls stopped dancing. They were still holding hands; they looked as if they were at a fancy dress ball. Buttercup was beaming. "What do we do next, Marged?"

"I have to calibrate the Time Stones to when I came here the first time and go out and see how close I can get. There won't be a watch out there this time, so I will have to venture further out, to find out if it's the right year and day. It might take several trips out and back. So let's get started."

Marged picked up the ruler again and marked off some more lines and made some notes. Then she picked up her bag and took out the jeans, the pink sweater, and the navy jacket. "I have to change into these, otherwise it won't be right." She ducked into a nearby alcove and changed out of her school uniform and into the other clothes.

She came out and put her watch on her wrist. Buttercup stared at her. "Marged, how can you wear those terrible clothes? You are wearing trousers."

"They are not trousers, they are jeans. Just about everyone in my time wears jeans. When I get the times right I will bring you some."

"Oh, no, don't. I could never wear anything like that."

"Well, I have to, to go out there, when I complete this part of the calculations." She once more adjusted the Time Stones and placed her hands on the rock. The rock door opened again. She said goodbye, out she went and the rock door closed behind her.

It was drizzling but, not wet enough to worry about. She made her way up through the fields; continually looking about to make sure she wasn't being seen. The hayfield was as it should have been. Skirting around the edge she became more cautious as she realized there were no previous tracks through the field.

She knew she was early and it was then that she saw the stumpy man. What was he doing so close to her house? Then she saw herself again and he was watching her. Why? She didn't remember seeing him there and she didn't want to be seen either by herself or the stumpy man. How early was she? There were no sheep in the yard. Should she go back to the cave? She had to know what day it was. The time of day seemed to be right by where the sun was in the sky peaking through the drizzly clouds.

She continued to watch and was ready to run if anyone got anywhere near the far field, because from there she would be seen. An hour went by when she noticed a van coming down the farm lane. It was a farm tractor parts delivery van and now she knew what day it was. Her calculations had been close. The van had delivered parts to her father two days before she and her brother went to the cave. She turned and ran back as fast as she could. There was no way that she wanted to be seen, not by herself and not by anyone who might think she was in two places at once especially the stumpy man.

It didn't work. When she got to the cave he was there again. She was beginning to be frightened by him even though he was probably harmless. He spoke to her in his strange voice. "Marged Evans, beware what happens on your farm."

She glared back at him in defiance. "You're a nasty man. You stay away from me or I will tell my parents, and my father has a gun."

He turned and walked away again. Marged thought that she would not see him again. She was pleased.

Back in the cave she smiled at the others. "Phew! I saw myself again. I was three days early."

Buttercup asked "How did you find that out?"

"It was the tractor parts delivery van."

"I don't know what that means."

Once again Marged did her best to explain and the explanation was accepted.

"So you have to make some more adjustments."

"Yes, and then I will go out again." She recalculated and then moved the Time Stones accordingly once again and placed her hand on the rock. The rock door opened and she was on her way once more. This time she felt it was right. She got up to the hay field and noticed the previous tracks, where she had walked with her brother and then by herself afterwards. At the stile she noticed that the cattle in the field were all the ones she knew and they were grazing. This was a good sign. After climbing over the stile and crossing half the field, she noticed there were no sheep in the yard. She had got it wrong, she was late. There seemed to be a lot of vehicles parked in the yard. What was she to do? She decided to go back to the hayfield where the cover was better, to think about how she was going to find out how late.

As she turned to go back there was a shout. She turned in the direction of the voice to see two men coming through the gate with a big dog each. "Oh, no!" she thought, "The tracker dogs."

There was another shout. "There she is, we've found her! " She stopped, her arms hanging by her side. She was caught. Now she would soon find out how late she was.

The men and dogs joined her and marched her back to the farm. There were police everywhere. They escorted her into the house, she didn't bother taking off the wellies. She entered the living room to see her parents sitting on the sofa and opposite were the lady police officer and the CID man.

Her mother leapt to her feet and grabbed her. "Where, oh, where have you been? We've been worried sick about you. What happened to you?"

"I was in the cave."

"You can't have been, we searched the cave last night and you weren't anywhere to be seen."

She looked at her mother. "I've only been gone since yesterday?"

"Yes, since yesterday. What happened to you?"

"Nothing happened. It's better than being gone for a whole year."

"Marged, what are you talking about?"

"Last time it was a year and you had left the farm."

Her father who had hardly moved stared at her. "Oh, my stars, she's gone off her head."

The CID man spoke up. "Mrs. Evans, could I ask your daughter some questions?"

"Of course."

Marged thought. "Oh no, not again."

She turned to the detective and in a loud voice stated. "No, I am not answering any more of your questions. You asked enough the last time and you never believed any of my answers."

The CID man looked back at her with a frown. "Young lady, I don't know you, I have never seen you before in my life. You must have me confused with someone else. Mrs. Evans, has your daughter gone missing before?"

"No, never."

Marged was astonished. She stopped and realized the huge blunder that she had made. How would they know? The first time that she had met the man was a year into the future. "I am going to my room." She turned and left them staring after her.

Her father shouted. "Marged, come back here."

Megan spoke up. "Let her go, Emrys, we'll talk to her later."

The CID man rose and so did the policewoman. He nodded. "Well, you have your daughter back. If she reveals anything about what has happened please give me a call. You have my card. So now we call off the search. I hope this is a happy ending."

"Oh, we hope so too."

In her room, Marged began to work out how she was going to get back to the cave. She decided to slip away after supper that evening.

Once she had decided on her escape strategy, she went back downstairs making sure that all the police had gone. She explained to her parents and her brother about what she had seen in the cave. They shook their heads in disbelief as she smiled to herself. They had no clue as to the incredible adventure that she had stumbled upon.

After supper she went back to her room and found her original backpack and stuffed in some spare clothes including jeans and shoes and an electronic hand held calculator. She laid down on the bed, and as soon as the house was quiet, she slipped downstairs and crept out of the back door. It was a half moon night and gave her enough natural light for her to see by. In seconds she was across the yard and through the gate into the field where the cows were. They were quiet and lying down. She crossed to the stile, climbed over and made her way across the hayfield and then to the cave.

She got back inside, and as the rock door closed Buttercup said, "It's dark outside. It was light when you left."

"I know, I was a day late and I got caught, so I couldn't get away until it was dark."

"Did they do anything to you? Did they punish you?"

"No, they were upset, but at the same time happy to see my return, so there was no punishment. Now I must recalibrate so that the Time Stones are correct." She got down to work and made the adjustments.

Buttercup noticed Marged's other bag. "You have another bag?"

Marged smiled. "Yes, I've brought some spare clothes and shoes. I've got jeans as well. Look." Marged opened the bag took out the pair of jeans and held them up. "See."

Buttercup looked at them. "I am not going to wear them." She glanced into the backpack and grabbed another garment. She held up a pair of Marged's underwear. "What are these?" She asked.

"That's my underwear."

"Don't you wear bloomers?"

"Noo. No one wears bloomers anymore, in my time."

"You are very strange. So what do we do next?"

"Next we go back a hundred years and find an exact day and set out the watch again in that time and make our adjustments until we get the Time Stones right."

"How are we going to do that?"

"First we are going to need Rhys Edwards."

Buttercup expressed a very distasteful look. "Eoor, not that awful, smelly, nasty boy?"

Marged looked into Buttercup's eyes. "Oh, Buttercup, don't say those things. He can't help who he is and we need him to help us. Please be nice to him, so that we can all work together. Will you do that?"

"Alright, I will be nice."

"Thank you. Let's go and find him."

CHAPTER 5

Moving stones to make time right
Is even hard for a girl so bright.
Bring together mend fences all
And work as one to prevent a fall.
Find supplies and plan your trip
And be prepared to maintain your grip.

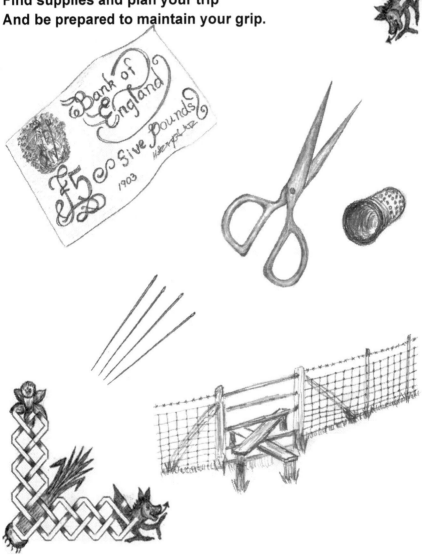

The girls found Rhys Edwards where Marged had seen him on her first visit. They approached him. He looked at Marged. "What are you doing with *her*?"

"Buttercup is helping to get the times right, and we've come to ask for your help."

"I am not helping her. She says I stink and that I am a crude Welsh boy."

"Rhys, we really need your help. Buttercup, say you are sorry."

Buttercup hesitated.

Marged frowned at her. "Go on Buttercup, say it."

She perked up. "Master Rhys, I am very sorry if I insulted you."

He looked at her. "What do you mean 'if'? You did insult me."

"Alright. I am sorry I insulted you."

He acknowledged with a nod. "That is alright."

Marged smiled. "Good, let's go back to the rock door and talk about what we are going to do."

Marged explained the marks and the Time Stones to Rhys until he understood.

"So what do you want me to do?" he asked.

Marged smiled. "We want you to help us find the exact time you came to the cave."

"I don't want to go back to that school." He moved his feet nervously ready to escape if they should decide to drag him back there. "I don't want to be beaten anymore."

"We won't let that happen. What we want is to pinpoint the year 1904 and the exact time you came into the cave."

"What is a pinpoint?"

Marged thought for a second. "What a pinpoint means is where you find something very exactly."

He nodded.

Marged continued. "We have established the exact position of the Time Stones for 2004. What we have to do now is establish their exact position for 1904, and then that way I can calibrate all the years, months and days in between. Once that has been done, all the people that came here during that time, in that hundred years, will be able to leave and show up in their right time outside. I have made some calculations with the ruler." She held it up. "Now, all I have to do is punch the numbers into my calculator." She removed it from the bag.

Buttercup's eyes widened. "What is that?"

"It's a calculating machine."

"So what do you use it for?"

"Well, I will show you both." They stood either side of her and she began a demonstration of how the calculator worked.

They both accepted it; however, they were very suspicious and the thought that perhaps she was some sort of magician crossed their minds.

Using the calculator she soon had answers to getting the Time Stones close to right. She turned to Rhys. "Now, where did you come from?"

"Llanymddyfri."

"Llandovery! Llandovery, that's miles away. How did you get here?"

"I walked every step of it. How else could I have got here?"

"Why didn't you get a ride?"

"I was afraid in case I got taken back to that school."

"But why did you come all the way up here?"

"Because my uncle lives up the valley and I was going to stay with him, but I never got there, I came in here instead because it was raining."

"How are we going to get you back to Llandovery?"

"I don't want to go back there." There was a touch of dread crossing his face. "I want to go to my uncle's farm up the valley."

"Alright, we'll get you there in your right time, but first we have to establish an exact year and time that matches the time you got here. So what was the date of your arrival here?"

"I don't know."

"You don't know?"

"No."

"What day was it when you ran away from the school in Llandovery?"

"It was the thirtieth of March 1904."

"Good, how long did it take you to get here?"

"Three days."

"So you must have got here on the second of April, right?"

"Yes, I think so."

"Well, I suppose that is about as accurate as we are going to get. Did you get here in the morning or afternoon?"

"In the morning, I think."

"Alright, I think that will do. Now, I have set the Time Stones to where I think they should be. But to know for sure, we are going to have to go out there and get an exact time and date." She turned to Rhys. "We can't go up the valley, because if it's not the right time your uncle might see you and if you are early you will still be in Llandovery and that will not be good."

Rhys responded. "I don't think it will hurt any. My uncle has never seen me before."

"He has never seen you?"

"No."

"Well, that's a point in our favour, but I still think you should avoid seeing him until we have calculated the time right, and that means we have to go outside and find out what year, month, day and time it is. Where we are going to find out this, I am not sure, but we have to, or we can never get you back to your right time. Once we find the time out there on our first visit, we will come back in and make further adjustments to get close to the time we want, and then I will leave the watch hidden outside. I can leave it in 2004 time, because 2004 and 1904 are leap years."

Buttercup, who had been listening very intently, asked, "Marged, why do you say we are going outside? Are you Royalty, now?"

Marged laughed. "No, of course not. I mean all three of us should go out there, because I am not familiar with these times. Not only that, we have to look like we are a part of that time. Rhys, does Buttercup's dress look like the girls' dresses in your school?"

He looked Buttercup up and down. "Yes, I think so, but a lot nicer."

"So if someone saw her in 1904 she wouldn't look out of place."

"No, I think she would look alright."

"Good, so now I have to find something suitable for me to wear for the time. I could probably find something here that would be close, but they would be on somebody else and they might not want to exchange their clothes for my clothes."

Buttercup looked Marged up and down. "I don't think I would want to change my clothes with you."

Marged smiled. "If we go out there, it might take a while, so that means we should probably take some food with us. So what I am going to do is go out in my time, go home and find clothes that fit me for the time around 1904, find out more about what happened in that year and bring some food back, so that we can go out without sticking out like a sore thumb."

She went over to the roll of paper and checked her marks and notes, adjusted the pebbles, placed her hands on the wall and the rock door opened. She picked up one of her bags and emptied it. She would need it to bring back the goods.

As she left she said, "This will take me some time, because I may have to make the clothes, I will be a little older when I return so make sure I make a note of it when I get here."

She walked out of the cavern, confident that this time her return to the farm would be exactly at the time she had set with the Time Stones. She crossed the lower fields through the hayfield, across the cattle field, and arrived very early at the yard. Her father was outside crossing to one of the sheds. He raised his eyebrows. "You're up early."

"Yes, I went to the cave."

"You must have disappeared in there, because we haven't seen you for a year."

 She stopped. It felt as if her shoes were stuck to the ground and a shudder went through her. In the distance she could see the stumpy man watching. She stared back and again he walked away. After what seemed like an age she realized that her father was teasing her. She smiled. "It's all true, Dad."

"What is true?"

"The myths and legends. I didn't meet Owain Glyn Dwr there, but the protector of Llewellyn the Last was there and he said that Owain was out."

"Oh, so he was out was he, pity, you could have brought him back for breakfast."

"Dad, I am serious and I saw the fisherman too. He was wearing his waders and had a plaid shirt on. He was carrying his rod and reel and I am going to go back and help him get out of there."

"Oh, you did, did you? What kind of colour and type of rod was it?"

"It was a dull yellowish, made of bamboo."

Emrys, stared at her for a second. She was right. "Did you hear me or anyone say what the rod was like before?"

"No, Dad, I saw it for myself."

He stared at her again. "Oh, well, there you are. Did you tell him that he had been gone for eight years."

"Yes, I did, but he didn't believe me. He thinks that it is the same day he went in. The cave makes the time outside all wrong."

Emrys shook his head. When he spoke next, Megan, was serving up the breakfast. "Have you been listening to this, Megan?"

She smiled, "Some of it."

Emrys smiled. "This girl's imagination has gone absolutely wild. Tell me, Marged, if the fisherman can't find his right time, how did you get back here at your right time?"

"This is the first time that I have. The first time I came back I was a year late and because you were all upset when I was missing, you had leased out the farm and you were living in town." She continued with the story and told them about everything that had happened on that day and how she had begun to recalibrate the pebbles and get all her times right.

They hadn't even picked up their utensils to eat. They were staring at her trying to think about what to say in response. Then Megan came out of her mini trance. "Well, my girl, you have certainly thought that story out; we will have to add that one to the other myths and legends."

Marged looked at her mother and rolled her eyes. "I know you don't believe me, you never believed me when I came out before." She picked up her spoon and began to eat her breakfast. After a while she turned to her father. "Dad?"

"Yes."

"Did you ever hear about a girl going missing in 1918, after her mother had left her in the cave to go and get her help?"

"Yes, their horse had gone lame, or so the story goes, and when the mother came back with help, the girl was gone."

"Well, she is in the cave too and her name is Buttercup. She is helping me recalibrate the Time Stones."

"That is very nice, Marged. So what are you going to do today, go back to the cave again?"

"No, I have to do some things first before I can go back, because I have to find an exact date in 1904."

"Alright, Marged. That's enough. Do whatever you want."

That afternoon Marged went to her room to plan out everything and what she would need to take back with her to the cave. She thought that three days' food for three people would be enough and what about money? They would have to have money. She made a note, "Try to find money used in 1904."

She went back downstairs and got her mother's permission to go on the farm computer. Her first search was for a dress from 1904. It would have to be simple if she was going to make it herself. After scanning for half an hour or more she found what she wanted in a theatre costume website. If she could buy it or rent it, it would be perfect. She checked, and yes she could rent it for a pound a day, with a small deposit in case of damage and the shop was in town. Thinking that she would only need it for a day she could, perhaps, get it back the same day that she rented it. "Now, what about money?" she thought.

She murmured to herself. "Old money. Who has old money?" Another computer search found just what she was looking for. There was a shop in Llandrindod Wells that sold old money and she could get ten pounds of old money in coins for one pound of new money. She was delighted. That would be perfect. Now she had to persuade her mother to take her into Builth and then on to Llandrindod Wells. Builth would be easy, but getting her mother to take her to Llandrindod would take some working out. So she began right away.

"Mam."

Megan was in the kitchen she came out to the living room. "What is it?"

"Can we go into town today?"

"What for?"

"Well, I'll be going to the high school soon and I thought it would be good to go and get some supplies and I am going to need a high school uniform."

"You are in a hurry. Do you know what you want?"

"Yes."

"Well, that's good, but I don't want to go today. Tomorrow, p'raps, but before we go I will need to look at the list the high school sent me. It seems that you are going to need more than just the uniform. You will need underwear, sportswear, shoes and gym shoes and I want to see which shop has the best prices."

"Where are the shops?"

"Well, there is one in town and two in Llandrindod Wells."

Marged smiled. "Let's get everything in Llan'dod. We haven't been there for a long time."

"I expect we could. The prices will probably be six for one and half a dozen for the other. Anyway, I shall think about it."

It was two days later on the Friday before her mother decided to take her for the school uniform, and they would go to Llandrindod.

Marged extracted eight pounds from her savings. She saved quite a lot because she never spent money unless it was absolutely necessary. Everyone said that she took after her great-grandmother who was known as: "That Cardi woman". The Cardi's, of course, were known to be tighter with their money than the Scots were.

They arrived in Llandrindod and began their shopping. She was measured up for a uniform and found there wasn't one that fitted her properly, so the shop keeper said that he would have to order one, adding that it was good that they came in early, so that they would get it in time. Marged thought that it would not have made any difference because she already had a school uniform back at the cavern. All Marged wanted to do was get to that antique shop and buy those old coins.

When she and her mother came out of the clothes shop, Marged suggested they go looking at some of the other shops.

Her mother smiled. "Alright, we have plenty of time. Where do you want to go?"

"Let's go this way." She pointed down one of the streets and off they went, stopping to window shop on the way. Fifteen minutes later they were in front of the antique shop and much to Marged's delight some coins were displayed in the window. "Mam, can we go in and look at the coins?"

Her mother smiled. "Yes, if you want."

They went in and looked over many of the antiques. There didn't seem to be anyone around so Marged shouted, "Hello."

After a few seconds, she heard some movement behind a curtain in the back of the shop, then the curtain was pushed to one side and an old man came through. He had a grey beard. If it had been any longer she would have thought it was Caradoc.

"What coins do you have?" Marged asked.

"I have quite a few. My son advertises them on the computer. I don't have anything to do with that part of it, but I can show you what I have." He reached under the counter and pulled out a large box full of old British coins.

There were a lot of them because the old man struggled with the weight of the box. Once placed on top of the counter, he invited Marged to go through and select what she wanted. She hoped she could find the ones she wanted, but she would have to make sure that they weren't newer than 1904. Looking them over she then realized that she wasn't sure how the values worked. "Mam," she asked, "How did this money work?"

Megan wasn't really sure because she was a young girl in 1972 when they changed to the modern decimal coinage. "Why don't you ask the man?"

"Alright, Sir, how did this old money work?"

He smiled. "Of course, you don't remember the old money, do you?"

"No," she replied. "Show me."

He soon began to explain how there were four farthings in a penny and two in a halfpenny, then he said that there were twelve pennies in a shilling and twenty shillings in a pound. She asked him to explain it over again and the second time he showed her on a piece of paper how it all worked.

She smiled. "I think I know, now." She continued to go through the coins and quickly found a worn 1904 penny and it had the head of Edward VII on it. She looked at the shopkeeper. "How long was this man king for?"

"Let me see." She handed him the penny. "Ah, this is Edward VII, he was the son of Queen Victoria and became king in 1901 and served until his death in 1910."

She smiled.

Her mother watched her as she carefully sorted through the coins. To begin with she had to ask what the values of the silver coins were. The old man explained the sixpence, the shilling, which he told her was equal to a 5p coin and then the half crown. "What is a half crown worth?" she asked.

He smiled. "A half crown is worth 30 old pennies."

"How many of them in a pound?"

"Eight half crowns or two hundred and forty pennies."

She began to set out as many 1904 and earlier half crowns as she could and even some 1905 and 1906 because their dates could hardly be seen. She found sixteen and realized that ten pounds worth would be very heavy.

She asked him if he had old coins that were worth more.

He told her that the half crown was the biggest.

She wanted at least ten pounds worth so thought that she would keep on going to see what she could get. She set aside florins, shillings and sixpences.   She smiled at the man. "Is a florin two shillings?"

He nodded. "Yes, that's right, 10p. Now, perhaps you might like to see these."

He took out a large folder from behind the counter and laid it out for Marged. "Here we have some of the paper money that was used back then." He opened it up and showed her ten shilling notes, one pound notes and five pound notes that were white with fancy writing on them and it seemed that there were people's names signed on them as well. "If you don't have enough money for the good ones I will sell you the worn ones that are cheap."

"Yes", the excitement was on her face and in her voice. "I want to see them."

He closed the folder and placed it under the counter, then pulled out an old cigar box and opened it to reveal notes of all the denominations. They were torn and very dirty. "You pick out what you want and we will see if we can come to an agreement."

"I want some of the coins as well," she said.

"Good, pick out what you want."

"How much are these big white five pound notes?"

"They are poor quality and they are no longer legal currency, so I can let you have them for 50p each."

"I will have four of them," She said quickly and laid them out. "What about the other notes?"

"They are also 50p each."

"And their old value is less than five pounds?"

"Yes, but they are not currency anymore, they are now antique money."

"Alright, I will take two one pound notes. So, what do the coins cost?"

"For the coins I will give you a deal, 50p for what you have selected and I will throw in a few pennies, a few halfpennies, a couple of farthings and one silver threepenny bit."

"Yes, I will take them."

Her mother was a little confused. "Why do you want this old money, Marged?"

"I saw some people on the telly talking about it and I thought it would be kuhle to have some."

She handed over the relevant modern money and the man wrapped up the old money and handed the package over to the beaming girl.

They left the shop and outside was the stumpy man again. Her mother didn't seem to notice him. Was he invisible to everyone else? He turned and walked away. He always did this. Marged realized that he too must be able to travel through time and decided to ask Caradoc about him.

Marged asked her mother if they were going on to Builth.

"No, if you want to go to Builth you can go on Monday with your father. He'll be going to the market."

"Oh, alright."

That suited Marged, she would be able to rent the Edwardian clothes she needed without her mother looking over her shoulder. However, she realized that she would need more of her savings to make sure she would have enough money.

On Monday, Marged went to Builth with her brother and her father in the Land Rover, towing a horse box with two steers for the market. They dropped her off in the High Street and she went immediately to the place that rented the costumes. It was a small part of a clothing shop and she was directed through the shop to a small back room. They had what she wanted and the items fitted her reasonably well. She asked about the rental and was told that she could rent for a pound a day or five pound for a week. Then she asked if she could think about it for a minute. They watched her as she walked up and down and couldn't understand why she couldn't make an immediate decision.

Marged was going through all the possible scenarios of going back to the cave and getting back again. If she rented for one day she would have to go to the cave that night and the problem with that was when could she come back again? No one was going to be going to Builth the next day or Wednesday, Thursday or Friday possibly, but it would probably be the following Monday, so she decided to rent for a week. They put the costume pieces into a bag after she had paid five pounds for the rental and ten pounds deposit, which she would get back when she returned them.

She had a shopping bag with her and placed the bag with the costume into it. It would have to be sneaked into the house and up the stairs to her bedroom, without her mother seeing it.

She walked up to the market with her purchases to meet up with Rhys and her father ready for the journey home. The market was busy. Farmers were everywhere, just like the smells, surrounding the pens that held the cattle. The cattle were being prodded and discussed with great gesticulations.

She could hear, over the general noise, the auctioneer in a brisk full voice selling the cattle as they were hustled through the sales ring. She found Rhys and her Father they were being watched by the stumpy man who on seeing Marged walked away into the crowd. Her Father had sold the two steers as stores and had got a good price.

At home Marged was able to sneak her costume package up the stairs to her room and hide it away. When she came back down her mother asked her what she did in town. She told her she had looked in a lot of shops and had bought some chocolate and some energy bars.

"Why did you buy energy bars?

Now, how was she going to explain this? Tell the truth. "Well, I bought them to take to the cave. Of course, no one eats in the cave because there is no time there, however, when we go outside to find out what the date and time is, we sometimes are out there for quite a while and so that is what the energy bars are for."

Her mother was beginning to wonder if Marged was taking this cave thing too far, but decided to go along with it. After all she would be going to the High School in a few weeks and embark on growing up. "So do your imaginary friends in the cave like energy bars?"

"Mam, they are not imaginary and I don't know if they like them or not, because they haven't tried them yet."

Her mother shook her head. "Of course not, I should have known." She turned and went into the kitchen.

Marged went upstairs to sort out all that she needed to take with her. The costume and other clothes that she might need were laid out, including a pair of cut off jeans that she could wear under her 1904 clothes. She placed the money in the pockets. Energy bars, chocolate and some packages of dried meat that was called jerky went into her bag. That would keep them going for a few days. However, she hoped that they could feed themselves on their journeys and conserve what she had got in the bag. After all they would have plenty of money. She included a small first aid package, a sewing kit and two brand new torches with bright LED bulbs. A small digital camera was also added as she wanted to record her adventures, although she knew that taking things back from the future would not meet with Caradoc's approval, but she felt that she could persuade him.

Then she realized that she wouldn't be able to take the backpack back to 1904, so she decided to take two hessian corn sacks from the barn and hide them closer to the cave, with three plastic quart bottles of water, a large scissors borrowed from her mother's kitchen drawer, a ball of string and a large woolsack sewing needle from her father's tool box in the barn. By Thursday she was ready, so she left another letter under her pillow. It was almost the same as the first one and like the first would probably not be seen.

She left the house on Thursday morning with the bag on her back and walked through the cattle field, climbed over the stile and on through the hayfield. As she approached the cave she retrieved the goods she had hidden and struggled with them into the cave. On stroking the stone the rock door opened once again and she dragged everything through.

Buttercup, Rhys and Caradoc were there waiting, although to them no time had passed at all. With them was the fisherman whose name was David Taylor.

"What did you bring?" Buttercup asked.

"Everything we are going to need in 1904. At least, I hope so."

CHAPTER 6

To meet the past we can but dream
But, it will be real for our timeless team.
Even dinosaurs from the past be seen.
Not yet fossils have they been.
Marged goes back a hundred years
And in that past she finds new peers.

Marged began to show them everything she had brought in, including the three plastic bottles she had wrapped with the sacking and tied tightly with the string. "We have to bring these back; we cannot leave them in the past. We will use them for water and when they are empty we can collapse them so they don't take up too much room. From the sacks we must make bags to carry the water and the food I have brought for the journey. She held up the costume.

Buttercup giggled. "That's what servants wear."

Marged smiled. "Good. Because as you are wearing that nice dress, Rhys and I will be your servants and you will pretend to be a young lady, the daughter of someone very important."

"I am a young lady and my parents are very important."

"I know, so this should work out for all of us. Now, how much money do you both have?"

Buttercup didn't have any and Rhys had two farthings left of tuppence he left Llandovery with.

Buttercup had a beginning look of despair. "We have to have money; we can't go out there without money. We would have to steal it and what if we got caught. We would be taken to the workhouse and never get out again."

Marged watched the expressions. The fisherman, David Taylor, who had been listening said, "I have money, but it won't work in 1904."

Marged let a big grin cross her face as she held up the cut off jeans. "The money we need is here." She shook the jeans and the money jingled in the pockets and then she reached in and pulled out one of the five pound notes.

Buttercup's eyes went huge, but they were relatively small compared to Rhys' eyes.

Buttercup exclaimed. "That is a five pound note! Where did you get it?"

"In an antique shop in Llandrindod Wells. I have four of them."

Rhys was slowly recomposing himself. "My father doesn't earn more than twenty pounds in half a year. We are rich! We will be able to buy anything we want out there."

Marged smiled. "We will buy only what is essential for us to have and nothing more. Buttercup will have one of the five pound notes, a pound note, two halfcrowns, one florin, a shilling, a sixpence, two pennies and one halfpenny. The rest of the money will stay in my cut off jeans which I will wear under my 1904 clothes."

David Taylor smiled. "My goodness you have thought it all out, haven't you?"

Marged smiled at the compliment. "We hope so Mr. Taylor, we hope so. When we have finished with this part we are going to need your help and that will mean we will get you out in your right time."

"Thank you, on my last visit out there I was years in the past and I got beaten up by a game keeper. I tried to tell him that I wasn't poaching or fishing without a license. I showed him the license that I had and he accused me of pulling a fast one. 'License from the future indeed, don't you give me that twaddle.' I tried explaining and he began pushing me around and beating me with his stick. He also told me that he could make his gun go off by accident. I managed to get away from him and came back here. I was covered in bruises and Caradoc took the pain away. I don't want to go out, if it's not right, any more."

They all listened to his story. Marged responded first. "Don't worry. We won't let you out there unless it is the exact time. However, you can help. If you are a banker, you know all about maths?"

"Yes. What would you like me to do?"

"Well, to recalibrate the Time Stones I have had to make very fine adjustments with very small measurements and I wonder if you could find a way to make those measurements bigger without changing the outcome of the calibrations and what they do."

"I could possibly extrapolate your measurements into larger ones, just like a scale."

"That would be marvellous and then it would be nice to make the stones fit accordingly." She turned to Caradoc. "Would it be possible to change the movement of the Time Stones so they work just the same on larger spaces?"

"They can move themselves for time and right.
But what motivates has been my plight.
There is a place that governs stones
And the knowledge should be in my bones."

Marged saw the flash of fear and sadness on his face again. "Oh. Caradoc, you have forgotten haven't you?"

"I am afraid I have my lovely dear
And it will now come back while you are here."

Buttercup piped up. "How can you be so stupid to forget something as important as that?"

Marged turned on her. "Stop it, Buttercup, it is not his fault. We must all be nice to one another. The main thing is they can be changed, and all we have to do is work out how.

Buttercup announced that she was sorry to everyone.

Marged then asked Rhys, Buttercup and David to make two bags from the sacks using the wool sack needle and the string. She explained that they were for carrying food and water when outside.

Rhys asked. "There will be three of us. Why are we only taking two bags?"

Marged smiled. "For a start we only need two bags and we can take it in turns to carry them. That way we won't get tired and when we are around people Buttercup will not be carrying one because we want to make sure people realize that she is a lady. That way fewer people will bother us."

"Are you going to help us make them?"

"No, not yet. I want to ask Caradoc some questions. Caradoc, could you show me the place where the light comes out of the rocks?"

"I will gladly show you them,
Each and everyone a gem."

They arrived at the strange illuminating rocks. Marged smiled. "Have you tried to make these things work properly?"

"I have indeed, with all due speed.
To all others I've paid no heed.
They have been moved and are ajar
The reason for it could be afar."

"Is the fault outside and not within?"

"It could be out there at worlds end
But it is here the solving we must rend.
The work for you will be no crime.
Just like the work with stones of time."

"So what you are saying is that we can fix these things so that they work correctly once again?"

"Yes, indeed my lovely dear
And you can do it without a fear."

"I will work on it once I have calibrated the Time Stones and have helped those people who want to go back to their time leave."

"I am pleased you've taken up this cause,
You drive ahead without a pause."

She relaxed a little and smiled. "Caradoc, are there dragons in this cave?"

"Ah, the creatures with the mouth of flame,
Do not exist but have great fame."

"I have seen some strange reptiles here, where did they come from?"

"Millions of time from great big herds,
They are the parents of the birds."

"You mean there are dinosaurs here?"

"I don't think they were ever sore,
But being around them is quite a chore.
Come with me and I will show to you.
In here there are still quite a few."

He led Marged through some passages and into a cavern that was so big you could hardly see the end of it and wandering around were dinosaurs and huge insects that were flying amongst them. She was totally gobsmacked. A huge Apatosaurus turned and stared at her and moved off past a Tyrannosaurus and above was a pterodactyl gliding through the cave. Marged watched the flying creature the wingspan of which must have been 20 feet or more. If she had been outside, not knowing the cave, she would have been totally mesmerized. "Look, most of them have feathers." Then she asked Caradoc. "Do you think that they might want to go out to their time?"

"I do not know their times desire,
So if out wrong it would be dire."

"They can stay. I have too much to do to deal with them. Perhaps later. Now, I have another question. You told me that no one over 16 can stroke the outer stone and get in here. How did those older people get in here? Like Mr. Taylor."

"They take electricity from overhead,
It strikes them close by and leaves not dead."

"You mean they have survived a lightning strike?"

"Yes indeed they have lived to see,
The wonders of what it is to be.
Others come rushing in with great fear.
So pursued in fear they come in here."

"Oh, so if someone is afraid when they come here the cave opens up for them?"

"Here protection from your fears you'll find
And once in here all enemies will be kind."

"I like it. Alright, how far into the future can I go if I decide to go there?"

"To the future you have already been
And much ahead if you are keen."

"I am, but I have not seen anyone here from the future. Do they come here?"

"You have seen people beyond your day.
So how would you know either way."

"In other words they are here and I haven't noticed them?"

"Here they are among all you see,
When you ask you will know that here they be."

"Thank you, Caradoc, and thank you for letting me help these people find their way into their right time?"

"I have tried so much and done a lot
But my results have helped them not.
You are the first that can make it right
And help these people from their plight."

They made their way back to the door. Marged was pleased. The bags had been made and the food was equally packed in with the sack wrapped bottles of water. She took the cut off jeans with the money and the servant's costume and changed in the alcove.

She came out and said. "I am ready, but before we go I have a confession to make to Caradoc. For our safety we are taking two torches so that if we have to travel at night we will be able to make our way without stumbling and hurting ourselves. If we are in trouble we will do our best to destroy them and if it fails and I can get back I will pick a time to go out and retrieve them. We also have three modern plastic bottles for water wrapped in sacking we will do the same with them. Also, I have a first aid kit in case we hurt ourselves on our travels. Do you approve of us taking these things out there before their time?"

"I do not approve of such a thing,
But for keeping safe you have to bring."

Marged smiled. "Thank you. Now here is a trickier situation. The money we have for this journey I bought in the future for very little in my time. We can do a lot for people if we can go to the future and trade rare things from the past for the common things from the past that will be very useful to us when we bring them back. I bought the money with money from my time at a shop that sells things from the past. If the things in that shop from the past are in excellent repair they can sell for thousands of times more than their original worth in the past. When we go back to the past we should find small things of normal value that can be brought back here for trade in the future so that we can finance our trips out there. Could we do this?"

"Your thinking for success is good
And your need for money is understood."

She picked up the tiny digital camera. "This little machine can take pictures, photographs, hundreds of them. I want to take pictures in the past and then bring them back with paper from that time to make albums for use in gaining knowledge of the times we visit so others can use them to prepare for their return to their times. Caradoc, would you approve of this?"

"When you do this it makes me pained,
But approve I must for knowledge gained."

"Alright, thank you, Caradoc. Are we ready? I will arrange the Time Stones and out we'll go."

The rock door opened and Caradoc and the fisherman watched the intrepid trio embark on their first adventure together.

Once outside, Marged was stunned by the difference in the scenery.

Large trees that she had become familiar with in 2004 were not there. The seeds they grew from had barely been produced. The weather was beautiful and the leaves were fully developed on other large trees. Marged pointed out to the others that if Rhys arrived at the cave on April the second then they had come out later that year or in the summer of the years before or the years after.

Buttercup asked. "Where do we find the date for the time we are in?"

"Well," said Marged. "The first place I think we should go is up to my farm and see what we can find there. Follow me."

She led them through the fields that she thought would be familiar to her. They weren't. There were no fences, just hedges and some old dry stone walls that she had never seen and which hadn't existed in 2004. The old oak tree was there. It was already big, but not as big as in her time. However, there were quite a few other large trees. They approached the farm house and Marged noted there were no iron gates. The sycamores were quite small. The house didn't look to be in good condition and there were only two outbuildings. The modern buildings that she knew hadn't been built yet.

Outside the house there was an old woman washing clothes in an old wooden tub. She was wearing a filthy apron over a long grey dress made of sacking. Around her shoulders she wore a mostly red coloured shawl, although the colours had faded and were masked by dirt and grime. On her head she wore the tall black hat that was the traditional Welsh hat. Marged stared at what she considered to be a living museum piece and wondered if this woman was an ancestor of hers. The three travellers approached her and as they did the woman stood and called a dog to her side in Welsh.

Marged smiled. "My lady, do you know what day it is?"

The woman looked at her and after a short while of assessing the visiting trio said. "Sais." And then spat on the ground in front of them and turned and went into the house, called the dog in after her and slammed the door.

Marged heard Rhys chuckle and she turned to look at him. He smiled back at her. "That woman doesn't like the English."

"Why don't you go and talk to her, then?" Buttercup retorted.

He glared at Buttercup. "Welsh or not I am not going in there with that woman. A woman like that could eat people." Marged chuckled and Rhys continued. "We can go somewhere else as far as I'm concerned."

Marged nodded. "No, we can't do any more here or they might start asking questions that we do not want to answer. We must move on. I think we should try Builth or Beulah. We could go to farms for days and not get anywhere."

Buttercup was frowning. "Where are Builth and Beulah? I only know Garth because that's where my mother and I get off the train."

Marged's eyes went wide and her face lit up."The train, the train, why didn't I think of that." She hugged Buttercup. "That is where we can find the date and time. If we go down past Troedrhiwdalar we will be there before its dark and the station will have what we need. Come on, let's get going."

Marged guided them toward Capel Rhos. The going would be alright from there albeit a rough old dirt track compared to what it was in Marged's time. After half an hour they crossed the Gwenwst stream, the same stream that ran past the cave. They came out on the road to Garth; it wasn't the road that Marged was familiar with. The road she knew was wide and had tar macadam. This road too was also a dirt track with ruts and large potholes, but it would be a hundred times better to travel on than cutting through the woods and fields.

They had walked fifteen minutes before they saw anyone. In a field to their right was a man cutting hay. Marged watched in amazement. There were two horses pulling a reciprocating mower not unlike the one her father used except this one had iron wheels with lugs on. The man himself was sitting on the machine controlling the horses and working a lever. When the horses had reached the end of the swath the man pulled on the lever and the cutting blade lifted off the ground. This was so he could turn the horses and reposition them for the next swath, when he would release the lever and drop the blade to begin cutting again. Marged asked, "How does that work?"

Rhys, coming from a farming family explained in his broken English that as the wheels went round they turned a series of cogged wheels on the machine which in turn made the blade go back and fore. They watched for five more minutes, then Marged reminded herself that they were still on a mission not a sightseeing tour. Half way to Garth they were caught up to and passed by two well dressed young men on horseback. They didn't stop or take any notice of the travelling trio who barely got a glimpse of their faces. The trio was seen in full view and it seemed that they didn't look out of place. This was good.

"Who were they?" Buttercup asked.

Marged responded. "I have no idea who they might be. They were dressed fancy."

"English gentry," said Rhys.

They continued their journey. There seemed to be more trees and the fields were a lot smaller. The farms and their buildings were very rustic. Every building was built with stone and the roofs were slate with an occasional building thatched with long straw. Marged didn't know of any thatch in her time. Soon they were looking down on the small village of Garth.

Marged pointed. "There's Garth. We'll be there in no time."

Down the hill into Garth they went and onto the main road, it wasn't much of one in this time. In Marged's time it was a wide, tar macadam road with white lines down the middle of it and was the main road from Swansea to Chester known as the A483. The road they walked onto was not much wider than the track-like road they had just left. They were able to walk up the middle of it without a care. They saw two gambo's, one pulled by a horse and the other by a mule and they had to move to one side when a man and two sheepdogs came along droving a flock of sheep. As the flock was passing they noticed a man driving a light carriage pulled by a fine-boned, high-stepping trotter. He came right up behind the man droving the sheep and began shouting abuse at him to make him move the sheep over so that he could pass. It took the shepherd a few minutes to comply and all the while the man on the carriage heaped on his abuse. Marged was horrified. "Why is he so rude? Why doesn't he have patience?"

Rhys answered. "He doesn't have to. He is gentry."

Marged scowled. "He could never do that in my time. He would be told what he could do with his rudeness."

They reached the small railway station and were able to walk right onto the platform. Marged noticed the smell, a residual smell that lingered after every train. After walking a few feet a man appeared in a doorway behind them. "Are you here to catch the train?"

The trio turned and stared at him. Marged addressed Buttercup. "Are we catching the train today, my lady?"

Buttercup glanced at Marged and then faced the man in his British Rail uniform of the day. "No, not today, my good man, I am here to make possible travel arrangements."

He responded. "Certainly, my lady, I have a schedule of times. Would you be going north or south?"

"Oh. Yes, er, north or south? South."

"All the way to Swansea or somewhere nearer?"

She didn't know how to answer and then remembered the name Llandovery. She assumed it was one of the towns on the line. "Landovery." She said. Being English she couldn't pronounce the double L sound.

"Would that be one way or return?"

"Return."

"First, second or third class, my lady?"

She tossed her head as if she was offended that he would even think to ask such a question. "First class."

Marged almost burst out laughing.

"Yes, my lady, of course. I can tell you right away."

He slipped back through the door. Marged nodded approval and looked around. She spotted a newspaper on a small stand. She went over. It was a *South Wales Echo*. She glanced at the date. It was August 27th 1903. She whispered to Buttercup. "Ask him if this is today's paper and ask to buy it."

He came out. "My lady, the first class return fair to Llandovery is one shilling."

"Thankyou. Tell me is that today's newspaper?"

"Yes, my lady. It came up on the train early this morning from Swansea."

"Good. I would like to purchase a copy."

"Yes, my lady, that will be a farthing."

Buttercup reached into her purse and handed him a penny. He took it and went back into his office. After the scraping of drawers he came out again and gave her a halfpenny and a farthing in change, reached for a paper, picked it up and handed it to her. She immediately handed it on to Marged. "Carry this for me, girl, please."

Marged took the paper. "Yes, my lady."

The man stood in front of them waiting. "Will that be all, my lady?"

"Yes, that will be all for now. No. Sorry, do you have a copy of a schedule for the trains on this line?"

"Yes, my lady, I will get you one." He returned to his office and came back with a schedule and all the running times of the trains.

Marged whispered. "Let's go back down there and check the date on my watch. The time is four o'clock." She pointed at the clock down the platform. As they turned they heard the steam whistle of an approaching train and then the sound of the engine. Marged had never heard the sound of a steam engine before. They watched the train approach from the south, belching smoke and steam. It was slowing down, preparing to stop in the station. They moved to the south end of the building and stood there to watch. Marged glanced up the platform to see the stumpy man standing there. Marged wondered why she was always seeing this man who made her feel as if a cold wind had blown through her insides. He stepped away and the same two gentlemen who had passed them on the road walked on to the platform from the north.

The noise, the smoke and the steam was unbelievable as the train came to a halt and then the smell was re-intensified around the station. There were five carriages, two third class, two second class and one first class. When the train stopped the first class carriage was next to the platform. The two third class carriages had not reached the platform and the two passengers in third class who wanted to get off had to jump down onto the gravel beside the tracks.

The railway man came out of his office and from another door there appeared a man with an iron wheeled, wooden dolly. The two well-dressed gentlemen were greeting two ladies and were helping them off the train.

The trio watched and then suddenly Buttercup cried out, "Oh, oh, that's my mother and father!"

She began to move toward them but Marged who was also shocked by the exclamation grabbed her arm. "Buttercup, you can't go to them."

She responded furiously. "Why can't I go, they are my parents?"

Marged held her firmly and moved her behind the end of the building. Buttercup tried to free herself and Marged pushed her against the wall of the building. "Buttercup, you can't go to them because you haven't been born yet. You weren't born until 1907, were you?"

A sudden fear came over Buttercup. "Oh, my goodness, no. Did they hear me?" She stopped her struggle.

"I don't think so, not over the train noise."

"Can I look at them from here, please?"

"Alright but don't say anything."

"Oh gosh, I won't, this is terribly shocking."

All three peered around the corner of the building and watched the activity up the platform. Buttercup pointed out her father who was one of the gentlemen who had passed them on horseback on the road.

"Oh." Buttercup almost lost her breath completely. "He passed me. He passed me on the road. my father passed me on the road." She then pointed out the younger of the two women getting off the train. "She is my mother."

Marged looked at them. "When did they get married?"

"In September 1904."

"So they are not married yet."

Buttercup's eyes widened and she sank back against the wall of the station. "Oh, my goodness, they are not married and I am here. Oh, dear, they mustn't see me."

Marged smiled. "That's what I told you. But we can watch them from a distance and even if they look our way they are not going to know who you are because they haven't had you yet. Let's see where they go."

The trio moved around the building to see the two ladies being helped into a carriage. Buttercup whispered. "The other lady is my grandmother."

The two gentlemen took the bags from the porter's dolly and loaded them onto the back of the carriage, once this was done the carriage moved off driven by a man in a top hat. The two gentlemen then walked a short distance to where they had left their horses which were being held by a young boy. He was given a coin and the men mounted up and followed the carriage. The trio watched them go down the road and then turn up the road they had come down. Marged asked. "Where are they going?"

Buttercup answered. "They are going up to the big house where I was staying. If they weren't my parents we could have got a ride with them back up to somewhere near the cave. I suppose, now, we will have to walk."

Marged nodded. "I don't think we have to walk back. We could hire someone else with a carriage. Let's go and ask the station master man. Perhaps he will know someone and I want to set my watch, anyway. So, Buttercup, ask him where we can hire a carriage to take us to Capel Rhos."

They went back onto the platform and Rhys and Marged waited while Buttercup found the station master. As she went, Marged checked the station clock and made sure of the time and date on her watch.

The station master came out of his office and greeted Buttercup. "I suppose you want to buy your ticket, my lady?"

"No, I wish to hire a carriage to take me and my servants to Capel Ross."

He looked at her and brought his hand up to his chin and cupped it. "Ooh, my lady, I don't think you'll be getting a carriage here today. I could find somebody to take you in a cart, if you don't mind a bit of a rough ride. You see the carriage we use around here has just left. What do you think, my lady, should I send George, the porter, into the village to find one for you. There is usually someone around who can do it."

She glanced back at Marged and saw her nod slightly. She turned and faced the station master. "Yes, that will be fine."

He called the porter and sent him into the village to find transport.

The station master turned to Buttercup. "It won't be very long, my lady. There are some seats at the front of the building you can go and wait there if you wish."

"Thank you, my good man."

They moved around to the front of the building and all three sat down on the same bench and then Marged said, "I don't think we should do this."

Buttercup asked. "Why, we've just ordered the cart."

"No, I don't mean that. I mean that you should not sit on the same seat as your servants. You should sit on that one next to this one."

"Oh, yes, you are right." She got up and moved to the other seat.

As they waited Marged got up and walked around to take in the differences she could see around the station compared to her time. She carefully took pictures and as she was doing this she saw the stumpy man again. She pointed the camera at him and clicked and then stared at him and smiled. He turned and walked away. She would show the picture to Caradoc.

Twenty minutes later a man driving an old farm cart, a gambo, showed up. It was being pulled by a poorly groomed pony. The man stopped the gambo beside them. "Capel Rhos then is it?"

Buttercup answered. "Yes."

"Well, you'd better climb on board then."

Marged spoke up. "I think my lady would be more comfortable riding up there on the seat next to you."

He nodded. "As you wish."

Marged looked at Rhys. "Come along Rhys, help your lady up onto the cart and then we shall get into the back."

Rhys did as asked and Buttercup made herself comfortable on some blankets, facing the front sitting next to the driver. Marged and Rhys climbed into the back and sat on the hard wooden floor among bits of hay, straw and dried manure. As soon as they were settled the man shook the reins and the horse moved off at a slow trot.

Marged noted that they left the station at four fifty and wondered how long it would take to get to Capel Rhos.

No one spoke on the journey. It was quite bumpy, but it was much better than walking and the cave was less than a quarter of a mile from where they would be dropped off.

The pony seemed to struggle on the hills and was almost as slow as someone walking, but they still arrived at Capel Rhos in about an hour. Marged and Rhys got off slightly bruised. The man asked for three pence and Buttercup reached into her purse and gave it to him and then Rhys helped her down. The man turned the gambo around and stopped next to them as they were about to embark on their walk back to the cave. "Where are your bags?" He asked.

Marged answered. "We have only been gone for the day. My lady wanted to walk to Garth for exercise."

The man stared at them for a moment, shook his head and the reins and then moved off back to Garth.

In less than ten minutes they approached the cave and Marged saw the stumpy man going in ahead of them. The others didn't see him and she thought that she would find out more about him inside.

Marged checked the date on her watch placed it in the plastic bag that she had brought along for it and hid it among the rocks again. They all moved to the end and Marged stroked the stone and the rock door opened and in they went.

David Taylor and Caradoc were there, seemingly waiting even though for them no time had passed at all.

The stumpy man was not there. It puzzled Marged. Surely Mr. Taylor and Caradoc would have seen him. Soon she would have to find out more about him and why he was watching her.

CHAPTER 7

Go back in time, become forlorn
To see your mother before you're born.
Some relatives are far from kind
But, friends for you will surely mind.
What to do to make things right?
Go to the future to see the light.

Marged smiled at the two men who were as far apart in appearance as you could possibly get. "Phew, we found the date and time and Buttercup saw her parents. It was quite a shock for her because they weren't even married yet."

David, the fisherman, asked, "What was the time and date? Were you close?"

"It was ten past six on August the twenty seventh, 1903 when we came in. We were seven months early and we bought the day's newspaper. Would you like to see it? It's like history live." She handed it to him.

He smiled. "Thank you. Now what do you do?"

"Well, now I have to adjust things to go out there in January 1904 as close to the twenty seventh, as I can, quickly change the battery in my watch and then come back in and set the rocks as close to April the second, as I can. Then I need to go out again and check to see if it is that day. Once we have that we will set Rhys off up the valley to his uncle's farm, hopefully."

Rhys frowned at Marged. She spotted it. "What's the matter?"

"Batteries are big. How can you put a battery in that tiny watch?"

"Easy! In my time batteries are very small. Here, I'll show you." She reached for one of her bags and retrieved a small package that held two tiny, silver batteries. "See, very small and let me show you the ones in the torches." She reached for the other bag and retrieved a torch, unscrewed the end and tipped out four AA batteries. "These are what make the torch work." She put them back in and turned it on. The light was very bright.

Rhys was amazed. "Those four little things make that light so bright?"

"Yes. Now let me adjust the stones." She went over to her work area and the sheet with her calibrations and noticed there were different marks on the sheet. She realized that David Taylor had done what he called 'extrapolation' to help her make the marks more accurate. "Oh,

Mr. Taylor, thank you. You have done it."

"Yes, and Caradoc will try and help you transfer the new gradations to the marks and Time Stones."

"That is marvellous." She made some calculations and went over to the Time Stones, made some adjustments to them, placed her hands on the rock and the rock door opened. She went out and her watch said 26th January 2004, 3:11pm. However, she knew that it represented 1904. She got a new battery out of the package, flipped the back off the watch, swapped the batteries and replaced the back. She estimated that she had lost fifteen to twenty seconds. Insignificant, she thought.

She hid the bag with the watch once more and went back to the stone and stroked it. The rock door opened and inside she went. She smiled at Rhys. "Next adjustment, April second, 1904 about noon, I think."

Back at her station she made some notes and did some more calculations, then adjusted the Time Stones, placed her hands on the rock and was soon outside again. It was raining heavily. She retrieved her watch, the date was right and the time was 10:32am. This would be close enough. A short way off in a field close by, she saw a boy running with a jacket pulled up over his head. He was headed for the cave and she realized it was Rhys. She stared for a moment, he hadn't seen her. She smiled to herself; she would now have an accurate time for his arrival at the cave. She ducked back in and the rock door closed behind her as he reached the cave entrance.

"Rhys! I have just seen you. You got here at 10:34am on the second of April. You were very wet. How did you get dry again?"

"That's easy. When I went out again the sun was shining and I was able to get dry."

"Why didn't you go to your uncle's farm then?"

"Because there were some people in the distance and I thought they might be looking for me, so I came back in once my clothes were dry and I expect I was out there at the wrong time."

"Well, if you want to go to your uncle's farm, starting out just after you got here; you are going to get very wet. The clouds are heavy and it looked as if it would rain all day. So, this is what I am thinking: Would it matter if you left the cave the day after the day you got here, the third?"

"No, I don't think so."

"Your uncle is not expecting you, is he?"

"No."

"Good, I will adjust the Time Stones."

She went through the whole thing again and went outside. The day was much nicer. However, this time the stumpy man was there. She stared at him. How did he get out? She thought. The rain had stopped and it was quite damp everywhere. The man was dry. She snapped at him. "Who are you?"

He turned and walked away again. This was beginning to frustrate Marged. She would have to ask Caradoc about him as soon as possible. She checked the watch and it was April 3rd. 12:36pm. She was two hours off and she could live with that and back in she went.

She smiled. "The weather is good, but it is very damp out there. So, Rhys, are you ready to go?"

"Yes, I am ready."

"Before you go, are you sure you don't want to go back to Llandovery?"

"I am sure. I don't want to go back to that school. I have had enough beatings."

"You do realize that your uncle will probably send you off to school, probably in Newbridge and you might find yourself in the same situation again."

"No, I won't go to school again. I will work on the farm."

"You know you should let your parents know where you are. They are going to be awfully worried."

"I think they know where I've gone. I was hoping that Father would go to the school and tell the teacher not to beat me, but he said that he couldn't interfere."

"Alright. Buttercup and I will walk with you some of the way. Now if you have troubles of any kind, come back here and we will see if we can sort things out."

He nodded. Marged placed her hands on the rock, the rock door opened and the trio were outside together once more. The girls walked with Rhys until he could see where he had to go to find his uncle's farm and then the girls turned back for the cave. Marged couldn't help but continue to marvel at how different things were, compared to how they looked in her time. They saw a farmer in a field; he had caught a ewe and was delivering a lamb. He was continually shouting at his dog to lie down as he worked with the ewe. A dog overly disturbing sheep when they are in lambing season was very stressful to the mothers and mothers to be. Marged thought to herself, "Lambing hasn't changed much." Most of it, however, was done indoors in her time.

By the time they got back to the cave, the bottoms of their dresses were very wet. They picked an area close by, where the grass was short, to walk around in. The air dried the dresses out enough so they could go back into the cave and be comfortable. If they were wet when they went into the cave they would stay wet until they went out the next time.

Rhys eventually found his uncle's farm. There didn't seem to be anyone around, so he knocked on the farmhouse door and after half a minute or so the door opened to reveal a straggle-haired, blonde woman dressed in scruffy clothes. She had flour on her face and was wiping her hands on her grubby apron and she asked him what he wanted in Welsh. He smiled and asked if it was the farm of Idris Edwards, his uncle.

"He's not here. He has gone to the hill on the pony to look at the ewes after the rain. We'll be lambing soon you see. I don't think he will be back till supper. I don't know if you are a nephew or not, so you had better wait in the barn until he gets back."

She took a step back into the house and closed the door, leaving him on the step. He was stunned. He turned and walked over to the barn and lay down in a pile of hay that still had its new mown smell, to wait for his uncle.

He began to watch the animal activity in the farmyard. Around the Wain house, where there actually was a Wain, there was an assorted flock of hens and a couple of roosters scratching and pecking, at what, Rhys couldn't see. Close to a nearby hedgerow was a broody hen with about 10 three-day-old chicks. At the lower end of the yard was a huge duck pond, on the bank of which were four geese and a gander and a dozen assorted ducks, all preening their feathers. A considerably large weeping willow occupied the far end of the pond. He looked it over. The buds on it had started to burst. The tree would give a lot of shade when full in leaf. On one side of the yard was a five foot high dry stone wall, seemingly in good repair. In the middle of it was an old wooden gate leading to the hill land above.

He dozed and thought about what Marged had told him the first time they had met. Was it really possible that he had been in that cave for a hundred years? He thought about the times he had left the cave and found that everything was out of place. Then in his daze his imagination kicked in like it had never done before, and he began to wonder about all the things he would see if he were to go back to the cave and take trips outside with his new friend Marged.

The next thing he knew he was being flung by his arm out of the barn to come crashing down in the mud. It wasn't just mud, it was a mixture of mud and animal droppings and as close as Rhys was it smelled quite strong. He looked up; he wasn't sure what had happened. Then he heard the voice.

"What are you doing in my barn you filthy, little tramp?"

119

Rhys struggled to his feet and stared at a huge man dressed in dirty breeches, a waist coat with a watch chain, a grubby looking overcoat and an old sack pegged around his shoulders. On his head was a very old and crumpled, mouldy green bowler hat, with the most unkempt hair he had ever seen poking out in all directions from underneath.

The man was in a tirade. "Go on, what are you doing here? What were you going to steal? You look like a nasty little thief to me."

In Welsh Rhys spoke up. "I am Rhys Edwards, your nephew."

"Are you indeed? What are you doing here? Did your father send you? You can go back to him for all I care."

Rhys was becoming very scared of this man. "My father didn't send me, sir. I ran away from school because the teacher was beating me."

"You ran away from school? I knew there was something bad about you." He raised his shepherd's crook and swung it at the boy.

Rhys dodged the stick that was coming down on him, tripped on a stone in the yard and fell over back into the mud and manure. There was another blow coming at him, so Rhys lifted his left arm in self-defence as he struggled to get away from this vile ogre of a man. The stick hit his arm with force and he heard the bone crack. The pain was excruciating. Before the stick came down a third time Rhys managed to get up and move his feet fast enough to get away. As he ran across the yard, he saw his uncle's saddled mountain pony tied to a gate. He thought for a second, his heart was pumping. If he kept running he should get away, but if that man decided to run him down on his pony, he wouldn't have a chance.

Holding his left hand to his body, he reached the lightly tied rein with his right and fortunately was able to free it. He was on the right side of the pony, but he didn't care, he had no time whatsoever for equine etiquette. Quickly flipping the reins over the pony's head he placed his right foot in the stirrup, grabbed some mane with the reins and swung himself up into the saddle.

His uncle had reached him and made a grab for the boy and the reins. Rhys kicked out at him at the same time urging the horse to run. The horse, fortunately took off in the direction of the open gate onto the farm lane. He sensed the pony struggling in his getaway and on glancing back his vile uncle was hanging on to the poor pony's tail. He didn't hang on long, because the pony kicked him and he let go. Rhys urged the horse onto the farm lane with the screaming voice of his uncle ringing in his ears.

"Horse thief! I will see you hang for this!"

Rhys glanced back over his shoulder to see his uncle waving his shepherd's crook with one hand and holding his kicked leg with the other.

At the end of the lane, Rhys turned the horse onto an old track that led in the direction of the cave. He was at full gallop for just over five minutes and then slowed the pony down. He decided that even if his uncle were to run as fast as he could, he would not catch him even if he decided to walk the rest of the way to the cave, instead of riding the horse. He looked for a field with a convenient gate and in a few minutes found one and rode up to it, dismounted, opened it and turned the pony, bridle, saddle and all into the field. If he'd had the use of both hands he would have unsaddled the horse and removed the bridle. The pony was a little sweaty and Rhys hoped he would be alright. After all, as far as he was concerned, the pony had saved his life. He hoped his uncle would find the pony later, but not too soon.

He watched for a moment as the pony was walking calmly across the field, sniffing the ground and nibbling on the grass. It would be difficult for him to eat as the bit was still in his mouth.

Rhys turned away from the field and began to walk as fast as he could toward the cave. Then he realized how painful his left arm was, and also realized that tears were streaming down his face. He had just got away from the most frightening experience of his life.

After a while he picked up on the route that he had taken out of the cave. Even though most of it was downhill, it was an agonizing journey; every step jarred his injured arm. It would have been alright if he had been following an open track, but he had to scramble over ditches and through the entanglements of hedgerows. He eventually arrived at the cave.

Rhys stroked the stone and the rock door opened. He staggered in and collapsed on the floor in front of Marged, Buttercup, David Taylor and Caradoc. Marged rushed to his side as he was struggling to get up. She couldn't believe what she was seeing. In all of her short life she had never witnessed any serious violence, nor had she ever seen a victim first hand, except on television. Rhys was covered in mud, manure and scratches, his clothes were in a terrible state. His agonized face was smeared with the mud and tear stains and he was clutching his injured left arm with his right.

Marged was shocked. "Oh, Rhys, what happened?"

"He attacked me."

"Who attacked you?"

"My uncle." He was breathless, but explained as best as he could all that had happened to him. "I thought he was going to kill me. I only just managed to get away."

David Taylor spoke up. "He should see a doctor; it looks as if his arm might be broken."

Marged turned to Caradoc. "Can you help him?"

"Take the pain from sores I can,
But for broken bones I am just a man."

"Please take the pain from his sores and we will have to see what we can do about the arm."

Rhys struggled to his feet and Caradoc put his hand on him and all the pain left the boy.

Buttercup had a moment of compassion. She took a handkerchief out of her pocket and wiped his face. "It looks to me," she said "As if you should go back to your real home. I am sure that getting beaten at school is a lot better than what you have just been through."

The mud splattered, forlorn boy seemed defeated as he allowed Buttercup to do her work. "I don't know what to do any more. I am sorry, I really am a smelly boy, now."

"Oh, dear, dear. It will be alright. We will help you."

Marged was animated, moving her feet as if doing some strange dance. "The first thing we have to do is get your arm fixed. The nearest hospital is in Builth, and it should be done in my time, because things are a lot more advanced than in your time. The problem is, how can we get you into my time long enough to get your arm fixed without creating too much suspicion and awkward questions?"

David Taylor spoke up, "If they fix his arm in your time, won't he have to stay there until the arm heals?"

Marged thought for a second. "No, once the doctor has fixed his arm he will be able to go home."

David thought for a second. "That will be okay, except that modern casts, in our time, are very often fibreglass and plastic, not Plaster of Paris as they used to be."

Marged felt a little stymied. "It is going to be a problem, but what if we can persuade the doctor to use Plaster of Paris, then, everything would be fine?"

"And what if he won't?" David was doing his best to keep Margeds' thinking on track.

"We will have to cross that bridge when we come to it. First we have to get him into our time and I am going to have to think about this one. As long as he is here he will be in no pain and his break will do nothing, but as soon as he is out there the pain will return and we will have to get him to a hospital as fast as possible."

"Would your parents get him there?"

"Yes, but then how do I explain who he is and where he came from?"

"Well, we have to work it out, or he will be here with a broken arm while millennia, after millennia, passes out there."

All of a sudden Marged's face lit up. "I've got it."

Buttercup picked up on Marged's flash of excitement. "What? What are you going to do?"

"I am going out there at my correct time, and I will go up to the farm and grab some of my brother's old clothes, bring them back here and Rhys can change into them. Then I will take him back to the farm and tell my parents that I met him near the cave and he was showing off his climbing skills when he fell out of a tree."

Buttercup smiled and then slowly the smile left her face. "Won't your parents want to know who he is?"

"Yes, but I can tell them that he is from town."

David had his hand on his chin and was obviously thinking, then he spoke, "Won't the doctor and others want to know who his parents are?"

Marged thought for another second. "We can tell them. It won't make any difference."

"Yes, but what if they want to call them?"

"Ooh." Marged thought and found an answer. "I can tell them that I had already called them and that they were on their way to meet us."

"That is very good, but what if your parents want to call his family?"

Marged was getting exasperated. "Why are you making things hard for me?"

He responded. "Marged, that is not my intention; I just want you to take into consideration all the problems that may arise. You want this to go right don't you?"

"Yes, I'm sorry. I know, he can say that he doesn't remember the phone number because of his fall."

"That would work, but he should just say that he doesn't know it. If he says he doesn't remember because of the fall, they might want to admit him to the hospital for observation in case of concussion and that will give you a real problem."

"Alright." She turned to Rhys, "When we go out there into my world, if someone asks for your phone number or your parents' phone number, you must say you don't know it."

Rhys was looking confused. "I don't know what a phone number is."

Marged sighed. "Oh, my gosh, that's right. In your time they had only just begun to be used."

Rhys looked at her. "What is it?"

She shook her head. "People use them to talk to each other over long distances."

"Oh, it's the telegraph?"

"Um, not exactly. Mr. Taylor could you tell him what it is."

David smiled. "I will do my best. Rhys, you know how the telegraph works, right?"

"Not really."

"Alright. You know that there are wires on poles alongside railway lines, correct?"

"Yes."

"Right. Those lines carry signals from place to place. The signal is a series of long taps and short taps on a key at the end of the wires so information can go back and fore and in the right combination they represent words. The telephone is the same thing, only instead of tapping out a signal, you can just talk into it and someone will hear you at the other end and be able to answer, just like a normal conversation. Do you get the idea?"

"I am not sure, but I think so." He looked at Marged. "If we go out there in your time, will you stay by me so that I don't make any mistakes?"

"Yes, I will. You can take on dull a little bit, but not too much, or they will think you were hit on the head."

"Yes, I will be watching points all the time."

"Good. I am going to go out now and steal some of my brother's old clothes. I hope he doesn't find out, although I am not too worried about it. He will think our mother has thrown them out. I just hope he doesn't catch me stealing them, but I don't think he will."

Marged changed into her jeans, pink sweater and navy jacket, put on her wellies, grabbed her bag and checked her marks and notes on the paper sheet and adjusted the Time Stones, pressed her hands on the rock and left, before the rock door was fully open.

Marged got to the farmyard a while after the time she last left. It was late morning when she entered the house. She went upstairs to her room where she waited for her mother to leave the house and went to her window to make sure. Her mother had gone into the garden to do some weeding.

Marged watched. Megan was one of the very few people who grew a proper garden anymore. Marged immediately went into her brother's room and found three pairs of his jeans spread out on the floor. She grabbed a pair and then opened a wardrobe, grabbed a T-shirt and a regular shirt she knew hadn't been worn by her brother for some time. Then she found a pair of socks. She didn't bother with underwear, because they wouldn't be seen, or so she thought, anyway, and Rhys probably had his own on. The last thing she wanted for him was footwear. She stuffed the clothes into her bag, ran downstairs and opened the boot cupboard and shuffled through the pile of footwear. She soon found a pair of old trainers that her brother had not worn for quite a while and stuffed them into her bag.

She went outside, where her father and brother were working in a nearby shed. She shouted over to them. "I am going back to the cave, I won't be long."

Her father shook his head and continued with his work. Marged took off across the yard, into the cattle field and headed for the cave.

In ten minutes she was there. She went inside. She handed the clothes to Rhys, and realized he was going to have difficulty changing with his broken arm, so she asked David Taylor to help him. Once he had changed, Marged felt that she had better explain the world that he was going to see out there in her time. The important thing was to explain the modern car to him, because if he had never seen one, it would be an amazing contrast to what he would see out there in his time. She also briefed him on what to expect at the hospital, although she wasn't completely sure what to expect there herself. Next she tried to coach him on ways to answer questions and what kind of things to say at certain times.

He nodded several times, but in his heart he wasn't really sure if he would be able to follow her instructions.

Marged looked at him. "Are you ready?"

He nodded, "Yes."

"Good. Here we go then."

She placed her hands on the rock once more and out they went. Once outside she wondered how people would react to his broken English.

On the walk up to the farm she told him to say he was from Llandovery, that his parents were visiting in the area, he didn't know where, and they had dropped him off near Capel Rhos, which in her time was not there anymore, so that he could go and explore the countryside, and that was when he fell out of a tree and broke his arm, adding it was lucky that Marged came along. She explained several other things and gave him instructions on how to deal with any problems that might possibly arise.

He promised to do his best. Marged picked up the pace as they crossed the last field, where they were watched by the cattle. As they went through the gate on to the yard, Marged began shouting, "Dad we've got to help this boy." She ran up to her father who was in the yard and pointed to the boy.

He looked up. "Who is he?"

"He's Rhys Edwards and he has broken his arm. We have to get him to the hospital."

"Alright, alright. Your mother can drive you."

Rhys was riveted to the ground as he looked around the yard. To his left was a shed, a Wain-house, and inside, facing out, was a large, green and yellow tractor. It had a large cab and a front end loader; he stared at it for a few seconds before turning to where the vehicles were parked. There was a Land Rover parked next to a horse box and next to that was an Audi car. The contrast to what he had seen at his uncle's farm was almost unimaginable. He hadn't a clue as to what he was looking at. Maybe these were the things that Marged had tried to explain to him, but anyway, it was enough to take his mind off the pain in his arm, which had returned since he had left the cave.

Marged came back. "Come on, my mother is going to take you to the hospital."

"How?"

"In the car, silly." Then she realized that he still hadn't much of a clue as to what she was talking about. She pointed to the Audi. "That's a car over there."

"Well, what does it do?"

Before she could answer her father came over. "Don't you worry boy, we'll have you at the hospital in no time. I've never seen you before.

Where are you from?"

Before he could answer, Marged jumped in and answered for him. "He's from Llandovery. His parents are visiting in the area and he was out exploring the forestry and he fell out of a tree. He's very Welsh."

Rhys, Marged's brother, joined them and the first thing that came out of his mouth was, "You've got clothes just like mine."

Marged had a twinge of apprehension. "What if he was to go and check his wardrobe?"

They all went into the house where Megan was putting the food on the table. Emrys spoke up, "Megan, we can help ourselves. Get this boy in the car and get him to the hospital. He's broken his arm."

"Oh, my gosh, right." She put the last plate she was carrying down on the table and said, "Come on then." She started to the door, closely followed by the boy and Marged. They got out to the car and Megan turned to Marged. "You don't have to come, stay and have your dinner."

"No, Mam, I have to come." She looked at Rhys, inviting him to say something.

He did. "I want her to come."

"Oh, very well, get in." Megan was already getting into the car behind the wheel.

Rhys was totally baffled. Marged reached for the front passenger door and opened it. "You can sit in the front by here, come on."

As he was about to get in, Megan started the engine. It startled him and he jumped back. Megan looked at Marged with a questioning expression. "Is he alright?"

"Yes, Mam. He's in pain that's all, and a bit of shock. I'll help him in." Marged helped manoeuvre him into the seat, reached for the seat belt, pulled it across his body and fastened it with a click.

"Why are you tying me in?"

Marged wanted to burst out laughing, but managed to control herself. "It's a belt for safety. See my mother is wearing hers and I am going to be wearing mine when I get into the back. Don't worry. I'll be right behind you."

Marged shut the front passenger door, opened the one behind it, climbed into the back seat and hooked up her seat belt. "See, Rhys, I have mine on too."

He turned and looked and then noticed Megan moving a knob that was sticking out of the floor between them.

Megan smiled. "We're off. Hospital here we come." The car moved forward and picked up speed as they went down the lane.

From the back seat, Marged could tell from Rhys' body language that he was scared. She reached her hand between the front seats and squeezed his right shoulder. He was tense. "I bet you've never been in an Audi before, have you?"

"No, I haven't," he said in a voice that indicated that he was mustering up as much courage as he could.

As the car picked up speed Rhys was pressed back firmly in the seat, his eyes wide open. Megan glanced at him and thought, "What is on this boy on? He's behaving as if he has never been in a car before."

Marged kept her hand on his shoulder. Around the next corner, coming towards them, was a stock lorry. Megan slowed down and steered the car part way onto the grass verge. The stock lorry did the same on the other side of the road and they passed each other, doing about 35 miles an hour.

Rhys blurted out, "What was that?"

Marged did her best to cover. "Rhys, you are such a boy. You'll be telling us next you don't know what a train is?"

Immediately, he answered. "I know what a train is."

Then Megan's mobile phone rang. Rhys watched her pick it up, flip it open and place it to the side of her head. "Hello," she said, and Rhys listened to her having a conversation with this thing pressed to her face. Then she said "Okay" and placed it back in the cup holder.

They overtook a tractor pulling a trailer with a load of big round bales of hay. Rhys was astonished. And when Megan accelerated up to 65 miles an hour, and was whizzing by cars, Marged heard him gulp. She squeezed his shoulder, an almost futile effort to reassure him that everything was alright.

He was beginning to get used to it when Megan slowed down and announced that a cop car was coming from behind. It sped past them, sirens screaming and blue lights flashing. A shocked Rhys sucked in air.

They got into town where there were cars everywhere and when they pulled up outside the hospital, Rhys seemingly began to panic. "Out, out" he shouted.

Marged leaped out of the car and opened the door to let him out and quickly leaned in to undo the seat belt. As soon as he was out, he bent over and began to throw up violently. Megan got out of the car with some paper handkerchiefs and handed them to him. "We'd better get him inside. It must be the shock from his broken arm."

Marged knew quite well what the shock was.

Once he had settled down and Megan had helped clean him up a bit, they took him into the hospital. They walked in through the doors that had windows in them and approached the reception desk. Rhys, even though he felt awful, stared at the pristine cleanliness of the building. The walls were painted with two horizontal colours of the same width, cream above and a light green below. They were shiny, the floor was spotless and that too was shiny.

The nurse behind the desk saw them come in and responded right away. "Is this an emergency?"

Megan answered first. "This boy has broken his arm and he has just been sick. Is there a doctor in?"

"Dr. Williams is in. Take a seat and I will see if I can find him. What's his name?"

Marged answered next. "Rhys Edwards. He's from Llandovery. He is just visiting."

The nurse picked up a phone and paged Dr. Williams. The whole hospital rang with her voice. "Calling Dr. Williams, calling Dr. Williams. Please come to reception. Patient in need of urgent care."

Rhys was astounded. How could she do that with her voice? He looked around trying to comprehend it all. Megan picked up a magazine. It was full of glossy coloured photos. He watched her flip through it and was overwhelmed by the pictures that populated the pages. He heard footsteps approaching and looked up. A man about six feet two inches tall, wearing a white coat, went up to the reception desk and the nurse pointed at Rhys. "He's over there, Doctor."

The doctor approached the boy. What Rhys and Marged did not know was that this doctor, Dewi Williams, was Rhys' great-grandson. "So what have you been up to?"

Rhys just sat there, staring up at the man. He was the tallest man he had ever seen. He continued to sit.

Marged nudged him with her elbow. "Go on Rhys. Tell him. Go with the doctor. We'll wait by here for you, alright?"

He nodded and nervously went along with the doctor to be examined.

Megan remarked to Marged. "Well, if that isn't the oddest boy I have ever seen, it's as if he has been plonked down here from another age."

"You are right Mam. He's from 1904 and he has been in the cave."

"Oh, Marged, please don't talk so dull. I was just saying how odd he is."

Ten minutes later the doctor came back. "Mrs. Edwards?"

Megan looked up, he was speaking to her. "No, I'm Mrs. Evans. I'm not his mother."

"Where are his parents?"

"They are visiting a farm up our way and we haven't been able to contact them, yet. How is the boy?"

"He is being X-rayed and I notice that he has many bruises on his back, buttocks and thighs. I am not sure if he could have got all of them from falling out of the tree. Not only that, his underwear is quite antiquated. I have no idea where he might have got them in this day and age. I will say this: He speaks Welsh better than he can speak English, and it is not often around here that I can have a conversation in Welsh with my patients."

Marged squirmed; she must remember not to do things by half next time.

The doctor continued. "Do you know the boy's parents?"

"No, doctor, my daughter, Marged, found him in the forestry by our farm; he was out exploring the area. Well, you know what boys are like?"

"Yes, indeed, I have one of my own. Well, I must continue my rounds." He turned, went over to the reception desk, said something to the nurse and then left.

As soon as he was out of sight the receptionist called Megan over. "Mrs. Evans, could you help me with some details?"

Megan approached the desk. "I will do my best."

"Good. Do you know who the parents are of this boy?"

"No, I just told the doctor I didn't."

"How long have you known the boy?"

"Today. Since my daughter brought him to the farm earlier."

"So you don't know where his parents are staying?"

"No. He doesn't remember the name of the place. Isn't that right, Marged?"

Marged stepped up to the desk. "I think he knows where they are, but not the name of the farm."

The nurse shook her head. "I don't even know what to write down on the hospital forms. Do you know his address in Llandovery?"

Megan shook her head. "No, we've only just met him."

"Alright. When he comes out, bring him here and I will ask him myself."

Twenty minutes later the doctor came out. "Well, it's his ulna bone and it is not completely fractured which is a good thing. I will set his arm in a cast and he can be on his way, although I would really like to talk to his parents. When you find them, could you have them contact me, I can be reached here at the hospital."

Marged spoke up. "Will his cast be Plaster of Paris? I think he might like that, then people could write on it like they do in America."

"We rarely use Plaster of Paris anymore; I will fit him with a fibreglass cast that will be held on with Velcro straps. We like that kind of cast, because it can be taken off occasionally and the arm gently bathed."

Marged's mind was spinning. If he wore this modern cast, he wouldn't be able to go back to his time with it and she would either have to keep him in her time, or change the cast to a Plaster of Paris one so that he could go back. So she asked the next question, "How long will he have to wear it?"

"Well, if it had been a complete fracture, it would take about three months, but as it is a partial fracture, he should be able to use it lightly in six weeks. "I have given him a Tetanus injection, because he has a few nasty scrapes on his face and hands. I've also given him some painkillers and he will have a prescription for some more, if you could fill that for him at the chemist. I haven't given him any antibiotics, however, if any swelling occurs, or any infection in his cuts and scrapes, let me know and I will fix him up with some. Good, well I'll go back and fit him with the cast and he should be ready to go."

Fifteen minutes after that the doctor brought the boy back to reception. His arm was in a sling. Marged stood up and greeted him. "How was it?"

He nodded. "Alright. I feel better. The doctor speaks Welsh. He is from Llandovery, but it sounds a lot different to the Llandovery I know. It changed after a flood that was in 1987. He told me that his grandfather was an Edwards. I wonder if he was a relative of mine."

The doctor nodded to Megan and they met at the reception desk. He looked at Megan very seriously. "Mrs. Evans, could you find out who his parents are? I would like to talk to them. I have reason to believe that this boy is being beaten on a regular basis. He wouldn't tell me a lot and I didn't want to pursue it too much because of his current stress."

Megan really didn't know what she could do. "I will try and find out, doctor."

The doctor's statement stopped Marged in her tracks and in a low voice she asked Rhys, "What did you tell him?"

"I tried not to tell him anything. I didn't tell him about the cave. What are we going to do now?"

"I am not sure; he gave you a prescription, right?"

"I don't know. He gave me this piece of paper which he wrote on, but I can't read it." He handed it to her.

"That's it, we have to take this to the chemist and have it filled."

He stared at the paper in her hand and then looked at her. "That's a bit of paper. How can you fill that? What would you put in it?"

She smiled and almost burst out laughing again. "No, silly, at the chemist they will take this and they will give you some tablets, just like the doctor gave you, and they will be for any pain you have. When you have pain you will take a tablet and the pain will go away for a while."

He nodded; he was having a lot of trouble trying to understand everything that was happening. Just when he thought he was getting to know something, something else would pop up.

As the doctor left the reception, he said goodbye to the boy in Welsh. After answering some basic questions, asked by the receptionist, Rhys left the hospital, escorted by the two females. They approached the car and Rhys balked at the sight of it. "No!" he said, "I want to walk."

Megan stared at him. "You can't walk back, it's eight miles."

"It makes me sick."

"Oh, you get travel sickness. Well, I tell you what; you walk with Marged into town and I will drive to the chemist and get your prescription filled. I will also get you some travel sickness pills and I will meet you there, alright?"

He nodded and so did Marged. Megan climbed into the car, started it and drove away through the hospital gates. Rhys and Marged followed on foot and walked down the hill to the main street. As they walked a noisy motorcycle sped up the hill toward them. Rhys immediately left the roadside and scrambled up the ditch and hid behind some bushes. He moved so fast that Marged had no time to react, and by the time she realized where he had gone the motorcycle had sped past. She turned to see him up the ditch holding the branch of a bush with his right hand.

"Oh, Rhys, you have to stop doing that, people will think there is something wrong with you."

He slowly returned to the road. "What was it?"

"It was a motor bike, people ride them around."

"There was somebody on it?"

"Yes, they don't run by themselves."

"It was faster than a horse."

"Yes, and so was the car, remember? Some racing motor bikes can do over two hundred miles an hour and that is a lot faster than a horse."

They continued on to the main road and walked through town toward the chemists shop. A mind boggling, dazzling walk for Rhys; all the while Marged was encouraging him to act as normal as possible to all that was going on around them and she did her best to explain everything to him.

In the high street a woman, who was a friend of her mother, approached them. "Hello, Marged. That's not your brother, is it?"

"No, Mrs. Jones, this is Rhys Edwards."

"Oh, indeed. You are a bit young to have a boyfriend, aren't you?"

Marged was flushed and became as red faced as an old boozing man. "Oh, no, Mrs. Jones, he's not my boyfriend. He's visiting from Llandovery."

"Oh well. There's nice. You mind to enjoy yourselves now."

Marged recovered. "We will, thank you, Mrs. Jones."

They met Megan at the chemists; she had the prescription pills and a small plastic bottle of travel pills. She handed Rhys the prescription. "It says on the bottle take one when you feel the pain in your arm and don't take more than four a day. I don't think you will need to take one for a while. Here are the travel pills. If you take one now you will have to wait for an hour or more before it works and then you will be able to travel back in the car without being sick. So what I am going to do is visit a friend until we are ready to go, so here is some money." She gave the money to Marged. "Why don't you go and see a movie? I will meet you at the car. It's in the car park."

"Yes, Mam."

Megan went off up the street and Marged turned to Rhys. "Do you want to see a movie?"

"I don't know what it is."

Marged did her best to explain what movies were. "I think you will enjoy it. Please, Rhys, try not to make noises, because you will upset the other people watching and they might ask us to leave. Nothing is going to hurt you in there so just remember, try and be like everyone else. You will like it I know."

CHAPTER 8

Go to the future a hundred years
And face a whole new set of fears.
Flashing cars on black topped roads.
Speeding lorries with heavy loads.
Then pop and popcorn is your meal
And a movie show is very real.

NOW SHOWING

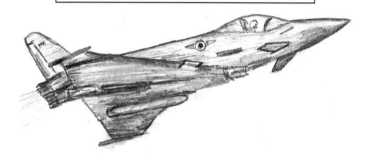

Outside the cinema there were posters for the movies. One was for "Uptown Girls". The poster depicted a modern school girl and a lady with a dress that only came to the knees and across it was a banner that said "Coming Soon".

Rhys looked at the picture, not realizing that it was a photograph.

There were other posters with "Coming Soon" on them as well.

The poster closest to the door had a banner on it that said "Showing Today". This poster showed a picture of a man looking as if he were about to kiss a horse. Rhys liked the picture, because he felt there was some relationship between the man and the animal that was good. He could never understand why people were cruel to their fellow creatures.

In the theatre Marged bought two tickets and they were shown to their seats.

Marged asked Rhys, "Would you like some popcorn and pop?"

The lights were going down as he looked at her. "I don't know." He had no idea about what she was asking him.

She smiled. "It's alright, I will get you some. It's been awhile since you were sick so it should be alright and you have taken the travel pill. Stay there and don't move. I will be right back."

Music began playing and on the screen were words. "WELCOME TO OUR CINEMA." He had never seen words so big and then they disappeared and in their place was a picture of a shop in town and a voice said, "Please support our advertisers." And all sorts of pictures appeared and disappeared.

Marged returned with a tub of popcorn and two cokes. She gave one of the cokes to Rhys. He held it and hadn't a clue as to what it was. He looked at the straw that stuck out of the top of this cold container and then he looked at Marged.

Marged smiled. "Put the end of the straw in your mouth." She pointed to the straw and lifted the container toward his lower face. "Put it in your mouth." He did. "Now suck."

He did, and did again two or three times. Then he stopped and looked at Marged and smiled.

Marged thought she had hit the jackpot. "I made him smile," she thought. She held the popcorn toward him. "Try eating this. It's good."

He placed the pop in the cup holder and picked out a small piece and put it in his mouth and chewed and swallowed and then reached for another piece. Then suddenly he was startled by loud music, which seemed to come from everywhere and on the screen were the words, "Coming Soon".

The screen exploded with a trailer for "Uptown Girls." Rhys, without thought, grabbed and squeezed the pop cup making the liquid shoot out of the straw. He pushed back as he saw the trailer unfold. A little white pig was shown and Rhys exclaimed, "They have a pig in their house!"

Marged nudged him. "Ssh. Don't talk."

He glanced at her and stared at the screen as the young woman and the girl interacted. Then all of a sudden again the screen went blank and then another preview came on the screen. PG13. "My Boss's Daughter." In this preview there was an owl and Rhys was dumfounded. "Look at that, it's an owl."

Marged nudged him again. "Rhys, you have to stay quiet."

That preview ended and another one began, a preview to tell all audiences that the movie was R rated. The movie was a Western, cowboys on horses and lots of shooting. Rhys began making noises. "Ooh, ooh, lookout, ooh." He glanced at Marged. She was trying to stop him making a noise by continuing to nudge him. He grabbed her arm. "But they are shooting and killing each other."

Marged could see that he was horrified at what he was seeing. She tried to reassure him, "Rhys, it's not real, it's acting."

"No, they're killing each other, look."

"No, Rhys, it's alright, they are acting. Keep quiet."

That preview went off the screen and then the opening credits appeared for "Seabiscuit."

The movie started and the demise of Red Pollard's family in the great depression was soon underway. Rhys was shocked that his parents had abandoned him alone with one ability, to ride horses. Rhys thought, "I left my parents because of a teacher beating me; they did not abandon me." He felt sad at what his parents must be feeling because he had abandoned them.

He decided that he would return home and do his best to speak English in the school to avoid being beaten. He watched the fortunes of Red Pollard fall and rise and watched the old horse trainer working with the horses. The movie continued to develop and moved onto the Buick business man getting together with the trainer and the jockey, all because of a horse.

Marged could sense Rhys' emotions and responses by the way he moved in his seat, and occasionally he would make noises of shock and surprise, but he managed to refrain from talking. However, when some of the races were shown, Rhys would try and get up in his seat to cheer the horse on, and on one occasion succeeded and blurted a cheer in Welsh, much to the amusement of the audience.

Rhys was feeling much better about his circumstances on leaving the theatre. He stared at the building they had just come out of, and although he somewhat understood what Marged had told him a movie was, he couldn't help but think that somehow they had got all those horses and race tracks inside. It was hard to believe that what he had seen was a whole series of pictures run together. He turned towards the streets with Marged, and was mesmerized by the traffic moving through the town and the cars barely missing each other.

He asked Marged, "Why don't the cars hit one another?"

"Sometimes they do, and sometimes people get killed in them when they do, but if people drive carefully and look where they are going, they don't get into accidents. Now we have to find mother and the car and then we can return to the cave and try to work out what to do next."

Crossing the roads made Rhys very nervous. The speed of the cars was something he was most definitely not used to. He was a bit embarrassed when Marged took him by the arm, but it gave him more confidence, walking stride for stride with her. They found the car and only had to wait five minutes for Megan.

She smiled. "How was the movie?"

Marged smiled in return. "It was great. Rhys loved it; he even cheered the horse on in some of the races."

Megan raised her eyebrows. "I bet that surprised the audience."

Rhys stared at the car. "I want to walk."

Marged stepped in. "You won't be sick this time, you took a travel pill before we went to the movie and that will stop you from being sick."

He looked from Marged to Megan and back to the car and then he nodded. Marged opened the front passenger door and Rhys got in. She helped him as she had before. All on board Megan started the car and pulled away and as she did she glanced at Rhys. "You don't travel in cars much, do you?"

He responded without thinking. "No, today is my first time."

There was surprise in Megan's voice. "You have never ridden in a car before today?"

"No."

"Do your parents have a car?"

"No, they have a horse and cart and a horse for riding."

Megan stared at him for a second as they drove out of town; if she had glanced in the rear view mirror she would have probably seen Marged squirming with mixed emotions, not knowing how to stop

Rhys and trying not to laugh.

Megan asked, "What do your parents do for a living?"

"My father works on a farm and works the horses and takes care of them and the cattle."

"What kind of work does your father do with the horses?"

"He does the ploughing and harrowing and harvests the hay and corn with them."

"Oh, now I get it. You live and work on one of those living history farms; that must be really fun."

He stared at her.

They were quiet for a while as they travelled back up into the hills and then Megan, having thought about the boy's responses, asked him another question. "So, if your parents don't have a car, how did you get up here?"

This question frustrated him and he gave a glance in Marged's direction. She came to the rescue immediately. "They got a lift with a friend."

That satisfied Megan.

As they came over the hill pass overlooking their valley an air force jet, travelling at about 500 miles an hour, passed right in front of them at their level, no more than 200 yards away from the car. Rhys violently pushed himself back into the seat and began breathing in and out rapidly. "Mawredd."

Megan casually commented. "I hate those things. I bet you don't get them in Llandovery. They like to fly up our valleys for practice. The Americans fly theirs up here too." Then a blast of sound enveloped the whole car. The sound coming from the jet engines always seemed to trail behind the plane.

Rhys, recomposed himself. "W... w... what was it?"

Megan looked back at him suddenly. This boy was very odd. "You've never seen a jet before?"

"Er, no."

"Well, if you spend time up here you will see a lot of them."

"How do they stay up in the air like that?"

Marged could do nothing. What her mother was thinking she wasn't sure, but it was more than likely that her mother thought the boy was a bit bonkers. The question was unanswered.

They got back to the farm. Emrys and Rhys had finished up their work in the shed and had just gone into the house themselves. Megan asked Marged when she thought the boy's parents would pick him up.

Marged said that they would go over to Capel Rhos before dark and hope that they would be there. She then led Rhys into the living room. "I have something to show you. You remember the movie? Well, in here we have a television and you can see all sorts of things on it. Let me show you." She turned it on and the screen came to life, displaying a man who was reading the news, and then it showed the President of the United States.

Rhys once again was shocked. "How do they get the pictures in that window thing?"

"It is transmitted through the air."

"How?"

"Oh, Rhys, I don't know how it works, but it does."

Rhys just stared at the screen.

Megan shook her head and spoke to Emrys. "That boy is like a complete stranger to everything around him. The doctor said he thought the boy had been beaten; perhaps his parents have kept him locked up and out of sight of the world. Anyway, Marged will go with him to Capel Rhos to see if his parents are waiting, so I might as well put supper now before they go."

They sat for supper and Rhys had never seen a table so clean or eaten food so tasty. Because his arm was in a sling he was unable to cut his own meat, so Megan did it for him. They observed that his table manners weren't the best, and watched him eat with aggressiveness.

When supper was over, Marged decided to get back to the cave and reached for a coat. Megan watched her. "Does Rhys have a coat?"

"No. Could he borrow one of our Rhys'?"

"Yes, why not. You can bring it back once he is with his parents."

Rhys and Marged set off in the direction of Capel Rhos and then doubled back and returned to the cave. As they approached Marged saw the stumpy man go in ahead of them.

Once inside Marged looked around for the stumpy man. He wasn't there so she went straight over to Caradoc. "A man came into the cave just before we did. I have seen him before. Who is he?"

"I have not seen the man who came before.
Tell me how he looks and of his core."

Marged described the stumpy man in detail and tried to show him the picture she had taken on her camera. However the picture she had taken was blank.

A look of great concern came over Caradoc.
"Beware of him you see about,
He can change events in the world without.

"So why isn't he here when I follow him in?"

"He can move through parallel caves
And in many, nasty work he surely paves.

"Is he bad?"

"He goes out to change things from the good.

146

Create problems for your work he could."

"So when I get things right out there he could change them to make them wrong for me?"

"When in your dimension he is found
Avoid him quick or go to ground.
When he has gone to another realm
Only then will you keep your helm."

"How will I know if he is in my dimension?"

"Out there to you he will be seen
And possibly to you be mean."

"Will he hurt me?"

"He has not the power to do you harm,
But change your work to give alarm.
Your friends out there could be in danger,
So please make sure they avoid this stranger."

"Will he hurt them?"

"Not in a way that you'd expect,
But in a way you must reject."

"How will I know what to do and what are his ways?"

"When you see the way you will know the wrong
And to beat him then you must be strong."

"Oh, Caradoc this is very scary."

"I understand you well my lovely dear
So do honest work without a fear."

"Will you help me?"

"From in this cave I will do my best
To try and rid you of this pest.
Out there with him you will have to deal,

But the cave will give you power that's real."

"Oh, Caradoc, I hope so. I didn't know that all this would be so hard."

They turned to the others.

Buttercup was impressed with Rhys' cast and sling. "Was it really broken?"

Rhys answered. "No, not really. It was cracked and it will heal in about six weeks. But Buttercup, we saw this movie thing with horses racing and everything and we saw a machine that was flying through the air so fast it was gone in a second. The future is hard to believe and now I have to go home to my time."

Marged detected a little disappointment in his voice at the thought of his going back to his time.

Marged looked at Buttercup and Rhys, each in turn. "We now have a problem; Rhys' broken bone will not heal here in the cave because time doesn't move here. With that cast from my time he can't go back to his time, unless we can change it to a Plaster of Paris cast and I don't know where to get it or how to make a cast out of it."

Caradoc spoke up.
"He cannot leave with your time cast
And return to his home well in the past."

Marged turned to David Taylor. "Do you know how to make a Plaster of Paris cast, Mr. Taylor?"

"No, I'm afraid I don't."

Marged thought for a second or two. "I could take him back with me and see if my parents would put him up until he is healed, but they would ask a lot of questions and that would be something I wouldn't like. My mother is very curious about him already. We have to find a place where he can be for six weeks without there being a problem. So please, let's think where and what time he could go to?"

David Taylor was the first to respond. "I suppose, if you got me out in my time I could take him home with me. I have two sons, 14 and 15. I am sure it would be fun for them to host a young Welshman, and once he has healed I could bring him back. Perhaps, he would like London and he would be able to see more movies."

Marged was excited. "Oh, Mr. Taylor, that would be perfect. Would you really do it?"

"Yes, I would. You help me get back to my time and I will do it gladly, and anyway I have been honoured to help you with this important work and I won't mind coming back to help from time to time."

Marged went over to him and hugged him. "Thank you. Will the clothes he has work in your time?"

"Yes, I think so, after all it is only 1996. My sons have clothes that don't fit anymore, so he should be fine. We can take his clothes from 1904 back with us and I can have them cleaned."

"Good. Alright, what was the time you came into the cave?"

"It was June the third, about three o'clock. I came into the cave to eat my sandwiches. When I was finished I stood up and went further in and then the rock door opened, so I came in. I had left my box of flies behind out there and planned to get them when I went out again."

"Alright, what I am going to do is, try and get as close to that time as I possibly can and then go out and try and find the date and time and leave my watch out there again. I could go up to the farm. No! I couldn't. My parents would be there and so would I. I would be three years old. Buttercup, you will have to do it."

"Oh, how?"

"Well, you will have to go up to the farm, ask my parents what the time is and then you make it correct on my watch, which you will take with you."

"I don't know if I could do that."

"Yes you can, you want to help Rhys, don't you?"

She looked at Rhys and nodded. "Yes."

Helping Rhys was a big change of attitude for her. Marged continued. "This is what you are going to do: You are going to change into my school uniform and you will wear my watch. I will show you how to change the time and date on it."

"I have to wear your clothes?"

"Yes. You can't wear your clothes. You will have to dress for the time you will be in."

Marged helped Buttercup change into the school uniform and showed her how to use the watch. The Time Stones were set and out they went.

On the way to the farm, Marged coached Buttercup on what to say to her parents and to get the right time as quickly as possible and return to where Marged would be waiting.

Marged noticed a few differences in the surrounding countryside. She realized that after visiting the farm in 1904 and knowing it in 2004 the countryside was always changing. The mountains seemed not to change, although according to Caradoc they did, very, very slowly. They got up to the hay field, but instead of hay the field was full of ewes and lambs. The lambs didn't look to be more than a month old. Marged led Buttercup to the old oak tree and from there she pointed to the farm and gave Buttercup instructions on how to approach it, and asked her a final time, "Now, you do know what to do when you get there?"

"Yes. Phew, I'm ready."

"Good. Don't forget it's the exact time and date we want."

"I won't. I will put it in the watch the way you showed me."

"Good luck. I'll be waiting here for you."

She watched Buttercup make her way to the farm, following the route that she had instructed her to follow to the letter. Squinting through the thick hedgerow she watched Buttercup tap on the door and saw her mother answer it.

When Megan opened the door with a three-year-old Marged clinging to her leg, Buttercup knew immediately who the little girl was and stared at her. Megan broke the momentary silence. "Hello, can I help you?"

Buttercup looked up at Marged's mother. "I am sorry to trouble you, some friends and I were walking and we have lost track of the time and we have to meet someone soon and we are not sure what the time is."

Marged watched as her mother invited Buttercup in and the door was closed behind them. Marged was hoping that the interaction could have taken place on the threshold, as she wanted to observe the action, but it wasn't to be, so she sat on the ditch in the damp grass to wait. She continually surveyed all around her. The one thing she could not afford was to be seen. However, in the distance she could see her father and Rhys coming toward her. Behind them was the stumpy man. It was as if he was driving them over to her. This scared her. She didn't want to face her father and brother at a time when she was only three years old. She crouched in the underbrush and felt that if they could not see her they would probably hear her heart beating.

 Megan took Buttercup into the living room and pointed to a clock on the mantelpiece. "That clock is right. Isn't your watch working?"

"It works, but the time is all wrong. I can put it right, now. Oh, dear I think I have the date wrong. What is the date?"

Megan stared at the girl. "You don't know what day it is? It's Saturday, of course."

Buttercup was wilting; she dreaded the questions that might follow. "I... I, er, know that, but I've forgotten the date."

"It's May the fourth."

"Thank you, Mrs. Evans." Buttercup made the adjustments to the watch and then she was faced with another question.

"How did you know that I was Mrs. Evans?"

Buttercup stammered. "Er, one of the other girls told me and said that you would help because you are very nice."

"Well, who was that then?"

"Oh, I don't remember which one, but I think it was Mary." Buttercup was becoming more uncomfortable by the second and realized that she had to get away before things got more complicated. "I must go now, the girls will be waiting."

Megan showed her to the door. "You're not from around here are you?"

"No, I'm English."

"Living in Builth are you?"

Buttercup answered with a quick "Yes" and took off across the yard.

As she crossed the field a man was coming to meet her and he had a boy about seven with him and a border collie. It was Emrys and Marged's brother, Rhys. "Hallo!" he said, "Out for a walk are you?"

Buttercup wished she could run back to the cave or disappear. "Yes, I am with some friends from the school."

"Yes, I know, there is someone waiting in the bushes over there. I think she was hiding, I didn't let on I knew she was there. I could come along and say hello if you like?"

Buttercup came close to panic and in a rushed voice said, "Please don't. She's very shy."

He smiled. "That's alright, enjoy your walk." Then off he and Rhys went in the direction of the farmhouse.

Buttercup got back to Marged.

"Oh, Buttercup, that was close. That was my father and brother. It was Roy, the dog that found me and he behaved just like always, as if he knew me. I thought that they were going to come into the bushes after me, but they called Roy out. Doing all this is very nerve racking. Did you get the time?"

Buttercup too, was breathing sighs of relief. "Yes, it's on the watch. Today is Saturday the fourth of May and I saw you at the house. You were so small then and you were hanging onto your mother's leg all the time I was there and your father wanted to come and say hello to you, but he didn't."

"Well let's get back before we run into someone else."

 The two girls moved briskly to the cave and entered after Marged had placed the watch into the plastic bag and hid it in the rocks.

Inside, Marged did her calculations, adjusted the Time Stones, placed her hands on the rock and watched the rock door open, then out she went and it closed behind her. It opened again, and in she came. "Not quite right," she said. "Three o'clock in the morning on the second of June 1996. One more adjustment and it should be right."

She made the adjustment and went out again. The stumpy man was waiting there and instead of turning away as he had been doing he spoke to her in his strange voice. "I know all your life and the lives of all you know, Marged Evans. So beware in the worlds and times you visit they might not be as safe as you might think."

She remembered what Caradoc had told her and bravely marched up to him. "Why do you wish to hurt me? I have never harmed you and I don't want to harm you. You can't hurt me, because I will beat you."

He looked briefly into her defiant eyes and then turned and walked away. Marged hoped that that would be the last she would see of him. She wasn't sure. She turned and checked the time and went back in with a huge smile, carrying a small box of tied fishing flies. "Ta da. It is four o'clock in the afternoon of the third of June." She smiled at David Taylor. "Are you ready to leave?"

"Yes, I am, there are no game keepers out there wanting to beat me up are there?"

"No, everything will be fine, but be careful. I will leave my watch out there and I will go out to see how the time is going and to see if you have left any messages, which you can do if there are any problems. But there again if you get this far, you might as well come in and let us know in person."

"Of course. Rhys, are you ready to go to London to live for a while in 1996?"

"Yes, I am. I want to see movies."

"You will see more than that, I can assure you."

Marged placed her hands on the rock once more and David picked up his fishing equipment and he and Rhys left the cave.

CHAPTER 9

A century's middle is to be found
And a person that has gone to ground.
Marged finds the man without great haste
Who has bombed our cities and laid them waste.
She helps him out but he won't last
Because of the evil in his past.

Buttercup smiled. "Will he be alright?"

"He will be fine, Mr. Taylor will look after him, you'll see, and he will learn a lot more English and that will help him if he goes back to school in his time. When he returns he will know more about a lot of things. More things than his teachers know. He will be the smartest pupil at his school."

Buttercup smiled with delight. "I am so happy for him." Then she glanced back into the depths of the cave. "What are we going to do now?"

"I thought we should try to get you back, but I can calculate your time better, if I can find a time in the middle of the twentieth century. First, however, I am going to need another watch, because the other one has to stay out there until Rhys returns from London."

"So you have to go out in your time again to get another watch?"

"Yes, and then I can come back and start calibrating again."

"Will there be anyone here you could help get back to their time in the middle of the century?"

"I am not sure, but we have to find out how people dressed back then, or in your case in the future. Wait a minute. I think there is someone who might want to get out."

"Who?"

"There is a German pilot in here from the Second World War he might want to get out but how he got here I don't know."

"Was he flying those big balloons that were dropping bombs on us in London?"

"No, that was the First World War; this man is from the Second World War. Come on, let's go and find him."

They trailed back to the area where most of the people were and found the German pilot where Marged had first seen him. As they approached, he straightened up, not sure why two young girls were coming toward him. The boy and the girl that were sitting on the rock looked up at the girls. The boy seemed to be about ten years old and the girl about thirteen or fourteen. "Can you help us? This man has made us his prisoners."

Marged walked right up to him. "Are you a German pilot?"

He replied in words that were very clipped. "I am a German Officer in the glorious German Air Force. I am waiting for dark so that I can escape from this cave. These children are my hostages to get me out of your country and back to Germany."

"How did you get here?"

"We were bombing Liverpool docks when the plane was damaged by the flak and we crashed into a mountain near here. We parachuted out and I found my way here."

"What day did all this happen?"

"It happened today?"

Marged could not help but be stunned by these people who were years, hundreds and even thousands of years after their time and didn't even know it. "What time, day and year was it?"

"You don't know what today is?"

"No. So please tell us."

"It is the fourth of May."

"Alright, what year is it?"

"You don't know what the year is?"

"No. Please tell us."

"1941. I don't understand why you are asking such questions."

"Well, I came here today also, and so did my friend Buttercup. She is from 1918 and I am from 2004. By my time you have been here for 63 years. Your war is over and you lost, just so that you know."

"You are stupid little girls. Are you mad? I have only just got here with my hostages and that man with the beard said that they are not my hostages and that when I leave here they still won't be my hostages." He raised his voice a little. "What does he know?"

Caradoc was nearby and came onto the scene and stared at the German with his timeless eyes.
"You do not threaten people here.
In this cave there will be no fear."

The German growled out a sneering laugh. "What can you do you silly man? Do you think you can stop me? A little girl could beat you."

"Girls have power as you will see
And mean no longer you will be."

"Your silly sayings are not wisdom. You can't even take my hostages away from me."

"Your hostages from you will go
And no more evil will you show."

The German became slowly enraged at Caradoc. It was then that Marged noticed how much the man resembled the pictures she had seen of Hitler. He even had a similar moustache.

In an angry, arrogant voice he spoke. "I have lost my patience with you and now I will show you and these children how useless you are." He unclipped his holster and pulled out his pistol.

Buttercup shrieked. "Stop it, you can't shoot him."

He turned and looked down his arrogant nose at Buttercup and waved the pistol in her face. "I can do whatever I want. First him and then you." Buttercup became petrified.

Turning back to Caradoc he pointed the pistol directly at him. "And now, I will prove it."

He was about to pull the trigger when Marged crashed herself into him from the side with as much of her body weight as she could put into one place. The gun went off as she glanced off his arms and landed on the floor sending small animals panicking away. As she landed she saw the stumpy man, just for a miniscule moment. He was smiling.

The bullet from the pistol had flown harmlessly across the cave and chipped a bit of rock off a distant wall.

Buttercup became suddenly animated and dived onto Marged to help her as she thought that she had been shot. She screamed out. "Marged, Marged, are you hurt?"

The boy and girl hostages were also screaming as the German turned the pistol back on Caradoc once again. "I will not miss now. The little girl will not save your life this time."

He pulled the trigger and there was a click. Nothing else happened.

Caradoc held his hands wide.
"All your power you will no longer need.
On no more violence you will ever feed."

The German took no notice. He pulled the trigger several times more and nothing happened. Then in a rage he lifted it high and brought it down on Caradoc's head, except, that it did not reach his head, it stopped three inches away as if it had hit a very hard rock. He was still a very determined German and tried again even harder and the same thing happened. The colours of rage drained from his face as his violent energy declined throughout his body.

Buttercup and Marged were doing their best to get to their feet. They were not hurt, but much shaken. The hostage children had calmed down. Caradoc had his hands still stretched out as a tempering tranquillity returned to the cave. He turned to Marged.
"You may continue your work to get him out.
He will harm no more you can have no doubt."

Marged, after all that had just happened, was a little sceptical. "Are you sure? I saw the stumpy man."

"He peered through from another cave
And failed completely by your act so brave.
As I have said, harm will never come to you.
So to all others you must be true.
You are free to continue all your work
And in all your efforts you must not shirk."

He then turned and calmly left the scene of the scariest altercation any of the young people had ever seen.

The German, although stoic, was demoralized.

A shaking Buttercup held onto Marged's arm. "What are you going to do?"

"We are going to help these hostages get away from this man and out of the cave so they can go safely back to their time." She turned to the stoic German. "You can put your gun away. You will never be able to use it again."

He put it back in the holster. "If it had not jammed, you would all be dead."

Marged smiled. "You will not be able to hurt anyone again in your life. Now, your hostages will leave and you will leave afterwards, by yourself."

"I will leave when I wish. I have only just got here."

"No you haven't. You have been here for 63 years. See those ancient soldiers over there?" She pointed to the seven Silurian's. He nodded. "They have been here for 1600 years."

"What you are saying is impossible."

"No, it is not. Once you have entered this cave, time does not pass. Didn't Caradoc tell you?"

"That old man is just a fool; if my gun had worked he would be dead now."

"He told you and I am telling you, you can never hurt anyone again."

"Go away from me you silly girls."

"I can prove it, but first I am going to ask your hostages questions."

"You can't do that without my permission."

"Try and stop me."

He moved toward Marged but she stood her ground. Then suddenly, he stopped and could move no further.

"See, you can't touch me."

She turned to the boy and girl. "Where are you from?"

The girl answered. "We're from up by the Elan Valley. We were out on the hill, checking on the lambs for our father, when we saw the four parachutes come down and we saw a plane that was on fire crashing in the distance. Three of the men were a long way away and they gathered up their parachutes and disappeared over the hill. The one closest was this one." She pointed to the pilot. "He was flat on the ground, so we ran over to help him. We didn't know he was German until we got there and then it was too late. He took his gun out and said he would shoot us if we didn't help him. He made us walk over the hill and we came into this cave. We want to go home."

"Don't worry, we will get you home, but we are going to need your help."

"But he won't let us go and he might shoot us."

"You can go anywhere you want and he can't do anything about it and he can't shoot you or anyone else ever again."

"How do you know this?"

"That is the way it is in this cave and, once you have been here, you can never hurt anyone again. Watch." Marged turned and faced the German pilot and got to within two feet of him. "Buttercup, take those two and go to the door area. Now, Mr. German, if you want to try and stop them, you will have to hit me first. Go on try it."

He lifted his right hand, pulled it back and only managed to bring it forward about a foot before it suddenly stopped. Marged smiled. "See, you can do nothing. What you should be thinking about is how you can get home to your family. If I were you, I would pick a time to go out there after the war is over. I know you don't believe all this, but if you come to the door area, I will prove to you how long you have been here, If you wish? Think about it."

She turned and left for the door. He shouted after her "You will be punished for this."

She stopped and looked back at him, put her thumbs on her temples, opened her mouth, waggled her tongue and hands at him and went "Bleeeh." She then turned once more to continue her walk.

Marged had to decide how to continue. She had to get the brother and sister out in their time, but it would have to be after the plane had crashed, so they would not run into the Germans again. An hour or two after would be OK and they would find their way home safely. Now all she had to do was find the correct time and that would mean going out again, close to it.

She turned to Buttercup. "I am going out in my time to get another watch and then when I come back we will have to send one of them out close to their time to get the right time and date, so that I can set the watch outside, like we have done before. Can you explain to them what we have to do. I think we will be okay in sending them to my family's farm. My great grandfather should be there and I think he will help. Alright, I will get another watch. If I manage to find the right kind of clothes for their time, I will bring them back and you can go out and do it." She turned to the brother and sister. "What are your names?"

The girl answered. "My name is Ceridwen and this is Brychan."

"Nice to meet you. Don't worry, we are going to get you home, but you will have to help us."

"Oh, yes, we will."

Marged readjusted the stones and stepped through the opening rock door once more, carrying her brother's coat. Outside she headed back to the farm, confident that she had got the time exactly right. She didn't even bother to be cautious.

Back at the farm she was asked if Rhys Edwards had found his parents.

She smiled. "Yes, his parents showed up and, they are nice."

At dinner Megan noticed that Marged was not wearing her watch. "Marged, where is your watch? You haven't gone and lost it, have you?"

"I'm sorry, Mam, it must have fallen off and I can't find it."

"Oh, Marged you have to be more careful. I have only just bought you that watch for doing well in school."

Marged snivelled and looked down at her plate. "I'm sorry; if you can take me into Builth I will use my pocket money and buy a new one."

"Alright, I will help you get a new one; we need to go in and take a look at what you might need for the high school in September, so we might as well go in this afternoon. And next time when you are out there take your watch off and put it in your pocket or leave it at home."

In town, Marged got her new watch and wanted to go to the shop that had the costumes, but her mother wanted to leave for home as soon as the shopping was done.

Once back, Marged left another letter under her pillow, although she knew she would be back again right on time.

Back at the cave she joined Buttercup in preparing the girl and her brother for going out. "I didn't have a chance at getting the right clothes, but I got another watch." She turned to Ceridwen and Brychan. "Now, here is what I want you to do. I am going to adjust the Time Stones to close to the time you came here and then I will come with you and point out where you have to go to find out the time. You will also have to find out what the date is and the year. All these things are important. At the house they will tell you this and as soon as you have the information you must come back to where I will be waiting. It is very important that you leave as soon as you have been told, do not delay. Do you understand?"

The girl looked at Marged. "I think so, but why can't we just go outside and go home?"

"That would not work because the mountain around this cave has slowly moved over thousands of years and you would go out at the wrong time. You could find yourself either in the future or in the past. You could go back before you were born or go back after you have died. So that is why we have to do it this way or it would never work."

"What about the German. Will he come out with us?"

"No, we will get him out on a different time, after the war is over would be good, that would be a shock for him. But, if he keeps behaving like he is, we might send him out into the Stone Age and see how he likes that."

The girl smiled for the first time since Marged had met her. "I will do what you want me to do, but I think we should leave Brychan here in case there is trouble. He is very scared."

"That will be alright. Buttercup can stay here with him while we are out there."

"How long will we be out there?"

"As long as it takes you to get the date and time."

"I hope it's quick, because if we are gone long, Brychan will get upset."

"No he won't, because even if we were to go for a year, no time will have passed for him in here. Do you understand?"

She looked at Marged sceptically and nervously said, "I think so."

"Good, I will make the adjustments." Marged changed into her 1904 costume, because she figured that would be more explainable if she were seen and questioned. After changing, she went over to her work station and made the calculations and adjusted the Time Stones and placed her hands on the rock wall.

Ceridwen was a little startled as the rock door opened, but she recovered when Marged took her hand and led her through to the outside. The rock door closed behind them and Marged noticed immediately the differences in the surrounding area once again. They walked together across the fields to the old oak tree. At the tree Marged found a spot where she could stay hidden, and yet at the same time have a clear view of the front door of the farmhouse.

She sent Ceridwen on her way, reminding her of what she should do when she got there. She got her watch out of her pocket and set the stop watch part of it to "ready". As she settled down to watch, she noticed that the farm didn't look a lot different than it did when she visited with Rhys and Buttercup. There were none of the buildings that her grandfather had built and of course none of the ones put up by her father.

She watched Ceridwen approach the door and knock. After a few seconds a woman answered and Marged could see a conversation taking place. It looked as if Ceridwen was getting questioned more than she had expected. After a minute or two Ceridwen disappeared into the house and about twenty minutes went by before she came out and began to walk away from the house. Marged hit the stop watch and watched the seconds go by. Three minutes later Ceridwen reached her. Marged asked, "Did you get the date and time?"

"Yes. The date is April twentieth, 1941."

"What was the time?"

"Well, when I went in it was half past two exactly and I couldn't leave because they gave me a cup of tea, but I was able to see the time on the clock as I left the house."

"What was it?"

"It was five minutes to three."

Marged pressed the button to stop the stop watch and immediately adjusted the date and time accordingly. She smiled at Ceridwen. "Good work, now we can get you home without meeting any Germans."

They briskly walked back across the fields to the cave. Marged placed the watch in another plastic bag, sealed it and hid it in the rocks. Ceridwen watched very closely. "What are you doing that for?"she asked.

"Well, when I place my watch here, set to the time it is, I can go inside the cave, make adjustments and then come out to check if it is the right time for you to leave."

Ceridwen seemed not to fully understand how it all worked, but she was interested in the plastic bag. "What was that bag you put the watch in? Was it a skin?"

"No, it's called plastic. You will see it and use it in your future. Let's go in and calibrate the right time for you to leave and get back home."

As soon as they got back into the cave they were greeted by the German pilot. He stood directly in front of the two returning girls. "Where have you been?"

Marged boldly stood her ground. "Out there. Making preparations so that Ceridwen and Brychan, in case you didn't know their names, can go home without running into you again"

"You are interfering with my hostages."

"Yes, I am, and you can do nothing about it. You can try if you want to, but you will be able to do no more than stand there and watch them go, so there. And Caradoc will make sure of that."

Caradoc, who had been observing all that had been going on without saying a word, suddenly spoke up,
"Marged now has the power, here within.
So you will be wise to curb your sin.

These children will leave without your stop
And all ill will you soon will drop.
You will watch it all become unrooted
And no more lives by you be looted."

Marged went to the work station and made calculations and then once more adjusted the stones and left, right in front of the now statue-like German. She came back in and smiled at him. "I am getting good at this. Only half a day off this time."

Marged made more adjustments and out she went again and when she returned her smile was bigger than the first time. "Got it right on this time. Alright Ceridwen and Brychan, you can go home now, it should take you a couple of hours up over the hill and I don't think you will be running into any Germans."

Marged opened the rock door once more and led Ceridwen and Brychan through. She laughed. "Say good bye to your captor. You probably will never see him again. I shall be back. I am going to go with them for a short distance."

Outside, Marged walked with them as far as the oak tree. She pointed the best way up to the hill and to where they would find their home and avoid any Germans, who, they had assured her, had gone in the other direction and no doubt they would eventually be captured. "Good bye. If you have any problems, come back here and we will help you sort it out. Just rub the rock."

They were about to say goodbye and then stopped. "What rock?"

"The one which opens the rock door from the outside."

"We didn't use that. The door just opened when we got close to it."

Marged realized that they had come in in fear so explained about rubbing the rock and getting into the cave if they should come back.

Marged returned, picked up the watch, and was satisfied with a job well done. The German pilot was still rooted to the cave floor. He spoke. "I want to leave now."

167

Marged smiled. "And where is it you want to go? Germany?"

"Yes."

"Well I'm sorry. When you leave here, you will still be in Wales. And if I were you, when you leave, you should give yourself up."

"I will find a way back to Germany."

"And you will have to do that without doing harm to anyone, because your pistol will not work again and you will never fight again in your whole life. Are you going to behave yourself if we let you go?"

"You are a foolish girl. I will fight my way back to Germany."

"You can try, but you won't succeed and you won't win. The war your Hitler started was lost, with millions of lives lost for no reason. Today, you might like to know, the whole of Europe is all together. All the countries there work together in harmony now and Germans are doing good work in it and are leading the way. So when you get caught, you will know that you will be in a prison camp until 1945 when the war will end, and you will be allowed to return to Germany and help put your country back together and make amends to anyone you meet, for all that leader of yours did."

"I don't believe it. The Fuhrer promised a thousand years Reich."

"Well, he didn't keep his promise, because he was a mean and nasty man. I will let you out in July of 1941 when people will be out on the harvest. They will see you and you will be captured and you will not be able to resist."

Marged adjusted the Time Stones, confident that he would go out on a nice sunny day. She went out first to make sure. It was ten in the morning on the 21st of July, the sun was blazing and farmers were harvesting. She came back, reopened the rock door and said good bye to the German.

CHAPTER 10

Back to school our Rhys must go
No more fears it will be just so.
Then by a train right to his school
And a teacher who will lose his rule.
Efforts to stop the Welsh will pale
And the cane of violence will surely fail.

When the rock door closed behind the German airman, Buttercup came over to Marged and grabbed her by the arm. "You were so brave." .

"I didn't think about it. Oh my gosh, Buttercup, I think I could have been shot. Thank goodness Caradoc stopped his power. I thought for a second he had lost it and we would all be killed. I am sure it is good now though, Caradoc made sure of that."

"Why was there another world war? In my time we were fighting Germany too."

"We won the war in your time, but in 1939 Germany had rearmed under this terrible dictator called Hitler. He wanted to conquer and enslave the world; he killed millions of innocent women and children as well as men. We beat him and the Japanese who were on his side. Now, all the countries in Europe are friends and will never go to war again."

"So when I am older I will have to go through another world war?"

"Yes, but I have a feeling you will be fine. But guess what?"

"What?"

"I think I have enough information now to calibrate all of the twentieth, century, right down to any day and time you would care to choose, and I want to start calibrating right away. Do you want to help me?"

"Yes. What do you want me to do?"

"I want you to take one of the ballpoint pens and make notes for me in the notebook while I make measurements and mark the large sheet and make transfers to the marks on the wall. Once in a while we'll go out to check our work by using the watches and that means we will have to go out every six months, so I will have to solve the problem of getting new batteries."

"Alright."

The two girls worked at the calibrations. Every year to start with and then every six months.

While they were working on calibrations, David Taylor showed up with Rhys Edwards. Rhys no longer wore a sling. He was completely healed.

David smiled. "Well, here he is and his English has improved. However, I found some Welsh speakers and he was able to use his own language whenever he wanted to, and it made him feel more at home. He also attended a couple of weeks in a modern school with my sons. We also took him to Heathrow Airport; so, now, I expect you have to figure out how to get him back to his own time. By the way, I've brought your watch in from outside. I hope you don't mind"

Marged was smiling. "That is good. I have already figured out how to get him back, we just have to prepare for the journey. It would be nice to find a way to stop those teachers beating him or any other Welsh speaker."

Caradoc was listening and spoke up.
"No more beatings on him will rain.
He can return to his school with no harm again.
When any stick is raised to Rhys
The wielder will be made to cease."

Marged's eyes lit up. "You mean that anyone who tries to harm him won't be able to."

"Once been here and healed within
No harm out there will ever begin.
From people that are known to him
He'll be protected life and limb.
There might be reasons to be alarmed
From those unknown he could well be harmed."

"So, if he speaks Welsh, at the end of the day the teacher that he knows won't be able to harm him?"

"For speaking his language he will not be harmed.
In the voice of the harmer, it will be charmed."

171

"Does that mean that the teacher will speak Welsh if he tries to harm Rhys?"

"It is true, as he will find
The teachers' language will be his kind."

Marged was delighted. "Rhys, that means you can go back to school and never be hurt again."

Rhys smiled. "You know what I am going to do?"

They waited for the answer. Buttercup couldn't wait for the few seconds it was taking for him to tell them. "What, what are you going to do?"

"When I go back to that school, I am going to make sure that I am the one wearing the "Welsh Not" at the end of the school day and that way no one will get beaten for speaking Welsh. I will speak English all day long and I am sure they will be impressed, and then at the end of the day, I will go over to whoever is wearing it, take it off them and loudly say in Welsh, 'Thank you very much, I will now wear it with pride.' And then, when the teacher takes out his cane in front of the whole class to beat me, I will smile and say in English, 'I think you will be the last one speaking Welsh today.'" He smiled. "I can hardly wait."

Marged and Buttercup were excited too. Marged headed for her calculations. "Alright Rhys, I will set the Time Stones ready for you and I think Buttercup and I should go with you. We can take the train from Garth, so let's get ready." Marged and Rhys changed and Rhys found that his clothes were not fitting very well; he had grown a little while his arm was healing in England. Buttercup examined the back of his trousers and the back of his waistcoat. She glanced at Marged. "We need a needle and cotton, then I could let his waistcoat and trousers out and then they would fit. His jacket would be alright as long as he didn't try to button it. So we need a needle and thread, a thimble and a pair of scissors."

Marged looked at the clothes. "Well, we can't send him back with them as they are, or his parents will think his clothes have shrunk. Or they will think that he has very suddenly grown. I will get the sewing kit so you, Buttercup, can get everything altered and then we can go out and on to Llandovery."

The sewing kit was handed to Buttercup and she got down to work. She cut the original stitching and found a thread of an appropriate colour, threaded the needle and began stitching. Marged was very impressed with the careful, precise stitches that Buttercup was using.

The waistcoat was finished. Rhys tried it on and it fitted perfectly, no one would notice that it had been altered. She moved on to the trousers and soon had them altered. Rhys went and tried them on and they, too, fitted perfectly.

When he returned, fully dressed, he announced that he was ready.

David smiled. "Don't forget, Rhys, you are welcome to come and visit me in London at any time. Of course, you will have to come back here first to do so. You have the right money. Use it when you want to visit. Good luck back in your time. My family and I have enjoyed having you stay with us. Marged, could you get me out so that I can return; the date is the twenty eighth of July 1996."

"I could do it now or I could do it when we return. It won't make any difference. If we do it when we return, we will be able to tell you how Rhys got on when he got back to his home and the school."

"Good idea, let's do it that way."

Marged, asked Buttercup for the train schedule. "Can you find a train from Garth that arrives in Llandovery with enough time to get to the school at the right time."

Buttercup took the schedule out of her bag and she and Marged perused it for a while until they had worked out what train to catch. Marged then calculated the time and set the Time Stones. She left plenty of time for walking, even if they had a long wait in the station and of course it would be a longer wait if they got a lift in a gambo.

Marged consulted her notes and calibrations and checked the Time

Stones once more. "Alright, is everyone ready?"

Buttercup answered, "Yes, but aren't you going out to verify the time is right?"

"No. I can set the Time Stones to any time from the years 1860 to 2060. That is 200 years, with enough precision to be within an hour of the time we want out there. There is only one problem that might interfere with our work."

Buttercup became alert. "What?"

"Well, there is a man out there and Caradoc knows of him and he will try and interfere with our work."

"I think I have seen him. Oh, my gosh, will he hurt us?"

"I don't think he can hurt us, but he might be able to upset us in all that we know. So we will have to be on the lookout to make sure he doesn't make things go wrong for us."

"Marged, I'm afraid."

"Buttercup, we can't be afraid all the time. We have the power of our cave, Caradoc's power and with all that we will be able to beat him and any power he has. We just have to make sure he doesn't harm the people around us."

"Oh, dear, I hope you are right."

"I hope so too."

The trio was on their way again, following a track to Capel Rhos to take the gravely, muddy roads to Garth. It took them the best part of two hours to get there. They saw one person on a cart pulled by a very nice looking white horse. They didn't get a ride in it because it was going in the wrong direction.

At the station they found that they had an hour to wait for the train. Buttercup went to the station master's office and tapped on the door. The same man appeared.

He stared down at her. "Can I help you, my lady?"

"Yes, my good man, you can. I would like three return, first-class tickets on the one-thirty train from here to Landovery. One for me and one each for my two servants."

He raised his eyebrows. "Servants don't usually travel first class, my lady."

"I want my servants to travel with me, to cater for any needs I may have on the journey, and that way I can also keep an eye on them."

Marged listened, amused.

Once the tickets were purchased they sat down on the benches, Marged and Rhys on one and Buttercup on the other. After a few minutes Marged got restless and decided to walk along the platform and look around. It was then that she saw a large coloured poster on a board attached to the wall of the station. She hadn't noticed it before, so she went and had a closer look at it. She was amazed. It was a poster with cowboys and Indians and it read, "Buffalo Bill's Wild West and Congress of Rough Riders of the World, Coming to Builth Wells, May 12th." Marged was excited. She took out the camera and took a picture of the poster. The camera worked. She had tried to use it in the cave. But, like her watch, in there it was dead. Except for showing pictures she had taken previously. She called to the others. "Hey, come and look at this."

Buttercup and Rhys joined Marged and stared at the poster.

Rhys scanned the poster with wonder. "Oh, I have seen movies with cowboys and Indians and these are real and they are going to be in Builth Wells in May. Oh, I want to go."

"Me too! What about you Buttercup? Would you like to see this?"

"I don't know. I don't know what my mother would say."

"But how would she know if you had been or not. This show is before you were born, so if you told her you were going, she would tell you that it is too late because it had already happened."

175

"That's right. Alright, I'll go." She looked closer at the poster. "Is that what it would be like?"

Marged didn't know a lot about the Wild West Show, but she did know that it had travelled the world. "This show has gone all over the world; I have heard stories about it, passed down from people who went to see it. Look, they do the Pony Express and Custer's Last Stand."

Buttercup stopped to think for a second. "But, how are we going to do it?"

Marged also thought for a second. "Well, Buttercup, you and I can go back to the cave and Rhys can meet us there closer to the time. He can use the return ticket to take the train back here to Garth. He could get a gambo to Capel Rhos to come back to the cave to get us."

Buttercup thought again for a moment. "And after the show couldn't Rhys just go back to Landovery?"

"Yes, if his parents allowed him to go, otherwise he would have to come back to the cave, so that we could get him out earlier, in time for him to catch the train and get back before he was missed, which is what we are going to do today."

It was Rhys' turn to think. "If I ask my parents for permission, they might want to go as well and then I couldn't meet you."

Marged asked, "If you asked your parents, would they say no?"

"I don't know. If they said no then I would sneak away and then at the cave you could get me out, so that I could get back before they knew I was gone just like you said."

"Or," said Buttercup, "I could meet them and say that my mother wanted to give them tickets for the show, because Rhys was kind to me."

Marged was listening. "You know, we should sort all this out when we get down there today. We will let Rhys ask his parents and if they say no, then he can get away and meet us and we will make sure he gets back in time. It will mean that he will have to walk back to Garth. We could go with him and get a gambo back. If his parents want to go, then we will see him on the train or at the show. The main thing is we will all get to see the show."

Shortly after their discussion they watched a train from Swansea pull in to the little station and stop. The station master came out and watched one person get off. Then, he blew a whistle, waved a flag and the train continued on its northern journey.

Forty-five minutes later their train pulled in. The station master came out and opened the train door into first class for the trio. Rhys and Marged had to stand to one side as the station master helped Buttercup on. They followed and made themselves comfortable and the train was soon picking up steam. It wasn't long before the train entered the Sugar Loaf tunnel.

Buttercup remarked, "I always get nervous when I go through this tunnel."

She was the only one of the trio to have ever been in it. Rhys and Marged thought it was exciting and very soon after coming out into the daylight they crossed the Cynghordy Viaduct, an amazing piece of engineering in its day, a tall brick and stone structure of multiple pillars and Roman type arches. Buttercup told them not to look down, because it would make them dizzy, but they did anyway. The houses, fields and trees looked tiny in their valley from the great height of the viaduct. Marged told them that the only time she had been on a structure that high was when she stood on top of the Claerwen Dam. They asked her what the Claerwen Dam was and she gave them a full description.

They soon arrived in Llandovery and the girls did their best to shield Rhys, in case someone who knew him was to see him. Marged asked "Where's your school by, Rhys?"

"It's over by there." He pointed to a large red sandstone building with blue grey stone quoins on the corners and around the windows and doors. It could be plainly seen from the station. Marged remembered travelling through Llandovery and her mother pointing it out to her.

177

"That's the Pantycelyn School over there," she had said.

Marged checked her watch. "Rhys, what time did you leave the school on the day you ran away?"

"About half past two."

"It's quarter past now. We will have to wait. Which door did you leave by?"

Rhys pointed to a door at the side of the building. "That one over there."

"Right, we are going to have to wait until after you have left, and then we can go in and nobody will have missed you. Here, you had better put this back on." She reached inside her costume, found her jeans pocket and retrieved the Welsh Not on its piece of string and hung it around Rhys' neck.

He looked at her in surprise. "Are you going to come in with me?"

"Yes, of course. After all we've been through for this, Buttercup and I have decided that we are not going to miss it for the world."

"But what if you are caught?"

"It doesn't matter. Like you, we have been in the cave, so we are now protected too and anyway we can tell your teacher that we are your cousins from Builth and we are waiting for you from school. We can hardly wait to see what happens."

Rhys asked, "If we are protected from being hurt, because we were in the cave, how was my uncle able to hit me?"

Marged responded. "That is a good question, I will ask Caradoc."

Buttercup nudged Marged. "Look." She pointed to the school door and running away from it was Rhys.

Rhys stared in amazement. He was watching himself leaving the school. "That's me," he said.

"Yes, it is," said Marged. "Weird isn't it?"

"What would have happened if I had met him?"

"I am not really sure. That's another question I will have to ask Caradoc. Perhaps you would melt into one another and become a combination in one. I don't know, but we are not going to try it until we have talked to Caradoc."

"Will my other self be in the cave when you go back?"

"Yes, but a different one to ours. At least I hope so; otherwise we will have to go through this all over again and again and again. No, that would be crazy. Come on, we have to get you back into the school before you are missed."

They got over to the door that they had seen him leave by and went in. Marged smiled. "Wow, where is your classroom?"

"Over there."

He pointed to an open door where the last class of the day was about to end. As they approached the door they could hear a loud voice. "Where is the boy wearing the 'Welsh Not'?"

Rhys smiled at the girls. "Here we go." He stepped into the classroom, followed by the girls. Marged was amazed at the wooden desks with old fashioned ink wells and sloped lids. She could even smell the ink. On each desk was a small chalk board and pieces of chalk in a groove next to the ink wells.

Rhys smiled up at the roaring teacher. "Here I am, sir."

The other students were rooted to their places in fear of this sadistic, bullying teacher. They could not believe that Rhys was cheerfully smiling in the face of what that man was about to do to him.

The teacher boomed "Come here boy! How many beatings will it take to stop you speaking that uncivilized language?"

Rhys smiled up at him again. "Until you are too tired to beat me anymore. I speak the oldest language in Europe and I will never stop speaking it, because it is the language of my country."

The teacher's eyes widened in shock at the boy's retort. "How dare you, you impudent little scoundrel. I will beat that language out of you if it is the last thing I ever do."

Rhys smiled again in defiance. "I will still be speaking Welsh long after the last thing you will ever do."

The teacher went into a violent rage and tried to grab Rhys. As his hand reached for the scruff of Rhys' neck it stopped three inches away as if it had come up against a solid object. He stared at his hand and in Welsh said, "What is going on here?"

Rhys looked up at him again. "It is lovely to hear you speak our language. Thank you, sir. Shall I bend over the desk here for you?" Rhys bent over one of the desks ready for the punishment he knew would not be coming.

The teacher stepped back and reached for his cane which was hanging on a hat stand close to the corner of the classroom. As he came forward he was speaking English again. "I will show you a lesson that you will never forget."

Rhys lifted his head. "It will be a memorable lesson for both of us, sir."

The teacher lifted the cane and brought it down swiftly with as much force as he could muster. It stopped in mid air and he started speaking Welsh again. Marged and Buttercup were cheering, jumping up and down and clapping their hands. Marged called out to the teacher. "See, you can't do it! That's because the Welsh language is pure and every time you try to punish someone for speaking it, you will speak it yourself."

With the cane still in mid air he glared at Marged and addressed her in a stream of Welsh. "Who are you? Are you in league with this impudent boy? I will beat you too you know, when I have finished with this one."

Marged understood most of what he had said and answered, "I am in league with him and so is our friend Buttercup. Are you going to beat her too?"

He stared at Marged and in Welsh he threatened her again. He lifted the cane once more and it stopped on the down stroke. It was then that he realized that he was speaking Welsh himself and it horrified him. His left hand lifted and he clutched his throat with it and in Welsh asked, "What is happening to me?"

Rhys stood up and smiled at him and said in English "You are speaking Welsh; you are the last one speaking it today, so here you are." Rhys took the Welsh Not from around his neck and placed it over the head of the teacher. The teacher could not do anything to stop him.

The girls' excitement was infectious and carried over to the pupils who were rooted no more. They were pointing and laughing at the demoralized teacher. Everyone filed out, leaving him muttering, still clutching his throat.

Outside the other children gathered around Rhys. "How did you do that to him Rhys?" one asked.

"Well," he answered, "I was given these special powers by an old man with a grey beard in a cave."

They all laughed. "Don't tell your lies. I suppose it was Merlin, was it?"

"No, his name was Caradoc."

Marged piped in. "He's telling the truth. We were there when it happened, weren't we, Buttercup?"

"Yes, we were."

One of the boys stepped up and looked into Rhys' face. "He might not be able to hit you, so it will be one of us he'll be hitting next."

Marged smiled. "You won't have to worry anymore. He won't be able to hurt anyone ever again. If any other teacher tries it, make sure that

Rhys is wearing the Welsh Not and that teacher won't be able to beat him either. Rhys is protected forever now."

They left the amazed students and headed back to the railway station, where Marged and Buttercup would catch the train for the return trip to Garth. Marged stopped. "Wait a minute; don't we have to find out if Rhys' parents want to go to the Wild West Show?"

"Oh, yes," Rhys said. "We have to find out. You had better come home with me and I will ask them. It's a two mile walk to the cottage where we live. I will walk you back when we've talked to them."

The girls smiled. "Lead on," said Marged.

They were on a beaten up road that Marged knew would become the A40 one day and be a major highway. They walked along it a short distance, then Rhys led them through an old wooden gate and onto a track that hugged the side of a field leading up to a brow of a hill. They walked diagonally across another field which held a few sheep that looked up at them casually and went back to grazing.

Marged asked if he had lived in Llandovery all his life. He answered that he had and told them that his family had lived there for generations and said that one of his ancestors was a seer or prophet.

Marged smiled. "What did he know? Did he know all about the future?"

"Lots of things that came true; he also said that one day there would be wires overhead that would bring light at night to the town. I saw all that in London and he said there would be horseless carriages in the streets and now I know there will be. He also said that Llandovery would be in a great flood with a great loss of life and a lot of damage and the doctor told me that had happened."

Marged stopped walking and a look of shock came over her face. The others looked at her. Buttercup spoke. "Marged what's the matter?"

"Oh my gosh. Rhys, that's right, in 1987 there was."

"There was what?"

"A great flood a dam that was built on the Upper Towy River burst and flooded the whole valley. It destroyed all the bridges and drowned a lot of people."

Rhys stopped and stood very still a look of deep thought on his face.

Marged was concerned. "What is it?"

Half a smile crept onto his face. "Now that we know I wonder if we could stop it from happening."

Marged looked at him and she too had a lot of thinking written on her face that quickly changed to a smile as she glanced at Rhys and Buttercup in turn. "We could do it, because I heard that it was some sort of sabotage when they built it that caused it to burst. We could go back and find out what happened and stop it. If we could do that the dam wouldn't burst, but it would mean that your ancestor was wrong."

Rhys laughed. "We should do it and I don't think my ancestor would mind being wrong. After all, I don't think he would want his prophecy to happen and all the people being drowned."

Marged nodded. "As soon as we have more experience going in and out of the cave we should prepare ourselves to put a stop to whatever caused the dam to burst. I shall put it on the list.

They came out on a second track which led them to the cottage and Marged asked Buttercup to make up a story about Rhys and give his parents a couple of pounds in thanks and tell them about the Wild West Show.

Rhys opened the front door of the cottage and the trio entered. Rhys' mother greeted them and asked in Welsh. "Rhys, who are these people?"

"Mam, this is Lady Buttercup, she wanted to talk to you."

"Oh, my goodness!" She had broke into English. "My lady, what happened?"

Buttercup raised her chin in a snobbish sort of way. "I am here to tell you how grateful I am to your son, who, earlier this week, saved me from being trampled by a horse and carriage and my parents have asked me to come here in person to give you some money for a trip, first class, by train to Builth Wells, so that you can see the Wild West Show in May." She handed Rhys' mother two one-pound notes.

The woman looked at Buttercup and back to her son. "I don't know what to say. James, that's my husband, and I was thinking about going, because they say it's a marvellous show. But we can't take your money."

Buttercup pleaded. "Please, Mrs. Edwards, if I go home with that money my parents are going to be very angry with me. Please take it, please."

"Alright, but I don't know what my James will say. You are very kind. Thank you very much."

"Rhys saved my life, Mrs. Edwards. It's the least we can do. Well, there we are then. Come along Marged. We must go back to the station."

Marged and Buttercup turned to leave when Mrs. Edwards asked, "Would you like a cup of tea before you go?"

Buttercup glanced at Marged and saw her give a slight nod. "Yes, thank you Mrs. Edwards. That is very kind of you. Shall we sit?"

"Yes."

They sat on chairs around an old table and Buttercup introduced Marged. "This is Marged, my personal servant girl. She could help you if you want. She's very good."

Marged almost burst out laughing, she could barely contain herself.

Mrs. Edwards smiled. "Oh, no, I can manage. I've got some Welsh Cakes. They are fresh, I made them today. I'll bring them out."

The best cups and saucers were brought down from an old Welsh Dresser and the tea was served, and some of the Welsh Cakes were eaten.

Buttercup rose from the table and instantly Marged and Rhys stood up as well. "Well, Mrs. Edwards, we must be off. Thank you for your generosity. We have a train to catch."

"Of course, Rhys you walk with them to the station and come back right away. I have some things for you to do."

They retraced their steps back into Llandovery and the station. They were in good time to catch the five-fifteen back up to Garth.

Buttercup went over to the station master and asked if he could telegraph to Garth station and tell the station master there to have a horse and carriage waiting for them. He nodded. "Yes, my lady, I will do it right away."

The girls boarded the train and said goodbye to Rhys. "See you at the Wild West Show, Rhys."

"You will," he shouted back through the clouds of steam and smoke, as the train moved out of the station.

CHAPTER 11

Native Americans in Mid Wales?
How did they get to the hills and vales?
It takes good medicine to help them out.
The girls are confident they have no doubt.
The train to Hereford they have to take.
Back to their time they have to make.

There was no one else in the carriage and Marged looked at Buttercup and smiled. "You should be an actress. It's nice to know that I am a very good servant." She laughed and Buttercup laughed. "I love doing this. Do you?"

Buttercup nodded. "Oh, yes, I could do this forever."

"Me too, but we have to keep going back to our times. Well, I do anyway; because there are always things there that I need to do for what we are doing."

"Could I go back to your time with you for a visit?"

"Yes. What I'll do is tell my mother that I've invited a friend of mine from school to stay for a few days. I don't think she'll mind, because I've done it before. We'll have to find you some clothes to wear; you've already used one of my school uniforms. You will need some old clothes as well as some best clothes, to go around in. No, we'll find you some good clothes and I will lend you some old clothes of mine."

"I don't want to wear trousers, those jean things."

"You can wear dresses, but they will be down to your knees, not like that long one you are wearing today."

"That will be alright. It will be the same as the skirt of your school uniform."

"Yes, so everything will be fine."

"When can we do this?"

"We could do it right away, but I will have to go out and arrange it first."

"I saw a very shiny blue carriage when I went to the house when you were three and two other ones. One was big and had small wheels and there were slits in the sides."

"That was a horsebox; we use it to take sheep and cattle to the market."

"You don't drove them?"

"We load the animals in there and we tow it into town with the Land Rover."

"Will I get to ride in one of the carriages?"

"Yes, we'll get my mother to drive us all over the place, even back to Llandovery. We can even find out who would be living in Rhys' cottage if it didn't get flooded. Perhaps we will meet a descendant of his."

"Wouldn't that be fun? Then we could tell him what kind of people his descendants are."

All of a sudden it went dark; they were back in the Sugar Loaf Tunnel. Buttercup grabbed Marged as if for some kind of protection from the dark, and as soon as they came out she let her go.

Marged smiled. "You know, we never noticed when the train crossed that huge bridge."

Buttercup smiled. "We were busy talking."

The train pulled into Garth station and the first class carriage stopped in the middle of the platform. The station master opened the carriage door and helped Buttercup down, but not Marged. It seemed that servants could help themselves out of the carriage. This Marged did, with a small amused smile on her face.

Buttercup slipped the station master a penny tip. He asked where her boy servant was. She smiled. "He is in Landovery attending to his education."

As the girls left they stopped to look at the Wild West Show poster again.

Buttercup smiled. "I am looking forward to this. Just look at how those Indians ride. They don't wear very much, do they?"

On the poster there was an Indian, dressed only in a breach cloth, half on and half off a horse at full gallop. There was no saddle or bridle, just a length of rope that was tied around the bottom jaw of the horse.

Marged's hand went back and touched Buttercup's arm. "Oh, my gosh."

"What?"

"There are two Indians in the cave. When I saw them I thought it was impossible for them to be there, because how would they have found the cave all the way from America."

"I've seen them there too, but I didn't think anything about it, because there are so many other odd people there."

"When we get back we will have to find out how they got to the cave. If they are from this show we must try and get them back there."

The station master came over. "The carriage you ordered is waiting for you, my lady."

"Thank you, my good man."

Marged had to suppress a giggle. They walked around to the front of the building where the carriage was waiting. The driver helped Buttercup up and was polite enough to help Marged up also. Then the driver got up on the front, shook the reins and off they went to the road up into the hills. Buttercup and Marged smiled at each other. This was a much more comfortable ride than the old gambo they had ridden in the first time.

It was getting dark when they arrived at Capel Rhos. Buttercup asked, "How are we going to find our way in the dark?"

"Don't worry. I have a torch, see." She pulled her costume to one side to reveal the torch sticking out of her jeans pocket.

"How will we see with that? It's too small to be a lantern."

"You'll see. I showed it to Rhys. Remember, it's from my time, so the driver must not see it until he is out of sight down the road. Although, I could tell him that it is some new invention."

The driver helped both girls down. "How will you find your way in the dark?"

"We'll manage." Marged smiled. "I've done it lots of times."

Buttercup paid the driver and then he proceeded to light a travelling lantern, so that he could see his way back, then he climbed aboard, grabbed the reins, turned the carriage around and trotted off down the rutted track for a road. As soon as they could no longer see the lantern on the carriage Marged took out the torch and turned it on.

Buttercup was gob smacked. "That is so bright."

Marged showed Buttercup the lit torch. "It is a tube, and as you know, inside there are batteries that send electricity to a bulb which is what lights up. I can turn it on and off with this switch which is right here." She pointed to the switch and turned it off and on. "We will only use it when we can't see properly, because we still have some light to travel by."

The girls set off on the trail back to the cave, periodically using the torch. After a while their eyes were used to the dark and Marged put it back into her pocket. A short distance from the cave they saw a smudge of a figure approaching them; they ducked behind some bushes and kept very still. As the figure came closer they could see that he was carrying four rabbits that he had caught.

Buttercup whispered to Marged. "He's a poacher and he's coming straight at us, what are we going to do?"

Marged removed the torch from her pocket. "I am going to scare him. Can you see to run to the cave when I do and then I will join you there?"

"What are you going to do?"

"You'll see. Get ready to run. Here he comes." Marged stepped out from behind the bushes and shone the torch right into the man's face, and began shrieking like an animal in awful pain. Buttercup took off, running towards the cave, tripping and stumbling as she went. The man cried out with horror, dropped the rabbits and ran off in the opposite direction to Buttercup.

Marged turned the torch off. The poacher didn't look back. She smiled. "I bet he won't come poaching around here anymore," she said to herself.

On meeting Buttercup at the entrance of the cave she burst out laughing. "Oh, Buttercup, you should have seen him run."

They entered the cave and David smiled. "How did it go?"

Marged was still smiling. "It went very well. You should have seen that poor teacher. Every time he lifted the cane to strike Rhys, it stopped in mid air and then he would start shouting at him in Welsh. When he realized he was speaking Welsh, he began to grab his throat. All the kids in the class were cheering, it was great."

David's smile got bigger and then dropped. "I suppose we'll never see Rhys again."

Marged said, "Yes we will and *you* invited him to come back as well."

Buttercup interrupted before Marged could finish what she was going to say. "Yes, we will! We are all going to see the Wild West Show in Builth in May. He is going to come up by train, with his parents, from Landovery and we will meet him there."

David's eyes widened with wonder. "You mean Buffalo Bill's Wild West Show."

"Yes. It will be amazing."

"Oh, my goodness. My boys, I know, would love to see that. They would be witness to a slice of living history." He turned to Caradoc.

Caradoc looked over at the two girls and David.
"You can arrange for them to see the Wild West Show
But no objects from the future there must go."

David thanked Caradoc and asked Marged to adjust the Time Stones to get him out in his right time.

She did and David left and as he went, he said, "I will be back with my two sons. I will find period clothing for them and myself. Bye." Then he was gone.

Marged smiled at Buttercup. "We have two Native Americans to find. But first I have to ask Caradoc two more questions."

Caradoc was attentive.

She smiled at him. "Alright, you have said that we can't be hurt by anyone out there, but Mr. Taylor was beaten when he went out and Rhys Edwards was beaten by his uncle. Why did that happen?"

"When you know here who might get you harmed,
With the caves protection you will be armed.
Others out there the cave can't stop
But, take a cave pebble and have the drop."

"You mean that you have a pebble here that we could carry with us out there and we would be protected?"

"Take any pebble from this cave
And all out there to you behave."

"That is wonderful." She smiled at Buttercup. They each picked up a small pebble from the cave floor and placed them in their pockets. "Now, another question. If I go out there and meet myself, what will happen?"

"Meeting yourself out there is fine and fun,
But if you touch you will merge to one."

"Oh my gosh, I would stay a long way from myself, that's for sure."

Buttercup nodded in agreement.

Marged thanked Caradoc for answering her questions and turned to Buttercup. "Let's go and find the Native Americans."

"You mean the Indians?"

"Yes, in my time they are called Native Americans. Come on. Let's go and meet them and find out how they got here."

Caradoc smiled once again as he watched the girls skip off to the area where most of the people were.

They soon found them, pretty much where Marged had first seen them. The two girls went up to them with smiles on their faces. Marged asked, "When did you come here?" She realized immediately what the answer was going to be; she had now heard it many times.

"We came here today."

Marged smiled. "Yes you did, but what year was it?"

They looked at each other and the one said to the other "Show her that bit of paper."

The other reached into his belt and produced a piece of paper with printing on it. He handed it to Marged.

She took it and opened it. It was the dates of the Wild West Show in 1903. Lots of English towns were listed and some in Wales. She held it so they could see it. "Tell me which Show was it that you came from, when you came here?"

The one who handed her the paper pointed to Hereford, July 2nd 1903. "We went hunting to catch food. We not like your food as much and we were going to meet back here." He pointed to Hereford, "And then we were going here." He pointed to Abergavenny, July 3rd 1903.

"You mean you followed the river Wye and came all the way up here? You would never have got back in time to get to Abergavenny." Marged looked at them with a serious, businesslike look. "You may think you came here yesterday, but you have been here just over 100 years."

"No, we came today."

"Have you tried going out?"

"Yes, it is not right place."

"That's right; you can't find your right time, because the pebbles, Time Stones, won't work for you to get you out at the right time once you have been in the cave. But now we have found a way to get you out in your right time. We can adjust the time and you will get out when you are supposed to."

"We tour with white man, Cody Chief. He bring us here to your country. We ride ponies in show."

"Yes, and we can help you get back to that show. Do you want to go back?"

"We want to go back. Our wives in America. We gone in your country for many moons."

"Alright, we will help you. We have to get you out so that you can get to Abergavenny before that Show starts."

"We got here today. Why can't we go out today? You have the medicine?"

Marged thought about this "medicine", and then she remembered a Western that she had seen and realized that that was the term for something, in their eyes, that was magic and good. She smiled. "I have the medicine."

"You are girls with medicine?"

"Yes, if you come with us to the rock door, we will show you the way back to your time. What are your names?"

The Indian with the spear answered. "I am Sharpened Stick." He pointed to his friend. "And he is Dark Sky Day."

The girls smiled at the unusual names and turned and walked towards the door area. The two Native Americans followed. On arriving at the rock door, Marged realized that they would have to take trains and she had no idea how to go about it. As far as she knew the railway line from Garth in either direction didn't go anywhere near Hereford or Abergavenny so she had to find out if there was a connecting train somewhere on the line. She decided to ask Buttercup.

"Buttercup, do you know what station we could go to from Garth to catch a train to Hereford or Abergavenny?"

"Wait a minute, I still have the schedule." She took it out and unfolded it. "There's a diagram. If we go to Builth Road we would have to get off the train and catch a different one that went through Builth and on to Hereford via Three Cocks Junction."

"But, there isn't a railway line in Builth anymore."

"Well, it says here that there is."

"Oh, yes, of course! I'm thinking of my time. It would be there in your time. So what we have to do is calculate the time to get to Garth and the time to get to Builth Road. How long would we have to wait to catch the train to Hereford?"

Marged turned to the two Native Americans. "Did you perform in Hereford on July the second, 1903?"

The one with the rifle, Dark Sky Day, looked at Marged quizzically and said slowly. "Performed?"

"Yes. Were you in the Wild West Show in Hereford on July the second, 1903?"

"Yes. We came here after show."

"Good, when the show moves to another town, do you take the train?"

"We take train all over your country."

"Yes, so, what we have to do is get you to Hereford sometime after the show ends, in time to catch the train from Hereford to Abergavenny."

"Take train before high sun."

"Good that gives us plenty of time to get you there. What times do you hold the show?"

"After high sun."

"So the show is held in the afternoon. Now what we have to do is get you to Hereford on the evening of the second of July, then no one will miss you." She turned to Buttercup. "Can you find an arrival time in Hereford around six o'clock in the evening and track it back to Builth, find that time and then find out what time we have to catch the train in Garth to arrive in Builth Road station, to catch the train to Hereford."

Buttercup went over to the work rock, picked up a ballpoint pen and started making notes in a notebook. When she was finished, she handed the book to Marged.

People would be curious to see two girls and two Native Americans on the road together, especially if they were carrying their weapons. They would have to take a chance. Marged began her calculations and was soon ready to adjust the Time Stones.

"We will go out at about half past eleven in the morning of the second of July. Is everyone ready?"

Buttercup announced that she was ready and the two Indians nodded. She adjusted the Time Stones, placed her hands and the rock door opened and out they went for another trip.

The Indians were delighted to be outside. It was a lovely day. However, they weren't too delighted when on the way to Capel Rhos, a gamekeeper came up behind them, held a shotgun on them and shouted, "Stop! What have you done with the rabbits you've taken?"

They turned to face him and the shot gun that was pointed right at them. The gamekeeper stared menacingly at the two Indians who were not sure what to do. "Drop your gun and that stick thing. I've a good mind to shoot you here and now. You won't get away with this."

They dropped their weapons and Marged stepped in front of them.

"They are not poachers they are American Indians from Buffalo Bill's Wild West Show."

"Girl, this is nothing to do with you. What are you doing with them? You shouldn't be consorting with these kinds of people. Perhaps you are in league with them."

Marged was facing the shotgun it was then that a short distance behind the gamekeeper she saw the stumpy man. Marged felt fear running down her spine; this was a very dangerous situation and realized that she was scared. She had placed herself in front of the Indians without thinking. She saw Buttercup out of the corner of her eye. She pointed to her. "My lady and I have been asked to help these people get to Garth, so that they can catch a train to Hereford, because that is where the Wild West Show is today."

The gamekeeper turned his attention momentarily to Buttercup. "Is this true?"

Buttercup had not realized the full extent of the danger and spoke up defiantly. "Yes, it is, and if you don't let us go now, I will inform my father and he will talk to your estate manager and you will be in serious trouble, because if you knew who I am, you would not question us. You must lower your gun and let us proceed to Capel Ross immediately."

When he heard her voice and its snobbish air he backed down, much to their relief. Marged watched the stumpy man walked away. The Indians picked up their weapons and they walked on to Capel Rhos and the road to Garth. Marged who was still shaking from the fear she had developed heard one of the Indians say to the other, "Girls have big medicine."

Buttercup heard it too. She turned toward them for a second and they both smiled at her.

The journey on foot was uneventful until they had just passed the Cribarth Farm. Marged saw the stumpy man watching them from behind a thick hedge. She could do nothing and then from behind, came a horse and carriage that was out of control. They could hear the clattering hooves of the galloping horse and above that noise a man was screaming, "The horse is bolting! The horse is bolting!"

Marged thought for a second that if anyone was shouting out like that around her, she would be bolting too. The runaway horse and carriage were gaining on them fast and she and Buttercup made for the ditch. They turned to see the Indian, Sharpened Stick, with the spear hand it to his friend, Dark Sky Day. The horse and carriage were galloping past, with the driver still shouting and waving his arms about. Sharpened Stick began running alongside the horse. Marged was stunned at how fast he was and was even more impressed when he leaped into the air and onto the horse's back. He picked up the reins and brought everything under control.

The driver of the carriage was dumbfounded and stared at the Indian sitting on the horse patting its neck. "Thank you, thank you. He was spooked by a bird coming out of the hedgerow and I couldn't stop him."

Dark Sky Day looked at him. "You make too much noise. Not good for horse."

"Yes, yes, I'm sure, I panicked you see. Thank goodness you were here to stop him; otherwise one only knows what would have happened. Thank you. Could I give you a lift? I am going to Garth station to pick up a train passenger there."

Marged wondered if the stumpy man had turned himself into a bird. After all, he always seemed to have the amazing ability to show up when something bad was about to happen.

Sharpened Stick who had stopped the horse slipped off its back and everyone climbed aboard the carriage and they were taken to Garth station. They decided to buy four second-class tickets to Hereford, instead of first class. Two singles and two returns. The station master was a little surprised to see the two young girls with these strange foreign men and barely took his eyes off them.

They had plenty of time to wait and Buttercup sat alone on her bench and the two Indians and Marged sat on the next one. A train pulled in from the north and the station master came out and so did the man with the dolly. The station master opened the door in the first class carriage and a woman stepped out right in front of Buttercup. It was her mother again. Buttercup cried out, but not too loud, and brought her hands to her face and peered through her fingers.

Her mother saw this and thought there was something wrong with the girl and came over to her. "Are you ill?"

Marged stepped in quickly. "She is fine, my lady. She had a terrible shock from a runaway horse. She is over the worst of it now."

Buttercup was patted on the head by her mother. "How awful for you. You can never be too careful today." Then she turned and went around the corner to where the carriage was waiting, followed by the porter pushing his dolly loaded with trunks and baggage. Buttercup still had her hands over her face.

Marged went over and nudged her. "It's alright now, Buttercup. She's gone. Wow, if she only knew."

Buttercup took her hands from her face and looked at Marged. "Marged, she touched me. She's my mother, I haven't been born yet, and she hasn't married my father yet, either. Oh, Marged, I was so scared. What if she had seen my face?"

"It wouldn't have mattered if she had. She wouldn't know it was you. She couldn't know you before you were born."

The Indians were looking on and hadn't a clue as to what had happened. Dark Sky Day asked "Was lady bad?"

Marged joined them again. "No, the lady was her mother, but in this time Buttercup has not been born yet."

There was a long silence of contemplation as they were trying to understand what Marged had just told them and then Sharpened Stick spoke up. "Lady, mother of girl, girl not born. How is girl here if not born? How lady mother?"

Marged took a deep breath and stared at the two of them; they stared back. She was thinking about how to explain what had happened. Staring at them for a second longer she spoke. "Because of the cave where no time passes, we haven't been born yet. You are in your right time, Buttercup will be born in 1907 and I will be born in 1993."

"Cave bad medicine?"

"No, the cave is not bad medicine. The stones were wrong in the cave, but the stones are good now. That's why we can get you back to the Wild West Show and nobody will have missed you. Do you understand?"

She waited quite a while for an answer as the Indians glanced at each other. "Not understand cave medicine. Your medicine good."

In an hour they boarded the train in second class as Buttercup and Marged had decided that if they were in first class someone there might object and they wanted to steer clear of that kind of trouble.

In the lower station of Builth Road people were staring at the Indians. One of them asked, "Are you fellows with the Wild West Show?"

Dark Sky Day nodded. "We with Wild West Show."

Then the person asked, "Isn't the show on in Hereford as we speak? Why aren't you there?"

Marged spoke up for them. "They are not in today's show, they are in the Abergavenny show, tomorrow."

A porter, who was wheeling his dolly past the waiting passengers, spoke to everyone and no one in particular. "You should have seen the trains this morning. People were standing as the seats were all taken up. Everyone was going to the Wild West Show in Hereford. There were people who wanted to travel first class, who had to stand in third class. I hope I get to see it one day."

The rest of the journey to Hereford was uneventful until they got off the train. There were people everywhere, whistles blowing, people shouting and porters with loaded dollies going in every direction. Marged thought they had landed in the middle of a riot.

They stood together on the platform, two young girls and two half naked, spear and rifle toting Indians being jostled by the crowd. They soon realized that the Wild West Show was over and the people were scrambling for trains that would take them back to their homes. Several spotted the Indians and came over and congratulated them on a great performance in the Show. One bellowed "Some of the finest horsemanship I have ever seen! Magnificent."

Dark Sky Day seemed puzzled. "We not in show today."

Everyone within earshot laughed. One fancily dressed man spoke up. "Did you hear that? Well, if you weren't in the Show, your doubles certainly were and they did a splendid job."

Marged was a little nervous and asked Buttercup to push her way through the crowd and lead them off the platform. Buttercup smiled as she went on ahead. Marged shouted to her. "You're a lady, so the crowd will get out of the way for you!"

Buttercup led the way and the crowd did their best to let them through. Young ladies of about eighteen were continually approaching the Indians and exclaiming how handsome and savage they looked, and then would retreat giggling and laughing.

Once off the platform and outside the station the crowd was a little thinner and Marged spotted a policeman who was nothing like the modern policeman she was used to seeing. She went up to him. "Excuse me, sir, but my lady would like you to point us in the direction of the Wild West Show."

He looked down at Marged. "You should tell your lady that she is a little late. The show is over."

"We know that. We have to get these Indians back there."

He looked at them. "How did they get here? I saw them down there a few moments ago." He was pointing to where, Marged assumed, the show had taken place. "And I came here fast in case there was trouble at the station."

Marged chose to ignore the question and she pointed where he had pointed. "So, is that where the show was?"

"Yes. They are striking the show and they will go back to their camps tonight and tomorrow morning they will load everything on a special train and go to Abergavenny for another show."

Marged thanked the officer and Buttercup led the way once more to where the show was held. Young ladies were continually approaching the Indians, and as they got nearer to the show site, Marged spotted the same two Indians leaving a tent and coming in their direction, and they too were being harassed by young girls. She turned to see if her two Indians had spotted them as well, but they hadn't, they were busy fending off their own young ladies. Marged went quickly over to Buttercup. "Look! They are over there and behind us., We have to keep them separated."

"Oh, dear. What should we do?"

"Well, perhaps if we stop for a minute and distract them, the others might soon move off. We know they will. I just hope it is soon."

Buttercup and Marged turned back to the Indians, and Marged pointed towards the station. "Just look at the crowds."

The Indians turned to look. Dark Sky Day commented "Many white men, like Buffalo on Prairie many moons ago."

Marged kept glancing back and then she saw the stumpy man watching the other two Indians climbing into a carriage and being driven away to the west. "So that's how they got up into the hills. They got a lift for quite a way, I bet, and it seems that the stumpy man was behind it?"

She touched Buttercup's arm and whispered in her ear, then nodded her head in the direction of the departing carriage. "They've gone, so lead on again."

Buttercup took the lead once again and Marged and the Indians followed. Marged said to the Indians "You left here by carriage didn't you?"

"Yes. We went long way in carriage."

Marged smiled. "Well, we have got you back. Now don't you take any carriage rides today. You get on that special train tomorrow and go and do your show in Abergavenny."

Buttercup stopped. "Look! There's Buffalo Bill."

And indeed there was the Wild West man himself, strutting around giving orders, as his crew were taking apart all the props used in the show. Tents and tepees were being taken down; native women were packing up pots and pans and folding up blankets and animal skins. Horses were loosely corralled in different areas and several individuals were distributing feed, which the horses seemed very grateful for, as others groomed them.

They stopped close to where Buffalo Bill was giving orders, and Marged smiled at the Indians, "Well, we have to say goodbye. Now, don't forget we will come and see you in Builth Wells next May."

They looked at her and Dark Sky Day spoke. "You come to see show?"

"Yes."

"You come now?"

"No, not now, next May."

"No, you come see Cody Chief. Follow."

Marged and Buttercup followed and they were led right up to Buffalo Bill. He turned and looked at the Indians and then at the girls and smiled.

Sharpened Stick said. "Cody Chief, girls have very good medicine. They help very much. You have paper for show next year." He pointed at the girls. "Tell him show."

Marged was nervous having to speak to this great man. "It's the show you are doing in Builth Wells on May the twelfth next year."

He stared in amazement. "How did you know this? I only planned that tour and dates two days ago and I haven't told anyone yet."

Marged thought. "Oh, dear. How am I going to explain this?" Then she smiled. "Well, I just guessed. I thought it would be a perfect day for you to come to Builth Wells."

He smiled back and glanced at the Indians for a second, and turned back to the girls. "You have good medicine indeed. I will write you a pass for you to attend. You come early, with your friends if you want, and you will be given a front row seat with the dignitaries." He took some paper out of his pocket. "Now, I have to go and find my pen and ink."

Marged spoke up. "I have a pen that will work here." She took a ballpoint pen out of her pocket and handed it to him, after pressing the top to expose the point. "You just write with it. You don't have to dip it in ink."

He looked at the pen and then at her, then wrote a note on the paper, resting it on the back of Dark Sky Day and signed it. He gave her the note and the pen. "Yes, you have good medicine, indeed; we will see you and your friends next year." He smiled and his blonde moustache twitched. He turned and began giving orders in all directions again.

The Indians waved goodbye to the girls as they left for the train. "You have good journey."

They smiled back and said "Goodbye" together.

There were still crowds jostling at the station. Marged asked Buttercup to upgrade their return tickets to first class and ask to get the next train back to Builth. It was getting close to seven thirty; it would be quite dark when they got back to Garth.

Buttercup went into the ticket office and had to queue for 20 minutes before she got to the window. She showed the ticket master her return tickets to Garth. "I would like to make these tickets first class, please."

This was done and she asked. "When is the next train?"

"It will be in ten minutes, my lady, but you won't be able to take it, because it is full. You will have to wait for the next one."

"Oh, dear. When will that be?"

"At eight thirty-five."

"Very well. Could you telegraph the Garth station and ask them to have a carriage waiting for our return."

"I can't do that here, my lady. You will have to go over to the telegraph window." He pointed to it. It was across the room. She waited in another queue and as she got to the window Marged squeezed through the crowd in a panic. "Buttercup we have to go now. The train is about to leave."

"It's alright. We can't take that one because it is full. We will take the next one first class. I am arranging for a carriage in Garth to take us back to the cave."

The telegrapher heard the words back to the cave and frowned. "Can I help you, my lady?"

"Yes, you can, my good man." Marged had to stifle a giggle. "I would like you to telegraph the Garth station and arrange a carriage for our arrival there."

"What time would that be, my lady?"

"Well, we are taking the eight thirty-five from here to Builth Road and then another train from there to Garth."

"I can work that out for you."

"Tell them the carriage is for Lady Buttercup and her servant Marged." She handed him threepence.

He thanked her and they moved out to the platform where the crowd had thinned out considerably. This time they sat together on a bench and watched the people and porters to-ing and fro-ing along the platform. Even though everyone was moving with purpose, it looked as if they were all confused about where they were going.

After an hour's wait, the eight-fifteen to Builth pulled in and Buttercup was helped into the carriage by a railway man. She was followed by an amused Marged, who received no help.

They arrived in Garth and the station master opened the carriage door and helped Buttercup down. "Are you Lady Buttercup?"

"Yes." She thought it curious that he should ask that, because he had seen her several times before and then she realized he had only seen her that morning, because the other times were in the future.

He smiled. "There is a carriage waiting for you."

Marged stepped down and thanked the station master. "Thank you. You must have had a very long day today."

"Yes, I have, but tomorrow I will not be working."

Marged and Buttercup rounded the station building, and in the dark shadows a horse and carriage were waiting. It was the same man whose horse was running away on him in the morning.

He helped Buttercup into the carriage and helped Marged as well. "Where do you want me to take you?"

"Capel Ross. We will manage from there, my good man." Buttercup was relishing her role as lady.

The carriage now had a stable lantern on each side of the driver, held up by rods with hooks on them. They swung gently as they moved off. It was a steady ride, but there wasn't much light even from the swinging stable lanterns.

Just past the Troedrhiwdalar crossroads the horse stopped and wouldn't move. The driver turned to the girls and said. "There is something in the road and I can't see what it is."

Marged reached through her costume and grabbed her torch and moved up alongside the driver. She pointed it in front of the horse and turned it on. The whole area in front of the horse lit up to reveal three cows lying in the road, happily chewing their cud.

The driver was astonished. "What is that light you have?"

"Oh, I bought it today; they are going to be using them in the future."

"Goodness me," he said. "I have never seen anything like that before."

Marged smiled and thought, "And you won't for quite a while."

"I will go and move the cattle," she climbed down off the carriage. "I will go in front of them and make them go back past the carriage. That way they won't be in front anymore."

The driver and Buttercup watched her go. Using the torch she moved her way through the resting cattle and shone it up the road, she had passed five and that's all there were except there was the stumpy man again. He turned and walked away into the darkness. She was puzzled at how he was able to show up in all these different places. Perhaps he was trying to find a place where he could do some harm. He had not succeeded, yet.

She turned her attention to the cows and slapped the last one on its rump a couple of times and it reluctantly got to its feet. She moved it back towards the carriage and then slapped the next one and that one got slowly to its feet. The third one rose on her approach and the last two quickly followed that one to their feet. Marged slowly walked them past the horse and carriage and then climbed back on board. They proceeded on to Capel Rhos. Buttercup asked him what his fee was.

He said he normally charged sixpence, but seeing that their Indian friend stopped his horse from running away he would charge them four pence, however Buttercup paid him sixpence anyway and thanked him. He thanked her in return then turned the carriage around and headed off back to Garth.

The girls got back to the cave, using the torch, and entered. They smiled at each other. They had successfully returned two more people to their right time.

CHAPTER 12

With a modern blower to answer why,
Hair that's wet will quickly dry.
Marged's puzzled by her mother.
Is it her or perhaps another?
Today spend money for the past
Back then much longer it will last.

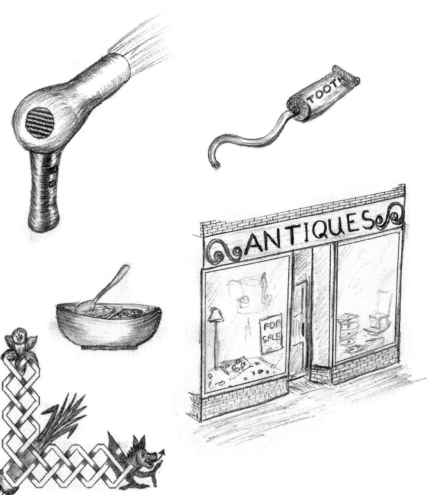

Although the girls were happy, they were tired. Marged suggested that they sleep. Caradoc, who was nearby, came over to them.

"Tired in, tired out,
You will get no rest in here about.
And no resting time in here you'll keep,
You need time to rest yourselves with sleep.
Out you must go to find a bed
And nice plump pillows to rest your head."

Marged shook her head. "I didn't think about that and I'm hungry too." She turned to Buttercup. "I will go out and let my mother know that I am bringing a friend home and get permission for you to stay at the farm with me, because going back to your time just to sleep will be too complicated. Change into my school uniform and I will be back."

"Won't your mother recognize it?"

"No. Because in the time we will go back to, she hasn't bought it yet."

"Oh, yes, of course."

Marged changed into her jeans, pink sweater, blue jacket and her green wellies. She adjusted the Time Stones and was out in a flash. Buttercup went to the alcove to change.

On her way up to the farm Marged was confronted by the stumpy man. It was sudden and she stood still and could slowly feel fear coming on and had to act. "You stay away from me. I do you no harm."

He responded immediately. "Things are not always what they seem, Marged Evans." Then he turned and was gone, just like the other times.

As she came through the gate onto the farm yard she saw her father walking into one of the buildings. She frowned. He had a moustache. When she left earlier he hadn't got a moustache. She checked her watch; she was not in the wrong time. He waved to her, so it seemed that nothing was out of place for him. Then as she was about to enter the house she noticed that the car was different, a different make and a different colour.

In the house Marged noticed that her mother's hair was different. She looked nervously at her. "Hi Mom, am I late?"

"No of course not. Have you been having fun?"

"Yes, lots of fun. Whose car is that outside?"

"That's a funny question to ask. You know very well it's ours."

Marged thought for a second and realized that something was not right and decided not to say anything further. After all, her parents looked at her as if nothing was out of place at all. So she decided to be her usual self and see what would happen.

She announced that she had a new friend called Buttercup, and that she had invited her to come and stay on the farm.

Her mother looked at her. "When?"

"Tonight. She can stay in my room on the hide-a-bed."

Megan frowned at her. "Oh, Marged. I don't think we should do that. It's too short notice. Do her parents know about this?"

"Mam, her parents know and they don't mind."

"You should have let me know sooner. I have nothing ready."

"Oh, Mam, that's an excuse."

"Where did you meet this girl and where is she from?"

"I met her at the cave and she's from Builth."

"How did she get to the cave?"

"Her parents dropped her off, so that she could go exploring. They used to stay with her until they met me, but now they leave her with me, and we have a lot of fun together in and out of the cave."

Marged had never told so many lies in such a short time in her life before. She felt a little ashamed, but when she told her mother the truth about the cave, she was not believed. She wasn't sure if telling the truth and not being believed was the same as telling lies and being believed or not.

Megan resigned herself to the situation, after all there was no real harm in it. "Alright, when is she coming?"

"About six o'clock. I am going to meet her at the cave and I will bring her right back."

"Well, after your dinner you can prepare your room. I don't know what I am going to do with you, Marged April Evans."

Marged spent the rest of the afternoon tidying her room and sorting out clothes that she thought would be suitable for Buttercup to wear. She chose dresses and skirts which she thought would do, and they would be better than wearing a school uniform. She also prepared the hide-a-bed with pillows, sheets and blankets.

After the preparation she went back to the cave. Buttercup greeted her. Marged adjusted the Time Stones, and they were soon crossing the farm yard. Buttercup stared at the car, the Land Rover and the horse box. "Tell me about the carriages, do I get to ride in one?"

Marged noticed that the car was the usual one and felt very relieved.

Marged explained the vehicles as best she could and assured Buttercup that she would get to ride in one.

Marged's mother met them in the living room and she stared at Buttercup. Marged introduced her, "Mam, this is Buttercup, my friend." Her mother was the usual one and Marged wondered if this one was expecting her to bring a friend.

Megan didn't say anything for about half a minute. She was still staring at Buttercup. She was puzzled, because she had a very strong feeling of meeting the girl before, but she could not fathom where.

Buttercup didn't notice that Megan was scrutinizing her identity; she was too busy looking around the living room. She had been in the house before, but she had been too preoccupied and nervous about the task she had to do there at that time.

Marged noticed her mother's curiosity and broke in. "Mam, I'm going to take Buttercup upstairs and show her my room and where she will be sleeping."

"Alright. I will call you when supper's ready."

Marged was surprised that her mother didn't object so she must have been expecting Buttercup. The whole dimension thing was puzzling. Marged wondered how many of them were close to the one she was in at this time.

She led Buttercup to the stairs; Buttercup was surveying everything around her. She lived in a nice house, but she had never seen a house like this before. There were no servants and yet everything was spotless. In Marged's bedroom she stared at the pop star-depicting posters on the walls. "Are those paintings?" she asked.

Marged smiled. "No. They are photographs made into posters and I will tell you who they are." Marged went around the room pointing out the different pop stars, why she liked them, and what they did.

Buttercup had great difficulty in understanding what Marged was trying to tell her about them, but didn't ask for an explanation either; she thought that she would get to know more as time went on.

Marged showed Buttercup the hide-a-bed. "This is where you will be sleeping. And now I will show you the toilet and the bath and shower."

Buttercup was taken across the hall into a converted former bedroom. It was clean, bright and airy; and she thought it was beautiful. Nothing like the toilets she was used to. She was shown the shower and asked how it worked. Marged turned it on to show her.

Buttercup was impressed. "So how do you use it?"

"Well, you take your clothes off and stand underneath it and you use soap and shampoo."

"I have heard of shampoo. Our maid washes my hair with it. I don't like it, I don't like it at all."

Marged smiled. "We have a lot of different kinds." She pointed them out. "Rhys and father use that one and mother uses one of these three. She changes them every so often, but I like this one. Smell it."

Marged unscrewed the cap off the florally decorated bottle, and held it under Buttercup's nose.

Buttercup was shocked. "Oh, that is exquisite. Where did you get it?"

"At the chemists' shop. Lots of people use it."

"I have to have some of that."

"Well, after supper you could have a bath or a shower before you go to bed."

"My hair takes a long time to dry."

"We have a hairdryer." Marged picked up the modern hairdryer. It was red and blue. She plugged it in, turned it on and waved it at Buttercup.

Buttercup backed up a little and gave a small shriek. "It's warm."

Marged laughed. "It blows hot air and it dries hair very quickly. You'll see."

Megan called upstairs. "Girls, come on down! Suppers ready."

They got downstairs; Emrys and Rhys were already sitting at the table. Marged was once more relieved when she noticed that her father did not have a moustache.

Rhys looked Buttercup over and seemed very curious. "What's your name?"

"Buttercup" she replied. "And you are Rhys."

Rhys kept looking at her in her Builth School uniform, and then he spoke again. "I've never seen you in Builth School before."

Marged cringed. "Well, she's seen you there. She told me, didn't you, Buttercup?"

"Yes, but I am not there much, because I go to school in England as well."

"Where in England?"

"In London."

Megan served the food, roast lamb, potatoes, carrots, Brussels sprouts, gravy and mint sauce. It was delicious. Then Buttercup asked why they didn't serve wine with the meal.

Megan and Emrys raised their eyebrows. Megan half smiled at the girl. "Your mother lets you drink wine with your meal?"

"Yes, of course. Since I was nine. It's very good. Our butler picks it. It comes from France."

"I have never heard of anyone giving a child wine before."

"I thought everyone did it. Perhaps they don't in your time."

Marged nudged Buttercup with her elbow and Buttercup made a small gulping noise and placed a fork full of food in her mouth.

Emrys asked Marged how her exploration of the cave went.

"That's where I found Buttercup."

"You found her in the cave, you say?"

"Yes, I did."

"And I suppose she disappeared in there many years ago."

He was teasing and Marged spotted it. She decided to go along with it and tell the truth, knowing that neither he nor anyone else would believe it. So she told her story about the cave, wondering if she had told it before in this dimension.

Emrys, mischievously, smiled. "Ooh, this sounds exciting! Tell us more."

Buttercup was looking horrified at Marged and was completely baffled as to why she was telling everyone about the cave.

Marged told him about the Time Stones and how the mountain had moved.

"So you met Buttercup in the cave?"

"Yes, she had been in there from 1918. She's the girl I asked you about."

"Oh, really? So where did she get the Builth School uniform? They didn't wear clothes like that in 1918."

"The uniform is mine."

Megan began to laugh. "But, Marged, you don't have a uniform yet. I was going to take you to Llandrindod or Builth tomorrow to get you one and get the school supplies you will need."

"I know. This will be the third or fourth time you will have done this, because I have been going in and out of the cave quite a lot, helping people get back to their right time. Even the fisherman that went in there eight years ago has been helping and he is now back in his right time."

Emrys, smiled. "What was his name, then?"

"David Taylor, but you don't remember that he went missing do you? Because we got him out to his right time. He would not have been reported missing."

"I met him on the brook the day before he left, and yes, he went missing and no one found him. Alright Marged, what was he wearing?"

"He was wearing green waders the same colour as my wellies and he had a bamboo fishing rod and he had a wicker creel and wore a chequered shirt."

"Marged, how did you find out this information?"

"Easy, I met him in the cave." Marged was a little puzzled that they should know that he went missing, when, in actual fact, she had got him back to his right time, so he wouldn't have gone missing. She thought about what Caradoc had said about other caves being where the one she had been in was, all at the same time. Perhaps there were whole worlds all in the same place and space. She began to wonder if she was with the right parents once again.

Megan shook her head. "Your imagination is going to get you into trouble one day. Now finish your supper."

Emrys wouldn't let it go; he was having great fun with it. After all he was delighted that his daughter was becoming a great story teller. "So Buttercup, what is life like in 1918?"

Buttercup was struck by the question and she just stared back at him, not knowing how to answer. Marged came to the rescue. "Just tell him. Tell him why you left London to come and stay in Wales."

Buttercup explained in detail about how she got into the cave and the fact that time didn't pass there.

Emrys smiled and shook his head. "Boy, you girls have come together on this brilliantly. You must have been practising to come up with something as good as this. You should be writing it down. It's an amazing story you have together.

Marged resigned herself once more to their not believing. "That's a good idea, Dad. We should do that, don't you think, Buttercup?"

Buttercup had realized finally what had happened and smiled. "Yes, we should."

Marged changed the subject. "Mam, let's go to Llandrindod to get the school uniform."

"Yes, that's a good idea, they are cheaper there than in Builth."

Marged wasn't sure if her mother knew that they had been there before and ordered it, or that she was in another close world. She didn't say anything. She would wait and see. "And Buttercup and I will have a look in the other shops." Marged wanted to buy some more old money, so that they would be well off when everyone went to the Wild West Show. She had forgotten to tell David Taylor to try and find some, so she wanted to make sure there would be enough for everyone.

After supper, Marged helped her mother carry dishes into the kitchen. Buttercup watched. She lived with servants who did that, and wasn't sure if she should help or not. After a minute or so she decided to help and picked up a plate. Emrys stopped her. "You are a guest; they will manage; besides we have a dish washer."

Buttercup peered into the kitchen, but could only see Megan and Marged. She looked back at Emrys. "Who is the dish washer?"

"It's not a person, gel, it's a machine you put the dishes in and they wash automatically. Don't you have a dish washer at your home in London?"

"We have a pantry maid and she washes the dishes."

"That's a bit old fashioned. You should get her a dish washer, she would love you for it. Alright, let's go and see what's on the telly. Come on, I suppose coming from 1918 you have never seen a television before?" He chuckled.

"No I haven't."

Emrys continued to be amused. "These girls give a heck of a performance."

He showed Buttercup to a seat, and he and Rhys sat down on the sofa. He picked up the remote control. Buttercup stared at it and saw him press a button. Then she turned to see the glass windowed box in the corner of the room come to life. She was dumb struck. "Where are those people?"

Emrys laughed. "They are on the television."

"They are inside that box with the window?"

"No, they are not actually in the box, they are in a studio miles away, and their image is transmitted through the air, the box puts the image on the screen so that you can see it. Why am I explaining this? You are having me on."

"I'm sorry." Buttercup went quiet; she decided to ask Marged about it later. She just watched, mesmerized.

They watched for two hours, before the girls went upstairs to bed.

As they went, Megan called after them. "Remember to clean your teeth. There's a new brush in the cupboard that Buttercup can use."

Marged called back. "Okay, Mam."

Marged led Buttercup to the bathroom. "You can wash your hair now if you want to."

Buttercup nodded. "Would you help me? A maid helps me at home."

Marged showed her how everything worked again and what to do, however, Buttercup was a little nervous. "You have to stay and help me."

"Alright. I will get the nightdresses; if I am going to help I might as well shower myself as well."

When Marged got back, Buttercup was still where she had left her, staring at the water coming out of the shower. "Buttercup, you have to undress. Come on."

Buttercup looked forlorn. "You will have to help me."

"Alright, but you didn't need much help in the cave when you changed. All you have to do is take off your clothes and step into the shower and wash yourself."

Buttercup resigned herself to the task and undressed and showered

219

with Marged's help. She liked the shampoo; her hair was a mousy brown colour and fortunately she had been following the fashion of the time and wore it medium length. She giggled and laughed as the warm water relaxed her. Soon it was over and she stepped out, greeted by a great big, soft, fluffy towel that Marged was holding for her. It was wrapped around the wet girl and then Marged picked up another towel and began to rub Buttercup's hair to remove the excess water. This was followed by Marged taking her over to the hairdryer, which she turned on as she picked up a brush and began brushing and blow drying Buttercup's hair.

Buttercup loved it. Her hair was soon dry and Marged helped her into a nightdress, and then it was Marged's turn and she didn't take long.

The showering done Marged went over to the bathroom cupboard and retrieved a new tooth brush. She took it out of the package and handed it to Buttercup.

Buttercups eyes widened. "What's this?"

"It's a tooth-brush."

"I know that, but what kind of bone is the handle?"

"It's not bone. It's plastic just like the hair dryer and the shampoo bottles."

"What are the bristles made of?"

"They are made of plastic too."

"The tooth-brush I use is bone with pig bristles for brushing."

"Oow er, I wouldn't like that. Here's the toothpaste."

"Toothpaste? Not a soapy powder? We use a soapy powder in my time." She manoeuvred the tube in her hands studying it carefully. "How do you get it out of this?"

"You unscrew the cap, like this." Marged undid the cap. "And then you squeeze a small amount onto the brush."

Not having squeezed a tube before Buttercup squeezed hard and a worm of paste four inches long shot out and into the sink.

It shocked Marged as much as Buttercup and they broke out laughing.

Marged got some of the paste on the brush and waited for Buttercup to stop laughing before handing it to her ready for her to use.

Buttercup, smiling, pushed the brush into her mouth and began to scrub her teeth.

Marged watched her eyebrows raise and her eyes widen. "Buttercup, are you alright?"

She stopped scrubbing, took the brush out of her mouth which was now covered in toothpaste suds and spoke through the bubbles. "This tastes good. It's much better than the powder, I use." She continued to brush.

Marged brushed her own teeth and once finished they were back in Marged's room, settling into their beds for a well deserved sleep.

In the morning, the girls dressed, Marged in her jeans and a sweater and Buttercup dressed in one of Marged's dresses. Downstairs Buttercup faced a bowl of Weetabix waiting for the milk and sugar. Megan smiled. "I thought you would like Weetabix too. Marged eats it every morning."

Buttercup stared down at it. "What is it?"

"It's Weetabix. Haven't you seen Weetabix before?"

"No, I haven't."

"That's very odd; I would have thought that everyone would know what Weetabix is."

Marged smiled. "Do what I do, Buttercup." Buttercup followed Marged's actions. She waited to see how Marged ate hers and then did the same.

Once they were finished, Megan gave them orders. "Take your dishes and spoons to the kitchen and place them in the sink, and then if you're ready we can go off to Lland'od."

The girls were ready. The day was a bit overcast and it looked as if it might rain later. Megan suggested that they take some Macintoshes with them in the car, which they did. Marged had Buttercup sit in the front and helped her with the seat belt. She asked the same question that Rhys Edwards had asked. "Why are you tying me in?"

Once Buttercup was strapped in and Marged was settled in the back Megan started the engine. Buttercup listened for a second and then looked at Megan as she was about to take off. "You don't have to get out and turn a handle to start it?"

Megan stared at her. "I would have thought that living in London you would have known more things than we do. Starting handles went out in the fifties and early sixties."

Buttercup put her foot in it a little deeper. "I'm sorry. I didn't know that."

Megan smiled broadly this time. "I am beginning to think that you are from 1918."

Buttercup, not unlike Rhys Edwards, was astounded by the speed and other traffic flying past.

They soon entered Llandrindod and went into the clothing shop. Just before they went in Marged saw the stumpy man again across the street and in the second she saw him he walked away. It was becoming very disturbing to Marged and she decided to find out more about him from Caradoc.

In the shop the man behind the counter smiled at the trio. "Ah, I remember, your timing is perfect; the new uniform just came in."

Megan stared at the man. "We've only just come in to see if you have one, you must be thinking of someone else."

"No, I don't think so, let me see." He went over to a computer. "Here we are: Megan Evans, uniform for daughter, Marged Evans."

Megan stood as still as a statue. She was puzzled. "Did I phone in to order it?"

"No. Mrs. Evans, you came in yourself with your daughter and we measured her here."

Megan shook her head. "I don't remember any of this; I must be going out of my head. Do you remember this, Marged?"

"Yes, Mam. We did come here."

The man said, "Well, there we are then; I will go and get it."

He soon returned with the uniform, covered by a flimsy plastic bag. He handed it to Marged. "Go and try it on."

Marged went off to change and came back wearing it. It fitted her perfectly. Her mother smiled, still confused about the whole situation. "How much do I owe you?"

"You owe nothing; you paid for it when you ordered it."

Megan was becoming a little stressed and concerned. She thought she was having some terrible memory lapse. She shook her head for the fourth time. "I'm sorry; I don't remember any of this."

Marged changed out of the uniform and as they left the shop, she suggested they go to the antique shop to look at the coins.

Megan smiled. "You really like that old money, don't you?"

"Yes. I really like collecting it and it's nice to lay it out and look it up on the computer to find what it would be worth in today's money."

Buttercup looked at Marged with another question on her mind. "Marged, what is a computer?"

Megan stared at the girl. "I'm worried about you. Don't you have a computer at home?"

"No, I don't know what it is."

"Haven't you seen one at your school?"

"No, I have a private tutor."

"Well, why were you wearing a school uniform? Don't you go to Builth School?"

Marged was shaking her head. If this was going to continue, her mother would probably either believe her about the cave, or go stark staring bonkers. Buttercup came back with an answer: "I borrowed it from my cousin."

That satisfied Megan for the time being, even though all she had heard was inconsistent. They got to the antique shop and looked at the window display before going in.

Buttercup stared at some of the smaller items in the window and was shocked at the prices. Two items in particular caught her eye. They were small decorative jewel boxes. One was £55.00 and the other was £76.00. "My mother bought one of those last year for a shilling."

Megan stared at her. "A shilling? We haven't used shillings for years. Your mother got a bargain."

They went into the shop and again there was no one around so Marged shouted, "Hello!"

Then a movement was heard in the back room and soon the old man appeared through the curtain. "Hello, again. Come to buy more old money, have you?"

Marged smiled. "Could we see some?"

"Of course. I have some more that have just come in." He hefted the box up on to the counter and opened it.

Megan was confused even more. She had never been in this shop, but it seemed that Marged was known there.

Marged began to sift through the coins and found some more half crowns dated 1904 and earlier. One in particular caught her eye; it had a distinctive mark on it. She picked it up and knew that it was identical to one she had bought previously. Was it the same coin? She would have to check. She laid it and many other coins on the counter, ready for purchase.

The old man then placed the folder with the paper money on the counter and Marged asked to see the cigar box with the damaged, cheaper notes. He reached for that and opened it in front of her. There had been some more added since her last visit. She picked out six £5.00 notes, three £1.00 notes and one ten shilling note. Then Marged smiled. "That will do for now. Could you show some of your smaller items, from about 100 years ago, to my friend Buttercup? Her mother has a collection of these kind of items."

"Yes, of course."

As he was coming from behind the counter, Marged whispered into Buttercup's ear. "Look for anything you can buy in your time, that would sell for a lot of money here in my time and I will make notes." Marged retrieved a little notebook and a pen from her pocket as they were escorted around the shop by the old man.

Megan, who was still trying to understand why she couldn't remember anything about their previous visit, had found an antique chair and sat herself down in it, holding Marged's uniform, folded in her lap. She watched the man show the small collectables to the girls. She noticed Marged taking notes, writing down all that the old man was telling her and Buttercup.

After their information gathering tour of the shop, Marged paid for her money and off they went back to the car. Megan asked, "So why were you so interested in those small antiques?"

Marged replied. "Well, Buttercup's Mom can get some of those things very cheap, so Buttercup can get some and we can sell them cheaply to the old shopkeeper, so that we can make some money and he can make some when he sells them to other people."

"Hmm," Megan muttered, contemplating it for a few seconds. "So now you are going to be dealing in antiques, is it?"

"It'll be fun, Mam."

"Well, I am sure it will be. Now, I have to understand what is happening to my memory."

Marged was wondering about that too. It seemed that her mother must be different from the one she came with earlier and the other one she had seen before that, and so as soon as she could get back to the cave she would ask Caradoc. She wanted to know how close together were all these seemingly, simultaneous worlds or dimensions he had talked about. It seemed to her that she was now popping in and out of a lot of them and it made her nervous. Was the stumpy man responsible?

The drive back to the farm was uneventful, unless, of course, you were from 1918. Buttercup was dazzled by the speed of all the traffic they encountered. She would have been even more dazzled if she had been on a modern motorway near London.

Back at the farm, Marged and Buttercup went up to the bedroom and counted the money that Marged had bought. The value of a £5.00 in 1912 to 1918 was about £450.00 in 2004 pounds. They had an approximate value of £3,500.00.

Marged opened her notebook and began to ask Buttercup the value in her time of the items that the old man had shown them. Marged was pleased; a few shillings in early twentieth century money could amount to a huge fortune in 2004. "Oh, Buttercup, if we can buy some of these things in your time or earlier, we can sell them in my time and make a lot of money, which we can use to get other people back to their times."

Buttercup agreed. "I should go out soon to meet my mother, but that would mean going back to London."

"How often do you travel to Wales?"

"Once every two months I think."

"That would be alright, because we could do a lot of things while you are at the cave and then we get you back to the right time again. We will have to do it at intervals that would amount to, say, two months work of visiting outside the cave, or your mother will think you are speedily getting older when you go back."

"That is good, because I have only been out about four days so far, since I went into the cave. That means we could do a lot more before I have to meet my mother."

"So what we have to do is find out who everyone is in the cave, and find out what time they got into it. Then we can sort out the ones that will be easy and the ones that will be hard. The people from the very early times may not want to go back to their time, so we will then have to find a time that is suitable for them."

"Marged, this could take forever."

"No, because, remember, there is no forever in the cave. It's just now."

"Oh, gosh. Then this is going to be such fun!"

"Yes, and there is something else we have to do."

"What?"

"We have to find out what all those rocks are, and how they work, and that might be a lot of work."

"Will Caradoc let us try and find out?"

"I think he will, because he wants to get back the knowledge too, and we won't do anything without him looking over our shoulders, because he will be a guide to the work."

"I don't understand why he doesn't remember what most of the things do in the cave. Do you think something has happened to him?"

"Perhaps it's because the mountain has moved over time, but I think he still has the most important powers."

"What are they?"

"Well, the power not to let people hurt each other and to be kind to animals. Just look how many are in the cave. He has held onto the power for total kindness and he accepts humans as we are, and understands everything about us. I think it is great that he lets us help him."

"You are right. Gosh, we should go back soon."

"Yes, we should, but I want to do some work on the computer."

"Marged, what's a computer?"

"I'll show you. There's one in the living room. Bring the notebook and we will find some things out, perhaps about the cave."

The two girls went downstairs and Marged got permission to go on the computer and show it to Buttercup.

Marged pulled up an extra chair so that Buttercup could sit beside her and watch what she was doing.

The computer was turned on and Marged clicked the mouse to connect to the internet. As she did she explained her moves to Buttercup, who could barely fathom what Marged was trying to explain.

With mouse in hand, Marged glanced at Buttercup and continued to explain what she was doing. She then smiled. "So let's try disappearances, Wales: Here we go." She typed in "disappearances Wales and UK."

The computer came up with a top ten of disappearances. One of them was the disappearance of some hippies that were camped in the middle of Stonehenge in 1971. A storm came in and some stones were struck by lightning, a massive blue light was seen and the hippies disappeared, never to be seen again.

"Look at this, Buttercup. Caradoc told me that one of the rocks that lights up sometimes has a shining blue light. I wonder if there is a connection? We'll have to ask."

Another was the disappearance of Oliver Thomas near Rhayader in 1909. "We will have to ask about him. Ooh, look at this one. A Welsh rock and roll singer and guitarist, Richie Edwards, disappeared in Wales on 1st February 1995. I wonder where he went; perhaps he is in the cave?"

Buttercup frowned. "What is a rock and roll singer?"

"I'll find something of his. Give me a moment." Marged keyed in Richey Edwards and soon she was able to click on a number that he had recorded. It played for about 30 seconds before Buttercup said very unemotionally, "I don't like that."

Marged smiled. "Here's what I like." Marged keyed in some more and a video came up on the screen. Buttercup stared with her mouth wide open as a stage appeared, in front of which was a crush of people clapping and screaming. On the stage were these weirdly dressed girls playing rock music, dancing and singing.

Buttercup raised her eyebrows. "What are they doing?"

"They are playing rock music for girls."

"It's awful."

"No, it's not. They are the Spice Girls. Don't forget, girls are made of sugar and spice and all things nice."

"I don't think that they are nice."

"Alright, what do you think of this one?" Some more keys were manipulated and another video appeared with a girl singer with a very nice voice.

Buttercup watched and listened. "She's the best so far. Who is she?"

"That's Charlotte Church."

"She's not in a church."

"No, Church is her last name."

"I don't mind her."

Marged smiled. "Alright let's get back to our search. Let's see. Ah, here. Look at this. 'Ninth Spanish Legion, was a legion alleged to have disappeared in Britain during the Roman conquest of Britain.' Wow, it happened in 117 AD. A whole legion? How many soldiers were there in a whole Roman Legion?"

Buttercup tossed her head and half smiled. "I don't know. I haven't lost one lately."

They both laughed.

Marged worked some more keys and came up with an answer that astonished her: 5000. "Buttercup, oh my gosh. 5000 soldiers just disappeared. Do you think that they might be in our cave?"

"Oh, Marged, I don't know. I have seen hundreds of people in there, but I don't think I have seen 5000 Roman soldiers in there as well."

"Well, we'll have to ask Caradoc; perhaps they are camped in another part of the cave like the dinosaurs are."

Marged perused some more. '1071, Hereward, a rebel in the eyes of William the Conqueror, disappeared while being pursued by William's soldiers.' "Wow, perhaps he got to our cave. Oh, Buttercup this is going to be so much fun finding out about all the people in the cave. The ones we are looking at are famous people in history. What about all the people who are not famous? There must be hundreds and hundreds of them. Oh Buttercup, this is going to be so kuhle."

"Why do you say cool?"

"It's just a saying that people use when something is good and I like to spell it K U H L E."

"Marged, I am so glad you came to the cave. I have never had so much fun."

"Me neither, and I am so glad that Caradoc told me about you. I think he really likes us, don't you?"

Buttercup nodded. "Yes, I think that he really wants us to help get people back to their times."

"Yes, and we are going to do that. Alright, let's see what else we can find."

Marged exclaimed, "Owain Glyn Dwr! Buttercup, he has been to the cave and is out at this time." She thought for a moment. "Whatever time he went out at, my father said that there was a story of him showing up in 1936 at the Red Lion in our parish. He disappeared sometime in 1412. He is going to show up at the cavern and I am going to have a talk with him. He will want us to help him to get back to his right time. History says that he became a humble teacher, because he was very smart and perhaps because of that, the people who wanted him killed never found him. They would never think of searching for a humble school teacher. Buttercup, that's what kings, queens, princes and princesses should do with their knowledge, teach people. Wouldn't that be wonderful?"

"Marged, I can't imagine my King teaching school."

"No, perhaps not; but our last true Welsh Prince did. Perhaps it was because of Caradoc. Alright, let's see what's next." Marged keyed into Wikipedia and announced aloud, "'In 1483 Edward V of England and Richard of Shrewsbury the sons of King Edward IV of England were placed in the Tower of London and were never seen in public again.'

"I bet they died or were killed. I don't think that they got to our cave. If they did I bet Owain Glyn Dwr would have met them. When we find him or see him we will ask him. Now, let's see, what's next?

"'Agatha Christie, the British crime writer, famously disappeared; although, she reappeared sometime later.'

"Wow, I wonder if she got into the cave?"

231

Buttercup frowned as she stared at the computer screen. "Who was she? In your time, who was she?"

"She wrote mystery novels."

Marged continued to work her way through all sorts of disappearances and wondered if the people were in the cave or in another cave or a cave in a different dimension.

Buttercup was now watching the screen with interest; she liked it, even though she had no clue as to how it all worked.

Another item came up. 'Richard John Bingham, 7th Earl of Lucan, the last person indicted for murder by a coroner's jury. His whereabouts have been unknown since the night his children's nanny, Sandra Rivett, was beaten to death with a lead pipe in the basement of his estranged wife's home. He was officially declared dead in 1999.'

Buttercup read the information. "Oh, Marged, what if he is a murderer and he is in the cave?"

"Buttercup, in the cave he can't hurt anyone."

"Oh, yes, that's right."

They clicked through lots of web sites and included some on myths and legends in Wales. They were too numerous to count. Buttercup was baffled by the Welsh words and smiled as Marged pronounced them with a flourish.

Megan came into the room. "Are you girls ready to eat? We're having a late dinner today. Marged, go and call your father and Rhys."

After dinner the girls went back on the computer and Marged looked up costumes through the ages and found plenty of pictures, which she decided to print out. Buttercup was astonished as the printer geared up and produced several pages of costume pictures with dates. "Does that thing paint pictures?"

"No, it prints them onto the pages, just like the newspapers."

"This is really magical, look at the colours!"

"If you like that, watch this." Marged got her camera and took a picture of Buttercup and then took the chip out of the camera and placed it in the computer. After a couple of key strokes Buttercup's picture filled the screen. "Now, watch." Marged pressed the print button and the printer whirred and produced a picture of Buttercup.

Buttercup was astonished by the whole process. "Thank you."

"Kuhle, don't you think?"

"Yes, very kuhle." She giggled.

Marged gathered up the costume pictures and then it was up to the room to put together the things they would need back at the cave. Pens, notepads and costume pictures were included. Marged packed her bag. "Alright, tomorrow we go back to the cave and start recording all the names of the people in there and the year and times they came in. If we use half a page a year in the notebooks we could get about 150 years in each one. We would need seven books for each 1000 years. I will have to get more soon."

"Do you think there will be people in there for all the years?"

"No, I don't think so. I went in this year 2004 and I bet I was the first since Mr. Taylor went in in 1996. What we should do is record people in blocks of years, say 20 years and then use another notebook to record the exact times and dates in that 20 years. I bet there won't be more than four in every 20 years and in a lot of periods there won't be any."

"So, we might only need two or three notebooks?"

"Yes. Now, batteries for the torches, money, energy bars, water. Tonight, we sneak out and get this stuff close to the cave and then we can get it in there quickly tomorrow."

As soon as Marged's parents and Rhys had gone to bed and been given enough time to be asleep, the girls crept out of the house with all the goods that they would need, mostly for the train ride to Builth for the Wild West Show.

It took over an hour to get the goods close to the cave and hidden, so they were late getting up in the morning. They ate their Weetabix breakfasts and said goodbye to Emrys, Megan and Rhys.

Megan smiled. "It was lovely having you here, Buttercup. You must come again, anytime."

"Thank you, Mrs. Evans, I would love to."

Off the girls went. It was another lovely day. They got to the cave and managed to get all the goods in that they had stashed during the night in one trip.

CHAPTER 13

In old vaults old money lies
And taken back much more it buy's.
There are lots of people to sort out
Within the cave and here about.
Not liking others can make you late
Especially, when dislike is hate.

In the cave the girls organized all they had brought in and Marged took the note books to her work station and began to make some headings on the pages. She hadn't got very far when the rock door opened and in came David Taylor and his two sons Richard and James. They were dressed in 1904 clothing. The boys were staggered by what they saw even though they had been briefed by their father. Marged and Buttercup greeted the visitors and explained the goods that they had brought in and then Marged showed them the money.

David laughed. "That's good, but I've done better."

Marged looked into his smiling face with a question on her mind and then watched him reach into his pockets and pull out packets of money. "What I have here is money from as many eras as I could find. For the time period from about 1860 to 1972 I have a small amount of coinage and hundreds and hundreds of notes. If you go back to any time before 1950, you will have enough money to do anything you want. This money in 1904 will make us all millionaires. What do you think of that?"

"Mr. Taylor, that's amazing, where did you get it from?"

"I work in a bank, remember, and my bank has a lot of old money stashed away in old vaults. It all should have been destroyed but it seems that no one got around to doing it."

"Oh, Mr. Taylor, this is fantastic! Thank you. We can help a lot of people with this as well."

"That's what I thought. Anyway, what have you been up to?"

Marged explained the research she and Buttercup had done and what they had planned to do and asked if he wanted to help.

"I like that idea. Could the boy's help too?"

Marged suggested two teams: Buttercup with David Taylor and Richard and James with her.

David Taylor smiled. "It sounds very good to me. I will be glad to work with Buttercup. Lead on Buttercup. Let's find out about all these people."

The two teams with their pens and notebooks and costume pictures headed deeper into the cave. Caradoc, who had witnessed the whole interaction, smiled. He had not said a word.

Every individual on the way to where most of the people were was stopped and asked: "What is your name? What is your address? What date and year is it?" It was useless asking them when they came in because it was always "Today." They were asked why they came to the cave and had they gone out of the cave since coming in and if so how many times.

Once the questions had been answered and noted down the people were told that they would be given help getting back to their own time. Many hadn't got a clue about why they were being asked these questions because they hadn't got around to going out for their first time and, of course, felt that they had only just got there.

Some answers were odd and Marged was going to have more questions for Caradoc. It seemed that quite a few of the people were from places hundreds of miles away and even from other countries. Many of them had not come into the cave the way the others had done. They said that they had been going about their normal life and in mid stride found themselves, suddenly, walking around inside the cave.

Marged was puzzled as to how this might have happened. How could they instantly be transported hundreds of miles from where they had been to find themselves in the cave?

The costumes helped a little bit to focus their attention on those they thought might be the ones most recently entered. That way they could put everyone on a reverse timeline list. However, Marged had not considered the people they may come across from her future even though Buttercup was well into the future in Marged's time.

Sorting people out was not easy because Marged could do nothing for people before 1860 without doing more calibrations, so these people were listed in the back of the notebooks to work with later. The major concentration was on the people that were from the two hundred years between1860 and 2060.

In the main area, if it was the main area of the cave, there were hundreds of people, mostly individuals; however, there were couples, trios, families, small groups, medium groups and large groups of about a hundred individuals. One of the things that was noticeable there was almost no communication between individuals and groups. Marged considered it as being odd, but then realized that it was probably because no time had passed for them. So they must have felt that they had only just arrived and felt no need to communicate with others right away.

Marged began informing them that they may have been in the cave seemingly in their time and if they went outside they could possibly find themselves before, or in the future of their time. Many could not grasp that fact, especially those who had not been outside. Others began to understand and accept the strangeness of their situation, and Marged recruited many of them to communicate with others and inform her when they found people in the timeline that she could deal with.

As the two teams roamed through the large area they noticed around seventeen or so groups of soldiers. One group in particular seemed to be a little odd to Marged. Before approaching them she asked David what he thought.

"They look like American soldiers from World War Two to me. I think there might be something going on between them."

"I am going to talk to them." Marged went up to the group and noticed that eight of them were white soldiers who were angrily facing down four black soldiers who looked very scared.

Marged smiled. "Hello. What year is it?"

A great big 6 foot, 4 inch white soldier sergeant looked down on her. "Why missy, we are hea to fight your war for you. It's 1944."

"So, how did you get here?"

"By ship."

"No, sorry. What I meant was how did you get into the cave?"

"Why missy, we was chasing these niggas and they ran in here."

Marged was shocked at the way he referred to the black soldiers. "Why were you chasing these other soldiers?"

"Cos they was talking to white girls in the streets and they as niggas should know better. So we was goin to teach them a lesson. Where we come from what they was doing is a hanging offence. We'd hang em here, but we can't get to em."

Marged was shocked. "You would hang someone for talking to another human being?"

"They is only niggas and they should not be talking to whites unless they is spoken to, and these niggas will be punished. If not here we will do it as soon as we get outside again."

"You can't do harm to anyone in here and Caradoc will make sure you can't hurt them out there either."

"That old man. He's a nigga lover. We'd hang him where we is from. We stamp that kind of thing out before it takes hold."

"So, you wanted to hang these soldiers for talking to white girls because they are black? You are all from America. Aren't you all Americans?"

"We is real Americans, but they is just niggas."

"Well, I think they are better Americans than you are. And I would be very pleased to have them talk to me."

The black soldiers appeared to be more scared, because Marged had made the white soldiers even more aggressive. The big white sergeant leaned right into Marged's face. She didn't move or back down. "Missy, don't you be contaminating youself with those niggas."

Marged stared right back into his face. "What are you going to do about it? You can't touch them here in the cave and you will never be able touch them again, anywhere."

She then turned to the four scared black soldiers and reached out her hand. "Gentlemen, I am honoured to meet you." She shook each of their hands in turn.

The white sergeant and his troop tried to move against the black soldiers. They could not move, it was as if they were up against an invisible rock wall.

Marged turned to the white soldiers and smiled. "How long have you been in the cave?" They answered as she had expected.

"We came in here afta these niggas today."

Marged continued to smile. "You said that you came in here in 1944. I came in here in 2004 so that means you have been in here for sixty years."

One of the white soldier's eyes went wide. "Man, are we AWOL?"

Marged didn't understand the statement. "What is AWOL?"

"The missy doesn't know what AWOL is. It means "Absent Without Leave.""

Marged turned to the black soldiers and asked them. "I still don't understand. What does it mean?"

One of the black soldiers answered her. "It means that you have to have permission to leave camp for a certain amount of time, and if you leave without permission, or you stay away longer than your permission allows, it means that you are absent without leave or permission."

"So what happens if you are?"

She was then interrupted by the white sergeant. "Missy, why you asking these dumb niggas your questions?"

Marged turned and smiled defiantly. "Because they give better answers than you do" She turned back. "So what happens if you are AWOL?"

"You get thrown in the guard house."

"What is a guard house?"

"It is a military jail and depending on how long you were absent, or if they have to find and capture you, it can be a complete reduction in rank, confiscated pay and anything from one month to three years in the jail.

Marged began thinking things over when the soldier added, "If you do it while you are fighting the enemy, it is called desertion and when you are caught you are shot by a firing squad."

"Well, I had better get you out of here at the right time so that you don't get into trouble." She smiled at the black soldiers. "You are going out first so these others can't chase you down, even though they will not be able to do you harm out there either. Come with me."

They followed her to the cave exit and they were followed by the eight white soldiers who could not get close to the others no matter how they tried.

Caradoc had been observing Marged at her work.

Marged asked the black soldiers for the day and the time of their arrival in the cave and they told her. She asked how long they would have left on their leave and when they were due back at their camp. They told her that they had a whole day.

Marged adjusted the Time Stones accordingly and then Caradoc spoke to the black soldiers.

"In twenty years from your time on
Many of your troubles will be gone.
A man of your kind with the name of King
Much freedom to you he'll surely bring."

Marged placed her hands in the usual place; the rock door opened and out went the four black soldiers. The rock door closed behind them. Marged then asked the white soldiers what time they had to get back.

Their answers were the same as the black soldiers. Marged didn't really care. She had made a decision and she adjusted the Time Stones so that they would be a week late getting back to camp.

Caradoc saw the move, smiled and turned to the soldiers.

"Your hatred for your fellow man
From your hearts one day will ban.
In hate, happy lives you will never see
If you don't lose it and let your hearts be free."

Marged opened the rock door and out they went, running to try and catch the black soldiers, not knowing that they had been gone a whole week before them.

There were the seventeen other soldier groups and Marged decided that these would be dealt with later.

They listed about 300 other individuals and groups in the timeline they could work with. There were many interesting stories of how and why these people wound up in the cave.

There was a family that was in a state of stress. The man looked dejected. He was holding a shepherd's crook with two dogs by his side, and a sack two thirds full of what seemed to be household goods; he was accompanied by a woman with a smaller sack and three children, two girls and an older boy. The one girl, about six, was crying and clutching a rag doll. The other girl, about eight, was not crying, but certainly looked as if she had been. Marged asked, "What year did you come into the cave?"

"1940," the man said. "We were at war and we had to move out by order of the army."

"Where did you come from?"

"The Epynt, of course."

Marged knew that Epynt was an army training range; after all she had just found 17 groups of soldiers and most of them were from that mountain. "So why did you come to the cave?"

"We came in to shelter, because we weren't sure where we were going to go. We thought we could stay in our home a bit longer because there were still some sheep around that had to be moved. The trouble was we hadn't found another place to live and it was no good moving into town, because I'm a shepherd, on the hill is where my work is. We were told to leave our house by the end of April or we would be thrown out. Then they extended it to give people more time, but the trouble was with everyone trying to get moved I was kept busy working the sheep. We were supposed to be gone by June the first, but I had to stay on to help move the sheep off a big area of the hill. On the fifteenth, I came home and Mam and the children had been locked out of the house, and there was a soldier guarding it, to stop them back in. We were told that we had to leave. I told the soldier that I still had some sheep to move, but he said he didn't care about that, if we didn't leave the area he would have us arrested. So we left and came here."

Marged was horrified. "They threw you out of your home?"

They nodded.

"That is terrible; I never knew that had happened. I know of some families that left Epynt and moved into our area; they bought farms with the compensation they got from the war department."

"It was alright for the farmers. They got compensation, not a lot, mind, but I'm just a shepherd, there was nothing for us. The house we lived in wasn't ours, you see. It was rented."

"Wow! Ah, er, I am going to do everything I can to help you."

"You're just a bit of a gel. How can you help us?"

"Well, this might be a shock to you," they stared and listened, "this cave doesn't have time and no one gets older here. I don't really know why that is, except Caradoc, the old man with the long grey beard, says that it is to do with the Time Tyrants, whoever they might be. I don't know what they are, or exactly what they do."

"You say you can help us, but how can you help us? We don't have any money. The last man I worked for didn't pay me because he has also had to leave Epynt"

"We will help you find money and a shepherding job."

"Can we help you do what it is you do?"

"Yes, but how much I don't know. I do know that we will be asking you a lot of questions, so I will be back."

Marged moved on and found another boy dressed like Rhys Edwards. Marged thought that perhaps he was running away because of the "Welsh Not". However, he was not wearing one around his neck. "What year did you get here?"

He looked her up and down. "1904, of course," he sniggered. "And what year did you come in here?"

"2004. In my time you have been here a hundred years."

The boy laughed. "You are not right."

"Alright, why did you come to the cave?"

"The soldiers were chasing me."

"What soldiers?"

"The soldiers guarding the railway line to the new dams, because of the Royal Train."

"I don't understand. When was this?"

"It was when the King and Queen came to open the Elan Valley Dams. I wanted to see the King and Queen, so I hid behind some rocks close to the new dam and close to the railway line. The tracks were lined with soldiers. When I stood up to wave to the train, a soldier thought I was too close and was going to hurt the King and he chased me. I didn't stop running till I was on top of the hill above the dam and I couldn't go back because he would be waiting for me, so I came on over the hill and came into the cave."

"Where is your home?"

"In Elan Valley. My father is a foreman of the masons."

"Have you been out since you came in?"

"No, I've only just got here. I am not going out until that train has gone back to England."

"The train went back to England 100 years ago."

"You are strange, you are."

Marged smiled. "You'll see. By the way, what is your name?"

"Dafydd Jones."

"Alright, Dafydd Jones, be ready to go home with no soldiers anywhere to be seen chasing you."

She met up with David and told him what she had seen. He was totally shocked when she told him about the shepherd and his family.

"Oh, that is awful. No wonder a lot of the Welsh don't like the English. This whole experience, I must say, has been quite a surprise to me. We will definitely do something to help them. Perhaps we should cheer them up and take them to the Wild West Show."

"That is a great idea and there is another boy here from 1904, a Dafydd Jones. We can take him too."

"So how did he get here?"

"He was chased from Elan Valley by a soldier; all he wanted to do was wave to the King and Queen who had come to open the new dams."

"Well, that's a coincidence; I found another shepherd who had been displaced from his home because of the building of the Elan Valley Dams. He and his family had been offered a job on a farm on the Epynt Mountain and they were on their way there, when they sheltered in the cave and their little girl opened the rock door."

"Oh, wow. So we have to get them to Epynt? Oh gosh, you don't think that the two families are related do you?"

"I have no idea; we had better make some enquiries. The main thing, however, is to find a home for the family you saw."

"They don't have any money."

"That will be no problem. We have money."

"Did you come across an Oliver Thomas?"

"No. We never got around to everyone."

"Don't worry. We soon will." She smiled. "I have an idea." Her smile got bigger. "Do you know what it is?"

"No!" they all said just about together. "What is it?"

"I think we should all go to the Wild West Show."

"Yea!" They shouted. "Let's do it."

CHAPTER 14

Cattle Fairs in Builth are in the street.
They crowd into town so watch your feet.
The noise and smells could disturb the dead
But, what relief in the smell of bread.
Steers in shops do not get served
Just like bulls it's been observed.

Marged was now buoyed up by the prospect of going to witness a great event in the history of Builth and the World. "Buttercup and I have to change and we have to sort some things out for the journey, especially the money, but we need to let the shepherd from Epynt and his family and Dafydd Jones from Elan Valley know."

David smiled. "What about the family from Elan Valley?"

"Ask them too. We have the money."

"Very good. Me and the boys will go and find them."

The girls changed then they got the money together and began to count it out. Marged put down the first half crown she got, the one with the distinctive mark on it, and then picked up the second one she had bought. They were identical. "Look at this, Buttercup. These two half crowns are identical." She picked the first one up again and held the two side by side. "See."

She brought the coins together and touched them. In an instant they appeared to melt into one another and become one with a small flash of blue light. Marged shrieked and dropped the coin. "Oh, my gosh. Did you see that? They're one now!"

Buttercup saw what had happened, but she still had a fixed stare on the coin; her bottom jaw had almost fallen off her face. "What happened?" she finally asked.

"Buttercup, those coins were in two different worlds until they touched, and then the two worlds they were in became one. Wow, that is amazing!"

"Will it happen again?"

"Oh, my gosh, yes it could. We must keep the two lots of money separate, just in case we have more that is identical and in two different worlds. We must tell Mr. Taylor and keep his money separate also."

David and his sons came back with Dafydd Jones and the Epynt shepherd and his family and their two sheep dogs. He told the girls that the Elan Valley family had already seen the show, so they had decided not to go. They didn't believe that they could see the same show twice, especially if it had already happened.

The girls told David what had happened to the half crowns.

"Would that happen to people if they met themselves?"

Marged nodded. "Yes, it would.

"What about inside the cave?"

Caradoc answered.

"Inside the cave life can't be two.
Other things become one to view."

Marged looked over the shepherd and his family and decided that their old fashioned clothes from their time would probably pass in 1904. She smiled at them. "I forgot to ask you for your names and I should have done that when I first met you."

The shepherd straightened up. "I am William Williams and my wife is Heulwen, the boy is Thomas and the girls are Branwen and Rhianon." He gave a small smile. "And the dogs are Mott and Bryn. How is it that we are going to see a Wild West Show? We don't have any money for that sort of thing."

Marged smiled. "We have enough for everyone."

Dafydd spoke up. "I saw the Wild West Show when it was in Builth. I didn't know that it was going to be there again."

Marged and Buttercup laughed.

He looked at them. "Why are you laughing at me?"

"We are laughing because the show you are going to see is the same one you have already seen."

"Well, you can't see it again. It's already happened."

"Well, if you go with us, you will already be there and if you touch the other you, you will become one and I don't know if that will be one or other of you or a combination of the both of you."

They did their best to explain what might happen to the unbelieving boy.

David turned to Mr. Williams. "I think that I might be able to help you find another home. Have you ever thought of buying your own farm?"

"Oh, yes, I have always wanted to have my own farm. Heulwen is from a farm and her father has told us that he would help a bit, if I could come up with some money of my own."

"Well, when we get back from the show we will see what we can do to make things happen for you. I think you have gotten a bad deal from the government, and I don't believe that people should be taking advantage of other people, especially hard working people like yourselves. They have treated you very badly and I am going to help make it right. Well, we have a show to go to."

They all glanced at Marged; she had her serious, thinking face on. "Don't you think that we might have a problem? There are eleven of us going to the show and Rhys Edwards and his parents. We are all going first class because we have the money. Mr. William Cody gave us a pass for some good front seats at the show, but I don't think he was expecting eleven of us."

Mr. Williams spoke up. "We shouldn't be imposing on you people, you are being more than helpful to us. We should stay, so that we are not a problem for you." His children looked disappointed.

David turned on him quickly. "Certainly not. After all you've been through, you are more deserving of this than anyone. You are going. I will stay behind."

Marged lifted her arms and began waving. "Stop it! Everyone of us is going to go to the show. What we need to do is go out about a month before and make arrangements."

David nodded. "Yes, I agree. We should make sure of everything. It would be awful if we couldn't take the train because it was full."

"Alright, we'll go out and make the arrangements and then come back and reset the Time Stones, so we can all go first class to the Show."

Marged made three attempts before she found a dry day. It was the 13th of April.

After a discussion they decided that it would be Buttercup, Marged, David and his boys. David thought it would be a good experience for his sons.

They got out onto the rough road by Capel Rhos and walked toward Garth, picking their way around pools of water and the deeper patches of mud. It took a while to get down to the Troedrhiwdalar crossroads, but once there, the going was a little easier.

They saw three people on the journey; they were shepherds in fields checking on the ewes and lambs, some of which were still being born. Lambing was always later in the hills, timed for when the new spring grass was emerging. They passed many farms and they knew when they were about to pass one that was close to the track. The first thing they noticed was the smell, a strong unspecific smell, a combination of smells unique to each farm. The next thing was a couple of sheep dogs, racing out to greet them with barks and just as quickly settling down to have their ears stroked. The dogs would walk with them for a hundred feet or so past the farm before returning to their yard. Most of the farms had children and they could be heard playing from a long way off.

At the station they decided that David would be Buttercup's estate manager and carry the money.

Buttercup tapped on the station master's door and he opened it. He smiled, "Hello, my lady."

"Now, my good man, I would like to reserve eleven seats in first class for May the twelfth, on a train that can get us to Builth Wells in time for the Wild West Show."

"The trains are filling up fast, my lady. It's a good thing that you decided to book early. Come in and we shall see what we can do."

Everyone followed Buttercup into the station master's office and she placed herself in front of the ticket window. The station master faced her. "Eleven first class return tickets then, is it?"

"Yes, it is. Thank you. Mr. Taylor, my estate manager will pay you."

David paid the money and Buttercup asked for a carriage to pick them up at Capel Rhos and then asked about tickets for the Wild West Show.

She was told that she would have to go into Builth for those.

They bought tickets for the train to Builth and while they waited Marged got up to have a look at the poster for the Wild West Show again; it was still there. She noticed that there was an address in Builth Wells where the tickets could be purchased. It was a shop in the High Street. Marged took out her ballpoint pen and made a note of it in her little notebook. She was just turning away when she spotted a line in the poster. "Grand Parade through Builth at 10:00 am." She made a note of that as well.

The train was a few minutes early and the station master wouldn't let the train go until the time was correct for it to move. Then, he blew his whistle and waved a flag to let the signal man know, and the train moved off. The boys were stunned by the noise, the smoke and the steam. They had watched the train pull into the station with awe, and now they were on board with all the sights and smells of the age of steam. They were living real history, something that in their time was only done in re-enactments.

In Builth Road they caught another train for the short ride into Builth station. When they got off and made their way out of the station there were cattle everywhere. It was market day in Builth and it was a Spring Cattle Sale. Cattle were being brought in from the surrounding area and they were being funnelled over the Wye Bridge by drovers and farmers with their dogs. Marged had been to Builth for cattle sales with her father, but she had never seen anything like this in her life.

All the cattle had horns, some were quite small, some quite large and every few seconds the sound of them clashing against each other could be heard through all the other noises. Some of the cattle had even been gouged and scraped by them. Marged realized why cattle in her time had been dehorned.

Buttercup seemed totally bewildered by it. David and his boys had never been this close to a large animal in their lives, let alone large groups of them. Marged could see the shock and stress on the faces of her friends and knew that she had to take command; after all she was the only one with any farm and cattle experience. The smell of the animals hardly bothered Marged, and Buttercup seemed to tolerate it as well, after all London in her time would be full of such smells and far worse. David and his boys however were almost overwhelmed by it and every now and then he would hold a handkerchief over his nose.

Marged spoke up over the noise of the drovers, the clashing of the horns and the bellowing animals. "Alright, everyone, stay close to me and we will be alright." She led them between two groups of cattle and up to and alongside a young man with a crumpled top hat, and an equally crumpled, dirty, three-piece suit, a knotty blackthorn stick and two dogs.

The entourage was visibly scared and stuck very close to Marged. They kept looking back because of the other group of cattle that was coming behind them. The herd in front was quite large and made up of a few Welsh Blacks and mostly rangy looking Herefords. Marged remained calm and asked the young man if the cattle belonged to him.

"No, they belong to seven farms. I have been droving them since five this morning from out Hundred House way. You might want to push your way through if you want to get into town. They will be holding me up on the bridge while they clear some of the cattle, which have been sold off the street down to the Groe by the river."

"How long will it take for you to get into town?"

"Last year I had to wait over two hours and there are more cattle here this year."

Marged had to make a decision, either to wait or try to make their way past the cattle, get in front of them and beat them on to the bridge where there would probably be more cattle. She knew that she could do it, but would her scared friends go with her. So she decided to take a chance and get around the herd and get in front. She turned to David. "The boys should follow me, followed by Buttercup and you should be behind. We must stay close to each other. The cattle won't hurt you, they will want to move away from you, but as there isn't a lot of room, you are going to find yourselves very close to them."

The noise was amazing, people shouting and whistling, mostly commands to the dogs, the cattle were lowing and bellowing and the horns were clashing. There were cattle droppings everywhere and the smell to the boys and David continued to be pretty awful. Buttercup could bear it. It wasn't as big a problem for her.

They followed Marged as she negotiated a route around the cattle, every now and then she would push against them and slap them with her hand. "Come on, move." Slap. "Come on, move it."

David was astonished that this little girl seemed to have no fear of these large cumbersome animals. In a few minutes they made it to the front of the herd and found themselves behind another herd. This herd was smaller and was a mixture of a few Welsh Blacks, Herefords and several brown spotted cattle, which Marged thought were Shorthorns. They were being driven by an older man who was perfectly dressed for his trade and the time he was in. He had a sack pegged around his shoulders, a broad brimmed, dirty bowler hat, breeches, hobnailed boots and gaiters. He had a shepherd's crook and one dog. Marged moved alongside the man. "Can we get through?"

"You might. We are getting close to the bridge and it will get pretty tight on there."

Marged rallied her group. "Come on, we have to pass these before they get to the bridge." She took off, slapping and shouting at the cattle that weren't moving out of her way quickly enough, the others nervously followed as close as they could. One of David's boys got swished in the face by a very mucky wet tail.

He screeched out, "Oh, my gosh! Dad, do something." He was reaching for his handkerchief.

His father shouted "I can't do anything; you will just have to put up with it."

They got in front of the tight, scrambling herd due to Marged's valiant efforts and made it onto the bridge. Because of the narrowness of the bridge, the cattle dung was quite deep and slippery in places, so they had to be very careful where they were treading. They came up behind a horse and carriage, following another herd of cattle. These were young steers born at the end of the previous summer. Marged thought that the farmer would probably get a good price for them if they were bought to go down country into England to fatten, and down there they would gain weight quicker.

They followed the horse and carriage and kept turning to see the herd they had just passed catching up with them. Then all of a sudden there was a shout, a man was running over to the parapet of the bridge. One of the steers had clambered over it and fallen into the River Wye below. Fortunately the man was able to stop others from following it over.

Marged and her little group peered over and they could see that the animal was severely injured, because the water where it had fallen in was less than a foot deep. There were men splashing over to it with ropes, to pull it out. It was then they noticed that other cattle had gone over previously and they were being slaughtered by two men on the bank of the river to put them out of their, broken bones, misery. Two more men were skinning and dressing out the carcasses.

David averted his eyes and those of his sons as there was blood all over the bank which was running into the river, it could be seen flowing downstream and under the bridge. The dressed out carcasses were twisted and misshapen from the fall and they were being loaded onto carts.

The hides were piled up next to the horned heads that had been cut off the cattle, beside some bushes. The tongues lolled out of the mouths and the eyes were still open and dull, their life's light gone completely out of them. Several women were sorting through the piles of intestines, cutting and placing them in tubs and baskets. They were also fighting off several dogs that were milling around, trying to steal odd parts and lick up the blood.

Marged took in the shocking sight. She glanced back to find that the cattle following had really closed up. When they got closer Marged could see everyone getting scared even more, so she turned, moved back and stood her ground and the cattle stopped in front of her. She shouted to her group, "I will hold them for a while!" Then she shouted over the cattle to the farmer, "Can you stop for a minute? It's very crowded over here."

He used his crook to acknowledge her request and then leaned on it to wait.

Marged waited until the front cattle started clearing the bridge and began moving up the main street and then she turned and walked briskly, being as careful as she could not to tread in too much manure, and joined the others in front once again.

David looked at her and shook his head. "Marged, you could have been trampled by those cows."

"They are not cows; they are steers, mostly stores."

"Oh, I see. What are stores?"

"They are cattle that are sold to someone else to fatten, like farmers in England."

David momentarily lost his nervousness. "Do they fatten a lot of farmers in England?"

"No, silly, I mean the cattle." They both chuckled.

They followed the carriage past the end of the bridge and it turned off and went down the Hay Road towards the east avoiding cattle coming in from that direction.

The little group turned the other way onto the main street of Builth. There were cattle as far as the eye could see and they were being kept in small crowded groups by a lot of men. They weren't in pens or tied, they were just kept together by the men with sticks and their ever keen working dogs, which included Corgis, the traditional Welsh cattle dog. Marged had never seen one working before. There didn't seem to be the same chaos on the main street as there had been on their walk from the station.

This was a Builth that Marged had never seen before and never could have imagined. Just about every shop had a bowler-hatted man outside who would accost the passers-by, trying to persuade them to go in and buy things. They also were moving away the cattle that came too close to the shop they were promoting.

In the spaces where there were no shops, individual vendors were selling their wares. Each had their own handcart, which had the merchandise laid out on it; carts with eggs and butter, others with seeds for the garden. There were baskets and sticks being sold, socks, hats, aprons, shawls and other things that were stitched or knitted. Some had baked goods, which you could smell over the smell of the livestock as you got close. David stopped in front of a cart with baked goods and they all gathered around him. Marged asked, "Are you going to buy something?"

"Not really, I just want to savour the incredible change of smells."

They continued on up the street, sidestepping cattle and doing their best to avoid the shop promoters and the manure. Marged smiled to herself. She couldn't decide which was worse, the promoters or the manure! Children were running and playing around the cattle, completely fearless.

Amongst the cattle, men were arguing, stamping their feet, gesturing and turning to prod a steer to emphasize a point. They were shouting out numbers and smiling at each other before shaking hands after spitting on them.

David asked, "What are they doing that for?"

Marged smiled. "That's how the cattle are sold and some of the older farmers do it in my time."

"Marged, your world is so different."

She smiled again and led her group to the shop that sold the Wild West Show tickets and in they all went. There was quite a queue, but fortunately they weren't all there to buy tickets. After twenty minutes of waiting, it was their turn. They were facing a white-haired, red-faced man in a black pin-striped, three-piece suit. "Can I help you?" he bellowed. He was almost as loud as the bellowing cattle.

Buttercup smiled. "Yes, I wish to buy first-class tickets for the Wild West Show."

"How many would you like?"

She glanced at David. "Ten, don't you think, Mr. Taylor? We do have some complimentary tickets from Mr. Cody. "

"Yes, yes, indeed, my lady."

"Give him the money, would you?"

"Yes, my lady." He handed the man a five pound note and got ten tickets and two pounds change. Even at that time the tickets were not cheap.

Marged suggested that they find a tea shop and have something to eat before the journey back. They all agreed and found a very pleasant place on Broad Street and watched the cattle chaos. The tea shop was nice, but the smells from the day's activities were permeating their way through the whole place. They ordered cakes and teas and once again Buttercup ordered David to pay.

Just before they were about to finish, there was a huge commotion across the street at a shop that had pots and pans hanging on the outside and glassware and china for sale inside. Three men with sticks and a couple of loudly barking Corgi dogs had been chasing a very large steer, which had panicked and crashed through the door of the shop. The three men followed it in, dogs and all. There was a lot of shouting, women screaming and the terrible crashing noise of breaking glass and china. This went on for almost a minute, then all of a sudden the glass window at the front shattered, with broken glass and mullions going everywhere, as the steer, with his big horns, came crashing back out of the shop on to the street once more. The steer was mad with panic, upsetting the other cattle and the people who were trying to do their shopping. Screams and shouts filled the air. Two ladies fell over each other in their hurry to get out of the way.

David looked at his boys and smiled. "There you are. Now you have seen a bull in a china shop."

They all laughed, even though it was a serious happening. Someone could have been badly hurt.

David asked Marged, "Does this happen all the time here?"

"Not in our time it doesn't, and I don't know what other days here in this time are like. I have never seen anything like it before."

They left the tea shop and made their way down the town. There were still cattle coming in, so they would have to wait. As they got toward the bottom of the town, a rush of cattle came around the corner from the bridge; it was the young man they had seen earlier. The cattle slowed down a little, but they were crushed coming up the street, so Marged guided her entourage up into a narrow side street.

To the side of them was a shed at the back of a butcher's shop, and there were three fat steers in a pen, one of which was being held by two men. One man was holding onto the tail and the other had his right arm around its neck and the fingers of his left hand in its nostrils. Another man approached the front of the animal with something that looked like a mason's mallet in his left hand, and a large hammer in his right. He placed the mallet thing on end and pressed it against the middle of the steer's head, and he hit the other end with a hammer. It sounded as if a gun had been fired. The big animal dropped to the floor, kicking, and the two men wrapped a chain around one of the kicking back legs and the stunned animal was quickly hoisted up on a pulley, attached to a heavy beam that was sticking out of the shed roof.

As soon as its nose cleared the ground, the man who had used the mallet thing and the hammer put them down, picked up a large knife and cut the throat of the shot animal. Blood sprayed out everywhere, but mostly into a bucket. David was horrified at this spectacle and hustled his boys away from it.

Buttercup was in shock. "Oh, how awful! The poor animal!"

Marged had seen her father slaughter sheep, but she had never seen anything as brutal as the slaughter of that large steer.

Things had calmed a bit in the main street, so they continued their journey to the bridge. They made it just in time. The cattle which were down by the river after being sold were now moving up to the bridge, to be taken across to the railway station. There they would be loaded for their journey to England to be fattened or to the London meat markets. They crossed the bridge as quickly as they could avoiding the last of the groups that were still coming in. They picked their way through the manure that was just about everywhere. Marged wondered who would have to clean it up if they ever did.

They got to the station and had to wait for half an hour to catch the train to Builth Road station, where they would have to wait for another half hour to catch the train to Garth. In the ticket office Buttercup asked the telegrapher there to let Garth know the time of their arrival. David paid him with a smile and fourpence.

As they waited they watched the activity in the rail yard, where the cattle were being loaded for their journey to England. They also watched a man in a cart that had a framework on it, adorned with hundreds of dead, paunched rabbits approach a freight carriage of the train. The man stopped the cart at the carriage and a big door opened and they watched as two men loaded the rabbits off the cart and into the carriage.

At Garth, the station master helped Buttercup down, but the others had to help themselves.

"Thank you, my good man."

They went out of the station to where a carriage was waiting, it would soon be dark. They all boarded to find it was the same man who had driven Marged and Buttercup before. They made arrangements to be picked up at Capel Rhos early enough on the twelfth to catch the train and be in Builth for the grand parade.

By the time they reached Capel Rhos it was getting dark, although there was half a moon, that looked as if it were racing through the fast moving clouds, there was enough light to just about see their way. The carriage driver lit up his carriage lanterns, and headed off back to Garth. Marged flashed her torch. "Follow me." And off she went with David bringing up the rear once again.

David and his boys had never been out in the country in the dark before, so for them it was a little bit scary. Their eyes soon got used to the dark and Marged hardly had to use the torch.

They were about a hundred feet from the entrance to the cave, when they spotted a man that seemed to be carrying a bundle of sorts. Marged turned and placed her finger to her lips to shush the others, they heard her but barely saw her action. Fortunately they were quiet and stopped and peered ahead to where the man was ambling toward the cave. Marged whispered, "I think he might be a poacher. I am going to scare him like I did with the other one, because we don't want him in the cave. Wait here. When you see the torch come on, make a lot of noise."

Marged slinked away to the left and made her way quickly and quietly until she was in front of the poacher. He didn't see her coming. She was behind some foliage and about six feet in front of the man when she turned on the torch and shone it straight into his face. She began shrieking and once the others heard her, they too began shrieking. Marged Evans expected the man to run, as the other one had run, but this man dropped his bundle and immediately drew a huge sword, lifted it with both hands above his head and came at Marged.

She was totally unprepared for this turnaround of events and staggered backwards but managed to keep the torch on the man. It was her turn to be scared, and on staggering back, she tripped, fell over and found herself sitting on her bottom in a tuft of wet grass. This took the focus of the torch off the man, and then she saw the full height of him and the huge sword that was flashing swiftly down on her.

She screamed like she had never screamed before. "No! No!" She wanted to move, but she was so petrified it was impossible. The sword was going to cleave her in half from her head down her middle, but it came to an abrupt stop about a foot above her head, and no matter how hard the man tried, he could get it no further.

David approached, he had made Buttercup and his boys stand back. He was horrified, he thought Marged was going to be killed and wanted to stop this man, but by the time he got to him it was all over. Marged was struggling to her feet and recovering from her horrendous fright. "It's alright, Mr. Taylor, he can't hurt us. He has been in the cave and we are protected."

David stopped and stared at this strange man, who seemed to have two beards on his chin, instead of one in the middle. Marged moved the torch so that it pointed to the ground nearby. It cast enough light that everyone could see each other.

The man lowered the sword and stared at everyone in turn and then back to Marged. She pointed at him, "Owain Glyn Dwr?"

He nodded.

She was still shaking from the fright but managed a smile. "Come on everyone, back into the cave, I want to talk to this man. He is the greatest Welshman of all time, our last true Prince, Owain Glyn Dwr." They got back into the cave, the rock door opened and they all trooped in to the vastness of the interior.

CHAPTER 15

**A more modern dress for our ancient prince
And espouse he may, but wont convince.
The Wild West is in our streets,
Noble people perform great feats.
The horses move by spur and quirt
And all the men with danger flirt.**

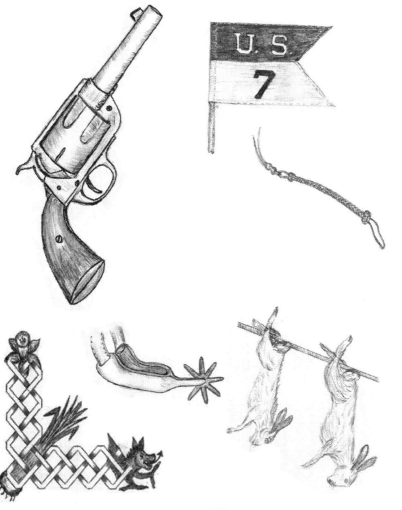

Caradoc smiled at the sight of his helpers accompanied by the great Prince. He had seen Owain go in and out of the cave many times and fail to get to where he wanted to go. But now, Marged would get him out to his right time. She turned and faced the great Prince; he was still holding his sword and staring back at Marged. David stood by his side, holding the bundle that he had been carrying; it was the medieval costume that he normally wore in his time. He looked very peculiar with a band of bronze on his head, his hair down to his shoulders, his twin beard and wearing a 1930s' three-piece suit with a sword buckled on around it.

He was intensely focused on Marged. "You are a girl, a small girl. I nearly killed you. What magic is it that you have that you could stop my sword?"

She smiled. "It is the magic of Caradoc and the cave that saved me. I have heard and read much about you. In my time you are still a hero in Wales."

"What is your time?"

"Six hundred years after yours."

"Have you been out on wrong times as I have?"

"Yes, twice; but now we are correcting the Time Stones to make things right."

He looked at Caradoc. "You have not told me of this girl's magic."

Caradoc looked at him as if looking at an old, old friend and no doubt for the number of times the Prince had gone in and out they probably were.

"You were out when she came here.
She has tackled Time Stones without fear.
Soon we'll know of all the times out there
And all go out without a care.
Marged knows the times for many years
And will get you back to all your peers.
Your trial and error will now end
And all the times for you she'll mend."

Owain, who had mostly been looking at Marged, gave her his full attention. "How will you help me find my place out there?"

"You have to tell me the time and date you came here, and the time and date you would like to go out on."

"I don't know where to start to get an idea." He looked at everyone in turn. "I know it was after a battle."

"If you know the battles then we can get close. If you don't know the times of them, I can get them for you, because they are all recorded in history. Can you think about them all? You were there so you should remember all of them."

"I do, I do, I will order them in my head. There have been many. We lost the Battle of Bryn Glas, not by a lot, but it set us back for awhile. Then more followed and we were mostly successful in those."

Marged stared at him for many seconds, allowing what he had just told her to go through her mind. "But, you didn't lose the Battle of Bryn Glas. I was told you won it."

David spoke up. "She is right, you won it very decisively. We called it the Battle of Pilleth."

"No, no, we didn't."

Marged wondered if this Owain was from a different world or dimension. "You did capture Edmund Mortimer?"

"No, not at all. He nearly captured me."

Marged was a little confused. Had the history that she had heard been wrong? She began to wonder if all the things that she had done in the cave had affected some important events in history. She thought, "No, it had to be a different world." But, different or not, she felt that she had to do something to make the Battle of Bryn Glas fit the history that she knew.

She looked at Caradoc, then she turned to Owain and with great deference spoke. "In my history, my Great Prince, you won the Battle of Bryn Glas, and you will win it again. From this cave you can go out and fight it again for the first time. I will help you, because I know I can find out what you did to win it in my history. What you should do is think about all the things that happened in that battle, then we will compare so you can win in a way that Mr. Taylor said. What was it?"

David smiled. Here he was aiding and abetting the Welsh against his own ancestors. "Decisively, you will win decisively."

The Prince listened, even though he was a little confused. He looked at Caradoc and then David and back to Marged. "I will do as you ask, little girl, I will think over what happened at Bryn Glas, the beautiful green hill that was stained with blood."

Marged had a grim half smile. "The next time you fight that battle you are going to win. Now, we are going out to see a Show. You would be welcome to come along and we will tell you how this Show came to be. Come with your suit and leave your other clothes and sword behind, and since you and we will not understand each other out there, I will explain here what will happen."

Caradoc smiled and stepped over to Owain and touched his shoulder.
He will now speak forth your tongue
No matter who he is among.

Marged cheered. "Hooray," and with David's help explained North America.

He half smiled. "I will go with you to see this man who is King of the Wild West."

David explained modern democracy to the curious prince.

He listened carefully and looked from Marged to David. "And does that work?"

"Yes it works." David smiled.

He looked a little puzzled. "I want to hear more about this. You must tell me when we go to the show."

Marged nodded and smiled "This is going to be wonderful my Great Prince. You have seen the motor vehicle. Have you seen the train?"

"I have seen many things out there where I did not belong.
You tell me of what I see
I would like to know what becomes of me.
I wish to know what the world will hold
For all the descendents from my fold."

He was sounding like Caradoc.

Marged forgot herself and hugged Owain and kissed him on his cheek. He was stunned; none of his subjects had ever dared to do a thing like that. She let him go and he was a little embarrassed, but he liked the enthusiasm and passion of this young girl.

She looked around. "I have said this before; let's go to the Wild West Show."

Two carriages were waiting at Capel Rhos. Owain's face lit up. "Are these chariots?" he asked.

Marged was amused. "They are carriages. Climb aboard, you will see."

They were past the Cribarth when they came up behind a cart pulled by a mule that was loaded with paunched, dead rabbits, hanging on long horizontal poles attached to the cart itself.

One of the carriage drivers shouted at the man driving the cart to move out of the way. The man shouted back. "You will have to wait until the road gets wider."

The carriage driver shouted back. "Well, move it along, we have a train to catch."

"So have I," he shouted back.

Owain stood up and he, too, shouted, "I am Owain, your Prince and I command you to move out of the way."

"I don't care if you are King Edward, you will have to wait."

"You will be punished for your insolence."

Marged tugged at Owain. "My Prince, we are in plenty of time and he doesn't know who you really are, and he won't believe you anyway. As far as he is concerned you have been dead for 500 years at this time."

The carriage driver was shaking his head and laughing. He would have some stories to tell his friends after this day's work.

In about a quarter of a mile the rabbit laden cart pulled into the end of a farm lane to let the carriages by, and as they went the man on the cart shouted at them, "My load of rabbits is worth more than the whole lot of you."

Dafydd, in the other carriage, shouted back, "Yes, and we know where you poached them."

Marged, David and his boys burst out laughing and Marged waved to him. "It was lovely meeting you too."

Then everyone laughed, even Owain gave a chuckle as he realized that he couldn't do much to anyone in a time different to his own.

They arrived at Garth station and Buttercup put the carriage drivers on notice that they would be needed later in the day. The platform had more people on it than Marged had seen before at the other times. She admired the ladies' dresses and the exquisite hats of the day. The men too were smart in their suits of the time, some with flowers in their buttonholes. Bowlers and top hats seemed to be the male head fashion of the day.

Buttercup and David managed to buy another first-class ticket for Owain. It was the last one available. It seemed that the Wild West Shows were the most popular event in the whole of the British Isles.

As the train arrived and came to a stop Buttercup noticed her mother once again, sitting in first class. So she slipped into the group of people, hoping to conceal herself. However, her mother didn't get off; she was being joined on the train by Buttercup's father.

Buttercup went up to Marged and David and told them what she had seen. "We can't sit in the compartment where my mother and father are. I couldn't stand it."

David smiled. "Your parents are here?"

Marged stopped him. "Mr. Taylor, her parents are not married and Buttercup has not been born at this time."

"Oh, dear. Yes, of course, we had better find our own compartment."

In the meantime Owain was attracting attention. His persona was unusual to those around him to say the least. Some asked him if he was part of the Wild West Show.

"I am going to see it. In which part of it would I be?"

Marged pointed to an empty first-class compartment. "This one is ours and we won't all fit into it, so some of us will have to sit with Buttercup's father and mother in their compartment."

David nodded. "Right, me and the boys can do that and Owain can sit with us."

"Good. Oh my gosh, I just thought of something. What about Rhys Edwards and his parents? I will see if they are on the train." Marged turned and walked slowly down the platform, doing her best to avoid people getting on and off the train. She didn't see them in first class, but as she reached the first second-class carriage she spotted them and waved.

Rhys opened the window and poked his head out. "See you at the show, Marged. Is the Lady Buttercup with you? My father wants to thank her."

"Yes, she is and so is Mr. Taylor and his boys and a surprise guest. Let's meet when we get to Builth."

As she turned to go back she could see the rabbits that they had passed being loaded onto the train. She boarded, after showing the station master her ticket and sat opposite Buttercup in a window seat. Buttercup wanted to be as far away from the entrance door as possible, in case her mother came by, so she had asked the shepherd and his wife to sit in those seats. Everyone else sat in between.

It took a while before the train moved off and Marged wondered if the delay was due to the number of people boarding or the number of rabbits being loaded down the line.

Builth Road was busier than Garth and there was quite a crush of people descending the stairs that were enclosed in the wooden tower to the lower level, to catch the train into Builth. Buttercup was wary of seeing her parents and asked David what had happened to them. He told her that he had seen them catching a fancy carriage, which was going to take them into Builth, instead of the train.

There was such a cram on the short trip train into Builth that all twelve of the travellers were crowded into one compartment and Marged found herself sitting on Owain Glyn Dwr's lap. She smiled and wished her parents could see this. She would tell them, but of course they would never believe her, unless she took them into the cave and she didn't think that she should. After all, this was her great adventure.

In Builth station there were even more people milling around. All the siding tracks were full of carriages, freight and stock wagons. Marged could see that they were the trains that transported the Wild West Show around the country; many were emblazoned with pictures of events in the show.

There were dozens of people unloading wagons, horses, equipment, even a group of twenty buffaloes, North American Bison. They were huge.

Whenever Marged thought that she could get away with it, she would take pictures with her camera and slip it back into her pocket.

Rhys Edwards and his parents approached the group and they were a little confused as to how their son knew David Taylor and his boys. Marged whispered to Buttercup, "Talk to them about Rhys saving you, so they don't ask too many questions."

Buttercup spoke up. "Mr. and Mrs. Edwards, I am honoured that you could come and join us on this day. I can't tell you how grateful I and my parents are for what Rhys did for me."

Rhys was trying not to laugh, as his embarrassed parents were struggling to find words to answer Buttercup. "Thank you, my lady, you are very kind." This was about as much as they could manage.

Owain was watching the reunion and asked who they were. Buttercup stepped in. "This is Rhys Edwards who bravely saved my life and these are his parents."

"You are honourable." He looked at Rhys, "You would make a great knight in my army."

Rhys wasn't sure who this man was even though he had seen him in the cave. He would ask Marged later. Rhys' parents were also puzzled by this man with the two beards, who talked of knights in his army.

Marged led the way toward the Wye Bridge. The bridge was crowded with people this time, not cattle, as it had been on her previous visit. She noticed the residue of dried and flattened manure still on the bridge and wondered why no one had cleaned it up. Anyway, in the throng of people, hardly anyone else noticed and Marged realized that it was probably because it was normal for the time they were in.

They got across the bridge and passed the Assembly rooms, better known to Marged as the Wyeside Arts Centre. They forced their way through the crowd onto Builth Main Street to watch the parade. She turned to the group. "Let's try and get up to the top of the street, so we will be able get a good view as they come up through the town."

They made it up the street and found a suitable spot opposite Strand Street and claimed a piece of Builth street territory.

It was 20 minutes before a man in western garb came galloping around the corner, firing a pistol into the air and shouting at the crowd. Marged couldn't make out what it was he was shouting. The rider disappeared on Broad Street, because of the narrowness of the street higher up. Owain was wide-eyed, although he had been outside his time from the cave on many occasions, he had never heard a gun being fired. The rider then reappeared just below the watchers. As the rider approached, still firing his pistol, Marged finally heard what he was shouting.

"Make way for Buffalo Bill's Wild West and Congress of Rough Riders of the World."

Marged slipped out the camera again and was able to take pictures of the whole parade. It was easy because everyone's attention was focused on the parade itself. Then she exclaimed to herself. "Oh no, he's back!" The stumpy man was watching her from down the street. She hoped that he wouldn't interfere with the show.

Owain was almost mesmerized by the activity. "Why is that hand cannon so very small?"

David smiled at the Prince. "That is a gun. It is a weapon that came after your time and followed the hand cannon."

"The hand cannon is not a good weapon. It makes noise and burns the soldier who makes it work."

Everyone was cheering in reply to the pistol firing rider. Then around the corner at the head of the Grand Parade came Buffalo Bill himself on a magnificent, high-stepping, Palomino horse. The cheering was incredible as he led the parade, at a horse walk pace, up through the town waving his broad brimmed hat. A whole host of western riders followed him, and behind them were the buffalo, followed by about 40 Indians, whooping and hollering.

They were followed by a small Western Wagon Train, a stage coach and US army Cavalry. The wagons were several different kinds, some were pulled by four horses, others pulled by four oxen. One very large wagon, heavily loaded with what looked like hay and animal feed was being pulled by a team of ten mules.

As Buffalo Bill came to the top of the street, he spotted Marged and Buttercup and lifted his hand to stop the parade. Marged was astounded. Everyone else was wondering why he had stopped and then he shouted at the top of his voice, "A greeting to the medicine girls."

His horse reared up and flailed its front legs in the air and then landed. The great man approached the girls and he made the horse bow to them before continuing with the parade.

Owain was bowing with respect to the resplendent hero of the West. "He is a great king indeed."

Marged smiled. "I have told you before, where he comes from they have no kings."

The Rough Riders of the World filed by and it seemed that they were from all around the world. They were followed by the carefully controlled small herd of buffalo. There was a space of about fifty yards to the Indians on horseback. They were milling around as if in a wild state of confusion, their screams and shouts were frightening the women and even scaring some of the men, many of the children were frightened into screaming and were clinging to their mothers.

They didn't frighten Marged and Buttercup, who were shouting along with the main crowd. One of the Indians on a beautiful paint Appaloosa horse dashed out of the group. He carried a spear adorned with feathers, and, spotting Marged and Buttercup, he pulled up. The horse was wildness itself; Marged could see it in the eye.

The Indian was Sharpened Stick. He smiled. "Ho, medicine girls." Buttercup and Marged were smiling up at him and then in a second the whole host of Indians joined him, hoisting rifles, bows and spears in honour of the girls. The crowd surrounding them thought that perhaps the girls were part of the show. The Indians milled around in front of the girls for over a minute, holding up the rest of the parade. Marged was cheered when one of them almost trampled on the stumpy man which sent him off down the street to retreat into the crowd.

The Indians moved off, some of them wore beautifully feathered bonnets, denoting their status as chiefs. Further on they would turn on

Church Street for the Groe, where the show would take place later that day.

Four beautiful oxen were pulling the first wagon of the Conestoga type, with the saddle back canvas top and complete with a going west family. Most of the wagons following were also pulled by teams of four large oxen, then came the world famous Western Stage Coach, pulled by a team of six dark chestnut, lighter weight horses. Up front was the driver and the classic "riding shotgun" man. In the coach were Builth Wells dignitaries, including the Mayor, decked out in his mayoral finery and his chain of office. They all waved enjoying their celebrity status. There were about 40 US Cavalry following the stage coach, all in perfect step, four abreast. The four leaders carried a US flag with 45 stars, a Union Jack and a couple of colourful US Cavalry Guidons.

There was no Welsh Flag, which disappointed Marged. "Wow," she thought, "The English must have really been afraid of the Welsh."

Behind the cavalry were two American Civil War wagons with supplies, pulled by a mule each. These were followed by the team of ten mules, pulling the huge wagon with the large wooden wheels. The wagon was as long as a modern articulated lorry of Marged's time. There was a man on either side of the driver, carrying a rifle each. In the middle of the wagon were two more men with rifles and three more riding on top of the freight at the rear of it. David made a comment with a big grin on his face: "There must be something very valuable on that wagon for it to be defended like that."

The large wagon was followed by a marching band, playing music that excited the crowd of people along the street. Then came a whole crowd of Indian women with children. Some of the Indian women were on horseback, pulling a sledge of two poles with animal hides stretched across it, loaded with other poles and hides. Someone in the crowd pointed out that they were called "Travois."

"Oh, look at the little papooses," a woman cried out when three Indian women passed, wearing boards on their backs, on which their little babies were strapped, facing backward. The babies seemed quite indifferent to all the activity and the noisy spectators.

Other groups of riders and marchers followed. Further down the street a hunting horn or trumpet of some sort was blown by a rider, who was coming up the street at full gallop, alongside the parade, brushing the people on the edge of the crowd, who were having great difficulty getting out of the way. Then right across from Marged and her group, the crowd parted on the top of Strand Street and a cowboy came through, leading a saddled horse that he held in the middle of the High Street in readiness. He shouted, "Clear the way for the Pony Express Rider!"

The galloping rider coming up the street had put his horn away and pulled up alongside the led horse. He leaped off as the cowboy grabbed its rein. As quick as a flash he lifted a large square of leather off the saddle and dropped it over the saddle of the led horse. On each corner of the square of leather was a leather box with a flap that was padlocked. The rider leaped onto the led horse, sitting on top of the leather square. He dug his spurs, which had large rowels, into the flanks of the pony and took off up the street in an instant gallop, leaving the cowboy holding the other horse, which he led back through the crowd and back down Strand Street.

David asked to nobody in particular, "Was that some sort of saddle bag?"

Someone in the crowd nearby heard and answered, "That's what held the post, the letters; it's called a 'Mochila.'"

David thanked the person for the information.

CHAPTER 16

Five pound notes take to the bank,
When one meets itself it is no prank.
Monies invested can gather more
And over years you won't be poor.
Down to the Groe to see the Wye,
Where row boats through the waters vie.

11:30am The parade was over. The crowd dispersed and found things to do until the show started at 2:00pm. David decided to go to a bank to change a couple of five pound notes into smaller change for everyone to use during the day. There seemed to be only one bank, as far as he could tell. David entered and the others waited.

There was a queue of half a dozen people, mostly making small withdrawals of spending money for the Wild West Show. There was a stern-looking man just inside the bank. He watched all the activity with his hands behind his back. David smiled: 1904 security. Two tellers were taking care of this seemingly brisk business. When David's turn came, he handed two five pound notes to the teller and asked him to change them into smaller amounts. The teller looked at him suspiciously and asked him if he had an account in the bank.

David told him that he did not, as he was visiting from London. The man then asked him if he was in Builth to take the waters. He didn't know what the man was talking about and said no.

The teller then gave the five pound notes some close scrutiny and called a manager. The manager nodded to David, looked over the notes and could see that they were genuine and then straightened up. "We don't usually change this amount of money unless you have an account with us."

David smiled. "How much money do you need for me to open an account in your bank?"

"Five pounds would open an account, sir."

"I see. What about 500 pounds?"

The man raised his eyebrows. Was this a serious question? "Yes, sir, that would be very acceptable."

"What sort of interest could this money earn?"

"For that amount of money, about three percent, but that can vary."

"Could you guarantee that it would never earn below three percent?"

"I would need to telegraph our head office in London for you."

"Very good. Do it and I would like to open two accounts not one. And while you are telegraphing, I will fetch the man who I will want the other account for."

David stepped outside and asked the shepherd, William Williams, to come into the bank with him. The shepherd followed him and David told him that he was going to set up an account for him.

In the bank they were shown through to an office where they were asked to sit and wait for the manager. They waited 15 minutes before the manager came back and told David they could guarantee his interest request.

David thanked him, reached into his pockets, and pulled out wads of old five pound notes. The bank manager's eyes opened wide. "Where did you get that?" the manager asked.

William's eyes opened wider than the managers.

David kept his cool and smiled. "I have been a high stakes gambler for many years. Much of this money I won in New York and had it changed to pounds to bring back to Britain."

"I see. Why are you bringing it to us in Builth Wells?"

"I want to set up some funds to help shepherds and farmers in the area and to possibly buy an estate."

"I see," the manager said again. "How do you want to go about this?"

"First I would like to set up an account in the name of David Taylor, with the sum of 100 pounds to accrue interest and not to be touched until May the twelfth, 2004. I might add more money to that account later. There is to be no communication from you or your bank until May the twelfth, 2004, and the communication is to be sent to this address." David wrote down the address with a bright red ballpoint pen, with black ink, on a slip of paper he had pulled from his pocket and handed it to the manager. "Over time, I will check in with you and the account."

The manager was staring at David and the ballpoint pen. "This is highly irregular, sir. I may need to contact headquarters again."

"That will be fine, but before you do, I would also like you to open an account for a William Williams." He stopped. "Do you have any other names, Mr. Williams?"

"Morgan. Morgan is my middle name."

"Very good. Then the account should be opened in the name of William Morgan Williams and allowed to accrue interest until the middle of June 1940, and all notifications withheld until that time. The notification at that time is to be sent to Mr. William Morgan Williams at," he stopped and asked the shepherd his address on Epynt.

William gave the address, "Ty Beth Cottage, Llangammarch Wells, Breconshire."

The manager made a note of it and turned to David. "How much do you want to place in this account?"

"Five hundred pounds now and more will be added later."

"That is a lot of money. I will have to telegraph London again for approval. I hope you don't mind?"

"Not at all. Please make sure that Mr. Williams is notified at his address no later than June the fourteenth, 1940."

"Very good, sir.

"Just a moment, before you go." David thought about this date; it would mean that the Williams' would have to go back to the Epynt before they had left and that would not work. If he made the date later, the notification would be turned away by the army. He paused for a moment or two to think about it. He almost popped outside to ask Marged what she thought of the situation when it came to him. He turned to Mr. Williams. "Would you be able to pick up your letters at a Post Office?"

"Yes. Llangammarch, Post Office."

"Excellent." He turned to the manager. "Please have any correspondence from your bank for Mr. Williams sent to the Post Office in Langammack Wells and remember; none before June the fourteenth, 1940."

"Very well, sir. And no correspondence to his home address."

"That is exactly what you must do."

Outside the crowd was still milling around and Marged was staying close to Owain, who didn't say much but did a lot of observing.

The shepherd's wife, Heulwen, asked, "Why did Mr. Taylor ask William to go in there to the bank? We don't have any money, you know."

Marged smiled. "I don't know, but remember you haven't been born yet, so you wouldn't have money in the bank any way."

"I will never get used to this. They are not robbing the bank, are they?"

"No, but Mr. Taylor works in a bank in his time. Perhaps that is why they are in there."

The five boys were chasing each other, playing some sort of tag game and Buttercup was in the thick of it, doing her best to make them behave like young gentlemen. The two shepherd girls and Rhys Edwards's parents were laughing as they watched.

Back inside the bank while the manager was checking the telegraph, William looked David up and down. Then, he asked the question: "You are putting money into an account in my name. Why are you doing that?"

"You are being turned off Epynt without recompense, and your livelihood has been taken away from you. In my time, this money is worthless, and there is a lot of it in the bank vaults where I work, so if I bring it to this time where it is still legal tender, I can do some good with it, like helping you out and perhaps others."

The security man overheard some of the conversation but not all of it. He frowned.

"This is very kind of you. And you an Englishman. How will I pay you back?"

"I don't want you to pay me back. It is my contribution for what has been done to you and your way of life. It's not going to cost me anything. I will continue to add money to the account and you will not have access to it until the middle of June 1940. By then there should be enough money in the account, with the interest that has accrued, to buy a farm outright and all the livestock you will need. What you must remember to do is to go to the Post Office in Langammack and pick up the details of your account. You could go there directly from the cave."

The security man overheard the word cave and frowned again, but didn't comment.

William was a little confused about the whole situation. "Well, I don't altogether understand what is going on with this time thing. We are here in 1904 aren't we?"

"That is right, yes we are."

"This is a very odd thing, because I won't be born until next year."

"Yes, it is an odd thing and takes some getting used to. At this time you are probably older than your parents."

The security man's eyebrows were almost hitting the top of his forehead.

William shook his head. "Boy, I never thought of that."

"Did they come to the Wild West Show?"

"I don't know. Perhaps they did."

"I think you would know if they did and if they did they might be here and you will see them."

"Oh, duw. I don't know if I can manage all this. Please, don't tell me anymore."

The bank manager returned. He looked down at them. "I have talked to the manager in London and yes, we can accept your money into the accounts that you have requested. Follow me into my office. We will count your deposits there and I will have my assistant present to verify."

David turned to William. "Come along. Let's get you an account." They followed the manager back into the office.

In the office David and William were asked to sit facing a large desk. The manager sat opposite, next to his assistant, who had several important sheets of paper in front of him.

The manager stared across the desk with such a stern look that David thought that perhaps he was going to be sentenced to jail. It seemed that stern looks were required in the 1904 banking business.

"Now, Mr. Taylor and Mr. Williams, we have some paperwork for you to sign and fill out." Sheets of paper were handed to David and William and a bottle of ink and a nibbed pen with a wooden handle.

David smiled, reached into an inside pocket and produced the red ballpoint pen. "We will do it with this. It will be easier for me. I got it in America. Very clever those Americans, you know."

The manager nodded acceptance and pointed to the areas of the paperwork which David had to fill in. Once David and William had signed the papers the manager looked them over with an air of great importance. "Thank you, gentlemen. Now, the deposits."

David reached back into his pocket, hauled out the wad of five pound notes and began counting them out into piles of ten. The manager picked them up and counted them out again in front of the assistant, and then the assistant counted them and placed them to the side of the desk, making a note on a piece of paper with the nibbed pen.

David counted out twelve piles of five pound notes and sat back while the two very serious, dedicated men verified everything. When it was over the manager instructed the assistant to place the money in the safe. They all stood up. "Thank you, gentlemen, for doing business with us. Is there anything else we can do for you?"

David smiled. "Yes. I still want to change two five pound notes into smaller units. Say four one pound notes, six ten shilling notes and various denominations of coinage."

"Yes, of course. I will have a teller take care of that for you.'

David and William were led back into the main area of the bank and the manager spoke to one of the tellers who was serving others. One teller nodded to his manager and looked up and acknowledged David. In a couple of minutes David was in front of him and made the transaction for the change.

He placed the money in his trouser pockets and he and William Williams turned to leave, when they heard the teller shriek in alarm. They turned back and the teller was as white as an old five pound note. The manager who had gone back to his office came out again to see what was going on.

The teller was pointing to the cash drawer under the counter; he was totally speechless. The manager looked at the drawer and asked what the matter was. After a few seconds the teller regained his voice. "I, I, er put the two five pound notes in the drawer and there was a flash of light. I shut it quickly without thinking. Something has happened in there."

David and William waited and all transactions in the bank had stopped. All eyes were on the teller, including those of the security man.

The manager looked sternly at the teller. "Well, you had better open it so that we can take a look."

Cautiously the teller opened the drawer and a very faint, almost unnoticeable, wisp of blue smoke came out of it. The teller reached in and picked up the two five pound notes which David had passed to him and in a split second his face went whiter than ever.

The manager looked at him. "What's the matter?"

"Ah,er, Sir. There is a five pound note missing."

"What do you mean? What did you do with it?"

"Sir, it was there when I put these two notes in the drawer and there was a blue flash."

"A blue flash. What are you talking about?"

"When I put the money in the drawer there was a blue flash; I shut the drawer quickly, I didn't know what else to do."

"Where is your ledger?"

"Here on the counter, Sir."

"Hand it to me." He did as he was asked and then he was instructed to sit on a seat against the wall, behind the teller's desk. The teller sat down with a lot of stress on his face, the manager called to his assistant to verify the ledger, and count the money in the drawer. It took about four minutes and yes, there was five pounds missing. The manager turned to the teller sitting on the seat. "You will stay there until the police get here. You will be searched, so you might as well confess and return the five pounds right away."

The teller was horrified. "I didn't steal it, sir."

"Well, we'll soon find out." Then he instructed his assistant to go and find a policeman and he ordered the security man to stand over the teller.

The assistant rushed out of the bank on his mission. David knew what had happened and was wondering how he could make things right for the teller, who he knew was innocent.

He approached the manager while he reached into his pocket. "I think I might have made a terrible mistake when I gave your teller the money. I might have inadvertently taken back the one five pound note, when I put the pounds and ten shilling notes in my pocket." He produced a five pound note from his pocket.

"Are you sure of this, Mr. Taylor?"

"Yes, I am. I am completely certain."

"Well, I hope you are right. But I am still going to have him searched by a police officer when he gets here."

He had no sooner said it, when the door opened and in came a constable with the manager's assistant. The manager showed him through to the office where David had been and had the teller follow him in to be searched. In about ten minutes the officer came out and announced that no five pound note had been found.

The manager was frustrated and looked at David. "It seems that you are right, Mr. Taylor, but I am afraid I will have to let that boy go, because he should have spotted the mistake."

David shook his head as he handed the five pound note in his hand to the manager; then he took him aside. "I do not want you to fire him. I am going to insist that you keep him in your employ." David looked at him sternly. "If you do fire him later and I hear about it, I will withdraw my accounts immediately."

The manager sternly nodded. "Very well, Mr. Taylor."

David and William left the bank and David began to wonder about the five pound notes of his that had been placed in the safe. Would they meet up with their doubles?

Outside, David smiled at everyone waiting. "I have spending money for the day. Thanks to Lady Buttercup, each young person gets five shillings."

Dafydd Jones was astounded. Rhys' parents were astonished that this young lady would dole out money so readily. They were even more astonished when David handed them a pound note each. They tried to resist, but Buttercup stepped in. "It is my wish that everyone have money to enjoy the day, so please me by taking it and do not offend me by refusing."

Although they took the money reluctantly, they were grateful and were impressed with what they assumed was the chivalrous act of their son for The Lady Buttercup.

The shepherd's children were also astonished at such riches being handed to them. Their mother was almost in tears at such generosity, and William took her aside to explain what David had done for them.

Owain, was doing his best to understand what a bank was, as well as the shops and the hundreds of people milling around. Marged stayed close to him. Whenever he asked a question, she did her best to answer him and was often surprised at how he had his own method of understanding the world around him.

She described in her own way what a bank was. "A bank is where people put their money for safe keeping. The bank lets other people use that money and they pay the bank back with a little extra money."

The great Prince frowned. "Why would a person take money from the bank and give it back with extra?"

Marged smiled. "When they take money from the bank, they do things with it that help them make more money, so then they can give the money back to the bank with a little extra money, out of what the bank's money made for them."

"Hmm. So why would your King keep his money here? Why wouldn't he keep it where his palace is?"

"It is not the King's money. It is the people's money and the King only spends his money for the good of the people, but the King's money is controlled by representatives of the people. If the King kept his money in the palace, it wouldn't be there for the people, so it is placed in banks all over England and Wales."

"Many of the times I have been outside the cave, Wales and England are together. I do not understand why Wales would let this happen."

"You were the last person who tried not to let it happen. After you, no one else tried until a Welshman claimed the throne and his son became King of all Wales and all England."

"Who was this great King?"

"He was Henry Tudor. Since then, England and Wales have been together, but in my time Wales has its own parliament as well."

"So my work freeing Wales from that English King Henry IV was in vain?"

"No. My father says you laid the seeds for a united Wales, and it's because of you that Wales has stayed Welsh, even though it is a part of England."

"I have learned much since I went into the cave, and I am pleased about many of these things. In my time I have travelled far and learned Latin and French and gained much knowledge that I would use to rule Wales. With the new knowledge I have been learning, I will be able to teach much in my time and prepare people for the future I have seen. It troubles me much that I can't get back to my time."

"I have said that I can get you out, so that you can make things right at the Battle of Bryn Glas. I will also help you get back to the time you first came to the cave. I have more calculations to do and then it will happen. You will never go out of the cave at the wrong time again. Now, let's follow everyone else."

They turned and walked briskly to catch up on the others, who were on the trail of the Wild West Parade.

They got to the gate to the Groe at the end of Church Street, but were not allowed through because of the preparations and the setting up of the show. So they turned and walked west to the fields close to the Irfon River. It was there that they met people coming from the Mineral Wells who were on their way to see the show.

Marged took the lead and turned to the Wye on the west edge of where the show would take place. There were a few people boating on the river. Marged thought the scene to be lovely; there was no boating in her time. The weir that was across the river just in front of the bridge was washed away many years before her time, so the water was not held back for boating anymore. The group watched for quite a while before making their way back into town.

At the bottom of Strand Street people were beginning to queue up at the Groe's east entrance.

CHAPTER 17

The Pony Express runs in Mid Wales.
Mail delivered through wind and gales.
Wagon trains and a cattle drive
On prairies and our Groe yet thrive.
Sharp shooting marksmen from east and west,
But its horsemanship that comes out best.

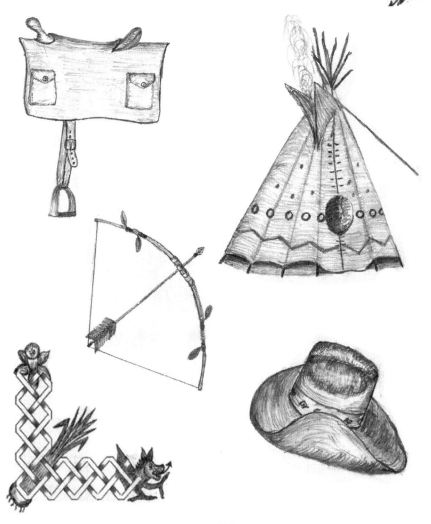

They got themselves to the end of the queue, and within half a minute there were hundreds of people behind them.

At the entrance, Marged handed in the pass signed by William Cody and the tickets they had purchased. The man in the booth called over another man standing nearby. "Tom, these are the medicine girls the boss was talking about. Could you escort them and their group to the first class privileged area and place the girls in front."

"Yes sir, Mr. Rowlands. Follow me please."

The man led the group to a set of stands that the Wild West crew had constructed for much of the audience. He placed them in front, on seats which were specifically reserved for them. The show had not started, but the entire arena where the show would take place was a vibrant muddle of activity. In the middle to one side, five tepees had been erected and two fires had been built between them. There were about 20 Indian women and children involved in all sorts of activities. The crushing of grains, weaving, cleaning hides, cooking and all sorts of domestic actions were taking place around the tepees.

Groups of men with saddled horses had stationed themselves around the arena and a couple of them seemed to have a farrier on hand.

In the middle at the other end of the arena, the herd of twenty buffalo grazed peacefully as if they were back on the prairie. No one seemed to be caring for them or even bothering to watch them, and neither were the beasts taking any notice of what was going on around them.

Between the sections of the stands were platforms, and on each stood a man. Marged was curious about what their role might be. She didn't have to wait long; they were the announcers.

Using a large horn the first called out. "My Lords, Ladies and Gentlemen. Please stand for the anthems." And he was quickly echoed around the arena by the others. The band struck up "Hail, Columbia." Marged wondered whose anthem it was. For America, she had expected "The Star Spangled Banner." Nobody sang until the band played "God Save the King." David enthusiastically joined in the singing and gained a few curious looks, not because of his voice but because he was singing "God Save the Queen." Marged had done the same thing; however, nobody overheard her and she quickly realized her mistake.

As soon as the anthems were over the announcers spoke up in their loud voices. "My Lords, Ladies and Gentlemen, Colonel William F. Cody."

Marged was curious as to why they didn't play the Welsh National Anthem.

At the end of the arena a rider entered at full gallop. It was the great man himself. He rode around the arena once and stopped in front of the girls for the second time that day. This time it was because it was the centre of the stands, and this was where he greeted the crowd. He took his hat off and waved to the roaring people for about four minutes. Then, he wheeled his horse and galloped back to where he had come in, turned, pulled the horse up and positioned himself like a mounted sentry, so he could observe the arena and direct the parts of the show that didn't involve him.

The announcers yelled out again, "My Lords, Ladies and Gentlemen, the Pony Express! Mr. Johnny Fry leaves Saint Joseph, Missouri for Marysville, Kansas, on the first leg that will take the mail all the way to Sacramento, California."

Again at the end of the arena a rider came through at an incredibly fast gallop past the crowd. He completed the circuit in just over a minute. As he rode, his horse's hooves picked up clods of turf and dirt. He came half way around again, blew a horn and then there was a repetition of what had occurred earlier in the street parade. A horse was led out in front of the stands and the rider pulled up, dismounted and switched the Mochila, remounted and continued to gallop around the arena.

There followed another announcement: "My Lords, Ladies and Gentlemen the Pony Express has to be supplied and maintained. Behold the Mule Train!"

The large laden wagon, pulled by the ten mules, entered the arena and began its journey around the circuit. The guards they had seen before were on board, and this time there were also four horses being led, tied onto the back of the wagon. Two of them had saddles. While they circled the arena the Pony Express riders galloped around and changed horses. The first rider had been joined by three others, two of them galloping in the other direction.

The announcers continued with a narration. "Every rider rides ten miles and changes horses at a relay station. When he has completed about a 100 miles, he himself is allowed to rest and return later in the other direction with the mail from Sacramento. What is this we see? A horse has thrown a shoe and has become lame. The rider has to lead the horse into the station."

The horse was led to where another horse was waiting to be mounted. The rider swapped the Mochila, mounted the fresh horse and galloped away. The lame horse, that was trained to feign lameness at the rider's signal, was led over to a farrier, who made it look as if he was treating the foot and replacing the shoe.

The riders continued and did two more circuits before there was a shout and four Indians came into the arena, whooping and hollering in pursuit of one of the riders. As they passed the girls, the closeness of the horses was breathtaking, coupled with the thundering hooves and the scattering dirt. The rider had drawn his pistol and had begun to fire back at his pursuers. One of the Indians made a spectacular fall off his horse and this was followed by another crashing to the ground, horse and all. The rider had gained on the remaining two and the announcers continued the narration.

"The Pony Express rider has beaten his pursuers and the mail gets through once again."

The crowd roared their approval and then about ten more Indians came galloping into the arena, and headed for the mule train wagon. Two of the people riding on the wagon undid the two saddled horses and led them up alongside the wagon as it was moving. They leaped into the saddles with their rifles and raced ahead of the mules. The five guards remaining on the wagon began firing their rifles at the Indians who were catching up fast. Three of the Indians made spectacular falls off the horses, then the two riders came back past the wagon and rode toward the oncoming Indians, firing their rifles, and two more Indians came off their horses. The wagon driver had whipped up the mules and they were soon pulling the wagon at full gallop. The two riders turned, holstered their rifles and were now galloping alongside the wagon, firing back at the Indians, with their pistols joining the fire from the five firing from the wagon itself. Two more Indians went down, horses and all, and the remaining group pulled up, turned and retreated.

The narrative continued: "The supply wagon has been saved and they will reach the next relay station safely."

The crowd continued to approve as the Pony Express left the arena.

"My Lords, Ladies and Gentlemen, to survive in the Wild West you have to shoot, so let's see what our sharpshooters can do." Several men and two women came into the arena from between the stands, all dressed in gaily embroidered buckskins. Half of them carried rifles and shotguns. They all wore gun belts with pistols.

Two of the men without rifles or shotguns began throwing things in the air, and those that did have weapons began to shoot at the objects in the air. None were missed. Then, the rifles and shotguns were handed to assistants, and the shooters began using their pistols. Again there were no misses.

The announcers continued with more narration: "Shooting from the saddle is vital for your survival on the prairies."

In front of the stands some of the shooting staff had erected a row of plates about ten feet apart, in front of a section of bank on the far side of the Groe which was clear of people.

Two riders came into the arena and began galloping toward the targets; as they closed in on them, they held their rifles using both hands; the horses continued to gallop, being guided by the knees of their sharp shooting riders. There were eight plates. The first rider fired four shots in quick succession, taking out every other of the plates. The second rider, right on his heels took out the other four. The crowd once again roared their approval.

After a few more spectacular trick shots the announcers called attention to the Indian camp in the middle and to one side of the arena. "My Lords, Ladies and Gentlemen, the Indians are about to go on the warpath."

Lots of Indians, faces painted, began appearing from the tepees. They wore breach cloths and little else. Soon, they were dancing around the fires, to the beating of a very large drum played by six Indians sitting around it.

"And here's the reason they are going on the warpath. My Lords, Ladies and Gentlemen, we introduce to you, George Armstrong Custer and the United States 7th Cavalry."

Entering the arena was Buffalo Bill as George Armstrong Custer at the head of two columns of cavalry. A band at the end of one of the stands played the Gary Owen. The Indians mounted their horses and began to gallop around the arena, as the cavalry gathered on a mound close to the middle but opposite the Indian camp. The Indians then turned to gallop around the cavalry who had dismounted and had laid down their horses as a living breastworks to defend themselves. The Indians were firing rifles into the group of soldiers, who were pretending to die in many different ways, some unimaginable. The Indians too were collapsing off their horses. Whiffs of smoke and the cordite smells from the guns were drifting about the arena. It made people think they were in the middle of a real battle. The whole re-enactment went on for 20 minutes. Finally, Buffalo Bill, as Custer, was shot down and the Battle of the Little Bighorn ended.

The crowd roared as before. As the noise died down the Epynt shepherd William Williams and Prince Owain enthusiastically discussed the incredible horsemanship they had witnessed, as if they were old friends, neither concerned for the rank of the other. Marged thought it was wonderful and was beginning to grasp that a commonality between people could easily overcome rank and elitism.

As she turned her attention back to the activities in the arena, two men walked up to them and asked for the medicine girls. Marged and Buttercup made themselves known, and the men asked them to stand on the front seats about 20 feet apart. They asked what for.

The men smiled and the senior of them said, "You will have to wait and see, but whatever you do, you must not get off the seats under any circumstances. You will not be hurt. We are making you part of the show."

They both smiled and climbed onto the seats. The men moved off and the announcers piped up once more: "My Lords, Ladies and Gentlemen, the American Stage Coach."

At the end of the arena, the team of six dark chestnut horses came galloping in, pulling the stagecoach which they had seen earlier in the parade. It pulled up at the first set of stands, and several local dignitaries climbed aboard including the mayor, once again. Boxes and luggage were tossed up onto the top of the stagecoach, and the driver and his shotgun rider packed them there and tied them down. They were in full Western gear, including the classic cowboy hats. Once the packing had been done, they moved to their positions at the front of the coach. The shotgun man picked up his rifle. The driver picked up the reins, and the horses were galvanized into action, almost pulling the coach off its wheels.

The coach sped past the girls, it was so close they were almost blown off the seats by the rush of wind. As it completed its first circuit, about 20 Indians came in and chased it. The driver whipped up the horses. They were now galloping faster than ever. The man riding shotgun moved up and lay down on top of the luggage, firing his rifle at them. There were more spectacular falls of Indians and horses, one right in front of the girls as they went past.

On the next circuit the Indians were chased by the US Cavalry and the crowd went crazy with their cheering. The stagecoach was completely surrounded by Indians, as it again approached the girls, but this time the Indians were beginning to disperse as the cavalry gained on them. However, two of the Indians came galloping along, right in front of the stands. The first one passed Buttercup so close he brushed against her dress and in the next split second he had picked up Marged in his arm and hoisted her behind him onto the horse. Before Buttercup could understand what was happening, she too was picked up and was sat on the horse in front of the next Indian.

The announcers were doing their best to describe what was going on, but not everyone could hear them due to the noise of the crowd. "The cavalry has saved the day, but, oh, oh, what has happened!? The Indians are out of control! They have captured two members of the audience. Where's the cavalry? Stop them!"

Marged was hanging on for dear life as they galloped around the arena. The fear she felt didn't occur until she realized what had happened and then she also realized she was riding with the Indian she had helped, Sharpened Stick. Her fear then subsided a little. He spoke to her as they galloped. "Hello, medicine girl. Chief Cody say that you are to be honoured by being part of our show. Hold on tight."

The Indian who had picked up Buttercup, Dark Sky Day, told her the same thing. They were galloped around the arena in one complete circuit, then they were taken to the edge of the camp in the middle, where the girls were lowered off the horses and loosely tied to poles, as part of the show. The two Indians told them that they would be rescued by the soldiers and invited them to visit their camp after the show was over.

The melee between Indians and cavalry continued around the arena for another four minutes and then dispersed. The Indians gathered at their camp and the cavalry left the arena where they regrouped.

The announcers continued: "The captives have to be rescued, and who better to get on the trail than the great scout and buffalo hunter, Colonel William F. Cody."

The far end of the arena opened up and in came Buffalo Bill on his incredible horse at the head of a double column of US Cavalry. Everyone cheered and even Owain got into the excitement of it all. Every 200 yards or so Buffalo Bill would lift his hand, and the whole column would stop while he got off his horse and pretended to look for a trail leading to the Indian camp. Then, he would point ahead and climb back onto his horse. Eventually he pointed towards the Indian encampment, and as soon as he remounted the whole cavalry took off at full gallop, right into the Indian village. The Indians scrambled in a great performance of panic, some pulled soldiers off their horses, others managed to get to their horses and were then pursued by some of the cavalry. Buffalo Bill rode right up to where the girls were tied to the posts, dismounted and untied them. He picked Buttercup up and lifted her up to a mounted soldier, who sat her down in front of him. Buffalo Bill remounted, reached down and picked Marged up and placed her in front of him, and the two riders took off around the arena.

The announcers yelled to try to be heard over the roaring crowd. "The captives have been rescued! Three cheers for Buffalo Bill and the United States Cavalry!"

The crowd continued to roar and give three cheers all at the same time. After two trips around the arena, the girls were dropped off onto the seats from which they were picked up and the announcers cried out! "Three cheers for the medicine girls!" And another round of cheers erupted from the crowd. Marged and Buttercup waved as they expressed huge smiles at their new found fame, a fame that came to them before either girl had been born. Marged wondered what the crowd would say to that.

The cavalry regrouped and filed out of the arena with Buffalo Bill once more at their head. The Indians went back to their camp area and the announcers were heard once more: "My Lords, Ladies and Gentlemen, we will now have a shooting competition between our sharpshooters and the Indians, who will use bows and arrows."

Three wagons were brought into the arena and were placed about a 100 feet in front of the stands. They had high wooden sides that faced the audience and in front were targets. Six sharpshooters came into the arena from between the stands and six Indians with bows and arrows came into the shooting area from their camp.

The targets were discs of paper, about three inches in diameter, on sticks.

Three Indians and three sharpshooters stepped up in pairs, to about 40 feet from the targets, in front of a wagon each. One sharpshooter fired and hit the disc. It was replaced. Then an Indian stepped up and fired an arrow, and the next target was disintegrated as the arrow split the target, shattering the wood to which it was pinned. The next pair did the same, followed by another pair. There were three rounds of shooting and a perfect score each time. The targets were changed to discs two inches in diameter and there was another three rounds of perfect shooting.

Marged noticed that when the shooters stepped up, there was absolute silence from the thousands of people watching as if everybody was holding their breath at the same time. The contrast from the noises earlier was stunning. The only time the silence was broken as they stepped up was the singing of an occasional bird and the calls of jackdaws flying between the houses nearby.

The next targets were set up and this time they were less than an inch in diameter. The following three rounds were exciting. In the first round one Indian missed, in the second round a sharpshooter missed and it was down to the last round to see who would win. The last sharpshooter to fire missed, and then it was up to the last Indian to shoot; he hit the target fair and square. The third and last hit won the competition.

Instead of stepping up and shooting his bow, he handed it to the sharpshooter to hold and then did a little dance. The crowd applauded and laughed and then he took the sharpshooters' rifle and took a mirror from one of the assistants and turned to face the crowd. Marged and Buttercup, who were now sitting back with the audience, recognized the Indian at once. It was Dark Sky Day, their Indian with the rifle. He smiled at the girls and gave a big wink; he lifted the mirror and placed the rifle over his shoulder, pointing toward the target. He adjusted the mirror a couple of times, then adjusted the rifle and fired. The bullet hit the target.

As the audience applauded his skill, he handed the rifle back to the sharpshooter, took back his bow and quiver of arrows; he turned and walked back toward the audience, and as he did he knocked an arrow firmly into the bow, and in a split second turned on one foot and fired the arrow at one of the missed targets, it split straight through the middle and thudded into the high sided wagon.

The announcer declared that the Indians had won the competition.

The crowd cheered and applauded and a voice in the back of the stands screamed out, "Can you hit this?" It was a man holding up his top hat. He was about 80 feet away.

The Indian smiled and shouted back. "Put it on your head and stand at the back behind the people."

The man did as he was asked, the arrow was fired and it went straight through the hat and got stuck in the canvas behind him. The crowd were astonished and cheered again as the man took the hat off his head and stuck his thumb through one of the holes that the arrow had made.

Marged wondered if the man was part of the show or just some squire doing it for a bet.

Owain was beside himself with admiration for the Indians' skill with the bow. He turned to the shepherd, "I have many skilled archers in my army, but not one of them has those kind of skills. That was very impressive."

The wagons stayed in the arena and the two inch targets were set up again as the announcers introduced the next part of the show. "My Lords, Ladies and Gentlemen, the west and east has to be fed and what could be better than Texas Beef? Behold, the Cattle Drive!"

At the far end of the arena a cowboy came in, followed by a herd of about a hundred cattle flanked by more cowboys. The herd was a mix which made Marged curious. The leading cattle were genuine Texas Longhorns; two of them had a horn span of almost seven feet. There were about a dozen of them in the lead altogether, followed by horned cattle of all sorts, even Welsh Blacks. Marged wondered if they would have Welsh Blacks in America and if so why would they bring them to Wales where there were hundreds of them in that time.

The cattle were herded around the arena and every so often the cowboys would demonstrate some of the skills for which they were famous-lassoing calves by skilfully roping the back legs and pulling them off the main track, to where four cowboys were demonstrating a branding operation. Some calves were captured by cowboys who leaped off their horses and grasped the running calf around the neck and pulled it to the ground. The cowboy would then tie its legs, ready to be branded.

Other displays included cutting out specific cattle. This was done by requests from the audience. It was amusing to hear the requests from local cattle farmers who knew their cattle well. The cattle they picked out were not the easiest to cut out: cross-bred, fierce-looking steers, cows that had to be separated from their young calves and an angry looking bull.

The cowboys were enjoying the requests. After all, they were performing for people who knew cattle as well as they did, if not better. It was almost alarming to watch a cowboy thrust his horse into the middle of the moving herd of horned cattle and separate the animals out to the edge. The horse was instantly controlled by the slightest movement of the rider, using knees and neck reining. When a cow or steer tried to regain the main herd, the horse would face it five or six feet away and whichever way the animal moved, the horse moved to block it. It was a movement that was unusual for a horse to make; it would lift its two front feet together and plant them wherever they had to be, to face down the steer or cow. It was as if the horse was dancing in front of the cow to control it.

The cattle drive was a marvellous display and Marged smiled and turned to David and Buttercup, "I wonder how these cowboys would have managed the cattle crossing the Wye Bridge when we came to get the tickets."

David chuckled. "That would be interesting to see, wouldn't it?"

They laughed.

The cattle left the arena and the announcers piped up again. "My Lords, Ladies and Gentlemen, Buffalo Bill and the Congress of Rough Riders of the World."

Buffalo Bill entered the arena once more. This time he was at the head of the most amazing assortment of colourful riders anyone had ever seen. There were, of course, cowboys, followed by Cossacks in beautifully appointed tunics and pantaloons. Following them came a whole troop of Mexican riders in exquisitely embroidered jackets and wearing huge sombreros. Behind them were eight white Lipizzaner Stallions of the Spanish Riding School, their riders dressed in dark maroon tunics, white breeches, knee-high boots and on their heads were hats that looked as if they were being worn sideways.

Marged nudged Buttercup, "I don't think that they are rough riders. I think that they are more like smooth riders."

Buttercup giggled.

Following the Spanish School, in amazing contrast, were six mounted Indian chiefs in full ceremonial dress, with flowing feather headdresses. They were leading an undisciplined troop of war painted braves. Right on their tail was a British Army cavalry unit, resplendent in their uniforms. There was nothing rough about the way they were dressed. Behind them came horsemen from the steppes of Mongolia. The announcers called it the land of Genghis Khan. There were riders of the French Cavalry and a couple of gaudily dressed groups whose names were not announced. However, they did announce the last group that came into the arena.

"My Lords, Ladies and Gentlemen, please welcome our President Mr.

Theodore Roosevelt's true Rough Riders, the heroes of San Juan Hill."

Marged approved, because they really did look like a rough lot of riders. The groups all galloped around the arena, led by Buffalo Bill himself, who every few yards would take off his large wide-brimmed cowboy hat and wave to the crowd.

After a complete circuit, the riders broke into their respective groups and began showing their incredible skills in horsemanship. There were horse and rider activities all over the arena. Each group would perform for about three minutes and then move into another position and perform again and this continued until everyone in the audience had had a close up view of all the groups, except the Indians and the Mongolians.

They waited for the others to finish. Then these two groups went into action. A Mongolian took off at a gallop, followed by an Indian, followed by another Mongolian, and then another Indian and they continued like this until they were all in line. They galloped around the arena at top speed. As they went, they drew their bows and arrows, and as soon as they came around to the stand side of the arena, they began firing arrows at the two inch targets. The Mongolians never missed, the Indians missed twice, but all in all it was an incredible display of marksmanship and horsemanship combined.

Owain was astounded by this display of skills and exclaimed, "If I had those men in my army I could defeat all the English soldiers in the land! I have heard of this Genghis Khan. Why are his people so good?"

David Taylor heard his question and was able to answer him because he had seen a documentary on television about these people. "They train to fire arrows accurately from a horse, but they only fire when all the horses' feet are in the air at the same time. The two Indians who missed, did so because at least one of their horse's feet was on the ground."

Owain shook his head. "My archers are said to be some of the best in the world, but I doubt if they could hit that target, even if they were stood still taking careful aim."

The Rough Rider extravaganza was over, so they filed out of the arena, followed by the high-sided wagons.

The next event was a buffalo hunt. Several Indians rounded up the buffalo and chased them around the arena. The announcers explained that normally the Indians would ride up close to the buffalo and fire arrows or throw spears into them. One of the Indians the girls had helped, Sharpened Stick, was in the chase. He got ahead of the buffalo by a good distance. His horse stumbled and off he came. Marged was afraid for him because he was right in the path of the galloping beasts.

The announcers cried out with panic. "There's an Indian down! He's going to get trampled by the buffalo! This is terrible!"

People picked up on the urgency in the announcer's voice and gasped with the horror of what might happen. Nobody was more worried than Marged and Buttercup. Then, just in time, Sharpened Stick was on his feet. Instead of getting out of the way, he began running, as a buffalo came up at full gallop beside him. He reached out, grasped the thick mane of the animal and swung himself up onto its back and rode it around the arena.

The crowd went wild and the announcers, who could barely be heard over the noise, continued with the narration, "When you lose your horse, a buffalo will do."

Sharpened Stick, slipped off the buffalo as it passed the Indian encampment. The rest of the Indians gave up the chase. There was a blast of music and the announcers spoke up again: "My Lords, Ladies and Gentlemen, the greatest buffalo hunter of all time, the great buffalo hunter himself, Buffalo Bill Cody."

The crowd cheered and hollered as Buffalo Bill rode into the arena at full gallop. As he got close to the buffalo he extracted a rifle from a large holster strapped to the front of the saddle. He let go of the reins completely and steered the horse with his knees. He rode up to one buffalo at a time and fired his rifle at point blank range. The buffaloes continued to run, as he was only firing blanks. If he had been firing bullets, every one of the animals would have been lying dead in that arena. It was an incredible display of horsemanship. If one of those giant beasts had decided to turn against the horse when it was so close, the great man would have probably been killed or severely injured.

The noises died down. The only activity was in the Indian camp, where a war dance had begun again. The announcers described the situation. "The Indians are celebrating a successful buffalo hunt or are they getting ready to go on the war path?"

There were more of them dancing this time and the drum was beaten faster. After about five minutes, the end of the arena opened and a wagon pulled by a team of oxen entered. Just ahead was a rider in western garb leading the way. Eight more covered wagons followed into the arena, all but one pulled by oxen. That one was pulled by mules. Men, women and children were walking alongside and there were several outriders on horses. There were a couple of small carts in between the wagons, pulled by single mules. In these carts were various farm tools and a couple of wooden ploughs. In one there were a couple of pigs and in a couple of others there were geese and chickens. Behind some of the wagons there were cows being led along. It was a true going west wagon train.

As soon as they were well into the arena the announcers spoke up again, "My Lords, Ladies and Gentlemen, the wagon train moves west, taking our hard-working citizens to new lands."

People applauded and some cheered. Marged watched closely as the wagon train passed the warrior Indians, in full war paint and bonnets. The Indians had stopped dancing. They were now mounting their horses. She turned to Buttercup. "I think the Indians are going to attack the wagon train."

Buttercup nodded. "It will be alright. I expect that silly cavalry of theirs will come to the rescue."

"Yes, I expect you are right, but it's a lot of fun, though, isn't it?"

Buttercup smiled, giggled and nodded in agreement.

The Indians moved off and began to trot around to the other side of the arena. They positioned themselves so they could pick up speed and chase the wagon train. As the wagon train rounded the far end of the arena, a rider galloped in at the other end. He was shouting at the top of his voice, "The Indians are coming! The Indians are coming!" He galloped after the wagon train and caught up with them as they turned on to the back stretch of the arena. "The Indians are coming! Form a circle!"

He kept repeating his alarm and the wagons picked up speed, but not much because oxen are not prone to gallop. However, the wagons turned into the empty spot in the middle of the arena and began to form a circle, as the Indians went in pursuit past the stands at full gallop. They rounded the far end and got to the wagons as the circle was completed.

The people in the wagons were unloading pieces of furniture and bags of what must have been grains or potatoes, and began placing these items between the wheels. The oxen and mules had been unhitched and were actually grazing in the middle, oblivious to the action which was unfolding all around them.

Indians were soon galloping around the circled wagons, firing arrows that were going over the heads of the defenders. To shield themselves from the wagon train defenders, the Indians hung off the sides of their horses, with an arm around the middle of the horse's neck and fired their arrows from underneath. It was spectacular horsemanship.

The defenders themselves had two muzzle loading guns each, and as soon as they fired one of them they handed it to a woman, who passed the second one to him and then ram-rodded the next shot into the barrel of the first gun. There was no live shot however, even though they made a lot of noise as they were fired. Clouds of smoke came out of the muzzles and drifted across the arena.

The Indians were spectacular pretending to be shot and falling off their horses. Marged was wondering why they weren't hurting themselves. The Indians certainly made it look real and they were hooting and war whooping. That alone would have been enough to frighten most people.

After about seven minutes of this intense activity, a bugle was heard at the other end of the arena and in came Buffalo Bill, once again at the head of the United States Cavalry, all at full gallop.

Marged nudged Buttercup, "Here comes your silly cavalry."

"Our poor Indian friends must get really tired of being beaten all the time."

"They did beat Custer, though."

"Custard, why would anybody want to be called custard? Perhaps it was because of his silly name that he was beaten."

"It's not custard, its Custer, C, U, S, T, E, R, and he was beaten because of bad decisions. Also, I think there were more Indians than he expected."

The cavalry raced past the stands. The horses once again kicked up clods of damp soil. The main track around the arena by now had lost most of its grass and was pocked and rutted. It would take a bit of effort to get it back to normal, probably the rest of the summer.

Once they got to the other side of the arena, they began to chase the Indians around the circled wagons. There was an incredible amount of noise, between war whoops, shouting, screaming and gunfire. Smoke and smell was everywhere.

The scene was about as real as one could get. To the audience, it looked as if soldiers and Indians were actually being shot, because of the dramatic way they came off their horses and also the way they came down with the horses, as if the animal had been shot from under them.

The battle went on for another five minutes. Then the Indians withdrew from the scene and galloped out of the far end of the arena. The people in the wagon train were on their feet, waving their hats and cheering their rescuers.

"My Lords, Ladies and Gentlemen," the announcers shouted. "Again the United States Cavalry has fought another battle to make the West safe for the courageous settlers."

Everyone cheered and applauded except Marged and David Taylor and his boys. After all, they were from a different age, an age where, finally, ethnic differences, human rights and equality were becoming a lot more acceptable.

The cavalry formed up and led off with Buffalo Bill at their head, followed by the unwinding wagons but instead of leaving the arena, they came around for another lap and as the last wagon passed the entrance, the Indians entered and followed. There was no whooping and hollering, the whole procession was moving at a walking pace. The mounted Indians were followed by the families, some with travois and others carrying their babies. Behind them came the sharpshooters and behind them came the stream of the Congress of Rough Riders of the World. This was the final parade of the Wild West Show.

Buffalo Bill rode proudly at the head of the parade, as he had done many times before. He could well be proud as it was one of the most spectacular shows of its kind in history. When he got to the far end, he moved to one side of the entrance as the rest left the arena, all except for one US Cavalry man, a US Rough Rider and one Indian Chief, resplendent in his feathered war bonnet.

Buffalo Bill turned for a final lap, followed by the three riders who rode abreast, the Indian between the other two. Marged wondered about this arrangement; as they moved forward, the Indian was surrounded to the front and sides, his only way out was to retreat. She thought of how much this represented what had happened to all the Native Americans.

As they went around the arena they would turn and face the people in each stand and Buffalo Bill and his horse would bow, as they had done to Marged and Buttercup in the High Street.

After the circuit had been completed, they left the arena and the announcers spoke up for the final time. "My Lords, Ladies and Gentlemen, thank you for attending this great event and please show your appreciation once more for Buffalo Bill and his Wild West and Congress of Rough Riders of the World."

The crowd rose to their feet as one, erupting in cheers and applause. This went on for over five minutes and just as it was waning Buffalo Bill galloped into the arena and did a final lap. The cheering was revitalized for another five minutes before it died down and everyone began to slowly leave the stands.

CHAPTER 18

To the Indian camp go the medicine girls
Honoured with better things than pearls.
Beaded moccasins for feet they bring
And fine feathers from an Eagles wing.
Touch your other self and you will blend
And one from two will be your end.

CROWN HOTEL

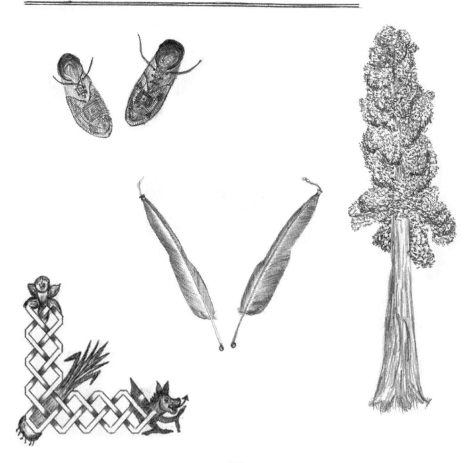

Marged and Buttercup invited everyone they were with to accompany them to the Indian camp, which was still in place to one side of the middle of the arena. The Indians, who had been on the outside of the arena, came back into the camp. They were ready to eat and make preparations for the move onto the next show.

As Marged and her entourage approached the camp, they were greeted by Sharpened Stick and Dark Sky Day, who enthusiastically welcomed them into their world. They were introduced to the chiefs and a medicine man who was very kind in acknowledging the girls as having good medicine. Several of the Indian women handed them small bowls of food, which consisted of fry bread, beans, some dried fruits and assorted meats. They found the food quite tasty and were soon offered more. The Indian ladies also proudly showed off the tepees and explained how they worked, even when a fire was lit in the middle of them.

After the meal the Chief, resplendent in his costume, beaded buckskins, breastplate and a feathered war bonnet, the ends of which almost touched the ground, approached the group and made an announcement. "We have come a long way from our lands across the great sea to the white man's many lands. Not all white men are good people, but we have here today two girls with good medicine." A young Indian girl came up to his side. She had a beautifully cured deer hide with beaded trim draped over her arms and on this hide were two pairs of beaded moccasins and two bald eagle feathers.

The Chief turned to the girls, picked up the two pairs of moccasins and gave one pair each to Marged and Buttercup. Marged was so impressed that she had tears in her eyes. Then the chief picked up the two eagle feathers. "These feathers are from the great bird of our land and they, like you, are good medicine." He handed each of the girls a feather. One was a left wing primary and the other was a right wing primary and on the ends was attached a little tuft of white fur. The quill end was made into a loop which would have been used to attach the feather to a head dress.

As the Chief handed over the feathers, there were small yips and hoots of appreciation from the Indians who were gathered. Then they did a very European thing; they applauded, along with the rest of the girls' group.

Marged wanted to hug the Chief but decided that it would be better not to. Sharpened Stick and Dark Sky Day came over with huge smiles on their faces. Dark Sky Day said, "You have good courage and your medicine helped us much. You shall never be forgotten. Those feathers will protect you for all your lives, because they are sacred to our people and the spirit of our people is carried in them."

Marged didn't hold back this time. She stepped up to the Indian and threw her arms around him and looked up into his eyes while the tears streamed down from hers. "Thank you," she said. "I am so glad we met you. We shall treasure the moccasins, and the feathers will be kept safe forever."

It was at that moment when Marged spotted the stumpy man again. He had a sadistic smile on his face, and as soon as he knew that Marged had seen him he quickly walked away.

Dark Sky Day continued. "We will never forget what you did for us in helping us get back to our people."

They turned away to leave and Rhys Edwards shouted, "Marged, Dafydd has gone to meet himself."

Marged's emotional reverie was over. "Oh, my gosh, where?"

Rhys pointed to where the people were leaving the stands. "He saw himself leaving. His other self was following his parents and he said he was going to meet him."

"He can't do that. If they touch it will be terrible. Come on Buttercup. We must stop them meeting." They both handed their gifts to William Williams and his wife. "Take care of these until we return."

Marged ran off, followed by Buttercup, who was running while holding up her skirts. David Taylor watched them go before realizing they would probably need help, so he too took off after the girls, closely followed by his boys.

After about a minute of running the girls spotted their Dafydd and he was shouting at his other self. "Dafydd, I want to see you!"

The other Dafydd stopped and turned to face the other while his parents, seemingly oblivious to what was happening, walked slowly on with the leaving crowd. The boys approached each other and the other Dafydd asked, "Who are you?"

And the response was: "I am you."

"You can't be me, because I am me. Who are you?" he asked again.

"I am you and I can prove it."

"How can you prove it?"

Easy. I live in Elan Valley and your parents are my parents. I was born on November 6 1892."

"Are you my twin brother?"

"No, I am not. I am you."

"I'm going to knock your block off. I don't like you." They approached one another as Marged and Buttercup arrived on the scene.

Marged was the first to step in between them and tried to push the other Dafydd away from himself and then Buttercup stepped in and tried to do the same with that Dafydd, but the boys were too strong.

Just as David arrived to help they touched. There was a blinding flash of blue light and the girls were thrown to the ground, David too was thrown off balance and also fell over. His boys had stopped running and were wide-eyed, totally stunned. Several individuals who had been in close proximity were also on the ground, two of them had been hurt, but not seriously. They rubbed their arms and elbows.

Only one Dafydd remained. His hair was standing on end and he had an expression of total terror on his face. Marged and Buttercup got to their feet, as a crowd gathered, to see what was going on. The girls were not injured, due to the magic of the cave. Many of the crowd asked what had happened and were answered by those who had witnessed the happenings, even though they could not grasp what they had seen.

A woman who had seen the event spoke up. "There was these two boys and they was fighting with these girls, see, then there was this huge flash of light and one of the boys vanished into nothing, just like magic it was."

At that moment Dafydd's parents came on the scene and went up to him. "Dafy, what has happened?" his mother asked.

He was composing himself. Marged wondered which Dafydd he was or was he a combination of the two.

He stared at his parents. "Mam, I met myself, and when we touched we became one."

"Don't you be telling me your nonsense, boy? What happened here?"

"Mam, I am telling you the truth."

"I have never heard such rubbish. You expect me to believe that pack of lies. What have you done to these people?"

"Nothing."

Marged came to the rescue and stepped up to his mother. "There was another boy that looked like him. They were about to fight when there was a flash of gunpowder from the show and the other boy ran very quickly off into the crowd. It wasn't Dafydds' fault." That was the best Marged could come up with.

Dafydd wouldn't let it go. "No, it was myself! I know it was."

His mother then grabbed him by the ear and began to drag him away. "Meeting yourself indeed and fighting in public. You should be ashamed. You wait till I get you home; it's the last time we'll take you to any shows."

His mother continued to drag him away and Marged shouted after him, "Goodbye, Dafydd."

He shouted back. "Goodbye, Marged!"

And that set her wondering again. Was he their Dafydd or was he a combination. Perhaps she would never know. Anyway, she no longer had to worry about how they were going to get him back to his own time. The rest of the group caught up and Marged led them off to the end of the Groe where there was a large crowd gathered at the entrance near the bottom of the Strand. The group went over to see what was going on. A speech was being made but the group was too late to hear what was being said. However, it had to be something to do with some trees that were being planted in honour of the Wild West Show coming to Builth. Someone had made a gift of them to the town and it could only be assumed that it was Buffalo Bill.

David asked for anyone to hear, "What kind of trees are they?"

Marged answered him immediately. "They are Giant Redwoods. They come from America. When they are fully grown they are the largest trees in the world."

David looked quizzically at her. "How do you know that?"

"Well, they are still there in my time and the one by the stone pillar over there is very big. The trunk is about seven feet across. It is the tallest tree for miles."

"And here you are watching it being planted. Isn't that amazing!"

They watched all of the Sequoias being planted before moving onto the Wye Bridge. Hundreds of people were crossing; just about all of them were going to be catching trains. Marged wondered how long they would have to wait to get seats, even in first class.

David stopped and turned to everyone in the group. "You know what we should do? We should go back into town and find a place where we can eat. We might have to wait a couple of hours or more to catch a train with seats."

Rhys Edwards' parents agreed immediately, even though they and everyone else had eaten some of the Indian food.

Marged smiled. "Yes that is a good idea, but we won't need much, because it hasn't been long since we ate at the camp."

They turned and trudged through the crowd going in the other direction. They got into town and decided to try the Crown Hotel. Marged, asked Buttercup to take the lead as the Lady in charge and defer to David who would speak for everyone.

There was a man standing in front of the door, whose job it seemed was to keep out the riff raff. They approached him and he looked down his nose at the two families, first the Llandovery trio and then the Epynt family. The disdain, verging on total disgust, written on his face as he looked them over was something that horrified Marged and David.

After a few seconds, he spoke. "I will have you know that this is a first class establishment and our other patrons would be offended if I were to allow you to enter. You will find a third class establishment more to your liking at the Kings Head further up the street."

Buttercup stepped up firmly to confront him. "I will have you know, that I am the Lady Buttercup and these people are workers on my estate. Today I am treating them for all the hard work they do. Mr. Taylor, attend to this please." She stepped back to make way for David.

He stepped up. "We would like to eat here and if you object then I would like to see your manager."

The man could see the persistence and asked them to wait; he turned and went into the building.

A few moments later he returned with a large, round-faced man with a moustache, accompanied by a friendly, black Labrador dog.

He looked the group over. "I don't know if we have enough room for all of you."

David smiled and slipped his left arm around the man's shoulders. The man was immediately alarmed until he saw the five pound note that David was offering him in his other hand.

The man coughed and spluttered as he took the note. "W... w... well, indeed, yes, I think that we should be able to accommodate you. Please, er, please follow me."

He led the group into the spacious first-class dining room. The tables were exquisitely laid and each could seat four individuals.

Marged whispered to Buttercup. "You and me, Owain and Mr. Taylor should sit together so we can talk. So tell them I will make the seating arrangements."

Buttercup made her announcement. "I have asked Marged to decide where everyone sits. Marged, would you show everyone?"

Marged then assigned the seating, much to the astonishment of the hotel manager and his staff. She had the Epynt parents sit with their two daughters, Rhys Edwards with his parents, the Epynt boy with David's two boys and that occupied one section of the dining room, so Marged, Buttercup, Owain and David were on a table a little further away.

Once the assignments had been made, the staff began scurrying around pulling out chairs and seating everyone. There were six of them and it didn't take long to get all 14 people seated. Menus were handed out and perused. As they were looking, Buttercup noticed how uncomfortable the shepherd and his wife were, and it seemed it was because the price of a meal was more than a shepherd's monthly wage. Until Buttercup had met Marged she would have never noticed such a thing. Buttercup waved over one of the staff, who was by her side in an instant. "I wish to stand to make an announcement." Everyone else in the room stared at her, including all the other patrons.

As she began to stand the staff person pulled out the chair. "To all my staff here today, please order anything you wish off the menu, because I will be paying the bill." She then sat down again.

All other patrons in the dining room stared for a few moments longer, then turned back to their meals, talking in hushed tones, no doubt, about who Buttercup was, and some no doubt were wishing they could work for her! Of course none of them would think it was possible that Buttercup, in reality, had not even been born yet.

The menu was quite formal; at the top in an almost calligraphic print was "CROWN HOTEL" and underneath was "Menu for May 12th 1904" and underneath that was written:

> In Honour of Buffalo Bill's Wild West Show we are proud to serve the following:
>
> SOUP: New England Clam Chowder
>
> ENTRE: Medallions of Texas Beef, with Anoka roast potatoes, Sweet potatoes, Carrots and mushroom sauce
>
> DESSERT: Cranberry Apple Pie with fresh cream

Underneath this, the main menu of the day, was a list of other culinary options.

Marged explained the menu to Owain. He would have no problem accustomizing himself to table etiquette; he had had plenty of experience in his multiple travels from the cave into the many different times.

Everyone ordered the main food event in honour of the great show that they had enjoyed so much. None of them were sure if they would be able to eat it all after their sampling of the true North American meal.

Marged smiled at Owain. "You have tried many times to get back to the time you belong in and with no success. We now have a way to get you back. You told me that you had lost the battle of Bryn Glas but my father told me that it was a great victory, and that you had captured an Englishman called Edmund Mortimer, who came over to your side."

"No, it didn't happen that way. As I have said, he almost captured me."

David then asked the question: "What did happen at this battle?"

Owain looked him in the eye. "We were prepared. Under my General Rhys Gethin we had placed ourselves on the high ground and the English, under Mortimer, appeared below us. We were in a good position. Their archers were out of their range. However, we were well within ours, so we launched volley after volley into their ranks. Not one of their arrows reached us. This excited my army. They could taste victory, but that was unfortunate, because after a while the English began to retreat, in what seemed like a panic. Before I could stop them, my soldiers gave pursuit and as soon as they reached the spot where the English had first engaged us, our right flank was hit by many archers. We turned to face them and did our best to reform, but then we were hit from below by those who were retreating. They had reformed. I shouted to my captains to call a retreat before we were routed. Many lost their lives, but most of us managed to get away. It was every man for himself. It was several weeks before we were able to regroup."

Buttercup stared at him. "The English are not bad people."

David smiled. "Back then I think perhaps they were." He turned to Owain. "We might be able to change a few things. Of course, it will have to meet with Caradoc's approval."

Marged nodded. "If we help we might have to go a long way from the cave and there will be no trains. It could take days or even weeks to sort things out."

David also nodded. "This will be quite an adventure."

Owain fixed David in a stare. "You are English. Why do you want to help me?"

"That is very easy. Just over a hundred years or so after your time there was an act of union, and even though Wales still maintains its culture and language, it is attached to England and England is attached to it in every other way."

"Has it been good for Wales?"

"Much of the time. However, there were some bad spells. But today, uhm, in my time and Marged's, Wales has a prominent place, not only in England but in mainland Europe as well. I do believe that Wales has been very good for England."

"Should I be fighting to free Wales or is my whole effort futile?"

"I think I can assure you that taking up your cause has been looked on favourably in your future. What you have done, or what you will do, will be good for Wales and its cultural identity. And that has been vitally important to all the people who live in the country right up to the times we know."

The meal was served and at once they realized how hungry they were from all the excitement and activity, even though they had eaten recently. Marged pointed out that as soon as they were back at the cave, they would have to go back out and rest.

David stopped for a second. "Oh, dear. William Williams and his family won't be able to go out, as there is nowhere they will be able to stay. Rhys and his parents will be OK, they can go on to Landovery." He looked around. "Perhaps they could stay here and go back on the train tomorrow."

"We could all do that. It would be marvellous. We would all be rested and we could just go straight back to the cave and do some other things."

Buttercup nodded as she delicately spooned up the last of the clam chowder. "I've never had this before. It is very good." Then she turned to Marged. "I think I should get back to my time for a while. The problem is if I do my mother will want me to go to London with her and I won't be able get back to the cave when I want to."

Marged thought about this. "How often has your mother been coming up to Wales?"

"She comes up every two months."

"Would she bring you along each time?"

"Only if I am not in school or my Governess is not present to teach. I would try to persuade her to take me along each time, but I think that she would think it rather odd."

311

"Why?"

"Well, every time she asks if I would like to come with her to Wales, I tell her that I don't like Wales and would rather stay in London."

David chuckled. "Your mother is going to wonder about what changed your mind."

Marged laughed. "I think our Buttercup will come up with something." She paused, "We should let them know that we would like to stay here right away. I hope they have rooms available. Mr. Taylor, could you make enquiries?"

"Yes, I will, but I won't stay. Me and the boys will go today. We should be fine. If we are tired we can stay somewhere on our drive back to London and Rhys and his parents will probably want to return to Landovery. I will ask and then book rooms. I just hope they have some available."

David went over to the other tables and asked. His guess was right. The Llandovery family wanted to return that day, so then he went over to the manager chap and asked about the availability of four rooms.

The manager told him that he would have a look in the register for that day. "We were full last night because of the Wild West Show but I do believe many of them will be leaving today. I will see what I can do."

David returned to the table where the main course had been served.

Owain had found a tough piece of meat. It was barely a spoonful. He picked it up and tossed it through the air. It travelled across the dining room and landed in front of the nose of the Black Labrador dog, who snaffled it up almost instantly. The other diners were shocked; Marged thought that one of them was about to become uncontrollably enraged, but he settled down again. The dog swallowed the meat whole and lifted his head to look around to see where it had come from. It was obvious that he wasn't sure as he stood up on the verge of a trip around the room to investigate, but before he could move a paw in that direction, a shout of "Stay" was heard from someone out of view and the dog lay down again.

As they were finishing the main course the manager returned and informed them that, yes, they had four first class rooms that contained large beds. David told him he would pay cash in advance on behalf of the Lady Buttercup.

Just as the dessert was placed in front of her, Marged looked up. "The trains. We have tickets for today, not for tomorrow."

David smiled. "When we go to the station today, I will get them changed; I can't imagine that it would cost that much more. I will also sort out the carriage situation."

They ate the dessert with little or no conversation. As they finished up, the shepherd boy looked over at Marged and asked if he could have more, and as soon as he asked David's two boys nodded at their father. David smiled, called over a waiter and requested second helpings of the dessert for those who wanted them. Marged and Buttercup were the only ones who declined.

Once the second dessert was eaten, David went off to find the registration desk to pay for the rooms and the morning meal.

William Williams and his son were booked into one room, his wife and daughters in another, Owain in the most expensive room. David thought it would be the most appropriate room fit for a Prince. Marged and Buttercup would share the last of the four rooms that he had booked.

They all, except Owain, indulged in a cup of tea following the meal. They had been offered coffee and Owain was intrigued to try it. He had tried tea and now was his opportunity to try coffee. Tea and coffee were not known in Europe in his time.

The dinner over, they decided to see Rhys Edwards and his family and David and his boys off on their journey.

When they got to the bridge, there were far fewer people, and most of those were hauling carts and wagons with some of the equipment that was used by the Wild West Show.

At the station David made inquiries about first class tickets to Garth the next day and was told that there was still a crush for seats on this day and they were grateful that he asked to move the eight seats to the next day, so there would be no additional charges.

There was a complete round of goodbyes and Marged asked David to return to the cave as soon as he was able so that they could help Mr. Williams the shepherd and his family and others who would have to remain in the cave until they could be helped. David smiled. "I have plans that will help just about everyone that needs help. I will be coming back once in a while to do some things that will make some big differences for us all."

Marged was immediately curious. "What are you going to do?"

He smiled. "You will have to wait and see won't you?"

Marged invited Rhys Edwards to come and visit the cave, so that he could be involved in some of the things that they would be doing there.

Rhys smiled. "I am going to have some very interesting questions from my parents, especially about Owain. They're very proud of what I did for Buttercup, even though I did nothing at all."

Buttercup glanced to her right and there was her mother again about to board the train. Their eyes met briefly and her mother was coming toward her. She tugged on Marged's elbow, "My mother is coming over to us."

Marged turned, but it was too late. Buttercup's mother spoke. "You're the medicine girls. Aren't you part of the show?"

At least she wasn't totally focused on Buttercup. Marged spoke up. "We are friends of the show."

"Oh, how lovely. What are your names?

"My name is Marged and this is the Lady Buttercup."

"Nice to meet you Marged and you, Lady Buttercup. What a lovely name! If I have a daughter I shall call her Buttercup."

Marged almost blurted out "you did" but was stopped when the train whistle blasted and the station master shouted "all aboard." They were saved by the whistle. Buttercup's mother turned and got onto the train just as it was about to move off.

The two families leaving waved until the train was out of sight.

Marged smiled at everyone. "What a wonderful day. Let's go back into town. I would like to look at the shops there. They are very different from the shops in my time."

As they crossed the bridge they paused, because it gave them a splendid view of the show site. There was still plenty of activity. Some large tents were being taken down, the stands were being taken apart and the pieces, along with other equipment, were being loaded onto the wagons that had been used in the show. The horses and livestock were being fed and groomed. Smaller tents were being erected, no doubt to accommodate many of the participants until their early morning train to the next venue, where all the equipment would be waiting for them.

They watched for almost half an hour before moving on. As they came down off the bridge Marged pointed out the Assembly Rooms. "In my time that building is the Wyeside Arts Centre and over there is the Lion Hotel. In my time it is still the Lion Hotel." She continued to point out shops that were different in her time, and as they passed the Crown Hotel she informed them that in her time it had been demolished and was rebuilt as a bank.

They reached the top of the street and Marged pointed out the Swan Hotel. "It is still called the Swan in my time, but now, it is the Builth Wells Rugby Club. Over there is the Barley Mow. In my time it is the favourite place of the farmers. My father goes there when he goes to the market."

They turned and went back down the street. As they crossed Strand Street a crowd of people tumbled out of the Drovers Arms in a brawl. It was four locals picking on three Indians. Marged didn't recognize the Indians but she could see them getting into trouble. "We must stop this." She turned to Thomas. "Thomas, run and find a policeman."

"Where?"

"I don't know where. Look! Ask. Do what you can, and when you find one bring him back here. Buttercup, could you go back to the Groe? Go down here." She pointed down Strand Street. "And try and find our Indians and bring them back here."

Thomas went off down the main street and Buttercup, without hesitation, went off down Strand Street to the Groe.

Marged, seemingly oblivious to the danger, marched across the street and stood between the locals and the Indians. "Stop it!" she screamed, and both groups stopped and stared at her.

One of the locals said, "Get out of the way, gel. We are going to teach these injuns some manners."

She defied him and glared into his face. "No. You will not hurt them."

Heulwen ducked behind Owain and her husband with her arms wrapped around her girls. Owain and William stood deathly still as they watched Marged go into action.

The half drunk man reached for Marged and was surprised when his hands stopped three inches away from touching her. They could get no closer; he pulled back his hands and looked at them for a couple of seconds. "Why, I will teach you something, gel." This time he took a violent swing at her and once again his fist stopped abruptly three inches from her face. She didn't even flinch. He tried again and he had put so much force into his swing that when his fist came to a sudden stop he could not prevent himself from falling over.

He stared up at Marged from his flattened position on the pavement and realized, along with his friends, that Marged possessed some very special powers. "You are a witch, you are?"

Marged smiled. "Yes, I am. And if you make one more move I will turn you into a wounded rat and set you off running down the street, where the first man who sees you will stomp on you."

He took her seriously, got up and backed off with his friends. What Marged didn't realize was that all around a crowd had gathered, and they had witnessed this strange power that she had shown. Many of them gasped and began exclaiming the magic of this young girl. One of them commented, "She is one of them medicine girls! She was in the show!"

As they were about to start asking awkward questions, Dark Sky Day and Sharpened Stick ran onto the scene, followed by Buttercup about 20 yards behind them. Marged explained what had happened and the two Indians launched into a telling off of the other three in their own language of Lakota. As this confrontation was coming to an end, Thomas and a policeman showed up and the constable immediately wanted to know what had been going on. By now Marged wished that she hadn't sent Thomas on the errand.

"Alright, one at a time," he boomed.

A woman five feet from Marged spoke first. "That girl there." She pointed at Marged, "She stopped a fight by using magic. She is probably a witch." Another spoke up. "No, she is one of the medicine girls from the show."

The policeman shook his head. He didn't believe what he was hearing. Soon Marged realized that none of the witnesses would be believed either, even though what they had seen had actually happened. However, things wavered a little when Dark Sky Day spoke up. "This girl is the medicine girl and her medicine is very powerful. She helps Indians."

The policeman looked around. "So who was fighting here?"

Marged pointed through the small crowd to the four locals who were almost running down the street. "There they are."

"Very well. I shall apprehend them and find out what has happened here." Off he went in pursuit.

The rescued Indians were escorted off down the Strand. Buttercup was panting and had to get her breath back before she could talk. The melee was over and the small crowd began to disperse. Buttercup looked at Marged. "When I told them that there were three of them up here about to fight some locals they ran so fast I couldn't believe it. It seems that they are not to go to saloons and places that serve alcohol. Mr. Cody doesn't allow it. If they had been caught he would have sent them back to America straightaway."

"That was very close then. I think we should return to the hotel and go to our rooms to sleep so that we can catch the early train tomorrow."

As they turned to walk back down the street, a woman came up to Marged and nervously smiled. "Can I touch you for luck?"

Marged looked at her for a second before nodding, "Yes, of course you can."

The woman placed her right palm on Marged's face. "Thank you." She withdrew and Marged and her friends went back to the hotel.

Before they entered they noticed that the policeman had caught up with the four locals and was busy threatening them with arrest.

The Crown Hotel rooms were quite spacious and everyone was in bed by 9:00 p.m.

Marged and Buttercup were up in the morning and downstairs in the dining room by six a.m. Marged looked around, and apart from a man in a very smart suit for the time, who was eating breakfast, there was no one else around. "We should let the others know so we can get an early start. Why don't you ask the manager to go and knock on their doors?"

"Good idea." She took off to find the manager. In two minutes she was back.

They chose the same table as they had the evening before and sat down. No one helped with the seats this time. In five minutes Owain joined them and in another ten everyone was seated and breakfast quickly followed.

Halfway through breakfast the manager subserviently approached the table where Marged, Buttercup and Owain were seated. He bowed his head slightly. "My Lady, I am sorry for the intrusion, but your estate manager arranged a carriage for you from the hotel to the station. The next train leaves at twenty minutes past seven and I can have the carriage standing by at the back of the hotel. Once you have finished breakfast you should have enough time to get there. I take it you are travelling first class?"

"Yes, of course. Thank you, my good man."

Whenever Marged heard her say that, it always made her want to laugh.

The manager backed off as if Buttercup was royalty. "Very well, my Lady."

After breakfast all eight individuals climbed into the carriage and were taken the short ride over the bridge to the station. As soon as they had passed the Llanelwedd Arms they came face to face with a hive of activity. There were wagons loaded with all sorts of equipment and supplies from the Wild West Show. They were waiting their turn to drive up on to the flat bed carriages of the train, which would take them to the next venue. In a huge pen next to the river, several local farmers were sorting through a herd of about a hundred cattle. They were the same cattle that were in the show's cattle drive. Marged realized that the cattle were hired locally, even though there were some genuine Texas Longhorns in the lead when she had seen them in the show. The Longhorns probably belonged to the show and local cattle were hired to fill out the herd.

At the station they had only five minutes to wait.

Everything went well and they were all able to ride in the same carriage from Garth that David Taylor had arranged. However, the horse struggled up the hills, particularly up past Tanyralt. By the time they got to Capel Rhos the horse was ringing wet with sweat. It was a cold morning. The sweat steamed off the horse and filled the air with a very strong horsey smell.

They got down off the carriage with the help of the driver; Buttercup paid him and included a handsome tip. The driver smiled. "Thank you, my Lady."

As they turned for the walk to the cave, they saw the driver take a blanket off his seat and throw it over the horse's back. He then reached under the seat, took out a small bundle of brown paper, climbed back on to the carriage and opened the package to reveal brown bread sandwiches.

Marged smiled. He was taking care of his horse and giving him a rest while he ate the sandwiches before the return journey. She appreciated anyone who took care of livestock.

At the cave Marged got Mr. Williams and his family settled in and assured them that it would not be long before they would go out to a better life. Although, she also assured them, there would be no time passing for them.

Marged turned to Buttercup and smiled. "Well, I think it's your turn now. Are you ready?"

Buttercup took a deep breath. "I think so."

"Do you want to take the gifts from the Indians with you?"

"I would love to, but I don't know what my mother would say. I think I will leave them here and come and get them if I change my mind."

"Alright, here we go then." Marged consulted her notes for confirmation, and moved the Time Stones accordingly, placed her hands and the rock wall opened. Marged went out with Buttercup to meet Buttercup's mother.

The timing was perfect. In three minutes Buttercup's mother showed up, with a man and two horses.

319

Buttercup hugged her mother. "Mother, I am well. I think the cave might have cured me. Oh, mother, this is my new friend, Marged. She has been very helpful to me. Say hello to her."

Buttercup's mother smiled. "Nice to meet you Marged. Haven't I seen you before somewhere?"

Marged had a feeling this was going to happen. "You may have. I live in the area on one of the farms and I come to the cave quite a lot to play."

"Yes of course. Well, Buttercup, we had better get you back. Say goodbye to your friend."

Buttercup turned and flung her arms around Marged. Marged did the same and they both cried, much to the amazement of Buttercup's mother.

Marged looked into Buttercup's teary eyes. "You have to come back soon, because we have a lot more work to do."

"Oh. Marged, I will, I will."

They parted and Marged watched as Buttercup was helped up into a side saddle by the man who had accompanied her mother. He then helped Buttercup's mother up. Once this was done, he picked up the reins of Buttercup's horse and led it off toward Capel Rhos, followed by the other horse carrying her mother. Buttercup and Marged waved until Buttercup was out of sight.

Marged returned to the cave and went over to Caradoc and Owain. "I am going to leave for a while. Don't worry, my Prince, we are going to help you and many of the others who are still trying to find their way back to their times. The problem is distance, so we are going to have to make journeys that will take us a long way from the cave."

Caradoc looked at Marged.
"The Time Stones here you have made to right
And saved many from an awful plight.
Your work with them is mostly done
And from that task you did not run."

Once more she set the Time Stones. The rock wall opened, and she turned to say goodbye. "My Prince, you must not venture out until my return. Please promise me that?"

Owain nodded with a smile. "That is a promise I will keep for you."

"Goodbye then."

The two old men waved goodbye. In a second, she was gone back to 2004, but soon to return for more adventures.

ABOUT THE AUTHOR

John Dingley grew up on a hill farm in Mid Wales and now lives in the Twin Cities area of Minnesota. He has been called a renaissance man who has shown a variety of notable talents. He is an animal scientist and his love of nature has involved him in a major role in wildlife reintroduction. He is on the board of directors of the Raptor Resource Project and the Decorah Eagle Cam.

His love of theatre has led to performances in a variety of roles, both in Wales and around the Mid West

A noted storyteller and singer he can occasionally be discovered performing his one man show, "John Dingley and the Biggest Pack of Lies You Ever Heard". Once in a while he sings the US anthem at sporting events.

He is a master glass cutter and engraver as well as being an accomplished stonemason.

This is John's first written work of fiction and he is currently working on the second and third books in the series; THE TIMELESS CAVERN - Marged Evans and the Pebbles of MORE Time and Marged Evans and the Pebbles of Distance

John takes a major interest in urban agriculture, sustainable agriculture and permaculture and has spent time teaching urban young people in the efficient use of gardening and agricultural hand-tools. His nonfiction book "Hard Work in Paradise - When all our Food and Lives were Organic" will be published soon.

Coming Soon

More from
THE TIMELESS CAVERN
series:

- Marged Evans and the Pebbles of MORE Time

- Marged Evans and the Pebbles of Distance

- Marged Evans and the Pebbles of Cave to Cave

- Marged Evans and the Pebbles of Space

Also

Short Stories and Poems

Non Fiction

Hard Work in Paradise

When all Our Food and Lives Were Organic

Reader comments

Enthralling! Sensational!

Just two words that I would use to describe The Timeless Cavern: Marged Evans and the Pebbles of Time.

Hello Mr. Dingley! I hope this finds you well.

I read your book this weekend and I cannot speak about it enough! This book and your tale is a story for all ages- it crosses all age barriers and appeals to all audiences. I found the story wildly exciting, riveting, entertaining AND educational. It really kept me on the edge of my seat the whole time, in fact I couldn't, I didn't WANT to put it down. I read it in less than one day's time. For me that is phenomenal, as it is usually hard to keep my attention and keep me awake no matter how good the book!

This book brings back the art of storytelling from days of old. It brought me back to the days of my childhood with my grandfather telling stories. I found it written such that I was immediately transcended to wherever Marged was in the story with vivid pictures of the scenery and people and their personalities.

I found the book to be crafted meticulously, so cleverly rolling in lessons of factual and accurate history, culture, acceptance, tolerance, kindness, intelligence, and morals. The inclusion of real names and places and the comparisons and correlations made between modern-day places/conveniences to previous times really keeps the reader in the story, allowing the reader to relate to these places and how they would feel if they had traveled back in time.

I can't wait for Book Two! Where will Marged go next and will she be caught? *Ann Lynch*

'I thoroughly enjoyed reading this book, a fantastic story, enjoyed by myself and my children alike, a great mix of fiction and real life events, and people, we can't wait for the next instalment.' *H. M. Powell*

"The Timeless Cavern: Marged Evans and the Pebbles of Time" introduces readers to Marged Evans, a young Welsh girl who explores a mysterious cave on the edge of her family's hill farm. What she finds inside will change her life forever. A wonderful book for readers of all ages, The Timeless Cavern will be of special interest to people who enjoy time travel fantasy. I was especially intrigued by the Welsh characters and setting, although the book explores a wide variety of real and imagined characters throughout history.

This reminded me a little bit of the Jack and Annie series (children time travel and explore history), but for older readers and with much more 'Welshness'. Looking forward to the next book. *Amy Ries*

"The Timeless Cavern: Marged Evans and the Pebbles of Time" is a book for all ages, especially those interested in time travel, fantasy, and fiction with a touch of accurate historical fact! I read the book in a couple of days because I found the story so interesting and engaging, and I could not put it down. I love fiction, and fictional mystery, so this book is a win-win in my mind. My Great Uncle was a Poet and writer of fiction in Ireland, and I have always loved the British-Irish-Welsh lore, myths, and history that accompany many of the stories by writers from those regions, and this book contains much of those things along with time-accurate depictions of the time that Marged Evans, the main character, travels through. This reminded me of the old Irish tales filled with the battles with England, and reminded me of my childhood, and I was left with a big smile!.

If you like fiction, and are a fan of the "Harry Potter" and "Lord of the Rings" stories, this book will entertain and engage, while looking forward to the rest of the series. I personally cannot wait for Book II, "Marged Evans and the Pebbles of MORE Time"!

I am a volunteer with Raptor Resource Project, and have great respect for John's work with wildlife, but was completely unaware of his writing, which belongs at the top of his list of many talents. I believe "renaissance man" would be an accurate description! *David L.*